Do You Solemnly Swear?

A Nation of Law, The Dark Side

Do You Solemnly Swear?

A Nation of Law, The Dark Side

Lin Wilder

Do You Solemnly Swear?
A Nation of Law, The Dark Side

Lin Wilder

FIRST EDITION

Print Edition ISBN: 978-1-942545-18-7
Library of Congress Control Number: 2015949009

Wilder Books
An Imprint of Wyatt-MacKenzie

Huntsville Prison, Huntsville, Texas

The more laws, the less justice.
— *Cicero*

C H A P T E R
1

The grin on Dr. Lindsey McCall's face was so broad that it nearly split her face in two as she gazed around the Huntsville Prison Emergency Treatment Center with an unusual sense of pride. McCall had felt no pride in the discovery of her new drug Digipro, yet the irrepressible joy in the new center was a tangible thing. The gleaming technology arrayed in the diagnostic room on her left, the state of the art eight-bed patient care area that dominated the Center filled her with joy. There was no echo left of the peeling and dingy walls, the 1950 style open patient care area, and the warren of small and relatively useless offices from the infirmary she had worked in as an inmate. The entire structure had been gutted and in its stead was a level one trauma and emergency treatment center rivaled only by those of the Texas Medical Center, sixty miles south of the prison.

Seventy miles north of Houston on Interstate 45 is Huntsville, Texas. Also called Prison City, Huntsville is home to seven prisons boasting about seventy-five thousand prisoners. Long known for its tough stance on crime, the state of Texas proudly boasts of a criminal justice system second to none. With a total of 122 prisons and accommodations for close to 168,000 prisoners, Texas ranks first in the United States and second only to Russia in its capacity for prisoners.

Lindsey had only one demand upon assuming the position of Medical Director at the Huntsville Prison System: a total renovation of the infirmary serving the over ten thousand prisoners in the system comprising seven facilities. Governor Greg Bell had laughed as he signed the executive order granting Dr. Lindsey McCall permission to renovate the infirmary.

"I'd have to be a damn fool to refuse you, Dr. McCall." Bell's dark brown eyes danced and one eyebrow raised," I wonder how many other Governors ever had the chance to grant a five million dollar renovation for which the state would pay nothing."

Winking at the cameras covering the ceremony, Bell answered his question by circling his thumb and forefinger, "Nada, not a one, I can guarantee you that."

Because of the family inheritance she had received upon the deaths of her mother and sister, Lindsey McCall had been a wealthy woman. But with the proceeds rolling in from the sale of Digipro, Lindsey could easily afford the five-million-dollar renovation.

Lindsey had spared no expense during the renovation. Prevailing on the wisdom of several trauma surgeons at the Houston Medical Center where she had been one of the leading Cardiologists in the country, Lindsey had followed their advice to the letter.

Taking a huge, shaky breath which caught in her throat, and feeling the tell-tale sting in her eyes, Lindsey whispered, "Thank You, Thank You, Thank You" in awe, wonder, and gratitude at the happiness she had never known was possible. She wondered if her dad could look down from the heavens he had once soared in, to see his smiling daughter and know the totality of her joy. She hoped so.

Shaking her head in exasperation at this unfamiliar incarnation of herself, Lindsey laughed softly, checked her watch and muttered, "Give it up, McCall, you've run out of time." The stacks of forms, paperwork, and charts awaiting her review would require a couple of hours to complete, they would have to wait. Lindsey calculated that she'd have just enough time to go home, take Max for a quick run, and then shower and change, but only if she left soon. Today was her first wedding anniversary and her husband and boss, Rich Jansen, Chief Warden at the Huntsville Prison, had made reservations at one of the finer restaurants in Houston, Perry's, to celebrate. But as Lindsey was packing her briefcase to leave, she heard Monica, the chief emergency center nurse and now one of her best friends, yelling at her.

Lindsey raced down the hall to the main clinic just in time to see Monica with Luke Preston, her favorite guard at the prison, transferring a severely injured man to one of the beds in the monitored section of the clinic. Monica did not stop her systematic emergency procedures to look at Lindsey, but the nurse was muttering under her breath with a most unpleasant scowl on her face. If this were any of the other nurses, Lindsey might have figured that she was merely angry at the late interruption of a quiet Friday afternoon, but Lindsey knew better. Something was bugging Monica big time, but this guy was unconscious, most likely in shock either from the extensive trauma or internal bleeding and looked as if he was barely moving his chest to breathe. There was no time to find out what her problem was.

While Monica applied electrodes so that they could

monitor his cardiac rhythm, oxygen saturation, blood pressure, and respiratory rate, Lindsey tried to find a vein to start an intravenous drip. Failing, she grabbed the cut-down set the ever efficient Monica had placed on a tray beside Lindsey, tore it open and quickly made a small incision on his forearm. Within seconds, she had threaded a large bore catheter into his brachial vein and started a drip of dextrose and saline. The man's face was unrecognizable; he had been beaten so severely that all Lindsey could make out were the vague outlines of mouth, nose and eyes. McCall's gaze rapidly traversed the man as her hands gently palpated his abdomen and chest, looking for abdominal injuries, bleeding or broken ribs. He was in shock, which was the reason she had not been able to start an intravenous line; the question was, why? Grabbing the portable x-ray machine out of the corner of the room, Lindsey waited until the guard and Monica had cleared the room, then donned a lead apron and took several flat plate films of his chest and abdomen.

While Monica was calling in Jake, a paramedic always looking for overtime, Lindsey walked rapidly into the x-ray room and clipped the films to the fluorescent wall readers.

"Jake can be here in thirty minutes, Lindsey," Monica said, glancing at her watch. "That should give you enough time to get home, change and still meet Rich on time."

"Ok Monica; thanks, this guy will need someone to watch over him pretty carefully but I don't see anything that looks worrisome on these films …." McCall stood and scanned the three films for the third time to make certain that she'd not missed anything on the x-rays. She viewed the new patient's monitor readings from through the window between his cubicle and the diagnostic room.

"His vital signs have stabilized, and his oxygenation saturation is up." Frowning, McCall looked over at the nurse,

"Funny, I was pretty sure that he had a flail chest but clearly I was wrong. He's pinked up and looks pretty good aside from a completely smashed face."

Sighing impatiently, Monica mumbled something that sounded like, "Like this guy's worth all this?" And then more forcefully, "Lindsey, come on, you need to go, or you'll be super late."

Turning to look at the usually pleasant dark features now rearranged in a fierce scowl, Lindsey asked, "Monica, what on earth has gotten into you? I've never seen you act this way toward one of our patients."

She was rewarded with a disdainful glare, "Are you telling me, Dr. Lindsey McCall, that you don't know who this guy is?"

Staring at her boss and shaking her head, Monica's features began to relax and soften into the attractive face of the Monica Bradbury that Lindsey had come to know and love.

Incredulous, Monica stared at Lindsey's bemused expression as she breathed, "Girl, you really need to get your head out of your books. This guy is Gabriel McAllister," and watched Lindsey expectantly.

McCall shrugged as she turned back to watch McAllister's monitor through the glass window of the x-ray room. She felt Monica's hand grasp her shoulder as she hissed, "He's the guy who raped that five-year-old little girl, it's been all over the news all summer, Lindsey … if there is one type of criminal that I detest, it's a pedophile," Monica added, shaking her head in disgust.

Still watching her new patient, Lindsey recalled Rich calling out to her on an evening late last week to come and watch the local television news. Her husband knew that she was cramming for her emergency medicine boards that she was scheduled to take in just over a month; rarely did he interrupt her, so she knew it wasn't a trivial issue. Deeply sighing as she closed a massive textbook on emergency medicine, Lindsey joined Rich in their bedroom to watch the late "breaking news" report.

Kate Townsend was being interviewed by the CBS news about her headline story in the Houston Tribune earlier that day. Ever on the prowl for a good story, the Pulitzer-winning reporter was commenting on a Houston juror who had recently pled guilty to juror tampering. According to Kate, the juror had sat on the jury selected for Gabriel McAllister's trial and had been concerned about the lack of evidence proving that McAllister had raped and sodomized the child. Because two of the state's medical witnesses had testified that the little girl had an intact vaginal hymen, this juror wondered if the state was going after an innocent man. After the first day of the trial, she researched on her computer at home the possibility of vaginal intercourse occurring in a child with an intact hymen. Once she learned that an intact hymen did not preclude sexual activity, she, along with the eleven other jurors, reluctantly found the defendant guilty of three counts of rape.

Bothered by the case, she spoke with a few friends about how badly she felt about this conviction. Then one of these friends informed her that she was expected to make her decision about the guilt or innocence of the defendant from courtroom testimony and that her online research was most likely against the law. After a good deal of reflection, the woman wrote a letter disclosing what she had done and why to the Judge who had heard the case. The unidentified juror wrote that she would have found the defendant not guilty had she made her decision based solely on the evidence presented by the state in the courtroom. She further asserted that there was only scant physical evidence of abuse found in the child and that her decision to find McAllister guilty was based solely on the accusations of the child.

The interview ended with the famous reporter commenting on what she called, "a worrisome trend" in divorce and break-ups between couples involving a small child. In more than 50 percent of custody dispute cases, there were allegations of sexual abuse brought against the father or live-in boyfriend. Somberly, Kate regarded her Houston audience as she declared, "In upwards of 35 percent of these cases, the accusations were later proven to be false."

Both Kate and Rich had stared at one another as they listened, wide-eyed, to their good friend Kate Townsend ignite yet another incendiary explosive device in the halls of Huntsville Prison.

September 5th, 2012

Criminal Court, Harris County Criminal Courthouse, Houston, Texas

Sometimes it is easier to see clearly into the liar than into the man who tells the truth. Truth, like light, blinds. Falsehood, on the contrary, is a beautiful twilight that enhances every object.
— *Camus*

CHAPTER

2

When six-year-old Annie took the stand to testify against him, Gabriel McAllister was brought to his knees. Until that very moment, Gabe had been confident that the truth would prevail. He believed in the law and the protection that it afforded American citizens, and he had great respect for fellow officers. During the shock of the arrest, when they tightened the plastic cuffs almost to the point of cutting off his circulation and when his head slammed against the cruiser as they threw him into the back seat, McAllister was confident the cops would soon realize their mistake. But they never did.

Raping Annie? For that matter, sexually abusing any child was inconceivable to him … the worst kind of perversion that any adult could inflict on a child. Of course, these guys would figure out that he was incapable of such behavior. McAllister was so confident that he ignored the advice of his boss, Captain Ted Stanley, to waive the court-appointed attorney and get him a good criminal defense lawyer. Stanley had even offered to call his high powered brother-in-law in Austin to see if he would take the case. And at the beginning of the trial, Gabe felt his hunch was right. This was America; people don't get convicted of something they didn't do; Americans were innocent until proven, guilty.

The first two days of his trial, Gabriel McAllister remained in a daze. He could not come to grips with the fact that he was here. And that the steady stream of cops, doctors, nurses, and psychologists testifying to the rape and sodomy of Samantha's then five-year-old daughter were talking about him. Most of the witnesses merely responded to the district attorney's questions in a purely perfunctory manner. But there were a few, like the nurse practitioner, who had quickly looked over at him while she discussed Annie's photos and pointed out the anal scarring, her repugnance manifested clearly in her expression. Gabe made the mistake of looking over at the jury at that exact moment, immediately sorry that he had done so. Four of the five men on the jury had followed the gaze of the nurse toward McAllister to look at him with expressions of intense hatred. Gabe could feel the inflammation of shame coursing through his body and inflaming his cheeks.

Yeah, right, try sitting here listening to a carefully orchestrated series of lies, each one worse than the one preceding it and not looking at the twelve people who hold your life in their hands.

But he knew his lawyer was right, he'd screwed up by looking over at those jurors. Gabe could easily imagine how guilty he looked to them. McAllister was aware in that moment that these men believed every word they heard, and he knew he was in the deepest trouble of his life. One of the few worthwhile things his court-appointed lawyer had advised him was to keep his eyes focused on the witness or the DA; to never, ever look at the jurors.

The testimony from a female pediatrician followed the nurse with slightly different versions of colposcopic photographs that testified to the presence of anal scarring; she too, somewhat hastily, mentioned the presence of an intact vaginal hymen.

Colposcopic cameras have become standard methods of demonstrating empirical evidence of damage to the anus and genitalia by magnifying the tissue, thereby making visible what would otherwise be invisible to the naked eye. In pointing out areas of scarring, vaginal tears and or irritation, the physician witness for the state can powerfully influence a jury through the use of these visual aids. But there is more than a little contention about the reliability of the colposcopic examination. Many practitioners contend that such abrasions could easily have resulted by vigorous wiping following urination or by tight underwear, and can be erroneously interpreted as proof of rape.

Increasingly, defense attorneys are becoming more aware of the subjectivity involved in interpreting the films and can present rigorous argument to the state witnesses to rebut what appears to prima facie evidence of sexual abuse. Unfortunately, Gabe's attorney was not among them. When the medical witnesses for the State completed their testimony, Prentiss had no questions. Even the Judge was surprised at Prentiss' silence; he had asked a second time, his voice a bit louder as if he wondered if Prentiss had not heard him. Strangely, it was one of the jurors who had been responsible for recalling one of the state's primary witnesses.

Out of the corner of his eye, Gabe watched a female juror write a note and hand it to the bailiff following the doctor's testimony. The bailiff brought the slip of paper to the judge who read it, nodded and instructed the bailiff to recall the pediatrician to the courtroom. Once the physician was seated in the witness chair, the judge explained that one of the jurors had asked for a clarification. Upon hearing the content of the note, the doctor answered in the affirmative, "Yes, the child's vaginal hymen was intact."

Once more eyeing the juror, an academic-looking strawberry blonde with brows furrowed and lips compressed, Gabe saw the frown on her face deepen and watched her jot another note to the bailiff. This time the judge refused to recall the doctor a second time. The juror looked perplexed and somewhat frustrated; a few of the other jurors were regarding the juror with interest, seemingly more interested in her reactions than in what was happening in the courtroom. Gabe was feeling pretty good at this point. This woman looked like an individual who could be persuasive with the other jurors and she was clearly dubious about how he, or anyone, could have raped Annie with such equivocal medical testimony. It only took one, after all.

Gabe turned to his lawyer, excited and hopeful, expecting to see some reaction from him but getting none. Somewhere between fifty and seventy, Gary Prentiss had passed his prime decades ago; his eyes, hair, and skin all lacked luster. When he stood to object to a question asked by the district attorney, Prentiss' voice was timorous, almost quivering, the voice of a very elderly man. Gabe sighed softly as he stared back at the opaque brown eyes and the almost lifeless expression of his defender. Too late, McAllister realized just how ill-considered was his confidence and how foolish he had been when he dismissed Stanley's offer of a real defense lawyer. He turned back to face the judge and was surprised to hear that the second day had ended. As the jury filed out, Gabe had kept his gaze on the redhead, beginning to believe that her doubt may be his only hope.

But this morning, here was Annie, sitting on that witness chair, dwarfed by the enormous wooden structure, legs dangling, happily answering the warm-up questions of the DA. Her bright red hair swung in two long ponytails on either side of her head, her big blue eyes were wide open and she cocked her head in that raptly attentive look. The look she used to shower on Gabe when he read her stories before she went to bed. Annie would not be here unless she were going to accuse him of doing all that evil; he could not listen, he simply couldn't and so he did what he'd been trained to do.

While forcibly directing his gaze back to neutral territory, the empty wall behind the judge, Gabe's mind began to wander back in time, to the night he had met Sam almost two years before; the night he decided to leave the Marine Corps. He'd spent that day delivering the news of the death of their only son to a rancher and his wife in central Texas. Slowly the courtroom receded as he traveled back in time; Gabe knew how he appeared to an onlooker, face impassive, devoid of any expression, the Marine he'd once been.

Like many young men and women in college around the time of 9/11, Gabe had been galvanized by the tragedy. A junior at the University of Houston, Gabe had switched his majors back and forth from business to pre-med to psychology, without feeling committed to any of the three. The armed forces recruitment day came at a perfect time for Gabe; while two of his buddies signed up with the Army, he walked over to the Marine Corps booth and signed up without a second thought. He'd never looked back; idly, he wondered how differently his life could have turned out if he hadn't quit the Corps. Just in time, he stopped the smirk threatening to appear as McAlister realized that he'd most likely be dead or severely injured by now. He sure wouldn't be sitting in a Houston courtroom watching his life unravel.

He was already fairly drunk by the time he met Sam that night, because Gabe had come to the realization that he couldn't go back again, but not because he was afraid he'd get killed; rather, because he knew if he did a fifth tour, he'd lose the last vestiges of the person he'd been before the Marine Corps and before this never-ending war. And that meant he would have to leave the Corps. He'd advanced to Captain in the ten years he'd been in the Marine Corps and had planned to be a career officer. But that was before these brutal soul extinguishing wars in Iraq and Afghanistan. All told, he'd lost close to nineteen men in the companies he had commanded. But it was the death of the kid from his home state of Texas that was his tipping point.

Gabe could no longer recall why he volunteered to do the visit to the parents of one of his newest recruits: a kid who had been obliterated by the business end of a rocket launcher, two months after arriving in country. His CO had initially rejected his request to fly all the way home to Texas and deliver the awful news but then looked at McAllister's file and saw he'd not been on leave for over a year.

The kid was from a small town east of College Station called Hearne; only a three- or four-hour drive from Houston. Although he knew Billy's parents would have received a phone call within hours after the death of the boy, McAllister was dreading the questions he knew they would have.

Their name was Stodgemont. The house was easy to find; it was a white clapboard farmhouse with a large porch with three empty, broad, wooden rocking chairs facing the street which should have looked welcoming, but didn't. They looked forlorn, exhausted, spent, matching the face of the woman who opened the door to let him in.

Mrs. Stodgemont said nothing as she opened the door to let him in. Her face was expressionless while her weary eyes scanned his dress blue uniform, stopped momentarily at the rows of medals adorning the right side of his chest and returned to his face. She invited him inside with a wordless tip of her chin. Walking heavily into the dark hallway of the house, the woman hesitated for a moment, deciding, then advanced to the back of the house into a large and surprisingly bright kitchen. A large man sat at the end of a red Formica-covered kitchen table, drinking coffee and reading the paper, an empty egg-smeared plate pushed away.

He looked up at his wife as she and Gabe entered the room, blinked a few times, and then stood. There was total silence in the room with the exception of cattle mooing softly in the pastures that must have been in the back of the ranch. For an interminable second the Stodgemonts silently stood facing Gabe, the lines in their faces deepening as the awareness took root. Awkwardly, the older couple and the soldier stared at one another in the kitchen, on the ranch where eighteen-year-old Billy Stodgemont had likely learned to ride, rope, and hunt. All the skills of a rural Texas boy had been acquired before he had decided to join the Marines and subsequently had gotten blown to smithereens in a country on the other side of the world.

The three of them simultaneously broke the silence—startling the cat that slept on the ledge of a high unadorned window facing the pastures and fields stretching endlessly into the distance—both Stodgemonts asking if he'd like to sit and have a cup of coffee and Gabe beginning to express his sorrow. Nodding once, Mr. Stodgemont extended a hard calloused hand to Gabe as he declared softly, "Billy's dead." The faded blue gaze flicked to his wife and then back to Gabe. "My wife and I thank you for driving all the way out here to tell us, Captain." And for the first time, Gabe saw in the older man an echo of the Marine he had been many years before.

During the entire drive, McAllister had been concerned about how he would answer their questions, "How did he die? Did he suffer? Were you with him when it happened?" And the unspoken ones: "Did he die a hero? Did he die for something worthwhile? Are we winning this war? Has his death hastened the time when our boys can come home?"

But as he regarded Billy Stodgemont's father, who was unconsciously standing in a close approximation of a Marine's stance, Gabe knew there would be no questions like that from him or from his war-weary wife. Instead, Gabe had held the older man's work-hardened hand, shook it, and said, "Semper Fi, Sir. Where did you serve?"

After spending a total of twenty minutes with the Stodgemonts and talking mostly about another fiasco of a war—Viet Nam—with Mr. Stodgemont, Gabe drove about ten minutes down the road, pulled over, stopped the car, and walked out through the thorny underbrush. He knelt down in the dust and vomited the three cups of coffee he had consumed while speaking to Billy's parents. He tried to tell himself that the tears pouring down his face were due to the nausea and vomiting, but he knew better.

The night he met Sam, Gabe had ended up at some bar in Montrose that he'd gone to when he was in college, a good place to get drunk. But when, after the second beer, he hardly had a buzz, Gabe decided to wander around the large crowded room. Drink in hand, Gabe made a pretense of checking out the photographs of Houston circa 1950. But he was much more interested in a covert look at the many attractive young women in groups of twos and threes. Five or ten minutes of this and his glass was empty, so Gabe wound his way back through the now tightly packed groups of people standing or sitting in small and larger groups.

Now standing at the long wooden bar, Gabe waited patiently for a third beer while a group of smartly dressed women ordered their drinks. There were five of them and their dress varied as much as did their drinks. Amusing himself by guessing what each woman would order based on her dress, Gabe struck out on each of the five: the gal in jeans and boots ordered the Cosmopolitan rather than the beer he had figured her for; and the dark-haired slim woman in the perfectly fitted business suit ordered the beer instead of the dirty martini that her chubby housewife-looking friend was drinking as quickly as possible.

Laughing silently to himself at the dissonance between dress and drink choice, Gabe turned around so that his back was leaning against the bar, and found her staring at him. Sitting alone at a small table close to the bar, a blonde caught his gaze and smiled, a slow comfortable smile. Her face was long and her nose a little too big for her narrow face. But the way her long blonde hair framed her large wide mouth and big brown eyes seemed to compensate by producing a most arresting face. When the busy waitress stopped at her table to take her order, she pointed to him as well as her empty glass and merely held up two fingers with that same sultry smile.

Condo home of Annie and her mother, Sam

My theory is that Clarence's problem arose precisely because he did not sexually harass Anita Hill.
— *Thomas Sowell*

C H A P T E R

3

Waking up the next morning with a headache bigger than the size of Texas, Gabe blinked several times as he tried to get his bearing in an entirely unfamiliar room. He was lying next to a woman whose name he could not remember while staring into a pair of dazzling blue eyes exactly at the level of his gaze.

"Who are you?"

Said simultaneously by Gabe and the child, there was a sort of perverted humor to seeing a miniaturized version of the woman lying next to him. The woman was snoring loudly, mouth gaping open with a small trail of saliva trailing down to the pillow while the child stood there staring.

Recovering first, the child frowned and replied, "Annie." Then said nothing more, staring at him with all the decorum that a five-year-old could muster while holding a large blue stuffed dog tightly against her thin chest.

His mind racing, Gabe considered his options and realized

there were none. Here was this woman's child, clearly unsurprised at the discovery of a strange man in her mother's bed, wanting to know his name. He was nude, his shirt and pants were thrown onto a chair in the corner of the bedroom, but too far away to reach.

"Gabe, I'm Gabe."

For a beat or three the man and the child stared at each other wordlessly.

Breaking the silence, Gabe said, "Annie, I would really appreciate it if you could grab my clothes off that chair," pointing over to the corner of the room where the clothes lay.

"Okay."

McAllister watched the child as she walked over to the chair, trying to guess her age. She was tiny, maybe 40 or 45 pounds. Despite her size, she still managed to grab his trousers, briefs, and shirt and bring them back to him without letting go of the stuffed blue dog that looked almost as big as she was.

Annie stood as if rooted to the floor while he took the briefs and pants to struggle into them while still under the sheets. The child regarded him solemnly while he swung his legs over the side of the bed, then stood up to pull up his pants and shrug into his shirt; her only movement was to step back a couple of feet so that he had room to stand.

The soft, rhythmic snoring of Annie's mother continued, the only sound in the sun-filled bedroom.

Man, I sure hadn't counted on this ... what do I say to this kid? Those blue eyes are huge; they seem to take up half of her face. And they look a lot older than the four or five years she must be. Shit, I've got to get out of here and fast.

"You're leaving now?"

Annie had followed Gabe out into the living room of the small condo and stood in the hall hugging the huge stuffed animal while staring up at him. Those eyes that seemed too large for her face conveyed a host of conflicting emotions. She was way too little to have learned to hide her profound loneliness as she waited for the door to close on yet another man who had slipped into and out of her life. It was so tangible, so obvious, the want of the child, her lonesomeness that he heard himself say, "What would you like for breakfast, Annie?" The words came out, even though he knew he was making a mistake, knew there was something off here; he did it anyway. His reward was a smile that stopped his heart. The kid's broad smile completely transformed her face, turning those huge blue eyes back into those of a child.

They walked into the small kitchen together, the six-foot-five, 225-pound former Marine and the 38-pound child. Her eyes danced as she watched him checking out the kitchen. It was spotless. But not from good habits of cleaning up after meals: there was a light layer of dust laying on the stove, and on the small table with three chairs. Even the chairs had dust on them; it looked as if no one lived here.

The story here was as ordinary as the proverbial nose on his face. This kid was on her own. The mother was a mom in the biological sense only. Gabe bet his commission that she had never cooked a meal here; the kid had to survive on fast food when Sam remembered to buy it. Suddenly startled, Gabe realized that the child had been alone here … all night. He was drunk when they got to her condo, but there was no sitter to be paid or driven home. The place had been empty and quiet as a tomb.

Opening the refrigerator door and expecting to see the damn thing empty, Gabe was pleasantly surprised to see eggs, milk, enough stuff to make breakfast for the three of them. He stopped, stood there looking into the refrigerator, "What are you doing here man? This whole situation reeks … little kid, left alone while Mom goes out to party, get out now. You know better than this."

Taking a deep breath, Gabe started to close the door and get out when a tiny hand reached around his bulk to try to grab the huge carton of orange juice. But she could neither reach it nor hold it; she was too little.

"Can I have a glass of juice? Can you pour it for me?" Turning to his left, he could look down to catch the somber expression in those enormous blue eyes.

"Where are the glasses, Annie?" Following the point of the tiny finger at one of the three cheap but clean cabinets on the left of the refrigerator, Gabe pulled out two glasses, one for him, and one for Annie, and poured. As he did so, the warning inner voice started back up.

Buddy boy, you spent a whole night, that's like 10 hours with the sleeping nude lady in the bedroom and you can't even remember her name. Even you aren't that coarse; there is something really wrong with this picture and you have no skin in this game. Nada. Get out, now."

The tiny hand was too small to safely grab and transport the full glass. Gabe walked Annie and the juice over to one of the chairs. He set the glass on top of the table in front of one of the chairs and watched as Annie scrambled up on top of one of the chairs to pick up the glass very carefully with both hands. She drank until she had emptied the glass.

"She's starving … the mother probably forgot to feed her! It ain't your problem, this ain't your kid … it felt as if there were two maybe three different people arguing in his head, making his head throb even more.

Sighing, McAllister walked back over to the refrigerator, and this time, pulled out the eggs and bacon. Opening cupboards below the electric stove, he pulled out a pan to fry some bacon, tore open the package and considered whether he should cook only half or all. Shaking his head at the absurdity of the notion that Annie's mother would cook any remaining pieces, he threw the entire pound of bacon into the large frying pan.

Well, I can feed her a good meal before I leave, that won't kill me; when did I eat last anyway? Sure didn't eat anything after leaving the Stodgemont ranch so we'll both have a decent meal before I get out of here … wonder if she drinks coffee.

Gabe searched through another cupboard and found a coffee pot that looked brand new, then looked around for coffee but found none.

"Mom keeps it in the freezer."

Startled at the sound of the little girl's voice, Gabe turned around to see that Annie had swiveled her little body around in the chair so that she could watch everything Gabe was doing. Annie had adopted a perfect yoga pose with the red hearts of her underpants peeking out, the blue eyes gazed somberly at him.

"You're looking for the coffee, right?"

Gabe nodded mutely.

"She keeps it in the freezer, says it stays fresh in the freezer."

Sure enough, there were three unopened bags of coffee in the freezer. Gabe chose the Dunkin Donuts, opened the package and added a liberal amount to the slide out container. As he did so, he thought about this woman whose name he still could not remember and this grave little girl who acted so much older than her years.

Gabe regarded the precocious child as his internal debate waged in his brain. Continuing to ignore the warning voice, he made the coffee, fried the bacon and eggs, and cracked the refrigerated biscuit tin against the sink to prepare them for cooking.

He never actually decided to move in with Annie's mother.

But by the time she stumbled, bleary-eyed into her kitchen, Gabe and Annie were already making a huge game out of cleaning up. They had each wolfed down a breakfast of biscuits, eggs and bacon, coffee for Gabe and three glasses of orange juice for Annie. The child had eaten as if starved and had put away two eggs, four pieces of bacon and two biscuits piled high with butter and Smucker's apricot jam. They were singing a song from Gabe's boot camp days and were unaware of Annie's mother until he felt her body pressing suggestively against his back as a mumbled, "Hmmm … and you're good in the kitchen, too," alerted him to her presence.

Supremely discomfited by the flagrant sexual posturing in front of Annie, Gabe shrugged her off, spun around and looked at the sleepy but alluring figure of Annie's mother. *Damn, what is her name?*

How can I restore what I have never stolen?
— Psalm 69

C H A P T E R

4

There was no sound in the cavernous courtroom as the ADA questioned the little girl with surprising gentleness. Allen Connors was good. He had started off by asking her age and her grade. Connors smiled broadly at the entire jury when Annie had replied that she was not in school yet, she was only in kindergarten, her voice ringing out clearly, like a bell. Her tiny body was poised confidently on the edge of the wooden chair and her face lit up with a smile that was larger than the entire courtroom. The little girl kept up her saucy self-confidence while demonstrating that sure she knew the distinction between what was true and what was false. The silly questions Connors came up with were designed to elicit laughter from both Annie and from the jury and did so.

The verbal and nonverbal changes in Annie's demeanor when he began the questioning about the sexual abuse were startling. Her small body seemed to seek a merger with the massive chair. The child shrank backward as if she were seeking safety. Gone were the smiles, the bell-like clarity of innocence;

a wounded animal had taken residence in the child as a voice devoid of emotion and which could hardly be heard told a disgusting tale of abuse. This was a textbook picture of trauma.

Stomach roiling, Gabe had all he could do to keep from tossing the small amount of food he'd been able to keep down since this nightmare had begun. He could feel the weight of the stares from the entire jury as Connors, a seasoned Assistant District Attorney, began the process of burying Gabe McAllister.

Out of the mouth of the six-year-old poured sickeningly detailed and accurate descriptions of the appearance of semen as it poured from a male penis. Along with simple but graphic language about the sounds and body language of a man as he climaxed.

While listening to the seemingly endless litany of descriptions of sodomy, fellatio and intercourse inflicted by him on this baby, Gabe felt nailed to the chair he sat on. That same nail felt like a stake through his heart. No way, he knew, would this jury find him innocent.

In fact, he didn't blame them. Were he sitting in the shoes of one of the jurors, he'd believe the little girl, too. Annie was eerily persuasive as she used words and images that no six-year-old should ever use. It was crystal clear to Gabe that the child knew what she was talking about: some creep who had preceded him had molested the kid, he had no doubt. Whether she had actually been raped seemed impossible due to her size but the hope he'd held while watching the juror who had questioned the pediatrician was obliterated by Annie's testimony.

Gabe was torn out of his reverie by Allen Connors' question, "Annie, can you point to the man who did all of these things to you?"

Without hesitation, the little girl pointed to him.

"Do you know his name, Annie?

"Gabe, his name is Gabe McAllister."

The child was holding an eight by eleven mimeographed diagram with two large stick figures. One facing front, the second turned so that the crudely drawn buttocks were demonstrated. There were circles around the areas which would approximate the mouth, vagina, and the buttocks.

Annie's eyes had the thousand-yard stare she'd had when she had first met him, the one that he recalled the night he finally moved out. She was staring at him, but he doubted that she saw him: her face was devoid of any expression as she stared down from the gigantic chair at him.

He'd known something was off with these two from that very first morning. But his affection for this little girl and the hope that maybe he could help her had kept him with Annie and her mother for eight long months. Gabe thought about the night he left Annie and her mother. The last time he saw the two of them, until now.

Although Gabe had put in a ten-hour day, he had to leave again for El Paso and Fort Bliss for a week-long training with his new assignment on the JTF. He was psyched about the new assignment because the job as a Texas State Trooper was getting to him. In a word, it was boring: hour after tedious hour of driving on the endless Houston highways rarely interrupted by a chase after a speeder or drink driver. He was grateful for the job and for the ease with which he had made the transition from Marine to the Texas Highway Patrol. Marines were welcomed into Law Enforcement Agencies across the country and the Texas State Troopers fast- tracked soldiers through an abbreviated training at their academy. For McAllister, the training had been condensed to several on-line courses which he had breezed through.

When his boss had announced the opening on the Texas

Joint Counterdrug Task Force in a briefing meeting the day before, Gabe had followed Stanley into his office at the conclusion of the presentation. McAllister closed the office door behind him. Stanley was ignoring Gabe and walked to his desk without turning around.

"Gabe, you need to know this; the criminals you will be dealing with are not your typical low-level thugs; they are extreme." Stanley had wheeled around so suddenly that he and Gabe were standing practically nose to nose. His voice was close to a growl.

Although he could see Stanley winding up to give more examples of why this post may not be the best move for a former Marine still recovering from four tours in Afghanistan, McAllister cut him off.

"Ted, that's what I need, extreme." Standing and staring at his superior officer, also a former Marine, Gabe adopted the Marine stance that was second nature after ten years in the Corps, said nothing else and waited. Ted Stanley was a good guy, and Gabe respected him. The wall behind the two men was plastered with Marine memorabilia from Stanley's past. Too young for Viet Nam, Stanley had enlisted in the mid-seventies and had seen action in Bosnia, Somalia, Beirut; after twenty years in the Corps, Stanley had joined the Texas State Troopers.

Waiting silently for the older man's reply, Gabe took note of the concern buried deep in Stanley's opaque dark brown eyes as the man stood and impassively returned his gaze.

"Report to Captain Elaina Rodriquez at 10:00 pm Thursday evening." Stanley's tone was gruff, his expression grim as he regarded the young former marine. The captain studiously ignored the broad grin on McAllister's face and the triumphal "yes" of his raised right arm and closed first.

"You keep yourself alive now, son. If those towel heads

could not get you then it would be a damn shame to let these cartel morons smash your butt into a million pieces."

Gabe figured Ted Stanley for mid to late fifties. Still wearing his hair cropped in the mostly hairless style of the Marine Corps, Stanley was more fit than most twenty-year-olds; certainly than most of the troopers in his department. Gabe and Stanley had started to work out at the barracks gym together three to four times a week. Gabe could see the work-out regimen that Ted put himself through in an up-close and personal way; it reminded him of boot camp. Gabe was aware that because Ted had three daughters and his only son had been killed in the first Gulf war, he was as close to Ted as any son could be. It mattered to no one in the Stanley family that Gabe was white and the Stanleys black. Since McAllister's parents had divorced when he was very young, it did not take long for Gabe to understand, appreciate, and be grateful for the affection and wisdom shown to him by Ted Stanley. Their relationship had strengthened as the months progressed.

Annie and Sam had been invited to several barbecues and holiday celebrations held by the Stanleys in the eight months he had worked for Stanley. Gabe knew that Ted and his wife worried about Sam and especially Annie; Sam's addictions were evident even to the casual observer.

Suddenly, Gabe had been transported back to the present as Stanley grabbed him in a bear hug.

"Get out of here now, son."

Walking out of Stanley's office, Gabe stopped when he heard, "Give 'em hell son." He raised his right hand in a quasi-salute and kept walking. The next time he saw Stanley he had been arrested.

When the shower door burst open that last night before he left for Fort Bliss, Gabe blinked hard to get the water out of his eyes. When he could finally see, there stood, inside the shower, a nude Samantha with a naked Annie soaking wet and giggling.

Gabe freaked.

Quickly throwing towels over them and wrapping one around himself, he got Annie dried off, into her pajamas and into bed. Then Gabe stalked into the bedroom where Sam waited with her "ready for sex" expression.

Trying to keep his voice down so the child would not hear him, "What the hell were you thinking, Sam?"

He had grabbed his bag and was hastily throwing underwear, socks, his fatigues, and most of his stuff into the bag while Sam watched him from the bed. Her face was devoid of any memory of the week-long training he had told her about last night.

It was weird, Gabe recalled, for he had felt schizophrenic: while half of him was seeing red, the other half was wired, exhilarated. The exhaustion of the long day had been erased because he was about to board a helicopter for the field training he needed to get before starting in the Counter Drug Task Force. The months of tedium were over, he was about to be blasted back into the dark yet strangely comfortable world of combat. After ten years in the Gulf Wars, McAllister realized he had no capacity for anything but war. And he couldn't wait to get the hell away from this drugged out, incompetent woman.

He had been furious at Sam—it had been only for an instant but the memory of the knowledge in five-year-old Annie's eyes, as she gazed at his nude body, chilled him, terrified him.

Sam had laughed off the entire thing, had seemed sincerely puzzled by why he had been so irate. But he knew what he'd seen in the child's blue eyes, had recognized the sensual and seductive turn to those huge expressive blue eyes of Annie's right before mother and daughter had left the bathroom.

Out of the corner of his eye, Gabe watched Sam watching him. Her eyes were at half-mast, so he figured she'd taken one of the seemingly endless supply of uppers and downers she had access to. That was another thing that drove him nuts; her stashes were everywhere. Sam had prescription bottles in the bathroom cabinet, the drawers of the tables on either side of her bed and even hidden behind a couple of spices he'd found that first morning he made breakfast. McAllister had learned very quickly that throwing them away resulted in the emergence of a new crop of a larger variety. Recently, Sam had become very adept at telling her story of her chronic back pain at the plethora of walk-in pain clinics around Houston. Obtaining prescriptions for relief of pain, anxiety, sleeplessness was all too easy in this vast city where no one bothered to check with anyone else. Each time he found a new bottle of pills, he flushed them down the toilet; his concern was not Sam but her little girl with her huge and knowing eyes.

Flipping the top of his well-used military backpack closed, he zipped it and then slung it over his shoulder.

"When will you be back?"

Her words were slurred and the pout now prominent.

"A week, maybe ten days," McAllister lied.

More than a little thankful to get the hell out of there, Gabe quietly closed the door and left.

The next time Gabe saw Sam and Annie was in the courtroom. ADA Allen Connors had totally shattered Simpson's defense strategy of a patriot. Simpson's naïve plan had been to dazzle the jury with the details of a war hero: heroic images of four tours in Afghanistan, of saving countless lives. A man who had sacrificed his life on numerous occasions. Simpson had very successfully used Ted Stanley to defend McAllister. Despite Connor's attempts to discredit and question the relevance of Stanley's testimony, the Judge had overruled the objections of the prosecutor. Stanley was a cop, a former Marine, and now Captain of the Texas State Police; his replies to Simpson, McAllister's lawyer, were crisp and convincing. When he claimed that in his opinion, there could be no way that Gabe McAllister was capable of molesting Annie, some of the jury looked as if they may be rethinking the entire case.

Simpson's defense ended with McAllister's own statements about his career in the Corps, the numbers of combat medals he had been awarded. For a very few minutes, it was looking as if the jurors had some doubts.

But the case was lost with one question by Allen Connors. Was it true that McAllister had showered with Annie?

There was only one answer. Yes, it was true, he had been in the shower with Annie and her mother. When Gabe attempted to explain what had actually happened that night, Connors cut him off.

McAllister had told his attorney about the incident. In great detail, he had explained how it had happened. How Sam had shocked him by dragging Annie into the shower and that she had most likely been stoned at the time. And that the child had been in the shower for less than a second before he got them out of there. But his lawyer sat there like a silent stone as every person in the courtroom visualized what he, Sam, and Annie had been doing in that shower.

*We must all learn to live together as brothers, or we will all
perish together as fools. We are tied together in the single
garment of destiny, caught in an inescapable network
of mutuality. And whatever affects one directly affects all
indirectly. For some strange reason, I can never be what I ought
to be until you are what you ought to be. And you can never
be what you ought to be until I am what I ought to be.
This is the way God's universe is made.*
— Martin Luther King Jr.

C H A P T E R

5

Kate Townsend sat at La Madeleine in the Rice University
Village shopping mall drumming her fingers and absently stirring her now tepid cup of coffee. She was frustrated, annoyed,
angry, disappointed, and close to being depressed.

Lips compressed, her thoughts ran wild.

I should be sitting on the plane to San Francisco. Checking
her watch, Kate saw that the plane she was supposed to be on
was rolling down the tarmac right about now.

*But here I sit, getting ready to give up my life yet again to
tell another story that just must be told. What is it with you
Townsend? You find the perfect guy, a guy who seems to have*

been made for you and yet, here you are, standing him up … for what? Another story? Just what are you looking for? Another Pulitzer? Come on, Kate.

Two years before, Townsend had brought fame to the Houston Tribune and herself with her Pulitzer-winning series, *Murder in the Texas Medical Center.* The newspaper had been on the edge of insolvency, but the investigative reporter's series had won Pulitzers not only for the reporter but for the newspaper. Suddenly, the Tribune had rocketed to rank among the most prominent papers in the nation.

Shaking her long dark hair impatiently, thirty-six-year-old Kate Townsend sighed deeply.

I have ten minutes before she gets here; she'll be on time, maybe even early ….

Dialing his number by heart, "Steve, it's Kate, sorry to call you at the crack of dawn, can you talk for a minute?"

Dr. Steve Cooper was Chief of Cardiology at the University of San Francisco Medical Center. He and Kate had met while Cooper had worked at the University Hospital in Houston, and she was gathering background on the experimental drug Digipro. Cooper had been intrigued and then interested and finally realized that he had fallen for this most unusual reporter named Kate Townsend.

"Kate, sure wait a sec." Cooper was surprised to hear from Kate. Looking at his watch, he smiled wryly to himself, *she's not on the plane, looks like I have a free weekend, after all.*

"Hey guys, I need to take this, go ahead and continue your presentation. Alicia, I'll be back in ten."

Cooper was addressing his Chief Cardiology Fellow, Dr. Alicia Simmons, who was leading the Morbidity and Mortality conference for the week. Cardiologists are like surgeons. Their meetings had to start very early because procedures in the Cath Lab begin at seven in the morning. Although Kate was calling Steve at a little before six in the morning, his long day was already well under way.

Outside the conference room, Steve quipped wryly, "Let me guess, Kate, there's another story with your name written all over it in lights, right?"

Cooper was only half kidding but frowned when he listened to Kate.

"I am sooo very sorry Steve; I don't know why I ...." her voice quavered and Townsend realized that she was dangerously close to tears.

"Hey Kate honey, it's okay. Really it is, whatever is going on, it must be important. Tell me what's up."

Cooper's voice had gentled, had lost any trace of sarcasm; he could hear the anxiety, the anguish in her voice. Sure he was disappointed; he'd planned a very special weekend, had spent as much time on the restaurant and seating arrangements as he did on many of the patients he had on his cardiac cath table.

Although Cooper was thirty-eight years old, he had never been married, had never even thought of asking a woman to marry him. Until he met Kate Townsend, that is. Listening to the woman he wanted to spend the rest of his life with breathe shakily, and try to get control of herself, the memories of the last year flooded him. Kate invariably mitigated her pivotal role in freeing his best friend and colleague, Lindsey McCall from a bogus murder conviction. Steve would always believe that all the complex forces that resulted in freedom for Lindsey had been galvanized by Kate, his intrepid reporter.

God, how I do love this woman ... and am so grateful she is in my life. It just is a real pain in the ass that she's in Houston, and I'm in San Francisco.

"She'll be here in just a few minutes, so I don't have time to tell you. But Steve, I just can't walk away from this. I'm meeting with a woman whose admission of juror tampering may result in a new trial for a guy named Gabe McAllister. He's a former Marine and Texas State Trooper now in Huntsville for three counts of rape of a five-year-old."

Cooper was delighted he'd left the conference room because Kate had succeeded once again in rendering him speechless. Leave it to his Kate, venturing to boldly go where no other reporter has gone before, to take on an untouchable case: child molestation. Steve could think of no other issue more controversial than the sexual molestation of children.

"Steve, are you there? Can you hear me?"

"Roger that, Katie girl, I'm here. You're coming through loud and clear.

"We're in a short time frame. I need to get back in that conference room and I have a bunch of reservations to cancel and you need to get yourself together to meet with this lady." He knew he needed to get back into the conference room, but his curiosity won out.

"What did she do that she is accused of jury tampering?"

Talking fast and low, the reporter he knew kicked in; Kate's voice was clipped and confident. "She's head of the Classics Department at Rice University. Her name is Dr. Alexandria Allbrite. She claims that she would never have found McAllister guilty had she not learned online the first night of the trial that an intact vaginal hymen did not preclude vaginal penetration, intercourse.

"A friend of hers told her he thought her actions were against the rules because jurors are to make their decisions solely on what was presented by the prosecution and defense. She wrote a letter to the judge who had heard McAllister's case to explain that she would never have found the guy guilty unless she had learned this information. At a hearing several weeks ago, she testified in court about her actions.

"Based on her admission, the state of Texas has amended their instructions to jurors to exclude online research along with the standard prohibition against discussing the case with anyone or watching and reading media reports." Breathlessly, Kate declared, "The Judge denied a mistrial which was upheld by the Appeals Court, but there is an appeal to the Texas Court of Criminal Appeals."

"Man, Kate … this sounds huge …." Suddenly, Cooper remembered the horrifying nightmare of a divorce case of an acquaintance of his. They had not been friends really but had worked together on a few cases when Steve had been at the University of Houston Medical Center. Ted was a cardiologist like Steve and had a lucrative private practice that he lost due to the indictment and conviction. Although Ross had been exonerated when his daughter admitted her lies on appeal, Ross had been forced to leave Houston due to the five-year media blitz surrounding the case.

Steve and Ted had each presented papers at the American College of Cardiology in Dallas. Theirs were the final two presentations of the meeting that year, meaning that most of the attendees had caught early flights home leaving only those with nowhere better to be on a Friday night in August. Following his own presentation, Steve had waited while Ted attempted rebuttals to the volley of complaints and criticisms about his methodology and conclusions of a study on pulmonary hypertension secondary to acute fibrosis in ten laboratory rats.

Steve had thought these guys were tough on him, but they had practically let him sail through compared to the older cardiologists' evisceration of Ted's data.

"Hey, let's go drown our sorrows in a gallon of alcohol." Steve had been smiling but when he saw the look on Ted's face, his grin quickly faded. "Hey, Ted, don't let these guys get to you. They're just pissed because the field they have commandeered for the last sixty years is changing. The 'Young Turks' are taking over." Steve knew he was babbling but did it anyway because of the concern he felt for his colleague.

Sighing, Ted nodded wearily, "Yeah, I guess that's not a bad idea."

The two men walked together to the central bar of the Ritz-Carlton in Dallas where the Cardiology meeting had been held. The bar was tastefully done. Dark mahogany merged with light woods on the tables and floor in an understated and cool elegance. An ambiance which could make one overlook the hot August day awaiting those who stepped out of the air conditioning and into the blistering heat of high summer in Dallas.

Barely five-thirty on Friday afternoon, there were only two other people in the bar. Steve walked over to the far and empty end of the bar, grabbed a table where he pulled out a chair, and told Ted, "I'm buying, sit down and I'll be back with ….?"

In less than five minutes, Cooper was approaching Ted, carefully balancing his vodka martini and Ted's Maker's Mark on the rocks. "To us 'Young Turks.'" Steve held up his glass until Ted raised his to clink Steve's martini glass.

At least that got a smile out of the poor guy. Cannot believe the rancor pouring out of a man who was once called "The Father of Cardiology."

Cooper was referring to one of the bitter cardiologists who had stayed to hear the last of the papers presented at the five-day conference that had just ended with Ted's paper. Why a man who had achieved such success in his career would let himself be consumed by rage was a mystery to Steve. His thoughts were interrupted with a comment from Ted said so softly that he couldn't hear the words.

"Sorry, Ted, I didn't hear what you just said." Looking up, Cooper was shocked to see tears standing in the hazel gaze now riveted on him.

As if to gain the courage to repeat himself, Ted gulped down a huge swallow of his drink, "I said that Marcie is accusing me of sexually molesting my Christy." Ted's wife of ten years claimed that Ted had raped their eight-year-old over the final four years of their marriage. "Staring down at the now half-empty bourbon on the rocks, Ted continued softly, "We are in the middle of the divorce from hell, Steve. She hired Jody Collins to make sure that there are no potentially lucrative rocks left unturned; but *this*, I had no idea Marcie would go this far." Jody Collins was a Houston divorce attorney well-known for winning huge settlements for her predominantly female clients.

"Steve, I've been *indicted* for God's sake … indicted for raping my own daughter … what kind of a pervert could do that to any child, never mind his own daughter!"

Although it had been over six years since that Friday night, Cooper could see clearly the anguish, fear, shock, and betrayal displayed on Ted's face as plainly as if each was affixed with a label.

Cooper had sat drinking and listening as the time for his return Southwestern Airline flight to Houston came and went. Finally at ten, the two men had ordered some food for the sole purpose of soaking up the prodigious amounts of alcohol they had consumed over the last five hours.

Steve was not a fan of Ted Ross, Cardiology Associates of Houston. He suspected that Ted and his group did lots of unnecessary procedures: cardiac catheterizations and stents in patients where the degree of coronary artery disease did not warrant the risks. But these procedures were the bread and butter of cardiology. Cooper was honest enough to admit that if, like Ted Ross, he were in private practice with a family to support, his academic medical center ideals could well be compromised. After listening to the vicious, slanderous attacks on Ross by Marcie Ross's lawyer, Cooper had been stunned by the speed with which a man's career, reputation, and entire livelihood could be imperiled. Ross had acquitted himself but only after years and hundreds of thousands of dollars ending up in bankruptcy for his practice. The last Cooper knew of Ted Ross, he had moved to Idaho and was practicing family medicine in a small town not too far from Boise.

"Steve, are you there? I think I see her coming in now."

"Kate, listen, this is important. If this guy is innocent, he needs you, Babe."

"Are you being facetious, Steve?" Her tone was curt, defensive.

"Not at all, Kate, far from it. I know a guy from years ago who went through hell … this guy was falsely accused of raping his daughter. He was later acquitted but only after a year, maybe two in prison—he lost everything, all because of a crazy wife. I had no idea something like this could happen to anyone. If this guy is in the same place as Ted was, you're his only chance."

"Give 'em hell, Lois Lane." Cooper took a deep breath, lowered his voice then said, "This is one of the hundreds of reasons I love you, Kate Townsend."

Kate grinned at Cooper's use of the sobriquet she had been given by a couple of research scientists while she was in Lausanne, Switzerland investigating her Pulitzer-winning series the year before.

I honestly don't know what I have ever done in my life to deserve the love, trust, understanding, and patience of this man but thank you for him. Not at all sure whom she was thanking, she did it anyway, more and more frequently.

Still smiling, Townsend stood and extended her hand to the fifty-something-year-old strawberry blonde standing in front of her, looking curious.

"You are Kate Townsend, right? I recognized you from your series of articles in the Trib a couple of years ago."

"That would be me, Dr. Allbrite, thank you very much for taking the time to meet with me this morning."

La Madeleine Coffee Shop

*Out beyond ideas of wrong-doing and right-doing there is
a field. I'll meet you out there.*
— Rumi

C H A P T E R

6

"So how did you find out about me?" Dr. Alexandria
Allbrite directed a pair of intense eyes of indeterminate color
at Kate. They could be hazel, brown, or a dark blue but in the
light of the bright morning sun streaming through the window
at their right, she could not tell. The beam of light aimed right
at the head of the Rice University Classics professor like a
halo.

The question was delivered in a measured tone with a
slight east coast accent. Kate knew that Allbrite's undergraduate
degree had been completed at Bennington College in Vermont,
her graduate at Tufts University in Boston and her doctoral
work in Classics at Yale. Dr. Allbrite's last ten years at Rice had
muted the broad "a" and barely heard "r" sounds of the eastern
intellectual, but they were there if you listened.

The Professor's question had come just as Kate had taken
a bite of the biscotti which would serve as breakfast and lunch.
Therefore, she had time to reflect on what she had learned

about this woman and to decide how much information she was willing to give her.

As if reading Kate's thoughts, Allbrite declared, "Listen Kate, I spend my days studying long-dead people and civilizations. And I attempt to persuade twenty-first-century teens that the art of writing and speaking exceeds one hundred forty characters. When I'm not in class, I write articles for scholarly journals that only I and a few thousand others in my world care about."

She took a sip of her tea and swallowed. "Quite frankly, I am stunned that I am sitting here talking with you; the truth is Kate, I have more to fear from you than do you from me. I *like* my quiet, orderly life and am fiercely protective of the seclusion my poet husband, and I enjoy. I have a horror of being on the nightly news or whatever show Oprah is doing now or Jerry Springer or whatever passes for breaking news these days …."

Allbrite picked up the decanter of hot water, poured a generous amount into the off-white ceramic mug with an Earl Grey tea bag tag looped over the rim while she stared out the window over Kate's right shoulder into the suddenly cloudy sky. She stirred the brew slowly and methodically; the motion looked rehearsed.

Kate waited as the seconds ticked by and then into minutes, appreciating the candor and the thoughtful reflection of Dr. Alexandria Allbrite. Hers was very clearly a trained mind; her speech was not hasty: this woman took great care to assure the accuracy of her words.

After at least two to three minutes of total silence, a very long time when two strangers are sitting together, Dr. Allbrite's gaze met Kate's. Flashing a quick smile at Kate, she continued as if she were in mid-thought, "But when I was informed that my research outside the courtroom was improper and constituted 'jury tampering,' I was," she hesitated as she visibly searched for the right word, "*relieved.*"

"This case has haunted me since I walked out of that courtroom ten months ago. We sentenced that man to three counts of rape: twenty to life for each orifice." Then a whispered plea, "My God, how I hope he did do this."

The troubled, dark blue gaze settled on her; now that the clouds had obscured the sun, Kate could see that Alex's eyes were a dark blue that seemed to fit her round, freckled face. Hers was the face of a redhead, skin so pale it looked transparent. Not a pretty face: her nose was too pug and her lips too full to be considered good-looking. At first impression, Alexandria Allbrite was ordinary looking; her hair was strawberry blonde, more carrot-colored than blonde, and she wore it at a casual medium length, tousled about her face. She wore very little makeup: only a touch of shadow and mascara, a reluctant and understated submission to the cultural mores of twenty-first-century females.

She was one of those quiet people, Kate thought, who you pass in the store without seeing because their features and body type are unremarkable unless you take the time to interact with them to sense the power of their intelligence and depth. If she'd had any doubts about taking on this case after getting the green light from Cooper, they were being whisked away, just like her biscotti crumbs were brushed away by the pleasant Hispanic waitress.

Kate had read the transcript of the first hearing for a new trial for Gabe McAllister. McAllister's new lawyer argued that the "jury tampering" by Dr. Alexandria Allbrite constituted sufficient reason to declare a mistrial; the judge hearing the case had denied the appeal.

There was only one witness: Dr. Alexandria Allbrite, who stated in the flat, emotionless prose of twenty-first-century jurisprudence that yes, she had researched information perti-nent to the case of *The State of Texas v Gabriel McAllister.*

The Court: Dr. Allbrite, you did this research despite being told not to discuss this case outside of this courtroom?

Dr. Allbrite: Judge, I discussed this case with no one. I am a researcher by profession and when ….

Mr. Allen: Please reply to the question that the Judge asked you.

Dr. Allbrite: I just did.

Mr. Allen: The Judge's question requires only a yes or a no answer.

Doug Allen was the ADA on the McAllister case and was obviously peeved at this new wrinkle in his excellent record of wins for cases he prosecuted for the state in Harris County, Texas.

The Court: Okay, Doctor, I will rephrase my question. Did you research information pertinent to *The State of Texas v. Gabriel McAllister* outside of this courtroom?

Dr. Allbrite: Yes, I did … I did this be—"

The Court: Thank you, Doctor.

Mr. Allen: Dr. Allbrite, what information did you research?

Dr. Allbrite: Whether the presence of an intact vaginal hymen precluded sexual intercourse.

Mr. Allen: And what did you learn from your research?

Dr. Allbrite: That it was possible for females to engage in intercourse without rupture of the vaginal hymen.

Mr. Allen: Where did you find this information, Dr. Allbrite?

Dr. Allbrite: I googled the subject and found several articles by gynecologists and obstetricians.

Mr. Allen: Do you recall the names of the journals?

Dr. Allbrite: I do not.

Mr. Allen: Did you share this information that was learned

outside this courtroom with the other jurors assigned to *The State of Texas v. Gabriel McAllister?*

Dr. Allbrite: Yes, I did, this info—"

Mr. Allen: Thank you for appearing today, Dr.—"

Dr. Allbrite: Wait, I need to tell you both something, Judge.

Mr. Allen: We are done here today, Dr. Allbrite.

Dr. Allbrite: No, Sirs, we are not done here. The reason I wrote to you and am sitting here is that if I had not learned that this was possible, I would never have found this man guilty of three counts of rape ....

Mr. Allen: Thank you, Dr. Allbrite.

The Court: Thank you, Dr. Allbrite. We are finished here, Doctor, The State of Texas thanks you for your time.

Kate's almost eidetic memory had flashed through the short transcript of the hearing denying McAllister's new defense attorney a mistrial as she'd listened to Allbrite. She had been impressed by the tenacity of a woman who quite obviously knew little to nothing about the law; and yet risked walking into alien territory with her eyes wide open—because she'd felt it the right thing to do. Now, listening to Allbrite's voice and the raw emotion still there after ten months, Kate was riveted.

"Ladies, can I get you something from the breakfast bar?"

While Allbrite scanned the menu the young woman handed her, Kate risked a glance at the time; she was due out at the prison by eleven and it was already ten. Mistakenly, she had planned only one hour with the professor.

You've done it again, Townsend, tried to pack too much into too little time. This woman may be the heart of this story. "Haunted" ... "relieved" at her discovery that she'd been guilty of jury tampering ... wow!

Glancing up, she found Allbrite looking quizzically at her, eyebrow raised.

"Dr. Allbrite, thank you very much for opening up to me like this. I cannot tell you how much I appreciate what you have just told me. If you'll permit me to make a very quick phone call to re-schedule a meeting I had planned out in Huntsville, I'd like to buy you breakfast." Waiting for a nod, Kate added with a smile, "And then I'd like to commandeer your morning. I believe you told me on the phone that this morning was free for you?"

Following a surprisingly excellent breakfast of bacon and eggs consumed by both women, Allbrite sat back and repeated her first question, "So, how did you find my name?"

Mirroring her posture, Kate sat back also, "I saw the notice in the crime section of the Tribune: that the state law had been altered because of a case of juror misconduct. Texas jurors will now be given instructions that prohibit them from doing internet research in addition to reading or listening to media accounts, and talking with others outside the courtroom while the case is in trial."

"Dr. Allbrite—"

Interrupting Kate, Dr. Allbrite said with a smile, "Kate, please, you've bought me breakfast, an excellent one at that, and it looks as if we'll be spending some time together. Let's dispense with the credentials? Please call me Alex."

Returning the smile, Kate responded, "Okay, Alex. The name suits you I think. Bet it comes as a surprise to colleagues at your meetings, who are expecting a man in a tweed coat and bowtie."

Alex laughed, coloring slightly at the reporter's insight. She had duped many an associate in the early years when accepting an invitation to present one of her papers at the Society for Classical Studies. But she said nothing, content to wait to hear more from Townsend.

"I've been a crime reporter for over ten years, Alex. I had

never heard of the phrase *jury tampering,* so I did some research on recent cases where appeals for new trials in Houston had been granted. A friend from the District Attorney's office got me the name of the case and the court reporter who had been assigned the hearing for the appeal: *State of Texas v. Gabriel McAllister.*

"You were the only witness." She smiled, "That's how I found you." Kate looked at the somber, intelligent face regarding her and made her decision.

"When I saw this short piece about you, about what you did, I thought I could read between the lines to guess your motives. And now, having listened to you explain what little you have, my gut sense about you is confirmed." Allbrite, Kate guessed, was one of those rare people who resisted the prejudicial thinking of most of us.

Early in her undergraduate years at Stanford, Kate had taken some psychology courses from a remarkable professor who had captivated Kate to the point that she had briefly considered a career as a psychologist. For his doctoral dissertation on the origins of prejudice during the late seventies, Dr. Simpson had studied thousands of people, expecting to find educational and demographic reasons behind those who demonstrated prejudicial views and those who did not. Simpson's study revealed no demographic predictors of prejudice. Age, gender, race, religion, and numerous other demographic variables had been controlled by the design of his study, and none was found which could reliably predict prejudicial attitudes.

Simpson determined that prejudicial attitudes *could* be consistently predicted by the way individuals processed new information and made decisions based on the new information. Most of the population was composed of two groups: those who analyzed new information versus those who synthesized it. Simpson was able to show that it was the analytic thinker who demonstrated the aptitude for prejudicial thinking and not the synthesizer. Rarely were there people who showed both methods of thinking: analytic and synthesis. Kate had applied them in her years as a journalist and believed that Simpson's methods had provided her with the insights into the motivation and attitudes of people that her editors and readers saw in her writing.

Allbrite, Kate was sure, was one on those rare individuals who were both an analytic and synthesizer. She remembered Simpson describing the person who naturally thought in both ways. They would be unusually intelligent, curious, highly intuitive, and could appear to be an erratic thinker; therefore, difficult to follow at times. Recalling all this so many years later, Kate realized that Dr. Simpson was describing Dr. Alexandra Allbrite entirely.

Kate used her fork to play with the detritus of her breakfast while she talked. "Frankly, Alex, it's eerie because I think you and I are in exactly in the same place here. Perhaps for not so very different reasons: neither you nor I really want to mess with this but we feel compelled." Looking up to gauge the reaction of her listener, Townsend was gratified by a look of surprise and a subtle but evident relaxation in the facial features of Allbrite.

"I cannot think of an individual more fitting of the term "a social pariah" than the child molester. Americans have more tolerance for suicide bombers than for child molesters." Steve's peculiar statement near the end of their conversation now rang in her ear. *"Kate, listen, this is important. If this guy is innocent, he needs you." That sounded strangely similar to Allbrite's statement that she had been "relieved" when she learned of her juror misconduct. Coincidence?*

Kate didn't believe in coincidence.

Alex was watching Kate intently; she was nodding very slowly as Kate made the comment about child molesters; her expression was grim.

"Alex, do you suspect that McAllister is not guilty, after all?" Kate had lowered her voice almost to a whisper because both women had noticed the silence in La Madeleine and the ease with which an interested onlooker could listen to a conversation that needed to exclude other participants.

Without waiting for a reply from Allbrite, because her question was rhetorical, Kate suggested they leave the restaurant. "If you have the time, I wonder if you'd like to walk off our breakfast for a few miles in Memorial Park while we talk."

An hour later, the two women were still strolling through Memorial Park. Although over four million people use the park each year, perhaps because of the threatening clouds and the time of day, there were on that day only occasional runners. It was nearly noon, and the famed Houston humidity hung heavily in the air. Houston's Memorial Park is one of the largest urban parks in the country. Opened in 1924, Memorial Park contains almost fifteen hundred acres inside the 610 Loop and across from the Memorial neighborhood.

Alex and Kate were able to walk two abreast on the narrow dirt running and walking path, so they could easily talk. With Alex's permission, Kate had her miniature recorder on so that both could walk at a reasonable pace while Alex filled Kate in.

"You asked if I thought then, or more accurately, think now, that Gabe McAllister is guilty. I haven't a clue. The only two people who know are a five-, maybe now six-year-old little girl and McAllister himself."

They were walking fast. Allbrite's pace seeming to speed up as she dug deeper into the memory of her experience.

"But from the beginning, his guilt was assumed by everyone." Alex slowed her pace so that she could see Kate's face.

"You know the maxim, 'innocent until proven guilty'? In this case anyway, it was a travesty. From the beginning of the trial, McAllister was doomed." Allbrite looked up at the darkening sky and picked up her pace.

"Too many things did not add up for me, Kate. First, there is the fact of the intact hymen attested to by the pediatrician and nurse practitioner. McAllister is a really tall, well-built guy, like six foot four or five, maybe two hundred pounds and Annie is maybe forty or fifty pounds?" Allbrite turned to Kate, an incredulous expression on her face.

"Second, the fact that Annie, the little girl, told a friend about all of this something like four or six months after McAllister moved out. Why wait all of that time? Then the little friend tells her mother. What does the mother of the little friend do? She calls the state. Wouldn't most people call the little girl's mother first? But in these Kafkaesque times we live in, I guess we no longer use common sense. We call the state to report a little girl's story about her friend." Kate turned to see Allbrite's mouth turn down into a frown.

"Something like six weeks maybe two months go by and then McAllister is arrested when he returns from a week-long training at Fort Bliss for some co-op team we have set up to fight the drug cartels. What were the police, the social workers, and the child psychologist doing all of that time?" Allbrite had ticked off her fingers as she named these disciplines. "Oh and the nurse practitioner and the pediatrician, forgot them."

By now, Allbrite was breathing heavily but seemed not to care.

"They were talking to this little girl, asking her questions and suggesting where she might have been touched."

Turning to look more thoroughly at Alex, Kate saw what she thought she would. That expression of intense concentration, the woman was reaching back into her experience as the juror on this case and was reliving it now.

Alex's generally porcelain complexion was fiercely red. She looked extremely uncomfortable but seemed not to notice as she stared ahead at the path they were briskly walking. Kate wagered Alex saw nothing but the disturbing memories that seemed to stalk her.

"I thought long and hard about that letter I wrote to Judge Gloria Bennett, Kate. I have a beautiful house in West U, which I share with my husband, Stanley." Turning to Kate with a grin, Alex quipped, "He of the bow tie and tweed coat."

Kate chuckled, increasingly enjoying her time with this bright and unusual woman.

"You asked how I learned that I had done something wrong. Serendipity really. A week give or take after the trial was over, I was emailing a friend I've known since we were both small children to tell him about the trial. About how I could not get this defendant, Gabe McAllister out of my head." Pausing for a beat, Allbrite glanced quickly at Kate and then at the slowly spinning tape in the miniature recorder in Kate's left hand, close enough to Alex so that the tape could record her voice, "Out of my *heart.* My friend Jeff replied that he had always thought that the responsibility of the juror was to conclude the presence or absence of guilt based solely on the information provided by the prosecution and the defense. Since I had told him the details of this case, Jeff added that he could understand why I had gone through the exercise of researching what seemed like a highly improbable event.

"I recall that I thought about his comment for at least two or three days. I had saved it and had returned to Jeff's email to read his exact words.

"I don't know why I didn't talk with my husband about all of this, Kate. Maybe it was because Stan had heard little else from me following the trial and because of my *guilt.*"

Allbrite practically hissed the word. "When we found him guilty of three counts of rape, he was sentenced to twenty years to life for each count; one for her vagina, one for her mouth and one for her anus, for God's sake." Her face was pale now, the perspiration providing a faint sheen. She was shaking her head from side to side as if in disgust.

"But I realized that I had to write to that judge."

Alex stopped there, still staring at the now empty jogging path. There were sounds of distant thunder and the sky was an ominous color, but Alex paid no attention. Kate was certain that Alex had a whole lot more to disclose and sensed that if they stopped now to return to Kate's car, they might not easily return to the place where Alex was now residing.

Kate stood quietly, waiting. *Worst case, I get soaked. Right now, not a terrible thought. I've sweat off most of my makeup and am sure my hair is already plastered to my head.*

Suddenly unable to resist asking the question a second time, Kate stopped suddenly, placed her hand on Allbrite's arm and quietly framed a question as a statement. "You really think this guy is not guilty, don't you?"

Alex turned to Kate and gazed into her eyes. She liked what she saw there: this woman Kate Townsend looked real, the expression on her attractive face was open; the expression in her warm brown eyes was pure compassion. Allbrite was glad she had come this morning if for no other reason than to feel as if she were doing something. Doing something for this man who seemed to her to have been railroaded and who she could not get out of her thoughts. "This little girl has obviously been molested. Anyone could see the change in her behavior when the ADA began to ask her questions and have her point to the places on the diagrams she had been given.

"But was it this guy? I was and am very skeptical." Alex took a deep breath. "But this is what I do know: he never had a prayer once he was arrested. This thing was a train, gathering momentum as it sped down the track faster and faster.

"I had never sat on a jury before, ever. And I hope I never do again." Allbrite's dark blue eyes searched Kate's brown ones. "Wouldn't you think that there would be twelve people willing to weigh the evidence? Willing to listen critically to the case presented against him by the DA?

"Wouldn't you think a jury of your peers would begin by assuming innocence? I waited for three hours while the judge, the prosecution, and defense eliminated potential jurors. Over thirty people were dismissed that morning. If they had a relative who was a cop or they'd had prior experience with sexual abuse, they were excused. But we still ended up with eleven people who believed the guy was guilty simply because he was there."

Allbrite, Kate knew, was talking about the process of voir dire. Voir dire is the process by which both the defense and prosecution get to disqualify potential jurors due to a stated bias or prejudice. The stated objective is to raise the threshold for twelve objective, open-minded jurors. In this case, people with a self-proclaimed history with sexual abuse would have been excused by the judge.

"Each one of the eleven people on that jury with me believed McAllister had done this, apparently from the start of the trail. *None* of them paid any attention to the fact of the intact hymen. Or to the fact that the mother had accused a man, not the father of the child, of sexual abuse of Annie before the child was a year old. Or that the mother could barely tell the ADA her name, she was so medicated.

"And my eleven colleagues bought the show cleverly staged by the use of six expert witnesses, each with impeccable qualifications, culminating with the testimony of the little girl herself. During the three maybe five hours we were in there, I tried to explain why I had so many doubts. There were a few who were listening to me when a former Marine in his mid-to-late sixties, suddenly opened his mouth to ask me if I was suggesting that Annie was lying. When I started to answer him that yes, kids have been known to lie, there were loads of studies demonstrating their suggestibility in a desire to please a questioner, the guy cut me off and stated that he had ten kids; none of them would *ever* lie."

Slowing down the pace of her walking again, Allbrite turned to Kate and said, "Sorry, I'm rambling, let me start from the beginning. Once the case was done, we were excused by the Judge and given our instructions. The bailiff led us into a conference room with a long table and thirteen chairs. We all avoided the chair placed at the head of the table; we took our seats and sat down. Several women began to talk to one another as if they knew each other and a couple of the men said something about electing a Foreman.

"They chose me to be Foreman. Probably because I was sitting there quietly. My head was down and I was staring down at my legal pad where I'd written a bunch of notes and several questions. I was trying to be anonymous when I heard the man sitting to my right say, 'Let's elect her.' I looked up, expecting to see some other woman move to the head of the table. But he was pointing at me and the others were all nodding their agreement.

"So okay, I thought, I can do this … I got up, moved to the head of the table and tried to get a discussion started." Sighing deeply, she added, "But it was just like every meeting you've ever conducted … one person started to talk and would not shut up. For several minutes, she talked about 'all the evidence' showing his guilt. She yammered on and on until I had to tell her to stop … that we needed to hear from the rest of us. I surveyed everyone seated around the table asking each person sitting there what he or she thought.

"Same thing, all the evidence shows without a doubt … he's guilty.

"After an hour or so, the man who had initially pointed to me as Foreman asked me why I had not said anything, had not given my opinion. I smiled at him in thanks because I thought that I could help them see that there was not any evidence—there were simply opinions by five witnesses for the state.

"They had placed a whiteboard behind my chair at the head of the table. So I stood and wrote the phrase 'Evidence' on one side. And I wrote 'Doubts' on the other side of the whiteboard.

"My list of questions under doubts was extensive. The presence of an intact vagina, the conduct of the mother, the time lag between McAllister moving out of the apartment and the child telling her story to her friend, the fact that the state had been working behind the scene for several weeks with the child. And that the child psychologist, social worker, nurse practitioner, and pediatrician were expert witnesses and were paid by the state to testify. The fact that McAllister's defense consisted of nothing more than three people saying he was a nice guy, he would never do this; and lastly, McAllister himself denying that he did this. That was the defense, pathetic.

"Never did his defense attorney question the mother about an accusation of sexual abuse made by the mother against someone not the child's father when the little girl was six months old.

"Never did the Defense question the pediatrician about how a five-year-old girl could have been raped but be found to have an intact hymen.

"And never was the little girl challenged by the Defense about her story.

"Then I moved over to the column labeled 'Evidence' and wrote 'extensive anal scarring.' Then I turned around to the group and asked my eleven colleagues, 'You've all been talking about all the evidence, but what evidence is there except the anal scarring?' Anal scarring which could have been there for years?

"Suddenly several people were talking at once. They were upset, a couple of them were freaked. One or two people asked if I was saying he was innocent, how could I deny the little girl's accusation? When I talked about day care centers where children had admitted to falsely alleging sexual abuse, a guy who was sitting at the far end of the table from me took me on. It was the Marine with ten kids; he knew that kids don't lie. Did I have kids? No? Well, he did, he had ten, and he could say for a fact that kids don't lie.

"We went back and forth with various people trying to understand why I was skeptical. There were two women who seemed to be really trying hard to see what I saw.

"Each time I would explain, one of them would say something like 'Would you feel more comfortable if we said only two counts of rape rather than three?' One woman kept saying, 'If the intact vagina is such a problem, let's say only two counts and leave out the question of the vaginal intercourse.' They were placating me … it was a negotiation, asking if I would feel more comfortable if …." Alex stared straight ahead and sighed deeply.

"None of these people had any interest in the conversation I wanted to have; no one wanted to discuss anything at all. They simply wanted to agree so that they could get out of there." Allbrite stood up, pacing, hair blowing in the increasingly brisk wind. Then she turned to Kate, "Wouldn't you expect twelve people to question an accusation as serious as this? Wouldn't you expect that they would want to explore other possibilities of what had happened here? Wouldn't you expect a group of 'peers' to need real, actual evidence that someone did something this heinous?"

Shaking her head in frustration, "I caved when the former Marine picked up a mimeographed sheet of paper we had each been given by the Bailiff. The ex-Marine instructed us all to pick up the page and read aloud the section that applied. He read: 'By law, in the State of Texas, sexual assault requires the testimony of only one witness for conviction.'

Standing at the opposite end of the table from me, he was waving the sheet of paper, "There's your evidence, the little girl, the victim *says* it happened! Are *you* going to argue with what we have been told by the State and by this judge?"

"So this is why I'm here with you, Kate; I should not have agreed with the three counts of rape—because I had reasonable doubt, a whole truckload of reasonable doubt."

Fittingly, the skies had opened, and both women were suddenly drenched.

Allbrite's hair was plastered to her head, her skirt adhering to her generous frame. "Well, Kate Townsend, I hope I look every bit as silly as you do right now!" Lifting her face up to the skies and the torrential rain, she said with relief, "I cannot tell you how happy I am that I had the guts to talk to you. I feel better than I have in months!"

They were standing in the middle of the path; as her smile faded, Alex asked, "How do you prove that you *didn't* do something, Kate?"

New Waverly, Texas

"Do you really want a cure?" The Holy One asked.

"If I did not would I bother to come to you?" The disciple answered.

"Oh yes," The Master said, "Most people do."

And the disciple said, incredulously, "But what for then?"

And the Holy One answered, "Well, not for a cure, that's too painful,

They come for relief."

— Joan Chittister in The Rule of Benedict:
A Spirituality for the 21st Century

C H A P T E R

7

Lindsey's eyes snapped open. She knew the futility of attempting to get back to sleep so she rolled to the side of the bed as quietly as she could, hoping not to disturb her husband, Rich Jansen. Although they had celebrated their first anniversary until well past midnight, Lindsey suspected that it was not yet five in the morning. The light of the brand new morning was just now beginning to filter through the tall pines of the Sam Houston State Forest where they lived in a "cabin" that had been built by Governor Greg Bell as a getaway from Austin. Each time she thought of this stunning, elegantly designed and furnished log home, she smiled to herself. Lindsey and Rich had attempted to buy the house from Bell but then the Governor had learned of their quiet marriage at the Co-Cathedral of the Sacred Heart in downtown Houston. Bell and his wife Cindy had insisted on giving them the house as a wedding gift.

Walking on bare feet over to her dresser on the far side of the enormous master bedroom, she grinned when she felt a cold, wet nose nudge her naked rib cage.

"Morning, Max boy." The red Doberman named Max at first intrigued Lindsey; she had never even seen a Doberman, never mind lived with one. The only pets her family had ever had were the koi in her mother's fish pond; none of the McCall family had been dog people. But her husband Rich had always had dogs and as an adult, his were Dobermans, bred from a Texas breeder of Dobermans who Rich's first wife, Laura, had found.

After living with Max for over a year, Lindsey's intrigue had quickly transformed into deep love. She could not imagine life without this intelligent being who behaved more humanly than many humans she had worked with.

The dog was tall, weighed about eighty-five pounds, yet had the ability to walk soundlessly on the all-wood floors of the house, like a cat. Lindsey had long ago become accustomed to the soft pressure of Max's nose as his signature hello. Glancing at the clock, she saw it was indeed only a few minutes before five. Max was standing still, watching her every move, on high alert for the sound of one of his favorite phrases.

Lindsey turned to see if Rich had stirred. There was no movement at all from the inert form of her husband, and the deep rhythmic breathing signaled deep sleep. Although she was eager to get to the infirmary to check on her severely beaten patient, Lindsey decided a quick run in the woods was in order. The run would clear the fog out of a brain that had enjoyed a surfeit of celebration last night.

Quickly finding her sports bra, underpants, running clothes and shoes, she gathered them into a pile and walked out of the bedroom to head down the stairs. Looking back into the bedroom as she stood at the head of the stairs, McCall could see Max, still standing at the door awaiting permission.

Whispering now, "Okay Max, let's go."

Immediately those expressive Dobie ears stood straight up. He was out the door and down the stairs, now standing, dancing a little, as he waited for her, excited at the prospect of a run in the woods.

Lindsey was donning her shirt and shorts as she descended the stairs, then sat down on the last step to step into and tie her running shoes.

Once outside, Lindsey stopped to do a few quick stretches and looked around the yard to see if there were any deer out enjoying the cool August morning. Seeing none, she started down the dirt path that extended for miles in the state forest, picking up the pace as she warmed up.

Max was, as always, in front of her, but stayed in close enough proximity that she could either see or hear him.

This feels good, just what I needed and good for Max too ... he spent a long time alone yesterday; the poor guy didn't get our usual run last night ... I barely had time to dress and get to Houston in time to meet Rich, never mind run with Max.

With that thought, Lindsey picked up her pace and ran for another thirty to forty minutes before she turned around.

Yikes, it's getting late, I need to get into work.

Within another thirty minutes, Max and Lindsey thundered up the stairs of the porch, and into the house, each heading for the water.

"Take time for breakfast, Linds."

Rich was standing in only shorts while he stirred the bacon with one hand and poured Lindsey coffee, added coffee cream, and handed her the mug with the other.

To the background sounds of Max drinking what seemed like gallons of water, McCall accepted the coffee with one hand and encircled the lean torso of her husband with the other. "Rich Jansen, I do love you! You make me soooo happy!" she said in a sing-song voice.Jansen grinned in reply, grateful for the miracle of this beautiful woman, for their love, and for the remarkable transformation of Dr. Lindsey McCall in a little less than two years. As he often did, Rich flashed back to the first time he saw her. She had been standing in the door of his office next to the Huntsville prison guard, Luke Preston; she was thin, almost gaunt, but incredibly beautiful.

Jansen removed her arm, kissed her soft coffee-tasting lips and then placed eggs, bacon, and a glass of tomato juice on the place mat at the bar dividing the kitchen from the great room. He sat her down in front of the plate.

"Eat."

Next, he turned to his grinning dog, "And you want some breakfast, too?"

The ears now at half mast, perpendicular to his head, Max sat.

"You are such a good boy, Max. Best Dobie boy in the world, aren't you?" Rich crooned to the dog as he fixed a couple of raw chicken wings with some chicken livers, placed them in his dish. Then gave the dog the okay to eat. In a flash, the dish was empty, so Jansen cut up a few carrots and an apple; within a few minutes, they were also gone.

Lindsey smiled as she watched her two men, surprised at how hungry she was after the huge dinner she'd eaten at Perry's the night before.

"I'm going to have to watch it, Rich—with the way you

feed me, I'll get fat."

"Right, fat chance of that." He watched as his wife took her plate over to the sink to wash it off; he loved the way she moved. And loved the way the ten pounds she had gained accentuated her curves in all of the right places. "Still worried about McAllister, aren't you, Linds?"

Nodding, she admitted, "Yes, very much so. And about Monica, too. The way she acted when the guy was brought in last evening just does not fit with what I know of her."

Monica was the nurse Lindsey counted on to run the Huntsville Prison Emergency Care Center. Her sudden hostility toward McAllister had come out of nowhere, and it worried Lindsey. Kissing her husband, on the cheek, she invited, "Hey, I'm going to shower and then get to the clinic ... will you be coming in as well?"

Rich had been making some comments of late about his feeling that his Chief Warden position had outlived its usefulness. Governor Greg Bell had created the job to deal with problems at the prison created mostly by the presence of the woman who was now his wife. The former combat Marine and homicide cop Rich Jansen was getting bored.

"I'm not sure Linds. If I do, I'll call you. When will you be coming home, do you think? Since Kate didn't go to San Francisco this weekend, she asked if she can come out here and stay overnight in hopes of interviewing McAllister. If he's up to it, that is. You remembered that, right?"

His voice was getting muffled because Lindsey had already reached the top of the stairs. Hearing what Rich just said, she trotted back down. "I did forget, Rich. Thanks for the reminder. Do you want me to go into town to get some stuff for dinner or what?"

Rich smiled and walked through the kitchen so that she could hear him better. Now standing at the foot of the stairs, he looked at her affectionately as he thought of her limited culinary skills, even when it came to shopping.

"Thanks, Linds, but I'll take care of it." Although the food had been delicious last night, they'd both had fish, and Kate Townsend loved a good steak. "How about I grill some steaks, mushrooms, and grilled vegetables from the garden? Sound okay?" Jansen had become close friends with the owner of a butcher shop in nearby Conroe who sold grass-fed Texas beef. He and Max could take a drive into the town to get the steaks after Lindsey left for work.

"Yum."

Within the hour, Lindsey was back at work. On a Saturday morning, she had no idea who would be working because Monica took care of the scheduling: functioning as would a nurse manager in a traditional hospital setting. McCall went straight to McAllister's bed and was surprised to see Monica standing there beside the bed.

Frowning to see her there, Lindsey said, "I'm sorry you had to come in today. Who called in?" Her frown deepened with Monica's reply about a nurse who seemed to call in sick regularly on weekends.

"You need some time off. I think you logged a couple of doubles last week, so why don't you take off and I can cover for you." Lindsey peered at the schedule posted on the wall behind the bed, "Until Jake comes in at four this afternoon?"

As she was speaking to Monica, Lindsey was carefully observing her patient. As if on cue, the visual data rolled in: deep, symmetrical breathing so no flail chest; lips, and nail beds pink; the absence of nasal flaring. The monitor screens flashed information about oxygenation, heart rate and blood pressure on a moment-to-moment basis, but Lindsey had been taught by a master diagnostician. The former Chief of Medicine at the University of Houston Medical Center had instilled in all his Cardiology Fellows that technology was best used to confirm the clinical impressions accumulated through observation, auscultation, and clinical intuition. Many a patient had been lost, Dr. Simon Bayer would declare over and over again, specifically because the physician permitted the technology to override clinical intuition. Lindsey's stethoscope confirmed the normal sinus rhythm she watched on the monitor at 48 beats per minute, and accompanied by a blood pressure reading of 118/69.

Gabe McAllister looked to be a lucky man except for the fact that he remained unconscious and that his face was badly bruised and beaten. McCall's gaze completed her sweep of the patient and returned to Monica just in time to see the expression of revulsion and disgust as she looked at McAllister.

"Okay, Monica. This is enough; more than enough. I don't know what your problem is but either get your act together or go home now." The words were whispered, almost hissed. Lindsey could hear the anger and disappointment with her chief nurse in her voice.

Two years ago, when Dr. Lindsey McCall had first begun working in what was the existing prison infirmary at that time, Monica had accepted McCall's help as an aide. McCall had lost her license to practice medicine due to her murder conviction. Yet when the life of a critically injured inmate depended on Lindsey's expertise, Monica had worked with the ex-doctor, risking her own license and livelihood in the process of saving the life of Devon Preston. The two had forged a deep bond that surpassed friendship during those tumultuous months.

Turning to face Lindsey, Monica's customarily gentle, attractive coffee-colored features were contorted with grief, and tears were streaming down her face. "Lindsey, I'm sorry, but I can't …." her words cut off by the nurse dissolving into tears and running out of the center.

Reaching for her phone, Lindsey looked at the schedule for the list of on-call people Monica had established and began to call.

"Hi, Jake, it's Lindsey. Monica and I have a bit of a problem here at the center. I know you're not due in until four this afternoon but I'm wondering if you can come in now to do a double?"

"Sure, Lindsey, I'm just down the street, and I can be there in under five minutes. Cool—I can use the overtime—thanks!"

> *"Rat," he found breath to whisper, shaking,*
> *"Are you afraid?"*
> *"Afraid?" murmured the Rat, his eyes shining with*
> *unutterable love. "Afraid? Of Him? O, never, never.*
> *And yet—and yet—O Mole, I am afraid."*
> — *Kenneth Grahame,* The Wind in the Willow

C H A P T E R

8

Lindsey and Monica were seated in Lindsey's office where Monica had been crying for over thirty minutes, completely overcome by something that was too overwhelming to speak about. Lindsey figured it had something to do with Monica's family, but she never expected to hear the words that finally emerged from the lips of her friend and colleague.

"My father raped me for almost six years." Her words were slurred and whispered as if she were revealing a huge, dark secret. Which, of course, she was.

"It started when I was six; he made me take a shower with him and touch him and then he taught me how ..." Her were words cut off with sobs, "... to make him come at first with my hand, and then with my mouth. Finally, he got on top of me most nights from the time I was eight." Shuddering sobs stopped her again and then, "He told me if I told Mama or my sisters, he would kill me."

Her face now in her hands, Monica said, "All these years Lindsey, I never said a word to anyone. I pretended he was the father my sisters talked about, then I read about this guy and …." She could say no more, the tears were beyond her control. Lindsey wrapped her slim body around Monica and held her tight.

Oh my God, she has never told anyone this. That's why the repugnance at McAllister, the disgust. She was trying to keep it all in, trying to deal with this, keep the lid on memories too awful to consider, keep herself under control—until I pushed her. And kept pushing her.

Lindsey sat holding her friend, dumfounded. She could not imagine the horror of a little girl being "taught" to service her own father. McCall tried and failed to imagine her own father doing this. The thought of the man who she had adored, perverting the custodial responsibility of a father to his child and *using* her in this most execrable of ways, caused a shudder to run through her entire body.

McCall was no stranger to trauma. She knew Monica needed help, professional help; but Lindsey was wary of psychiatrists, psychologists, and of therapists in general, with good reason.

Although she was a cardiologist and now boarded in Emergency Medicine, Lindsey had no psychiatric training outside medical school. But the three-month-long rotation in psychiatry as a fourth-year medical student had left her with a deep distrust of twentieth-century psychiatry and its reliance on medication for the vast array of human psychological conditions, including what she considered the everyday business of living a life.

Lindsey had postponed her psychiatric clerkship until the

last quarter of her senior year. She had no interest in the specialty and thought it a waste of time for someone who wanted a medical specialty like she did. The decision to postpone until her senior year nearly got her thrown out of the medical school since the Chief of Psychiatry at the University of Houston Medical School happened to be on service for that rotation. Holding her friend as Monica sobbed, Lindsey thought back to the primary reason she had such profound antipathy for the discipline of psychiatry.

Dr. Aaron Mazar and his entourage had been rounding in the in-patient psychiatric unit at the teaching hospital, and the Chief Psychiatric Resident had spoken with an attractive fifty-year-old woman who was recovering from a colon resection. The surgeons had removed over two-thirds of her colon, which had required a colostomy—perhaps for the rest of her life. Her doctor had called for a psychiatric consultation because the woman was depressed. Dr. Mazar had diagnosed the patient as an acute somatic-depressive reaction. He had conducted a pedantic discourse with the residents and medical students for fifteen minutes about his rationale for combining Lithium with Prozac in treating the woman's depressive symptoms. Mazar was a proponent of the biochemical school. A psychiatric approach which theorized that most, if not all, mental disorders were caused by imbalances in the neurotransmitters within the brain, requiring chemical treatment to restore balance—drugs and large doses of them.

The woman's responses were sluggish, and she moved very slowly. Her affect was flat, and she acted somnolently. Lindsey had been standing in the back of the group of white-coated medical personnel surrounding Dr. Mazar and had whispered to Dave, a medical student standing beside her, that the woman was stoned from all the drugs.

Mazar was an egoist and a bully; therefore, he expected

total deference from his underlings, and he had seen Lindsey whisper her comment.

"McCall!" he bellowed her name so loudly that every member of the group jumped, except the patient; she just looked more confused.

Lindsey had stepped to the side but had stayed in the rear of the group, hoping that this would blow over quickly.

"Get up here!" The psychiatrist was apoplectic, his face bright red and neck veins distended; even the nurses had gathered to watch the show.

Lindsey approached the front of the group and did her best to look intimidated.

"*Please*, McCall, *do* give us all the benefit of your entire four-year medical school education in your observations of this patient." The mockery in his voice was amplified to a point where even the patient looked concerned.

Lindsey knew no way to get around this, so she just said, "I told Mr. Williams, my classmate, that this patient looks stoned, Sir." Immediately hands flew up to cover mouths, and the smiles and laughter threatened to bubble forth.

Mazar's eyes darted around to each member of the group, daring anyone to laugh.

His voice dripped with sarcasm as Mazar began his trap. "Well, Ms. McCall, if you believe this patient to be overmedicated, how would *you* in your four years of medical training suggest that we treat this patient?"

"Stop the psychoactive medications, Sir. She is defecating through her abdominal wall; depression is a typical response to a change in bodily function of that magnitude. She needs time to accept what has happened to her; she'll not be able to if she is obtunded."

Suddenly the silence in the room became a tangible thing; even the Chief Resident was made speechless by the audacity of the fourth-year med student. By the end of the day, Mazar had McCall standing before the President of the Houston Medical School. Mazar had insisted on throwing her out of the school, but the President had refused. Dr. Chuck Morgan had been a pediatrician before "ascending" into administration. Upon hearing Mazar's account of the interaction between the medical student and the Chair of Psychiatry earlier that day, Morgan recognized a seldom-seen rare quality in this fourth-year med student: creative thinking buttressed by sheer guts.

After Mazar had stormed out of his office, Morgan had placed his head on the elbow resting on his desk and muttered, "Well, wasn't that fun?"

He had raised tired eyes to Lindsey. "McCall, if we place you in obstetrics for your last week in this medical school, do you think you can refrain from giving the Chairman of Obstetrics your opinion … about *anything*?"

All this flashed in seconds through Lindsey's mind as she regarded her friend and how she could best be helped. The last thing she would suggest was a psychiatrist out of the medical school in Houston. Lindsey knew that Monica needed to *deal* with these memories to heal. Psychoactive drugs would only suppress the memories, the rage, all the emotions associated with the betrayal of the man who should have been her protector.

Only another woman who had experienced incest could understand what Monica was dealing with right now. But Lindsey knew betrayal and loss and she had experienced the costs of refusing to deal with the emotion left by the perpetrators. She knew them exceedingly well.

Lindsey sat waiting for Monica to regain control of herself and prayed.

Strange that it feels so natural to call on You when not so very long ago, I had no idea who you were or even if you were.

People had assumed that Lindsey's conversion to Catholicism had occurred because she wanted to marry Rich. But her interest in the Catholic Church had begun long ago during her undergraduate years at Rice University. Lindsey's best friend, Julie Grayson, back then her *only* friend, had been a devout Roman Catholic and had introduced Lindsey to the lives of some of the mystics, like Teresa of Avila. Lindsey had attended Mass with her frequently. But after graduation and the two friends had gone their separate ways, life got in the way and Lindsey stopped thinking about church, about God.

When replying to those people who expressed interest, like Monica had, Lindsey never knew how to respond in a way that would be genuine but graspable. The minute she tried to explain anything about the faith that she now felt grounded her entire being, she used too many words and complicated theological terms while the gaze of her listener glazed over. She thought now about how it had begun, exactly how, when and why she had decided to join a church that seemed to function as a lightning rod for contemporary society.

Just a week after her release from Huntsville close to two years ago, Rich and Lindsey had sat in Father John Tobin's kitchen at the Sacred Heart Co-Cathedral in downtown Houston. Tobin had two doctorates, one in philosophy and the second in clinical psychology. Laura, Jansen's deceased first wife, had gone to Father Tobin for spiritual direction for many years. In fact, it had been Father Tobin who had helped Jansen deal with her sudden death in a head-on collision with a semi-trailer on a Houston freeway.

The priest was a trained psychoanalyst as well and had explained his concerns about the potential effects Lindsey's radical changes and decisions had made upon her battered psyche. Tobin had been very blunt with each of them in independent conversations about the importance of time apart from one another.

Jansen trusted the man's instincts implicitly.

Lindsey had been nervous; she had kept fidgeting with the spoon that she had used to stir the cream into the cup of coffee that sat in front of her, which was slowly growing cold. They had slept only an hour or so because they had spent most of the night talking, each dreading this morning's meeting and their upcoming separation.

John's appraising gaze swept over the two of them and then regarded Jansen soberly.

"Rich, I assume that Lindsey has told you that I suggested that you two spend some time apart from each other?"

Jansen nodded silently.

The priest's penetrating eyes did not leave Rich. "Lindsey needs some silence and solitude to come to grips with all the changes that have happened in her life before she then commits to a new job, and to you." The priest suddenly reached over to touch Jansen's arm. Very softly, Tobin murmured with a gentle quasi-smile, "And frankly, so do you Rich, so do you. Trust me on this, please." He held Jansen's gaze, waiting for the answering nod that came slowly; the hand stayed there for a moment.

Tobin leaned back in his chair and said, "My meetings today are at Holy Cross Monastery in Beaumont. Abbot Xavier is a good friend whom I called last night after you and I spoke last night, Lindsey.

"These are Benedictine monks who are accustomed to guests." John peered at Rich expectantly evidently waiting for an acknowledgment. For a few moments, Jansen was puzzled. His mind foggy with fatigue and sadness, but then he remembered that his wife Laura used to go to Beaumont for weekend retreats; she'd said it was Benedictine. Laura had said that her weekends at Holy Cross Monastery brought her back to those wondrous early weeks of their marriage, of the blessings of their covenant. He remembered because of the Benedictine monastery of Mont St. Michel they visited during their honeymoon in northern France. Upon climbing the hundreds of steps to the chapel at the top of the exquisite structure, they had arrived just in time for noon prayers.

Jansen smiled at the priest. "Laura used to love that place." Having said the words, Rich was surprised to feel the fear of losing Lindsey abate, and be replaced with that inner peace that he always associated with the presence of Christ. Jansen surprised himself by taking Lindsey's ice-cold hand in his and smiling into those sad, green eyes. "You will love it too, Linds. I know you will."

Ten minutes later, Rich had left to return to New Waverly, and Lindsey had been sitting in the passenger seat of Father John's Audi as they drove to Beaumont. For the first fifteen minutes, the priest rode in silence with soft classical music providing the only sound in the car. Lindsey's mind was racing, her thoughts frenetic. Part of that she knew was caffeine; she and Rich had devoured two pots of coffee as they had talked into the night, and she had finally drunk the tepid cup that the priest had given to her. But it wasn't all caffeine. She felt apprehensive and restless and was trying to identify the source of her fear. Lindsey thought about all the solitude she had endured in prison, the endless nights, and the nightmares; she was certainly no stranger to solitude, and so it couldn't be that. Although she already missed Rich deeply, she felt sure of him, his feelings for her, and of her conviction of a shared life together. She trusted Rich Jansen as she had never trusted any man she had ever known since her father. So what was her problem?

She saw the signs for the Holy Cross Monastery before

the priest did. Lindsey didn't know why it seemed strange to see signs for the monastery, but it did. Somehow she'd thought monasteries would be like Greg Bell's New Waverly place: hidden so that only an inner circle could get in—an inner circle who needed no map.

Following the signs, they traveled down a long gravel driveway, and then Father John pulled his Audi over on a cul-de-sac along which sat several medium-sized, white, wooden buildings. There was a small sign over the door of the middle building reading "St. Benedict's Holy Cross Monastery." Just as they got out of the car, a black-robed figure walked rapidly toward them. He stopped in front of Lindsey and smiled. "Welcome, Dr. McCall."

Lindsey stared back at the man, transfixed by his face and eyes. Like Father John, the priest was almost gaunt, cheekbones at right angles to the planes of his face. But his eyes were so *alive* and his presence so powerful that it was a second or two before she recovered enough to reply, "Lindsey, please call me Lindsey. And you must be Abbot Xavier?"

Father John was opening the trunk of his Audi to extract her suitcase, his briefcase, and a pile of books. He turned back just as the abbot replied with a huge smile, full of merriment, "Yes, that would be me, Abbot Xavier."

Lindsey couldn't help it; she stood grinning stupidly at this man in black who was looking at her as if he had been waiting to meet her for most of his life. The abbot was standing still but emanated vitality and energy from every pore.

"Xavier, where are you putting Lindsey? In the guesthouse or in the main house?" As Father John finished his question, he pointed in the direction of a smaller building to their right.

"Well, John, let's let Lindsey make that decision, shall we?" Turning to her, the abbot explained, "The guesthouse is about three-quarters of a mile down that path and is completely empty right now. If you'd like being in the middle of the woods and alone, then that's the spot for you. Or …."

Abbot Xavier turned at the sound of the front door opening, "Oh good, there's Brother Bartholomew; he can show you around to the guesthouse and the rooms in the main house so that you can make an informed decision." Checking his watch, the abbot added, "We have evening prayer daily at five; you're more than welcome to join us this evening. Brother Bartholomew will show you where the chapel is."

He strode off, long black robes flapping about his legs, but stopped short, and turned back. "If we don't see you at evening prayer, then please join us for dinner in the main house at six this evening."

Father John had stayed for dinner with her and the abbot. He then had walked her back to the guesthouse in the woods, ignoring Lindsey's protests that it was late and the mile walk would prolong his long drive back to Houston. The priest had handed Lindsey a dog-eared paperback when they reached the lighted porch.

Curiously, Lindsey had accepted it and stood holding the book while she regarded this priest at whose direction she had left Rich and the new life she had been busily constructing. Father John stood silently while Lindsey stared at him, almost as if he could read her bemusement. She blinked twice and then declared, "I have no idea how—or why—I have landed at this place, but it feels oddly comfortable, even familiar, here."

The priest merely nodded in reply but said nothing; he just gazed at her, gray eyes filled with patience, wisdom, and *love.*

Lindsey looked down at the cover of the book she now held and grimaced when she saw that she was holding Carl Jung's *Modern Man's Search for a Soul.*

"You don't like Carl Jung?" Father John was looking at her with a wry smile.

"I don't like psychiatry, Father. I hated my psych rotation in medical school. I thought the psych faculty was nuttier than their patients, and their Freudian fixation was absurd." Lindsey raised her eyebrows and sighed. "Unfortunately I was too stupid to keep that opinion to myself and came close to getting myself kicked out of med school."

Father John nodded. He knew who had been chair of psychiatry around the time that Lindsey would have been a student at Houston Medical School, and she was right: The man was deeply disturbed. But the priest quietly asked, "Have you ever read any of Jung's work, Lindsey?"

When she had said no, he'd replied, "You'll enjoy this book. I assure you." He had turned to leave but had stopped suddenly at the suppressed cry from Lindsey. Her eyes were wide, and she suddenly looked terrified and lost.

Father Tobin stood on the first step of the small set of stairs descending to the path that wound back to the main house of the monastery and asked, "That strange feeling of comfort and familiarity you feel here?" Father John waited for her answering nod. "It's not a feeling, Lindsey. It's a Presence."

"A presence?"

The priest smiled and nodded. "Talk to him regularly, figure out a place and times to do that, doesn't matter where or when."

"You mean Rich?"

"No, I mean Jesus. Lindsey, get to know the Man who has called you here. *Talk* to him; most people call it prayer, but that imposes all kinds of boundaries, conventions, and limitations. Think of it as a conversation with the person who has loved you from the beginning of time. Tell him everything. Or if you can't speak it, write it all down. There's nothing you've ever done or not done that he doesn't know about already." And then he disappeared into the night.

❖

"I am so embarrassed Lindsey. Good God, I don't know what came over me." Her voice was tremulous and though her face and eyes were swollen with the residue of the non-stop tears that had fallen for a couple of hours, Monica valiantly attempted a smile. "What have you been doing all this time while I have been blubbering like a fool, Dr. Lindsey McCall?"

"Praying and thinking that I know a man who can help you my dear, dear friend, a man you can trust: Father John Tobin."

"Lindsey, I can't talk to anyone about this … least of all, a *priest*," Monica's eyes were brimming once again, filled with what looked like terror.

Lindsey knew Monica's dislike of all things religious. She'd said very little, only that she had stopped going to church as soon as she could; she thought they were all hypocrites. Knowing what she knew now, Lindsey could see why; Monica's father had probably sung in the church choir each Sunday.

"Listen to me Monica Bradbury," Lindsey's voice was sharp, as she intended it to be. "You need help from someone who knows how to give it. Father John has more training than most of the shrinks I worked with at the medical school, and he will not try to force you back into the Church, I promise." Lindsey smiled at her friend adding, "But he *will* help you find your way from the darkness you're in now; I know it."

"I never told you this, Monica, and in fact, the only person who knows this is Rich … "I met Father John through some board members at the medical center right after I was released from here. And I asked him for help because I was such a complete mess. You can trust this guy Monica; he has absolutely no agenda."

Voice softer now, she added, "Please Monica, promise me you'll go see him."

Relieved at the answering sigh and nod, Lindsey dialed Father John Tobin's number, hoping he would pick up. She handed Monica the phone once the priest had answered and Lindsey whispered into Monica's ear, "You are on a paid leave of absence starting right now."

Closing her office door, McCall left Monica in the best hands available in the city. She felt relief on so many levels that her knees started to buckle as she walked back into the center. She offered a quick prayer of gratitude because had this happened two years ago, she'd have felt as alone and desperate as Monica did now.

God's timing ... remarkable ... then she grinned in delight.

New Waverly, Texas

God changes appearances every second. Blessed is the man who can recognize him in all his disguises. One moment he is a glass of fresh water, the next, your son, bouncing on your knees or an enchanting woman, or perhaps merely a morning walk.
— *Nikos Kazantzakis*

CHAPTER

9

Lindsey raced through the door breathless, "Rich, I am soooo sorry, the day got away from me and—"

Her words were cut off by a kiss from Jansen. "No worries at all Lindsey, Max and I had a simply splendid day shopping for dinner in Conroe, didn't we boy?" The Doberman was sitting on the Navajo rug in the great room, cocking his head at the conversation. His expression was expectant, alert.

"Bruce," naming the owner of the butcher shop where Jansen bought meat frequently enough to be on a first name basis, "risked the ire of the Public Heath Department of Conroe by letting us both into the store to select our steaks and bones." He looked over at Max, "Right boy?" Interpreting the question as an invitation, the Dobie trotted into the kitchen as if to agree.

Both Rich and Lindsey grinned at the dog, looked at each

other to chorus simultaneously, "Does it get any better than this?"

Taking a sip of what tasted suspiciously like the Alexander Valley Cabernet they had been saving for a special occasion, Lindsey asked, "So you said Kate was coming for dinner and staying for the weekend? I thought she was heading to San Francisco to see Steve last night?"

Rich had his back to her, while busy making some kind of pesto and all she could hear was a mumble.

"What? I didn't hear what you said."

"I sure look forward to September 5th, Dr. McCall."

Puzzled at the reference to the date she would be finished with her Emergency Medicine Board Exams, Lindsey cocked her head at what sounded like a non-sequitur. "Huh?"

"You look exactly like Max. You just need to grow longer ears, nose, and dye your hair a dull red."

Laughing, Lindsey acknowledged the dodge in conversation," Okay, fine, don't answer me, I'll take our dog and a glass of this spectacular Opus One Cab that I thought we were saving for a special occasion and go shower. Come on Max, let's leave the gourmand to his wiles."

A few hours later, Kate, Lindsey, and Rich were sitting in the now darkened living room; each proclaimed the meal they had just consumed to be an unqualified success.

"You know Rich, if you get sick of being Chief Warden, you could open an impressive restaurant."

Kate's long legs were extended in front of her. With her legs covered in tights, the short black and white skirt and sleeveless denim jacket worn over a white teddy, she looked about sixteen rather than thirty-six.

"Don't think I haven't thought about it, Kate." Jansen was feeling mellow and was savoring the feeling. He had liked Kate Townsend from the moment he met her. Back when he was

Head of the Homicide Department with the Harris County Homicide department, he had dealt with a lot of reporters. Most of them, he considered "talking heads": more interested, it seemed to him, in making sure their hair and their makeup were perfect for the evening news spot than in actually reporting the news. As he reflected back on those years, his impression was that the women had been far more aggressive in shoving themselves and their cameramen in front of their competitors than were the men. He wondered idly why that was so … and thought about how unattractive that quality was in women.

Townsend was different; she didn't seem to care when her hair was unruly, even tangled like it was that evening. Kate's hair refused to lie in the perfect straight lines that women favored today. Her dark hair tended to curl, and in the Houston humidity, did so frequently. And she was certainly aggressive enough when she needed to be, but hers was more of a quiet and comfortable confidence that seemed to radiate from her person; it was not unlike that of his wife.

Suddenly he realized that three pairs of eyes were on him. "What?"

"Kate's been asking you where you went just now. You were so deep in thought that I wondered if you were planning your next career."

Lindsey smiled as she said the words, but she had sensed the change in Rich over the last few weeks. He seemed restless and out of sorts and Lindsey suspected that the Huntsville Prisons were running too smoothly for her husband. He needed a challenge, she knew. Rich had replaced two of the wardens in the Huntsville Prison System, which comprised seven campuses, and the young Bob Cleary had been doing an excellent job at The Walls.

Staring at the sparkling green eyes of his beautiful blonde wife, Rich chuckled. "Linds, I should be accustomed to your psychic flare-ups by now. Woman, how can you get it so right, time after time?"

Lindsey shrugged mutely.

"What are you thinking of doing, Rich?" Townsend was intrigued.

Over the last couple of years, she had enjoyed immensely the deepening friendship she shared with these two rare people. Kate had very few female friends, a casualty of her dedication to her work certainly, but also because of her nature. She was intense, passionate; and when on a story she knew she had more in common with Max when he had a new raw beef bone than she had with most women. Lindsey had that same intensity, and Kate enjoyed being with a woman who had a similar commitment to her career but who also had a healthy interest in men. The four of them fit so well together when Steve could get away from his work in San Francisco. Thinking of Steve brought back the familiar, *Damn, I wish we could move Houston and San Francisco together.* As she thought that thought, Steve's curious and emphatic encouragement about this new series came back to her.

"A guy doesn't stand a chance with you two, do we Max?"

The Dobie was stretched out in front of Rich and at the sound of his name, plopped a paw onto the leather couch near Rich's left hand. At the signal, Jansen slipped onto the floor and rubbed the long, lean chest and abdomen of the big dog.

"Getting right to the heart of the matter, ladies, I cannot believe I am saying this but I'm thinking of returning to criminal defense." He reached over Max to pick up his wine glass, and took a long sip. Then he lifted it up in a toast, "Well, I have said it … my good Lord, I have said it. I want to return to criminal defense law. Am I crazy or what?"

Both women and the dog sat quietly, listening. Even Max

was aware that something big was happening; it was in the air. When Rich had taken his hands away and had started to speak, the dog had sat up, looking around at the three people with an expectant look on his face. Noticing, Rich quietly whispered, "It's okay Maxie boy, nothing to worry about. You can lie back down."

Prior to his years in the Harris County Homicide Department, Jansen had been a criminal defense lawyer in a lucrative Houston law firm. When he had left, he'd been relieved to go over to the other side.

"My problem is, I don't know what the next steps are. I have a call into Bell to let him know I'm resigning the Chief Warden job, to let him know that he can save the state six figures because there's no need for that job anymore."

Smiling at Lindsey, he told her, "What a white-water trip this has been, wife of mine!"

The three chuckled as each thought of the remarkable series of events that had transpired more than two years ago: Lindsey's murder conviction; Kate's Pulitzer Prize-winning series about her conviction; Rich's decision to risk his career by exploring the bizarre circumstances surrounding the then-Prison Medical Director's lawsuit against Governor Gregory Bell and the entire Texas Judicial System; the sudden and tragic admission by Lindsey's sister, Paula, in her suicide note that it had been she, not Lindsey, who had administered the unapproved drug to their mother; Lindsey's release from prison, and her refusal of reinstatement at the medical school. These were only the highlights.

The living room was quiet for a few moments; the only sounds were the soft strings of a Sibelius concerto and the occasional thuds of Max's paw to appeal for more rubs from Rich.

"That's a pretty intriguing decision on your part Rich,

and here's why."

Kate quickly explained her day to the couple: exactly why she had not boarded the plane to San Francisco that morning.

"Until I spent several hours with Alexandria Allbrite, guys, I was honestly only toying with the notion of getting involved with this case." Sighing, Kate said, "The thought of a man who would *do* that to a child made him someone I wanted to stay at least a solar system away from."

Kate shuddered visibly. "But after listening to this woman tell me about her experience on that jury, how she felt as she witnessed the patently, tangibly prejudicial attitude of everyone in the courtroom toward McAllister, the indifference of eleven people to several factors suggesting reasonable doubt about the guilt of this man, I knew I was hooked."

The reporter picked up her wine glass and stared into the half filled goblet as if expecting an Oracle. "Allbrite cannot forgive herself for not standing up against the eleven jurors who seemed so certain, *solely* on the basis of the testimony of a six-year-old; all the reasons she admitted to juror misconduct …." Kate realized she was not breathing and took a deep breath to calm herself down.

Staring at Rich and Max on the floor, Kate composed her thoughts. "And then I began to wonder … 'what if he didn't do this' … 'what if the little girl is lying?' and realized this was a most familiar feeling."

Townsend turned her body to face Lindsey, regarding her thoughtfully, quizzically, obviously puzzling about how to voice her next thoughts. "I felt *exactly* the same way I did as I learned more and more about your case Linds, the same horror: imagine if you get convicted for something you didn't do?

"What could you do … who could you turn to for help? Judged by your 'peers,' you were found guilty … and in a case like this one where the child is so young, the hatred of this crime is much deeper than of murder … I can see with no effort at all that because a guy is accused, the ease with which most people believe he's guilty."

"This morning, Dr. Allbrite must have asked me three, maybe four times, 'Kate, how do you prove that you did not do this thing'? According to her, there was no physical evidence—the only evidence the state had for the case was the testimony of the child … and the jurors kept telling Allbrite that kids don't lie."

The silence in the living room was a tangible thing; even the concerto was barely audible.

"And then, of course, I began to argue with myself, how likely could something like this happen *again* in the same city and at the same prison? Come on, self, no way …" lowering her voice to a whisper, "but I think it may have happened again, you guys, right here in River City."

Kate shook her tangled head of hair as she sardonically remarked, "Bet you two will think twice before issuing another invite to me for dinner!"

Lindsey was reeling with a riot of contradictory emotions as she listened to Kate's riveting story: anger at the secreted and perverse sexual abuse that her nurse, Monica, had been subjected to by her father was raging in her psyche. But shock at the reporter's revelations and incredulity at the distinct possibility that her patient may indeed be innocent was right behind the rage.

She shook her head vigorously as she, too, whispered, "My dear God, what if this has happened again? What if Gabe McAllister was nearly killed for something he did not do?"

McCall's eyes were wide as she grappled with the enormity of all of this as well as the torrent of memories from her own past experience as a convicted murderer in the Huntsville

Prison System.

Lindsey regarded her husband who still sat quietly on the floor, next to the dog, staring at Kate, still with that dark, pensive look on his face. As if feeling her gaze, Jansen looked up at his wife and drawled, "Well, honey, it's been kind of boring around here for the last year, don't you think? Looks as if it may be time to shake up our quiet lives again."

His irony was not wasted as all three of them began to chuckle and then laugh at the sheer absurdity of what may be facing them all.

Relieved at the tangible interest and support from Rich and Lindsey, Kate smiled gratefully at both of them and added, "There's more."

"Of course, there's more." The statement was said mordantly by husband and wife at precisely the same time and in the same tone, rekindling the laughter.

"Thanks, you two." Frowning, Kate continued speaking, "Here's the thing. When I called Steve while waiting for Dr. Allbrite to let him know why I wasn't on the plane to San Francisco this morning, he said the strangest thing. Something like, 'If this guy McAllister is innocent, Kate, he needs your help really badly.'

"Evidently, Steve knows a doc whose wife accused him of raping their daughter during a really terrible divorce; the guy was indicted and convicted and imprisoned. Steve said it happened here in Houston about six or seven years ago but apparently the whole thing was bogus …."

"Ted Ross."

Startled, both Rich and Townsend stared at Lindsey, who was nodding to herself, her face alight with recognition. "Right, Ted Ross, President of Ross Associates, one of the biggest and most lucrative private cardiology practices in Houston. He was my primary competition back in the day; his wife Marcie accused Ted of raping and sodomizing their eight-year-old daughter.

"Ted spent close to a year in prison, like me. A new lawyer got Ted's daughter to admit that Ted's wife had been behind the accusations of the daughter. The girl confessed that she'd been 'schooled' in the vocabulary of sex by her mother, brainwashed if you will, into accusing her father."

Lindsey regarded Kate thoughtfully. "I didn't know that Steve was friends with Ted, but it makes sense that they would know one another." She sat tapping her fingers on the arm of the brown leather chair she sat in. "The publicity was awful: he was tried and convicted in the media and declared bankruptcy as I recall. I don't know where he went but I think he left Texas."

This time the silence was peaceful; the light snoring of the dog accompanying the violin concerto.

"Not that I needed any more reasons to do this story," Kate summarized. "There are just too many coincidences here to believe they are coincidences. I'm in. I'll make sure I have the green light from Jeff, my editor at the newspaper, then the Philbin sisters, the owners of the *Houston Tribune*, to make sure they will go for this. That's why I'm out here this weekend; I wanted your take on all of this, both of you." Rubbing her flat stomach, "And of course for the gourmet meal prepared by Chef Rich Jansen!"

Glancing at Lindsey, she continued, "I am hoping to get to see McAllister tomorrow morning. Do you think that would be possible?"

Kate nodded, unsurprised at Lindsey's wordless "no way."

"Okay then." She glanced back to Rich. "Fully understanding that there are no fewer than four hundred million small questions and details that you would need to answer this question, Rich, would you be interested in helping this guy as his lawyer? Does the sound of this get your juices stirring?"

The grin she shot at Jansen could light up Conroe. "Think of how much fun we could have when we begin to lift up the rock of yet another wrongful conviction by the great State of Texas. This time for the alleged rape of a six-year-old; now that will liberate a whole host of creepy, crawly things sliding out from under the rock, I'll wager."

Despite himself, Jansen was intrigued. Townsend knew it: she could see it in the dark brown eyes glittering back at her.

"Lindsey?"

Kate and Rich both looked at Lindsey and were shocked to see the tears coursing slowly down her face.

"Monica."

After McCall had explained what Monica had disclosed to her earlier in the day, the horror the woman had endured from her father, Rich looked at his wife.

"My God, Lindsey. And I thought *your* case was complicated. This thing feels like a nest of vipers. There's a hell of a lot of poison here."

Kate Townsend's Condo, Houston

When it's over, I want to say: all my life
I was a bride married to amazement.
I was the bridegroom, taking the world into my arms.
When it's over, I don't want to wonder
If I have made of my life something particular, and real.
I don't want to find myself sighing and frightened,
Or full of argument.
I don't want to end up simply having visited the world.
— From When Death Comes, *Mary Oliver*

C H A P T E R

10

"Who did you say gave you my name?"

Dr. Ted Ross was stupefied to hear that Steve Cooper had given this reporter his name. And even more stunned that Townsend had tracked him down in Kuno, Idaho. Stupidly, Ross had believed that the horror of the five years he had fought to free himself from the lies of Marcie, her lawyer, and their daughter Christy, would have been erased by overhauling his life. Ross had relocated to this little town, quitting the practice of cardiology and becoming a family practitioner.

Ross heard her say Steve Cooper's name again and could feel the signs of the panic disorder he thought he'd conquered begin to overwhelm him. His mind and heart racing, Ross tried to persuade the hasty lunch he'd grabbed on the way to delivering Bob and Esther's eighth son to remain in his stomach. Desperately attempting to maintain a neutral expression, Ross gave his daughter Christy a tepid smile, hoping that would assuage the anxiety written all over her face. Gesturing to Christy that he needed five minutes to take the call, Ross picked up the wireless and walked into his home office, closing the door behind him.

You stupid, ignorant jerk, you should have known that Cooper would talk. You knew better than to trust anyone with a salacious story ... too good a story not to be repeated ... once she googled his name, the entire wretched tale became available in lurid detail. Ross took his hand, the one that was not holding the cell phone and sighed at the shaking right hand as he wiped the dripping sweat from his forehead. All the old fears took over, obliterating any other thought.

A reporter no less—are we going to be run out of this town, too? Will kids make Christy's life complete hell here? Jesus God, am I capable of starting over again?

"Dr. Ross, please, I am not looking to dredge up horrific memories for you; that is *not* why I am calling you."

Although the man had said only eight words to her, Kate could hear the unmitigated terror in his voice. She was almost sorry she'd called him but not sorry enough to hang up. If this guy McAllister really was innocent, he needed help, extraordinary help and maybe, just maybe, she, Jansen and McCall could be the conduit.

The only problem? The source of that extraordinary help.

After an early Sunday breakfast with Jansen and McCall, Kate had learned that McAllister was still comatose; therefore an interview with him would be impossible for the forseeable future. Kate had returned home to talk with Steve to find out if he remembered any more information about Dr. Ted Ross.

Once Kate began the online search, she'd been stunned by the prodigious amount of information about what read like the divorce from hell. There were hundreds of hits mostly from the local Houston media, but some national as well.

There had been two trials over the course of five years. The first ended with Ross's incarceration in Eastham Prison for eleven months until an appeal granted by the district court resulted in Ross's transfer to the Wynn unit. Ross was imprisoned there for another six months. The physician was acquitted of the crime in 2006 and was paid over a quarter of a million dollars by the state of Texas as compensation for the wrongful indictment. The case against Ted Ross had finally been dropped.

Ross had been acquitted when his new attorney put his daughter Christy on the stand where she claimed she'd had enough of the lies and the poison that had been directed against her father. The then twelve-year-old had confessed to the whole shameful mess. She had lied to please her mom. Christy had testified to the script her mother had given her, had persuaded both judge and jury with her extensive knowledge of the vocabulary of rape.

After 2006, there was no media attention on the case of Dr. Ted Ross.

Although Kate had witnessed the extremes of the human condition during her career as a criminal news reporter, the notion of accusing an innocent husband, boyfriend, or lover of this depraved act boggled her mind.

In her wildest dreams, she could not walk in the shoes of someone who lied like this. In McAllister's case, of course, she didn't know if they *were* lies. But after an entire Sunday at home researching what had happened to the once prosperous Houston cardiologist Ted Ross, and then having immersed herself into the prevalence of wrongful accusation of sexual abuse worldwide, she was hooked.

There was one hell of a story here; Kate could feel that unique combination of emotions which always signaled the beginning of something huge in her life: terror and extreme excitement.

What would move a woman to make those unspeakable allegations? And then coach her child to lie about her own father?

What could possibly be left of the relationship between this child and her mother?

How could this woman—Marcie Ross—live with what she had done to her own child?

Unsurprised at Ross's reaction, Kate said gently, "Dr. Ross, I would not blame you if you hung up on me after the hell that the Houston media put you through. But I am hoping you will not. Here is why I would like to talk with you, Sir, and why I think you may be willing to talk with me."

The next day, Monday, Kate was on the plane to Kuna, Idaho.

On the plane, Kate began to draft her first article in what she thought would be a total of three. Her working title for the series was: *A Nation of Law: The Dark Side.* After Ross had agreed to meet with her on Monday, Kate had talked to her editor, Jeff Simmons. The reporter provided enough detail about this story to explain why it would probably end up as yet another investigative series for the newspaper they both worked for, *The Houston Tribune.*

Once Kate had reviewed the high points of her interview with Dr. Alexandria Allbrite and the Readers Digest version of Ted Ross's horrific five-year crucifixion by the Texas judicial system, Simmons' silence had been so absolute that Kate thought their connection had been interrupted.

"Jeff, are you there?"

"Yes, Kate."

Kate knew her boss well enough to let him think in silence, so she waited.

"Errrr … Kate …." Jeff coughed and cleared his throat a couple of times. Then there was silence again. Still Kate waited.

This one hits below the belt, particularly for a guy with three daughters. Simmons and his wife Ellen had been married for over twenty-five years and had five kids, three of them girls. Kate could only imagine what was going through Simmons' mind as he pondered the complete and total ruin of a once prominent Houstonian; a destruction caused by the lies of his own wife and daughter.

"God Kate, this sounds like it has the potential to be another blockbuster." Jeff's voice was close to an awed whisper. "If this guy McAllister has actually been wrongfully accused, My Good God …." Simmons's voice trailed off.

"Honestly, I think we have no choice here, Kate. Go for it, I'll talk with Eleanor and warn her that we may be heading for the rapids again."

Eleanor Philbin and her sister Marguerite were two of the wealthiest women in Houston, and were co-owners of the Houston Tribune. The sisters had been active participants in the Pulitzer Prize-winning series, *Murder in the Texas Medical Center,* a couple of years ago. Consummate business women and staunch Catholics, the Philbins were native Houstonians who were keenly aware of the civic responsibilities evoked by wealth and privilege. Jeff had worked for them long enough that he could speak for them; moreover, their trust in Kate Townsend knew no bounds.

There was an attempt at a chuckle in Jeff's voice as he said "heading for the rapids," but it died, emerging as a muffled gulp, hiccup, and cough. Taking on the Texas prison system for yet another wrongful indictment and conviction was a gigantic risk for the paper; if they were wrong, the consequences could be catastrophic.

The flight from Houston to Boise was surprisingly pleasant; Kate flew Southwest Airlines whenever she could because the Southwestern Airlines staff never failed to impress. One of the cabin stewards acted as if he'd had stand-up comedy experience as he dryly delivered one-liners during the mundane cabin instructions and periodically during the cabin service, therefore making the two-hour flight feel like minutes.

Kate arrived by three forty-five at the cute coffee shop that Ross had described, fifteen minutes before their appointment. Boise airport had been wonderfully easy to navigate and the gal at the Avis counter had been efficient and friendly. Kate had been on her way to find Linder Street and Moxie Java in less than fifteen minutes after they had landed in Boise.

Each day of the past harrowing five years showed in Dr. Ted Ross. For all of it though, Kate thought as she extended her hand and smiled, he actually looked better than the photos of the urbane cardiologist he had been prior to his divorce.

Steve said he was about five years younger than Ted, so that makes him early to mid-forties; but he looks older, fifty-something. And it looks as if he's dropped fifteen to twenty pounds, leaving his face craggy and lined. Gosh, he hardly looks like the same guy ... his face is a lot more attractive than before somehow ... Ross's voice cut off her thoughts.

"I did not sleep at all last night, Kate. I kept replaying our conversation, twisting your words until I had myself convinced that you wanted nothing more than to dig up and re-pick the desiccated bones of the Ross family." Dr. Ted Ross was fidgeting with his coffee and a huge blueberry muffin; alternately he picked up a spoon to stir and then re-stir the brew and then break up the muffin into smaller and smaller pieces. Kate had not seen him take a sip of the coffee or even one of the increasingly small pieces torn from the monstrous muffin.

Ross gazed at the reporter, appraising her casual all-American look. The long dark brown hair was tousled, attractively so, and her makeup was subtle, her stillness calming; Ross found himself staring at the reporter, intrigued by something he couldn't yet put his finger on. Kate Townsend was pretty, maybe more than pretty but not beautiful: her face was too angular and her dark brown eyes too widely set to be considered beautiful. Despite himself, Ross found himself comparing Kate's looks to his ex-wife.

Marcie Ross was beautiful, a real Southern belle. Ross was surprised at the absence of bitterness as he recalled Marcie's naturally blonde hair, perfectly coiffured, her sky-blue eyes and the deep dimples at the corners of her mouth. Marcie's makeup was permanently flawless. One of the hundreds of things he did not miss about his former life was the time waiting for Marcie to do her hair, her makeup; she went to great lengths so that all could worship at the altar of her perfect face and body.

Regarding Townsend, Ross felt himself begin to relax. Smiling, he put down the spoon, picked up his mug of coffee and took a long swallow, "The coffee is magnificent. Try some, Kate."

She'd not ordered, not sure if she needed the caffeine jolt. Kate hadn't slept all that well last night, either. She'd tossed and turned well into the night, thinking about this guy and worrying that she'd get a call early in the morning that he'd thought it over and had decided not to meet with her, could not risk the exposure.

Kate had actually been surprised when Ross had agreed to meet with her. She had expected to hear a hangup during her lengthy explanation of the series she was planning to write. Or to hear the buzz of a phone line while she explained what had happened during her meeting with Alexandria Allbrite, the foreman of the Texas jury that had convicted McAllister to three, twenty to-life-sentences. The woman who had confessed to juror tampering because of her own nascent suspicion that Gabe McAllister was in Huntsville Prison for the rest of his life perhaps because his girlfriend and her little girl had lied. When she had finally said her piece, she'd heard only silence and feared that he was no longer on the line, so was greatly relieved when she heard, "This poor bastard. Okay, Kate, I'll free up my schedule."

"It sure smells good, Ted, yes, I'll join you."

Something had changed in Ross; for some reason, he had suddenly come to a decision about her, Kate realized. He had stopped fidgeting and he was suddenly still. She wondered if she had passed some kind of test.

"I suspect you already know most of my story, Kate. I am sure, like me, you did your research." Ross lifted an eyebrow quizzically. As he waited for her reply, he thought about the lengthy conversation with Zach Cunningham, the attorney who got him acquitted, the night before. Zach was both a personal friend and coincidentally also the lawyer for the billionaire Hank Reardon. Reardon and Townsend had worked closely together during a series that had ended up winning the Pulitzer for Kate and her newspaper, *The Houston Tribune*. Cunningham had nothing but praise for the reporter; had even suggested that talking with Townsend may benefit both Christy and him. Zach Cunningham was not given to effusive praise about anyone. There were few people Ted Ross trusted in this world any longer; Cunningham was on that very short list.

Kate cocked her head. She'd heard the "did your research like me" statement indicating that he had talked with someone about her. Kate idly wondered who but dismissed the thought, took a deep breath and dove in with all of the passion she felt about this grotesque behavior of Marcie Ross.

"Ted—is it okay to call you Ted?" Smiling at the affirmative nod, she continued, "I cannot understand, why a woman would do this, Ted. Yes, you are right. I have read a great deal about you and other men who claim this has happened, and I cannot grasp why your ex-wife would do this to you. But even more so, to your daughter!

"I've interviewed hundreds of people in my career. And I thought I'd seen most of the worst deeds one person could do to another. Even in the more despicable cases, I can almost get why the man or the woman is the way he is, why he did or didn't do it … but this …."

Taking a deep breath, Townsend stared at the former cardiologist. "People do things for a reason, there is *always* a reason. What on earth could be the motive behind a woman stuffing her little girl with the very worst kind of lies and taking her father from her?" Kate was stunned to feel the sting of tears in her eyes but did not look away.

Very softly, Ross asked, "You want to know what terrible thing I did to Marcie, right? To make her hate me this much? And to make her hate Christy this much, right?"

Seldom had Kate felt so uncomfortable. Even while writing her series about the homeless in San Francisco, living among a mix of psychotic, addicted, and dangerous men and women, she'd not felt like this. As if she were cutting away the top half of this man's psyche, without anesthesia and were using the dullest blade to do so. Her discomfort increased and she suddenly felt nauseated.

Good God, this is awful … who the hell do I think I am, prying into this man's life like this? But there is no choice … there is no other way to break open this most heinous of crimes. To defy the assumptions of most of us. If we are to get the attention of our readers, we must get them to walk in the shoes of these men, walk in the shoes of innocent men accused of doing the unthinkable. Get them to see that some of these men are victims … not all—certainly not all … there's also poor Monica and how many young girls like her?

Ross took a bite of the muffin and chewed slowly, reflectively. "It has taken me close to five years to get it, Kate, but the answer is insanely simple. Marcie was bored."

Kate had taken a large gulp of ice water and began to choke when she heard Ross's last words. Simultaneously coughing, and nodding that she was okay, she could breathe, in response to Ross's concerned look, she managed to sputter, "What did you say … *boredom?*"

The incredulity on her face was so starkly written that Ross laughed.

"That is just what I said, Kate. She was bored."

Ross explained that his former wife had been a beauty queen from Savannah, Georgia. Marcie Ross had all the requisite accouterments of a Southern Beauty Queen: Debutante, Prom Queen at Ole Miss, winner of countless beauty pageants, and then became enraged when she got pregnant with Christy.

"There are people, Kate, for whom life is very simple: They have only one interest and that is themselves. The psychiatrists have a name for people like Marcie: narcissist. Based on the Greek mythological Narcissus, who became so captivated by the beauty of his reflection that he fell into the lake and drowned.

"You are making Marcie's motives much too complicated and so did I … for too many years. Marcie cares only about Marcie; nothing, nor no one else, matters … certainly not Christy." Ross's gaze wandered to the door and then scanned the parking lot as if he were looking for someone.

"During the last several years of our marriage, I was

making millions; but to do that, I was in the cath labs forty hours a week. The remaining thirty hours of my seventy-to-eighty-hour week went to rounding on patients, traveling to give talks. I was never home and Marcie is extremely high maintenance: she requires attention, even adoration."

"Okay, I get that—but why not just tell you she wants a divorce?"

Ross smiled but without a shred of humor. "I was stupid, but not so stupid that I didn't know what I was marrying. I knew how selfish she was. Marcie signed a prenuptial contract, at the time, both even laughed about it. I was still in my residency when we married and wasn't making any decent money; but I was pretty sure I'd be earning big money eventually.

"The prenuptial contract required that she had to prove 'egregious lack of moral turpitude' in to get at the money I had accumulated over the course of our fifteen-year marriage. For five years, she did a bang-up job persuading the world that I was the worst of the worst." Unbelievably, the guy was smiling as he shook his head.

Suddenly he stood up and waved, "Here's someone who can give you the whole story." Ross was watching the door of the coffee shop, then smiled and waved at a stunning blonde teenager who had just walked in.

Kate was speechless and stared open-mouthed at Ross as his daughter gave a quick hug to their waitress and then approached them with her hand extended. "Hi Kate, I'm Christy Ross. We just finished your *Murder in the Texas Medical Center* series for my Global Studies class. What an honor it is to meet you!" The girl was even more beautiful up close: heart-shaped face, dimples on either side of the wide smiling mouth, long blonde hair tied back in a ponytail and two huge sapphire-colored eyes framed by long lashes.

Kate had recovered her equilibrium enough to take

Christy's hand and murmur a thank you. But she was so taken aback by her appearance that she could only stare at Ross and stutter, "How did … why … what did I ….?"

By now, Ross and Christy were seated again. "Kate, you have quite a number of fans." He smiled at his daughter and squeezed her hand. "In addition to Christy here, Zach Cunningham, the lawyer who gave us our lives back, happens to be Hank Reardon's best friend and thinks the world of you.

"Zach is not given to praising anyone with the exception of his wife and two kids. But he sure respects your work and told us we could trust you implicitly. He also told me to tell you that Reardon sends his love and expects a call from you very soon."

At the sound of Hank Reardon's name, Kate began to grin. There were very few men in the world whom she loved, really loved: her dad, Steve Cooper, and Hank Reardon.

Why am I not surprised that Hank Reardon is best friends with Ted Ross's lawyer? Of course, that would be the case … this gig is getting more and more unbelievable...

Laughing now, she promised, "Hank's right, it's been far too long since I have talked with him, and I'll remedy that when I get back to Houston." She wasn't sure how Ross wanted to handle things now that his daughter had joined them so she decided to play it safe.

"Well, Christy, there's nothing a writer likes better than talking about her own work. Do you have any questions I can answer for you?"

Eyes shining, Christy asked, "How did it feel to win the Pulitzer?"

I wonder how many times I've been asked that question ….

Kate studied the eager, beautiful face with those extraordinary eyes. She had to search a bit, but the last five years were there in the young girl's eyes; there was a woundedness, sorrow that was way too bottomless for a fifteen-year-old. Christy deserved more than a pat answer, a smartass reply from the famous reporter. Kate'd been stunned when the girl showed up but she knew what was happening here. For no apparent reason at all she was forming a connection with these two people: Christy was going to tell Kate about the whole horrid, evil mess with her mother. The awe that Kate felt was profound and the resolution to maintain their trust was total. She was crystal clear that the trust had to be reciprocal.

"I don't usually answer this question truthfully, Christy, because I think most people would not understand." As she regarded the girl, out of the corner of her eye, Kate could see her father's eyes widen in surprise and appreciation.

"It's nothing like what you think it will be; you expect that you would feel on top of the world, right? The most intense joy you've ever experienced because all of your hard work has been validated by the toughest critics of all: your peers." Kate stopped and gazed at Ted and his daughter, who were unconsciously miming one another as they listened intently, both leaning forward over the table, left hands cupping their chins.

"There were three maybe five feelings, each competing for first place in my mind and in my heart: shock, relief, numbness, disbelief, and anxiety: how on earth do I top *this?* The shock and the disbelief are connected—a kind of 'why me' and 'why for this series' kind of thing—because you know there are plenty of other reporters writing plenty of other stories as good, or better, than yours. Plus there were other stories I had written that were as good but no one had noticed them.

"And then there are the people at the top of the journalistic world who had never acknowledged me before. People who would never return phone calls or even say hello at a meeting, who were now acting like my very best friend." Kate shook her head and laughed sardonically. "It's comical, really, but it's hard to laugh off. I've ended up feeling sorry for some of the most powerful people in my field." Kate smiled ironically and shrugged as if to disperse the heaviness of the emotions she was reliving. "The relief is a feeling of, 'Okay, I did it, finally.' But the relief is short-lived: you think okay this is good, really good, but what do I do to top this? Another Pulitzer?

"For me, all of those competing emotions resulted in a numbness that lasted for weeks." Kate's gaze was directed at the wall of the Moxie Java where there were lots of photos of the kids who worked there, but she didn't really see them.

"But more than all of that, you guys," Kate regarded both Rosses somberly, "I knew I did not deserve all of this laudatory praise for the simple reason that despite all the acclaim for the series, this woman … this brilliant Dr. Lindsey McCall was sitting in prison for something I was convinced she did not do. I hadn't really done my job. I had not figured out what had really happened." She blinked hard a few times and stared hard at Ted Ross.

Her voice dropped almost to a whisper, unconsciously, and Ross and Christy had to lean forward to hear her. "And now, Lindsey is married to Rich Jansen, the Chief Warden who helped uncover the truth … and we have become the best of friends. Go figure."

Ross started to say something but stopped himself when he realized that Townsend was pausing to gain control, not because she had completed her thoughts.

"I am not a church-goer, but after witnessing the impossible happen with Lindsey, I now believe in Something or Someone and I sense Him." She smiled again this time without the ironic twist to her mouth, "or Her, here, now, with us."

Both father and daughter were nodding very slowly, almost

in unison. Kate cocked her head, cleared her throat, looked at both of them. "You know, I find it a whole lot easier to talk about really personal stuff lubricated with something a lot stronger than coffee. I hope at least one of you is old enough to drink?"

The laughter was spontaneous and a bit too loud—each of them feeling just a bit overwhelmed with what Kate had said, the intimate way she had spoken to people she had never met before.

Ross was feeling the exact emotions that Zach Cunningham had predicted he would once he spent time with Kate Townsend. He liked this woman: she felt authentic. Moreover, he felt that he and Christy could trust her with their story. Incredibly, he believed that maybe the three of them together could help this guy McAllister and in the process, help themselves.

"Kate, why don't we all go out to our house for dinner? That way Sheriff Vance won't be embarrassed by stopping Kuna's only doctor to give him a DUI."

Help O Lord for good men have vanished
Truth has gone from the sons of men
Falsehood they speak out one to another,
With lying lips, with a false heart
— Psalm 12

C H A P T E R
11

"A Nation of Law: The Dark Side

"'We now face an imminent social tragedy: the nationwide collapse of child protective efforts caused by a flood of unfounded reports.' Douglas Besherov, Director of The National Center On Child Abuse and Neglect (NCCAN) from 1976 to 1980, made this statement in 1986. The first Director of the NCCAN made the dramatic statement because over 65 percent of 1.1 million claims of child abuse filed in 1984 could not be substantiated. Of the remaining 40 percent, only half, or 20 percent were considered valid. According to Besherov, there were three fundamental reasons for the incipient crisis. The lack of standard definitions for abuse within and among the states, the total absence of penalties for spurious allegations, and vague to absent criteria directing what should and should not be reported. Besherov estimated that over half a million families were subjected to investigation by state authorities for unfounded reports of child abuse.

"The NCCAN was created by a 1974 Federal Law, The Child Abuse and Prevention Act, (CAPTA) by a government motivated by the best of intentions: protection of our children. Yet only ten years after the law was in effect, we read that the flood of unfounded reports was causing 'imminent social tragedy' and incalculable damage to those families accused in error.

"This is a grave matter to be sure, but child abuse takes on a byzantine complexity when we spotlight the sexual abuse of children. The NCCAN reports 9.3 percent (between 80 to 100,000 children each year) of the abuse of American children as sexual. Of the 80 to 100,000 sexual abuse cases in children each year in the US, somewhere between 2 to 30 percent occur in divorce, child custody battles, or following the break-up of an unmarried couple. Of these cases, somewhere between .2 and 40 percent are found to be spurious. Please note the broad range of the reported incidence of false allegations of sexual abuse: .2 to 40 percent, meaning that either 98 percent of the claims are valid, or possibly only two out of three.

"Does it hardly ever happen? Or are one out of three accusations false?

"A quick review of the literature justifies both claims; one can find copious support for each of these two opposing statements. If there is such wide variation in determining the frequency of valid versus false claims, how do we reasonably measure the scope of the problem?

"Unfortunately, we cannot. No one can. For the overwhelming majority of these cases, we have only verbal testimony by a child and or the child's mother with scant or no physical evidence. Frequently, the timing of the accusation precludes any of the routine testing for rape: semen, DNA, genital bruising or abrasion, vaginal tearing. These signs, if they were ever present, are long gone by the time these cases reach the authorities.

"For many social workers, police, and other professionals, the verbal testimony is prima facie evidence of guilt. Once the accusation is made, an indictment follows. In many states, only one witness (the victim) is sufficient to convict. These are the professionals who suggest that 98 percent of sexual allegations made by children are valid and for good reason.

"The child molester is universally despised and feared by American society, perhaps deservedly so; therefore, many states have ramped up the penalties for conviction equaling, and in a few cases surpassing, that for murder. That the child molester is among the worst of the social pariahs is no exaggeration.

"But what if the man accused of the horrific crime is not guilty?

"What if the child accuser lied?

"How does a man prove he did not do something when only he and the child were present and the child is lying?

"This is an ugly subject; one that most of us are loathe to think about, let alone talk or write about. At the very least, the sexual abuse of children makes us cringe; at the other end of that spectrum, we want justice, assurance that our kids are safe. We support the increasingly stringent penalties for sexual molestation; therefore, our law enforcement agencies follow suit.

"This reporter is no different from you. I find the horror of an adult man forcing himself sexually on a small child among the worst of the depraved acts I have reported in my fifteen years as a crime reporter. Recently, however, I have learned the relative ease with which an innocent man can be accused, convicted, and imprisoned for a conspiracy of lies. A conspiracy of lies fabricated by a vengeful parent and her vulnerable and impressionable little girl, and I feel compelled to write about it. I write because I know Houstonians, Texans, and Americans to be honorable men and women. We are people who share a horror of convicting innocent men and women.

"Dr. Ted Ross was convicted in a Houston courtroom on a January day in 2008 of sexually abusing his eight-year-old daughter, Christy. In 2012, as a result of his daughter's courage, Dr. Ross was found innocent. During the appeal that acquitted Dr. Ross, Christy Ross confessed that her father had never touched her sexually. Marcie Ross brainwashed her child into accusing her father of sexual molestation and accusing her father of sexual actions that had never happened.

"Her mother was relentless, recalls Christy. It began insidiously with Marcie Ross's manipulation of the meaning of affectionate gestures by Ross toward his little girl as sexual. And then the brainwashing escalated. Over the course of many weeks and months of listening to her mother's graphic descriptions of anal, oral, and vaginal intercourse, the young girl was forced to repeat the litany of lies over and over again. The now 15-year-old Christy Ross quoted Lenin when she explained why she fabricated sexual abuse by her father, why she had solemnly sworn that she was telling the truth in the courtroom: 'If you tell a lie enough times, the lie will become the truth.'

"Miraculously, father and daughter have reunited and now are living together in Idaho where Ted Ross practices medicine and Christy is President of her sophomore class at Kuna Idaho High School.

"A happy ending to be sure; but the cost to Ted Ross was bankruptcy, loss of his successful Houston private practice in cardiology, vilification by the Houston media, and imprisonment for just over one year."

Sitting on the Southwest Airlines return flight from Boise to Houston Hobby Airport, Kate read over this first draft of this first of three articles scheduled to be published in the Sunday edition of the Houston Tribune.

Needs some work but not a bad start … needs one or two actual statements from Ross and Christy but this is good stuff … I like it, has all the right ingredients: a subject that polarizes, universal appeal and forcing readers to think again about a subject that at first glance, seems black and white.

Happy with her work, Kate stretched and then replied back to the cabin attendant, "Sure, how about a glass of Prosecco. Do you have it on board by chance?" She grinned at the friendly Texan's drawl, "Of course, we have Prosecco. This is Southwest Airlines you're smart enough to fly!"

The dinner the night before had been sublime. Ted Ross's culinary skills rivaled those of Rich Jansen and that was going some, Kate thought. Ted and Christy had insisted that Kate stay at their place rather than driving back to the town where Kate's paper had reserved a room at the Marriott.

Smiling to herself as she thought of the evening, Kate recalled the silence in the car as the three piled into Ross's Ford truck and headed north from Kuna toward the mountains. After close to five minutes of silence, Kate broke it.

"Christy, I hope my reply to your question about how I felt about the Pulitzer has not dissuaded you from a career in journalism or as a writer? There are only a handful of people who have heard that story … perhaps I was too negative …."

"Honestly, Kate, I've just been thinking about why your words make so much sense to me."

The young girl turned around so that her earnest blue eyes could meet Kate's dark brown ones. "And they do—total, complete sense." Dark brown eyebrows were knitted together in concentration. "I thought that making head cheerleader last year would be the ultimate because I knew how hard I had worked to get the routines to be second nature." Christy's her clear voice faded just a bit and the look of concentration faded to sadness. "But my very best friend got so jealous, we barely talk anymore. And this year, when they nominated me for Class President, I ran as a lark thinking I'd never get it; we were too new to Kuna but then I did get elected." The girl stopped, gulped, took a deep breath, "And the cost of that one?" Kate could see Ted Ross's fingers grip tighten on the steering wheel. "My boyfriend decided I was *too much* for him." The sheen of tears was evident, but Christy shook her head as if in refusal to shed anymore. "So Kate, it helped … a lot … to hear what you had to say. And your willingness to say it to *me*," bravely ignoring the crack in her voice, "*matters!*"

Despite the awkward position of her body, somehow Christy managed to extend her arm and hand as if to reach out to touch Kate.

Deeply moved, Kate took her hand, "Christy, thank you," and chuckled uncomfortably at the depth of affection she felt for this stunning and incredibly gutsy young woman.

Bet this was Lindsey McCall as a teenager: beautiful, brilliant, intimidating as hell to everyone around her without a clue as to why.

Suddenly, they were there.

Their house reminded Kate of the house Rich and Lindsey lived in, simple lines, A-frame log home with windows everywhere and a wrap-around porch. But the view of the Rocky Mountains in the back of the house evoked a sense of majesty and awe. Kate drank in the clear mountain air, startlingly blue sky, and the sun just starting to disappear behind the mountains. The view strangely made her homesick for another mountain home: Hank Reardon's Lausanne, Switzerland home.

Abruptly, Kate became aware of six pairs of eyes fixed on her: both Christy and Ted were smiling at her from their porch along with a medium-sized gold and black dog of indeterminate breed. The pooch stood next to Christy with the wildest, wagging tail Kate had ever seen. The dog's tail was wagging in a perfect circle.

"Well, who are you?" The moment Kate crouched down and extended her hand, the dog was on her face, grinning, lapping and snuffling.

"Hey Lucy, stop that, you know better than that!" Christy had raced down the path to grab the dog. "Sorry Kate, she doesn't usually lick strangers like that. Come on Lucy girl, let's go now." The girl's voice was calm but firm and Lucy was quick to follow Christy into the house.

By the time Kate walked into the front room, Ted had poured a glass of wine and handed it to Kate. "I hope a local Cab is okay? There are some surprisingly good wineries around here, and this is one of my favorites."

Kate smiled and took a sip, "Thanks, Ted, yes, this is excellent."

About two hours later, after a splendid repast, the table had been cleared and at an unspoken signal between Christy and her Dad, Christy talked for over an hour about what had happened to her and her Mom.

"In class last year, I read a quote from Lenin, 'If you tell a lie enough times, the lie will become the truth.' That's what happened to Mom and me …." Her blue eyes had lost their brightness and there were shadows under them, shadows that had not been there earlier.

"It started slowly. Mom would come into my bedroom just as I was getting undressed." She looked at her father, "Had you moved out by my eighth birthday party, Dad?"

Ted Ross's facial expression was suddenly tense as he

nodded, pain evident in his eyes as he nodded to Christy. "Yes, honey, I'd moved out the month before your birthday."

Earlier, Kate had asked for and had received an okay from both Rosses to tape this conversation. Her miniature recorder was slowly turning, making a subtle hissing sound as the tape moved from one spool to the next.

Christy's expression had dulled. Impossibly, even her hair had lost its luster as she nodded in response to her father, clearly back to the night of her eighth birthday party.

"Mom came into my room just as I'd taken off my underpants and was starting to put on the new PJs that someone had given me that night. Mom stopped me and told me to lie down on the bed so she could 'examine' me." The girl's cheeks flushed as she went on almost robotically. "She spread my legs apart and had a flashlight shining on my genitals. 'He's been touching you, hasn't he Christy?' I started to cry as she turned me over to do the same thing—spread my buttocks and said that over and over.

"I kept crying, asking who she was talking about and that no one was touching me down there. Then she took the light and shined it on my chest, stopping at the nipples, saying 'How about there, does he touch you there, too?'

"After about the fifteenth time I had asked her who she was talking about, she said 'Your Daddy, of course, that's who.'"

Kate had closed her eyes as she tried to cope with the searing pain she felt in her gut for these severely wounded people. She tried to imagine the horror of Christy's eight-year-old-mind as she was slowly being manipulated by this crazy selfish bitch called her mother.

"Each time I came back from Dad's house," the robotic voice continued, "every other weekend for about …" Christy stopped, looking only at the slowly rotating spools of the miniature recorder, "six months." She looked over at her father, at the tears slowly coursing down his face, as if she didn't see them. "Yes, it was six months because my teacher wanted me to skip the fourth grade and you and Mom had a heck of a fight about it.

"It was a Sunday night and the routine was the same except that she hurt me with her fingers. 'He's putting his penis inside you isn't he Christy? And it hurts about like this doesn't it?'

"The only way I could get her to stop hurting me was to tell her that yes, Daddy was doing this to me … I remember screaming at her please stop, I'll say whatever you want me to say, just stop this, please …."

By now, Kate was crying, too. Stone faced, Christy sat staring off into space while her father and the famous reporter cried, the dog Lucy pacing nervously about, stopping only to shove her nose into Christy's lap and whine.

For what man can judge rightly concerning another?
Our whole daily life is filled with rash judgments. He of whom
we had despaired is converted suddenly and becomes very good.
He from whom we had anticipated a great deal suddenly falls
and is very bad. Neither our fear nor our hope is certain.
— *St. Augustine*

C H A P T E R

12

"Thanks very much, Greg, I appreciate your flexibility and understanding."

"Hell Rich, this sounds like it could be a fiasco if we don't handle it delicately. Frankly, we may even get some good press here." Rich could hear Texas Governor Greg Bell drumming his fingers rapidly on his desk while he thought. "I'll call a press conference on Wednesday to make the announcement. That should give you enough time to get all the details handled on your end."

The "details" loomed large in Jansen's mind: explaining to his new client what was happening behind the scenes with the former juror Dr. Alex Allbrite, obtain McAllister's consent to represent him legally, get the name of McAllister's current public defender, contacting Hank Reardon in Switzerland for an intro to Zack Cunningham, carefully considering Kate Townsend and her plan to do another major investigative series—this time with Gabriel McAllister as the star—and this was only the beginning. But he voiced none of these concerns to his now former boss.

"Yeah Rich, I think this will play well in Austin: *Huntsville Chief Warden Rich Jansen resigns to defend convicted sex abuser Gabriel McAllister.* We'll need to tweak that a bit, obviously." Bell chuckled. "But my guys can handle it. Can you make it up here if we wait until noon for the press conference, Rich?"

Suppressing a sigh, Rich agreed reluctantly, "Sure Greg, I'll get up there by noon."

"Great, then we'll grab lunch at the ACL Steakhouse." Bell was referring to a restaurant on Lamar in downtown Austin that had been favored by Austin legislators for years.

Spending all of Wednesday in Austin was the last thing Rich wanted to do, but he knew it was the right thing to do. Working for Greg Bell these past two and a half years had been a privilege. The guy was maybe the best boss Rich had ever had; Bell possessed the rare quality of being able to stay out of the way so that the person he hired could do the job. Not only that, but when the heat turned up, Bell backed his man, unafraid to take the consequences of tough decisions. Rich had grown to consider Bell a good friend, one he could rely on, he owed him Wednesday.

Stretching, Rich stood up to look at the clock. Lindsey had said to meet her over at the emergency center by 9:30; it was close to that time now.

Max was sitting on his bed, hoping for an invitation. When it came, he bounded over to Rich to stand there, his stub of a tail wagging furiously and his ears straight up. Grinning, Rich put his hand on his head. "I bet Dr. McCall will agree that you'll be good for her patient."

Opening the door, he called out, "Wanda, we're heading over to the Emergency Center. Where is Bob Cleary, do you know?"

Smiling up at Rich, the pleasant, heavy-set secretary replied in her Texas twang, "He's meeting with the other wardens, said he'll be back in a couple of hours. Want me to get him for you?"

"Nope, that's fine. Tell him he has his office back. Max and I are gone for the day. Yesterday I moved all the stuff that I want to take with me; tell Bob he can have whatever else is there … except for Max's bed." The last was added with a grin.

"Okay, Rich. Will you be back at all this week in case inquiring minds want to know?"

"Probably not, unless someone needs me specifically … most of them are getting used to going to Cleary, right?"

Wanda frowned and rotated her right hand back and forth in the air: *half and half.* "Bob's a good man, Rich. They will get used to him in time." Neither Wanda nor Rich made mention of the fact that Cleary was the first black warden in the history of the Huntsville Prison System.

Rich walked out of the office that no longer belonged to him, with Max padding along beside him; he turned left, and hit the double doors opening the new Emergency Center. The center was quiet. He could hear low conversation, but there was no other sound. Jansen had been here only a few times, so he and Max followed the conversational tones which were too soft to understand.

"Hey, you two. Did you get permission to bring your dog in here, Mr. ….?"

Lindsey was grinning ear to ear as she perched on the end of the bed on which he presumed Gabe McAllister lay.

"Hey yourself. This is no ordinary dog and I am no …

.”Rich caught himself as he realized he no longer had any authority here. His resignation had been accepted. No longer was he Chief Warden at the Huntsville Prison System.

Lindsey caught his verbal brake, raised her left eyebrow inquisitively and gave him a thumbs up at his answering nod.

Without missing a beat, Lindsey stood and moved up to the head of the bed where the still severely beaten Gabe McAllister could see her without straining.

"Gabe, this is Rich Jansen, the man we've been talking about, and that four-footed creature with him is our Doberman, Max."

At the sound of his name, Max padded softly over to McAllister and gently placed his nose in the man's open hand, seeming to intuit the injuries the guy had sustained.

"Wow, aren't you a beauty, Max? I'd smile at you fella, but my mouth's all messed up so I can't." McAllister's words were muffled as he tried to talk through the extensive swelling of his nose, lips, and jaw.

Through eyes that were mostly slits, "Hoorah Jansen, I hear you were in Beirut back in the day."

Rich winced as he regarded this man. "Yep, Beirut and a few other hell holes … you were in Iraq and Afghanistan?"

The grimace that appeared on McAllister's battered face when he tried to nod in reply to Rich was visible only to Lindsey, who had quietly moved over to one of the several intravenous lines snaking into him.

Gabe was lucky, Lindsey thought, as she increased the morphine drip; early this morning, her best nurse next to Monica had caught the sudden tension pneumothorax that could have killed McAllister. Jake had switched to days to cover Monica's sudden leave. Jake had worked in critical care in the medical center and had moved out to "the country" to raise his family. Lindsey was in her office catching up on paperwork around six-thirty that morning when she heard Jake's call for help. The deadly constellation of rapid breathing, acute cyanosis, and difficulty breathing accompanied by a shift in the trachea can kill in minutes. Jake knew exactly what it was and could probably have inserted the chest tube himself had Lindsey not been there. As it was, the emergency had been calmly handled by the experienced nurse and Lindsey, but now McAllister had another source of discomfort to add to the long list.

"Gabe, should I come back later today when you feel better?"

This time, Jansen recognized the answering grimace as an attempt at a smile, "I think later today may be more of the same so let's go ahead."

"Max, sit. Leave Gabe alone." The dog had moved close to Gabe when he saw the grimaces of pain. Rich suspected that the dog knew and wanted to comfort, but not everyone defined comfort as a cold, wet Doberman nose pressed into your hand.

"Let him stay, please. I was the handler for one of the only Doberman war dogs in the Corps." The grimace was the best McAllister could do for a smile. Lindsey had started to leave but turned back around when she heard what the soldier was saying.

"Baron was a 'misfit' when we met at Lackland. They were going to throw him out of the Corps until we hooked up." His words were muffled; the morphine was taking effect and Rich had to lean in to understand.

"Baron and I did two tours together, then when we returned for the third, I had just received my Lieutenant stripes so Baron became my captain."

Noting the raised eyebrow of Jansen, McAllister explained, "In the Marine Corps, dogs trained in sniffing out IEDs are given a rank higher than their handler to instill respect and admiration by the handler toward the dog. He was a black and tan Dobie; saved me and my platoon from an IED but he died doing it."

Now tears leaked out of McAllister's eyes, slowly making their way over the tortured flesh of his face. Looking up, Rich saw tears in his wife's eyes as well.

Leave it to the Corps to come up with ranking the dogs higher than their handlers.

Looking at his healthy and happy Dobie boy, Rich started to put himself where McAllister had been but stopped; he couldn't do it nor did he have any desire to.

"Okay Gabe, after a story like that, you win. Max stays right here. Can you tell me what happened, Gabe? Why you were accused of this?"

Close to two hours later, McAllister had drifted off to an exhausted sleep, but Rich thought he had a pretty accurate view of McAllister's side of the story. Despite his low opinion of the soldier's poor judgment, Jansen believed him; he could not see this guy raping the little girl.

McAllister could have shaved off twenty, maybe twenty-five years from his prison sentence by admitting what he had done. As a decorated vet and cop, he may have been able to get out of prison after ten to twelve years served, but would have been added to the sexual offenders list for his entire life. Between ninety-five to ninety-seven percent of all criminal cases are settled out of court, leaving only one to three of a hundred to actually reach trial. Settlements are reached between the prosecution and the defense in a type of legal bartering system. Indictments for crimes of sexual abuse are no different; often the defendant is advised to settle simply because of the extremely emotional nature of such kinds of courtroom trials and the social prejudice against crimes of this nature.

Because he had not pled guilty and had then been found guilty, the guy was in for life: three consecutive sentences of twenty to life, one for each orifice.

A settlement would have been the first thing offered by his lawyer. When Jansen had asked Gabe why he'd refused the plea bargain offered by the state, the prisoner had tried to sit up, he was so upset at Jansen. In the process, McAllister had nearly dislodged the brand new chest tube and had caused himself a boatload of even more pain.

Basically, Rich told Lindsey later that night at dinner, the guy had been drunk, horny, and stupid when he decided to move in with the woman and her kid. Deciding to stay with the troubled mother and her damaged child had been reckless, Jansen believed—especially when the signs of drug addiction in the mother and trauma in the little girl were so evident. Gabe had compounded his stupidity when he accepted a public defender and turned down the offer of his boss for a private attorney; quadruply stupid, Rich concluded.

"What would you have done?"

"What?"

They were sitting in their living room drinking the last of an excellent cabernet. Lindsey was stretched out on the dark brown, leather couch. Rich stood looking down at his wife with a quizzical expression; he had just emptied the bottle of wine, carefully pouring the remainder equally between their two wine glasses.

"Okay, then, I'll rephrase my question with more detail. You joined the Marines after 9/11. You work your way up to the rank of Captain fighting a war that no one understands and enemies that change from moment to moment. You want to believe that all this death *matters* and makes a difference, that your decision to join the Marines was the right one." Lindsey's eyes were focused on her husband like twin green lasers.

"You're considering a fifth tour in the hell hole of Afghanistan but you volunteer to do a visit to the parents of the latest dead soldier from your company before you commit.

"Suddenly, you're back in your home state of Texas, because you volunteered to do the personal visit to the family of an eighteen-year-old kid. A kid under your command who was blown to smithereens two months after he gets to Afghanistan. After you deliver that lovely message to a Hearne, Texas rancher and his wife, you realize that if you go back there again, any resemblance to the person you know as Gabe McAllister will be obliterated.

"So you quit. Summarily. To celebrate or mourn … or more likely to celebrate *and* mourn that decision … you go to a bar hoping to pick up someone, get drunk and laid, more or less in that order.

"The next morning you wake up next to what's-her-name and meet her kid … her lost, damaged, wounded five-year-old kid, named *Annie* and with *red hair*, for heaven's sake!

"You'd enlisted after 9/11 to protect your country against the 'enemy' of all enemies, the *evil empire*. And suddenly you find yourself at the other end of the world in desert hell. Nine years elapse, you make it to the rank of Captain. You watch your dog," Lindsey's eyes dart to Max lying on the floor next to them and up to Rich, "get blown to smithereens saving your life and those of nine others. And you realize that the only thing you know how to do is kill people you've never met, who may or may not be the enemy. You grasp that if you don't quit the only thing you know how to do, you'll lose yourself. And then you meet this little girl … would you have walked out on her, Rich?"

After Rich listened to her concise summary of the facts about his first client, he only shook his head, slowly back and forth. He was stunned at her ability to *nail* this guy's story, the bald precision of her recitation; she *got* it. She got Gabe McAllister in a way that Rich, despite all of his similarities to the ex-soldier, could not. Jansen was astounded at her sympathy … and somewhat shamed by his lack of it.

"I don't know what I would have done."

"That's not an answer; seriously, what would you have done, Rich?" Those startling green eyes of hers were on him, demanding that he open up his mind, compelling him to follow her into the heart and psyche of Gabe McAllister.

"Linds, you're right. I thank God I was never in his situation. But I probably would have stayed, too … I probably would have been quadruply stupid, just like this poor bastard."

Humility is the agreement of the mind with reality
— *St. Thomas Aquinas*

C H A P T E R

13

"Top of the mornin' to you all, what a pleasure to see you again. I just wish it were in person!" Hank Reardon's signature grin, electric blue gaze and intensity crackled across cyberspace from Lausanne, Switzerland to the three sitting together in Lindsey's conference room.

"Katie girl, I read your first article for your new series, *A Nation of Law: The Dark Side;* grin fading by a few thousand watts, "Rich, is your boss up for yet another shot across the bow of the Texas Jurisprudence System at America's favorite prison in Huntsville, Texas?"

Jansen coughed, still viscerally uncomfortable with his return to the other side. "Good afternoon Hank. Actually, the Governor is no longer my boss … technically anyway. I'm back with Todd Kensington's firm as head of their criminal defense department."

Jansen recalled Bell's request following the press conference the previous Wednesday. The Governor had made it crystal clear that he wanted to be kept apprised of all that was happening with this Huntsville inmate McAllister ... and that he wanted the reports from Jansen, personally. The Governor was not a fan of surprises.

Head swimming with all the happenings of the last week, Jansen grinned at Reardon." You know the drill well, Hank, I am sure ... some of us just cannot abide peace, lack of conflict, and calm in their work lives. And once again I owe you big time, this time for the introduction to Zach Cunningham. The guy is a piece of work."

As if in a fast-forward video, scenes from the past week flew across Jansen's mind. Monday had begun with a conversation with the recovering Gabe McAllister and ended with Lindsey challenging him on his rush to judgment of McAllister and forcing him to walk in the shoes of the man.

Once again, the insight and analytical ability of his wife had astounded him. True, she had rigorously trained her mind for most of her life. Also true was that training required the consummate professional to think beyond empirical data in order to make creative inferences; but much of the time, professionals resided in the low-risk, lower levels of thought, never daring to make the inferential jumps. Generally, Lindsey came across as the detached clinician she was trained to be, even in their personal life, so that Rich had come to expect only that; therefore, those times when her inductive, intuitive gifts manifested themselves, they presented in an almost shocking way.

Jansen knew the past week would never have gone so well if Lindsey had not effected that subtle but profound shift in the way he viewed his client. He could feel his energy change when he spoke about the case ... and mostly all he had done during the week was to talk about McAllister, his case and defense. He'd started with Kate.

Tuesday night, Jansen had driven into Houston to have dinner with Townsend, figuring that he could stay at a hotel downtown and fly to Austin for the Wednesday press conference with Bell. Fortunately for him and for the Governor, Kate had enough of a first draft of her upcoming article in the Sunday Tribune for Bell's people to prepare a message for his Wednesday Press Conference. The message given on Wednesday sounded as if all the changes at Huntsville had been carefully orchestrated by Bell and his administration; this idea would be reinforced the next Sunday when Kate's article appeared in the Sunday Houston Tribune.

Generously, the reporter had given Rich copies of her notes and the tape recordings of her interviews with Ted and Christy Ross, along with a copy of her upcoming article. To say the material was riveting was a colossal understatement. Like Kate, Jansen found the history of the Ross case the perfect combination of prurience, outlandishness, and heartbreak; one that guaranteed to titillate the Houston and Texan readers. Bell's people had been overjoyed with her notes that were hand delivered by Rich just a couple of hours before the scheduled press conference. Within minutes it seemed, they had massaged Kate's short-hand into a concise and coherent announcement by Bell which hit all the right political buttons of safety for our children while assuring that wrongful convictions would not be tolerated in Texas.

Kate had been unable to reach Zach Cunningham for his comments, though Cunningham's wife had assured her that Zach would return her call within a day or two. During their dinner at the Backstreet Café, Rich's phone had rung just as he and Kate were digging into the head chef's signature desserts: a warm apple tart with house-made vanilla bean ice cream the two had split.

"Shit, I am not going to answer that, the fragrance of this dessert is to die for! I will *not* thank you in the morning, Townsend. No way can I work in a run tomorrow and make my Austin flight but you are right, this is spectacular."

The two had worked their way through half of the enormous serving when her phone rang again. This time, he plucked it off of the table where he'd left it when it had rung, and looked at the caller ID.

"Ummm Kate, think I had better take this, it's Hank Reardon calling from Switzerland."

Quickly looking at his watch, he raised an eyebrow at Kate. "Where it is currently two in the morning!"

"Hi, Rich, Reardon here. Kate has told me of your need for a 'little help from a friend' so grab a pencil, give Zach a call now, he said he could move some stuff around so that he could see you sometime Thursday. His private cell is 405-782-3535."

"Hank, how can I—"

"No worries, happy to help out Rich, call him now. The guy is swamped but I got his attention with an offer he couldn't resist.

"Oh and Rich, when you have a minute or three, can you give me a call when you're not with Kate? Steve Cooper and I would like to enlist your help; Lindsey's too, for that matter. Gotta go, my other line's ringing … Liisa's team is having a whale of a time with our new epigenetic research; remember, not a word to Kate, please, Rich." Liisa Reardon, Hank's daughter, was head of research for Reardon's pharmaceutical company, Andrews, Sacks and Levine.

Dialing Zach Cunningham's cell number, Jansen returned Kate's gaze with a studied neutral expression, successfully masking his intense curiosity about what Reardon and Cooper could be cooking up regarding Kate.

"Sorry Kate, I am following Hank's instructions here, shouldn't be long, please don't wait for me." He pointed at the cooling apple tart with the best ice cream either had tasted in forever as he dialed the number that Reardon had given him.

"Jansen?"

The voice was gravelly and the tone peremptory.

"Yes, than—"

As if Jansen had not spoken a word, the gruff voice continued, "My assistant checked flights from Austin to Oklahoma City. You can make a Southwest flight leaving Austin at 3:20 Wednesday, getting in by 6:30. I've cleared my calendar so I can pick you up at the airport, do dinner and see if we can work out a deal for your guy. It's a full flight so tell me now and we'll book it for you."

"Sure, than—"

Rich sat listening to the dial tone.

Laughing and shaking his head, Jansen looked across the table at Kate, smiling at the big bite she had taken of the apple tart. "Zach Cunningham is not a man given to the use of superlatives," laughing harder, "or even basic conversation, it seems!"

Lifting up his wine glass, he grinned and toasted Kate, "Well, Ms. Townsend, let the games begin!"

Accessing the transcripts of McAllister's trial and the denied appeal for a mistrial based on Dr. Alexander's "jury tampering" proved unbelievably painless. Harris County Courts had decreed that all court reporters enter the entire transcripts of each trial at a secure site. Kensington and Associates, Jansen's new law firm and employer, paid a hefty fee for the privilege. But it sure beat the old days when the court reporter was the "owner" of each transcript and provided copies at a dollar per page. Since most transcripts numbered in the many hundreds of pages, the new system actually saved money for lawyers needing the entire transcript.

Upon return to his hotel room on Tuesday after dinner

with Kate, Jansen logged into the law firm's account, found the two transcripts for McAllister's original trial and the denied appeal. Then he downloaded them into PDF files which he saved on the desktop of his Lenovo tablet. McAllister's trial was only two days long so the entire case was under nine hundred pages. After scanning the critical sections, Rich was impressed with how accurately his client had related the events of the trial when they had spoken on Monday morning. During the flight to Oklahoma City the next day following the morning Austin press conference and lunch with the governor, he planned to outline the material he had read and jot down questions for his upcoming meeting with Zach Cunningham.

When Rich had googled Cunningham, he had found hundreds of pages of his entries under his name, but very little personal info; from the less-than-thirty-second "conversation" he'd had with the man, Jansen had devised a very clear picture of the guy who would be picking him up tomorrow night.

Just as Jansen stepped outside Will Rogers World Airport into the semi-tropical drizzle, a black Ford pickup pulled up next to the curb. In moments, the passenger door swung open and he heard that signature croaking rasp of a voice telling him, "Hope you like barbecue, Jansen, we're goin' to Saltlick. It's the only decent restaurant around here."

Climbing into the cab of the truck, Rich tried not to register his shock at how completely, totally, absurdly off he had been about his mental image of Zach Cunningham.

He was short and almost gaunt, could be called wiry; but Rich thought skinny was more accurate. Cunningham was so short that he sat on some complex type of seat adjuster which could raise him up so that he could see to drive but also allow his feet to operate the pedals of the huge truck he drove. And he was black … and ugly. Cunningham had a face even his mother must have had to work to love: his full mouth was stretched by a jagged scar, beginning mid-cheek and extending down to his lips. The scar caused the left side of his mouth to drop noticeably. Cunningham's nose would have fit the face of a Texans linebacker and looked far too big for a man who was maybe five-foot-four. The nose was big and crooked, the genetic source of that nose was Italian, not African.

Without taking his eyes off the wet road, Cunningham rasped, "Not the honky redneck you expected, huh?"

Rich Jansen was a man of contradictions. A former Marine turned Homicide Cop, now back to Criminal Defense, Jansen was at ease with the astonishing variety of his fellow humans; but what he loved the best was the wholly unexpected, the startling, that was personified by Zach Cunningham. His imagination was flooded with images of Cunningham's performance in a courtroom; a guy this whacky had to be a treacherous opponent.

"You got that right, Zach. I really appreciate you taking the time to consider taking on Gabe McAllister's case and me along with it. And barbecue sounds great—Saltlick started in Austin, and I haven't been in one of their restaurants in forever."

Jansen had spoken fast, expecting to be cut off but once again, the guy surprised him with his attention. Cunningham turned right on Terminal Drive, driving slowly in the drizzle that looked like it was thinking about turning into a downpour.

Soon, carrying two heaped plates of the best barbeque available in the country according to Saltlick in their ads, the two men walked to one of the long picnic-like long tables. They swung their leg over the bench and sat opposite one another. It was close to eight on a Wednesday evening; there were maybe ten other customers seated at the restaurant. Jansen saw a few look idly at them, then quickly look again as if to verify what they were seeing, as the unlikely pair wandered by.

Jansen was just a little over six feet, not all that tall; but next to Cunningham's five-foot-four height, he felt like a giant. To further compel people to notice the little man, he wore his graying hair in long Rastafarian locks which draped over the collar of a black and gray striped superbly cut Armani suit. Out of the corner of his eye, Jansen watched Cunningham wink at a female patron who stared with open mouth.

"I filed a writ of habeas corpus. Judge Bennett shot it down a few hours ago. I've written an appeal to the Appeal Court on both arguments. Meanwhile, we'll look for evidence that Annie and her Mom committed perjury. You can work on that end with my investigators; you'll need to find Harvey and Tony office space as they will be in Houston Monday morning."

Cunningham said all this so softly that Rich could barely hear him. They were sitting at the far end of the large room with no one close enough to hear them. Jansen had taken out his legal pad with the outline and questions he'd prepared during the flight from Austin to Oklahoma City, but had put both pad and pen down when Zach began to speak.

Nodding, as if in approval, Zach continued speaking, constraining his gravelly voice into a whispered rasp. "McAllister got shit for defense; hope that pitiful excuse of a lawyer is not typical of the quality of the Houston Public Attorney's Office.

"You've filed the writ and Judge Bennett has denied it."

Rich knew he was staring at this most curious blend of eccentricity, defiance, and genius. He knew he should pick up a piece of the barbecue that was slowly cooling and was so far untouched, but he had never encountered anyone like this guy. Ever.

Quite clearly, Cunningham had obtained McAllister's trial

transcripts, read through them and found the weakness in the case: inadequate legal representation. He had filed the writ of Habeas Corpus to Judge Gloria Bennett who had almost immediately denied the appeal for a new trial, all in less than twenty-four hours, eight of which had been the middle of the night.

Habeas Corpus (the Great Writ), a Latin term meaning "you have the body," derives from the English common law and is a constitutional protection from unlawful imprisonment. In a sense, the writ of Habeas Corpus is intended to serve as a check on the manner in which states honor the constitutional rights of citizens, assuring that the State has sufficient evidence to imprison an individual. Frequently, the petitioners are prisoners. Functionally, however, the criteria for satisfaction for Habeas Corpus are seldom met, because of steps imposed by the Federal Government in a 1998 law intended to limit the time consumed by the courts by desperate prisoners who filed frivolous appeals.

Although Cunningham had not revealed to Jansen the content of his petition for the writ he'd filed, Jansen knew there were only two possible arguments for Judge Gloria Bennett to consider granting the writ: evidence of incompetent counsel and jury tampering. Bennett had already denied the mistrial on the basis of jury tampering, as had the Appellate Court. The likelihood of her granting the habeas petition had been negligible, but the legal busy work had been essential to gain the attention of the Texas Court of Criminal Appeals. And Cunningham had already appealed Bennett's denial to the highest court in Texas.

Cunningham was dispatching his meal with surprising speed and finesse; barbecue was notoriously messy and required a good deal of dexterity to consume the meal without wearing it.

Without looking up at Jansen, Zach ordered, "Jansen, eat. This train is just startin' to roll, you need your Wheaties." The last was said with a smile and chuckle that made Cunningham's unattractive face look scary and his voice sound even stranger than when speaking normally.

Now, looking at the smiling face of Hank Reardon, Rich found his curiosity no longer bearable.

"Hank, I hope you don't mind my asking this but just how did you and Zach Cunningham get to be buddies?"

Reardon's reply was hilarity. Not laughter but uncontrollable belly-clenching hilarity. With tears rolling down his face, Hank Reardon finally was able to control himself well enough to reply. "Now, that's a story best told over an excellent dinner and a special wine or three to accentuate the meal. I promise to tell you the story the first time we're all together … okay, Rich?"

Reardon was staring intently at him. Wordlessly, Rich knew, Reardon was reminding him of yesterday's conversation with Steve Cooper, Kate's San Francisco cardiologist boyfriend. Jansen had not had the time to tell Lindsey about the surprise planned for Kate, so he adopted a fatigued pose, which was not tough at all. He was exhausted and covered a huge yawn with his hand, "Okay Hank, I look forward to hearing the story. Zach has my work cut out for me, that's for sure."

Kate and Lindsey had been silent while they watched Jansen and Reardon. Each was smiling without actually comprehending Reardon's reaction to the simple question Rich had asked because neither had met the most unusual, even bizarre, criminal defense attorney, Zach Cunningham.

Jansen looked over at his wife and friend and shrugged,

happy that he was so tired, or his mouth would open and he'd spill the beans. Yawning once again, Jansen thought about the weirdness of the genetic lottery. Zach Cunningham "should" be a loser: he had all the requisite physical requirements of a man who would be marginalized by this culture that is so obsessed with physical appearance. But Cunningham had spun his many negatives into a tightly-wrapped package of uniquely positive qualities.

History does not repeat itself but it often rhymes.
— *Mark Twain*

C H A P T E R

14

Kate waited impatiently in the temporary parking lot at the airport. Houston created the lot when the city decided to expand the friendly, easy-to-navigate-and-park airport by planning a two-year expansion for international flights at Houston's Hobby Airport. The expansion was huge, double-digit billions and was causing all the expected chaos and more. The idea behind the lot was brilliant: wait for your incoming person to text you so that you could go pick him up right at the exit door. But the reality was a bit more predictable: sitting in the late August heat and humidity while your hair frizzes, or run your car so that you can stay cool for the twenty or thirty minutes you wait.

Like many Houstonians who lived close to the downtown section of the huge, sprawling city of Houston, Kate and Steve were fans of Southwest, and Hobby was Southwest's preferred airport. The flight was late, understandably so because of thunderstorms over Dallas, which had re-routed the flight; but still, Kate was nervous, anxious, uncharacteristically so.

Something was up, she knew; her antennae were sensing changes in the ozone of their relationship. Kate realized she was indeed nervous about seeing Steve. The last time they had been together had been back in July before she had taken on the "Gabe McAllister" story, six or was it seven weeks ago?

What am I so jittery about? Why so frantic about seeing him? Frantic, wasn't that an overstatement? Nope, something is about to happen, I just know it. He was talking about all the reservations he had to cancel that weekend I was due to fly out … he doesn't get wigged out about that kind of stuff, it's almost as if he'd planned something special … very special … could he ….?

Cutting off those thoughts with deliberate intention, for the twentieth time, Kate checked herself in the mirror of her Audi.

Okay, you'll do, Townsend. Quit fidgeting, for heaven's sake.

When her phone pinged with his text message, she was startled but grateful for the immediate cessation of her ridiculous ruminations about some silly comment he'd made over a month ago. Putting the car in gear, she arrived at the passenger pickup lane just as he walked out the door. As she pulled up to the sidewalk and watched the tall lanky stride, the broad grin, and his sparkling eyes, Kate could feel her heart accelerate, and the thrill of the blood circulating through her body as she reached over the passenger seat to open the door for him. *This is the man I love … have waited for....*

Luckily, Steve had been able to get the Friday of a four-day weekend off. Despite the two-hour delay at the airport, the couple was seated upstairs at their favorite bar, Marfreless, by four thirty, within forty-five minutes after she picked him up.

The bar was a forty-year-old Houston secret known only to those who knew. Although there were many patrons who claimed to understand the meaning of the peculiar name, Marfreless, few knew for sure.

Located behind the River Oaks Theater on Peden, a blue door was the sole identifier for the bar. There had been great consternation among the devotees of the distinctive bar, among them Steve Cooper, when the bar had closed for renovations for close to a year. But Cooper happily observed that the changes were subtle and enhanced the romantic, cloistered feel of the place. There were fewer tables downstairs and the updated chandeliers cast a soft, subtle glow.

The staircase was new and unfamiliar with almost no light as Kate slowly picked her way up the stairs; she was careful, for she had on heels, and she'd never learned to walk comfortably in heels. Harry Connick crooned a ballad as they took in the details of the renovations: several plush dark brown booths lined the left side, terminating in a long couch along a mirrored back wall; the old tables had been replaced with marble-topped pedestal tables which sat on the dark red carpet; and to their left was an isolated booth with floor to ceiling sheer red curtains which could enclose for privacy. The overall effect was trendy chic with just a dab of decadence.

Sighing deeply with relief and gratitude, Kate lifted her martini and opened her mouth to toast him and them when Steve reached across the table and gently pushed the hand holding the martini back down on the table, remarkably without spilling a drop. Cooper's beautiful deep brown eyes were on her, devouring her as he continued speaking. "I figured this is even better than what I had planned if you'd come to San Francisco last month. Marfreless has a forty-year proud history that we are about to join."

Steve rose, walked around their table to the chair where she sat, speechlessly. He reached into his pocket, pulled out a blue velvet box, got down on one knee beside her chair, his intense gaze never leaving hers and huskily whispered, "Kate Townsend, will you marry me?"

The diamonds in the ring glittered in the dim light as he held it out to her.

Paralyzed, Kate only stared at Cooper, having no idea what to say.

"Yes, Kate my love, your word is yes, that's all you have to say."

"Yes, yes, yes …."

Gently, very gently, Steve lifted her to her feet and kissed her softly, then … not so softly.

Holding on to him for all she was worth, Kate buried her head in his shoulder, fearful of what her tears were doing to her makeup. Just as they parted, they heard a muted smattering of applause from the three other couples in the dimly lit room, along with that of the waitress who always seemed to be there, dressed in stiletto heels and blue jeans.

Steve placed both hands on her face. "From our very first martini here, almost two years ago, I *knew* this would happen, Katie, my girl. I love you … and want us to be husband and wife. I want to spend the rest of our lives together …."

Steve's right index finger tenderly dried the tears under both of her eyes, "Now, we can have that martini."

Seated once again, Cooper sat back, grinning for all he was worth. He loved the flush on her neck and cheeks as she gazed at her engagement ring. She looked more like an eighteen-year-old freshman college student than a thirty-six-year-old Pulitzer Prize-winning reporter.

The waitress approached just as Steve was looking around for her.

"Bet you would both appreciate some popcorn, we just made some fresh … ready for two more?"

"You bet, two more please." Steve ignored Kate's weak refusal.

Taking her first long drink of the martini, Kate shivered, "Golly, that is stout and good … have not had one of those since …."She stopped and trembled again, this time not from the drink, but because Steve had taken her hand and was holding it. He was saying nothing, just gazing at her; the love, the desire, the sheer *want* in his eyes were curling her toes.

Marfreless was iconic to those who knew of the blue door right behind the River Oaks Theater. In over forty years of operation, there had never been a sign over the door. The explanations of the meaning of the name, Marfreless, were as varied as were the numbers of couples who had made the decision to marry while enjoying the intentionally secluded, cloistered sections of the bar.

Laughing at herself as Steve caught her staring at the ring … the exquisite gold band with a one-carat diamond in a four-prong setting, she told him, "Steve, it is stunning, beautiful." Kate straightened out her long tapered fingers and watched the light of the candle shower a prism of reflected light from the diamond. Once again, Kate looked up and stared at this man she loved and would marry soon, deciding to say the words.

"I think we should pay the check, Dr. Cooper, and go somewhere more fitting for this occasion, don't you?" Whispering for his ears only, "Like my bed, before we burn up Marfreless?"

Four hours later, Kate stood, stretched, and arched her nude body, taking pride in her lean, athletic torso, butt, and legs. "So, Dr. Cooper, was it worth waiting for?"

His answering grab almost caught her but she darted away, shouting out a comment as she fled her bedroom, heading for her kitchen and the food for they were starving."I stopped taking the pill when you and I …." her voice faded and Cooper grinned in memory, for he didn't need to hear Kate's words to remember.

It was our first date or maybe the second but way before our fourth or fifth. No, it was the night she won the Pulitzer—we went to Marfreless to celebrate. We talked and drank for hours; but somehow, I never felt the vodka, only the conviction that she and I could be special … could have something unique: a relationship to treasure, rather than use up and discard, once we satisfied ourselves physically.

I told her then that we had a choice … we could do what we each wanted to do … what we'd done with plenty of others in our past … or we could wait. Decide to get to know one another … really get inside each other in a way that isn't possible once the sex takes place … once the sexual intimacy obscures the mystery of the selves we never reveal to another.

They were words he had never spoken to any other woman, words he didn't even know he knew until they came flooding out of his mouth that night.

We could have something. He remembered using the word precious that night as he explained what they would need to do, that they needed to pretend that this force of want and desire did not exist until it was the right time. They had to be 'friends' in the old-fashioned sense of friendship between a man and a woman. And they would need to impose a type of self-control on themselves

that was outmoded, almost unknown in these days of bedding down with everyone we meet.

Miraculously, she had understood, agreed, and had replied that his suggestion had made her more nervous than would the sex. She had laughed at her words, in nervous acknowledgment of exactly what they were saying, the pledge they were making to one another.

Two years would never have worked had they lived in the same city. Cooper knew that; there were too many times when the attraction between them was almost unendurable. Strangely, the one to cool off the moment was almost always Kate, who seemed to understand the echo of a promise spoken that night; a promise with all the beauty and fragility of new life. Interesting metaphor there, Cooper. Kate had warned him just now. She had been off the pill for two years; something unplanned may have happened this night.

Good. Boy or girl ... good, it's only four months to Christmas ... and closed his eyes.

New Waverly, Texas

When it comes to life, the critical thing is whether you take things for granted or take them with gratitude.
— GK Chesterton

C H A P T E R

15

Although it looked to be a scorcher of an August day in Houston, Rich Jansen decided to leave the top off his beloved Mercedes 380 SL. This was his first day in his new career as head of the criminal defense department at Kensington and Associates law firm in downtown Houston and Jansen felt uneasy in the suit and tie. For close to two years, as Chief Warden at the Huntsville prisons. his most formal dress had been a sportcoat. Despite all of the travel, and countless hours of study of last week, he felt ready to take on this new challenge as Gabe McAllister's lawyer. The chief reason for his sanguine outlook toward the potential nightmare of taking on McAllister's, Jansen knew, was Zach Cunningham. Without the force, vitality, and sheer *presence* of one of the more talented and unusual people he had ever met, Jansen would be toast.

Jansen's last criminal defense case had been close to fifteen years ago. The guy had been a total sleaze-ball but Rich and Todd Kensington had just incorporated Kensington and Associates and they needed clients. After graduating together from the University of Houston's law school, the two men had agreed to open a law practice specializing in medical and criminal defense. The Kensington family was composed of three generations of physicians with Todd being one of the rare exceptions as an attorney, while Rich's three-year stint in the Marine Corps between Harvard undergraduate years and law school drew him to the criminal defense side of the law.

At a population of four million and growing fast, Houston was in constant in need of public defenders. Therefore, granting the new firm of Kensington and Associates a contract for representing accused criminals lacking the resources to pay a private attorney was a no-brainer.

The accused was a twenty-three-year-old disinherited son of one of Houston's oldest wealthy families. Although Rich was convinced that the guy had beaten and raped the woman who accused him, there were enough holes in the case made by the prosecution for Rich to out-maneuver the brand new assistant District Attorney. When the jury returned the verdict of not guilty, his client had tried to "high five" Rich in victory. Jansen had walked out of the courtroom, disgusted with himself, and had told Todd he was done; he applied for the Police Academy. Fifteen years later here he was, back in criminal defense.

Quickly glancing to his right, Rich smiled as Max lifted his left paw and placed it on Rich's right hand as it lay on the gear shift. The dog curled the pads in his paw around Rich's hand for all the world as if his were a hand rather than a paw.

Max sat erect in the passenger seat of the car and, as always, got lots of surprised glances quickly followed by second looks from other motorists. Occasionally, the red Doberman would return the stare of another motorist, and Rich chuckled as he noted the expression of the other driver.

Maneuvering his Mercedes among the slowly building crowd that was heading south into down- town Houston, Rich was well aware of the prodigious blessings of his life. He breathed them in like the still cool early morning air that embraced him and his dog. He turned on his XM Radio to his favorite station, XM Vox and began to sing along with Puccini and Pavarotti. Passing the massive and stunningly pure white concrete statue of Sam Houston on his left, Rich slowed down a bit so that he could safely gaze at the edifice. Jansen grinned as he quickly glanced at the sixty-seven-foot statue towering over the freeway. This was Texas, he thought to himself, the Texas he loved; there was nothing unique about building monuments to national heroes. But leave it to Houston to commemorate the man for whom the city was named after with the tallest commemorative statue of any in the entire country. Well aware that this statewide addiction to the outlandish was frequently derided by other regions of the nation, Rich loved this quirky side of Texas. He had never adapted to the more subdued and tamer styles of speech and architecture so favored by the northeast despite his undergraduate years spent in Boston.

Forty-five minutes later, he and Max were striding into the lobby of the JP Morgan Chase Tower. The Kensington law offices were on the fifty-second floor of the tallest building in Houston at 601 Travis in downtown Houston. Had it not been just after six in the morning, he would probably not have brought Max to his first day of work. But when his internal alarm clock awakened him at just a little before four-thirty this morning, Jansen was immediately wired. Max was up sitting on his bed and watching as Jansen showered, shaved and dressed, quietly, so as not to awaken Lindsey. The observant dog knew there would be no run this morning; Rich's clothes were different. So he sat staring with those alert amber eyes fixed on him. Hesitating at the bedroom door, Rich considered which option: take him or tell him to stay so that Lindsey could take him along for her run when she got up in an hour or so. The dog's expressive gaze was unwavering.

"Okay boy, it's my first day, let's greet it together." It was a whisper in the still dark bedroom, but Max was up, out the door, and down the stairs in seconds, standing in front of the front door, grinning at Rich.

As he'd suspected, the lobby of the downtown building was deserted as was the elevator. Max's ears were straight up, his eyes alert, attentive in this foreign territory. Rich grabbed his collar tightly as the elevator silently ascended the fifty-two floors to 5252 where Kensington and Associates was housed. He doubted that his former and now current partner would already be in the office. However, there could be new associates working this early and he wanted to have a hand on the dog just in case there was someone standing in the hall when the doors opened.

But there was no one there when the elevator doors opened. Entering the suite, Rich stood quietly, Max at his side, admiring the foyer of the suite.

"Well Max, we've come up a bit in the world, haven't we?" Taking in the tasteful but opulent glossy mahogany furnishings, paintings, and carpet, Rich smiled at the contrast between his new workspace and his former office at the Huntsville Prisons. Even without his successful law practice, Todd Kensington was a wealthy man because of his generous endowment of family money. The decision to move his practice from the office that he had started with Rich years ago was easily made once the practice had grown from two to twenty-five, now twenty-six attorneys. Although Todd had offered Jansen a full partnership, Rich had turned him down, claiming that he was more than happy to fit under the rubric, "And Associates." Both men were tacitly aware that the real reason was Jansen's discomfort and uncertainty about his decision to flip to the "other side."

Can't deny it though, Toddster: these digs are magnificent … and the view of the city spectacular.

Todd had insisted on giving Rich a corner office and once in it, Rich was happy he had not argued. The northern wall was mostly a huge window and in the rising sun, he could see the bell tower of the Sacred Heart Co-Cathedral. Jansen happily realized that he could renew his habit of attending daily Mass, for the church was a mere ten- to fifteen-minute walk away.

In the center of the large room sat a large white block conference table with six white chairs arranged on three sides. In front of the fourth side, between it and the front of the desk, stood a portable whiteboard. Legal pads and pencils lay in front of each chair. Blinking, he started because the desk—

My desk … that's my desk! How did they get this out of there and move it so quickly?

"Max, look, there is my old desk!" Shaking his head and laughing at what had to be a conspiracy between Kensington and Lindsey, accomplished sometime last week. Rich was elated to see the desk he had used when he had been Chief of the Homicide Division at the Harris County Sheriff Department and then had moved to his office at the Huntsville Prison. He loved that desk, smiling even more widely now because Max had found his bed that sat beside his desk and was sitting in it, watching him.

"Good boy, Max. This already feels like home. Down, boy. We'll be staying here for a while, I think." The dog stood, circled the big bed twice and lay down, happily sucking on the Berber chew toy that either Lindsey or Todd had left on the dog's bed.

Walking over to the far left of his office, Jansen was enchanted to see another charming addition from the conspirators. The intimate grouping should not have worked with the stark design of the rest of the room, but it did, beautifully. During his first week in the decoratively challenged Warden's office at Huntsville Prisons, Jansen had purchased new furniture from an antique store in the center of Huntsville. The chairs were comfortable, unlike most antiques that he'd sat in; the fabric in the upholstery was lovely; each was upholstered in subtle variations of deep rose, green, and gold antique.

Beautifully displayed on the wall behind the grouping hung the three Boudin prints that he and his first wife Laura had bought in Honfleur on their honeymoon. Rich Jansen was an enigma. Every inch a Marine in discipline, character, and courage, Jansen possessed a powerfully accurate, intuitive sense about people, situations, and decor; his appreciation for color and design seemed an almost feminine trait. Laura had attributed the contradictory nature of her husband's personality traits to his June 11 birthday. He was a Gemini, the sign of the twins, which, when added to the date of his birthday, added up to at least four different personalities. For Laura, this fact explained her husband's inconsistent actions or statements. She would use that knowledge to make sense of an action or statement of Rich's that was in direct opposition to something he had said or done just the day before.

The honeymoon had been planned by Laura and financed by her parents as a wedding gift to the young couple. Laura's had been a military family; she'd lived in most of the Asian countries and all of Europe growing up. But her favorite part of the world had been the coast of Normandy in northern France. Rich and Laura had spent two weeks there, using a twelfth-century-monastery-turned-bed-and-breakfast as a base to take day trips throughout the beautiful and historic

Normandy coast.

One of their first trips was to Mont St. Michel, a rocky tidal island two miles off the northern coast at the mouth of the Couesnon River. Laura had been there as a child; her descriptions of its grandeur were so captivating that Rich was eager to see the thousand-year-old abbey. The islet is surrounded by a confluence of tidal forces that can rush faster than one can run. Jansen recalled his astonishment when he caught his first glimpse of the place. The highway runs along a topographically boring coastal plain when suddenly Mont St. Michel manifests itself in an almost ethereal way: One moment there is nothing, and then in the very next, there floats a spectacular gothic abbey on top of a rocky mountain. The young couple had spent the day there; first, climbing the nine hundred stone steps up to the Abbey and then gratefully joining in for Matins, the noonday prayers sang by the Benedictine monks as they celebrated their liturgy of the hours. Miraculously, there were very few tourists there, and none was photographing the Benedictine monks intoning the ancient and beautiful Gregorian chants.

Laura had insisted on these prints, Rich recalled, as he looked at the three Boudins hanging diagonally from one another. They had argued about the cost. He was just starting law school, and Laura made very little money as an art teacher, but his new wife had worn him down with her patient and relentless conviction that the couple needed a way to return to those magical two weeks.

"There will be times in our lives," Laura had predicted, "that we'll feel as if we'll never be happy again; but these clouds and this Honfleur light will dispel the darkness." Rich could sense her presence as he gratefully drank in the perfection of the clouds of Boudin's *Studies of the Sky* and his almost unearthly *La Havre, 1989,* a lone sailboat in silhouette against spectacular yet subtle colors of a setting sun in Honfleur harbor. Displayed underneath was the third painting, *Sea Painting on Oil*, a stunning depiction of the Normandy coast.

Laura had taught him a great deal in the twelve years of the marriage that ended tragically with her death in a head-on collision with a semi-trailer driven by a man who had fallen asleep at the wheel. Eugene Boudin, she had explained, was the real father of impressionism, not Claude Monet. In fact, Rich could recall the intensity in her lovely violet eyes as she clarified why they must spend all this money on three very high-priced paintings.

They were standing in the Boudin Museum in Honfleur while Laura explained that Boudin urged his younger friend by fifteen years, Claude Monet, to join him at Honfleur. Monet was making a reputation in Paris, drawing caricatures in charcoal.

Boudin thought Monet was capable of more.

Laura's eyes had sparkled as she spoke from memory about a conversation that completely changed the art world. Teasing his friend, Boudin admitted that Monet's caricatures were fun but were not "real art … I mean art; I mean painting, Claude, *painting!*" He claimed over and over that he wanted Monet to see the light, that fantastic light that in a flash transformed rocks and fields from brooding to brilliant. Once Monet agreed, he later described that it had been as if "a curtain had been opened in front of his eyes." Finally, he *understood.*

Recalling the months of grief he had suffered not so long ago when his critical injuries forced him to deal with her death, Jansen smiled at the fact that memories of Laura now brought joy, not heartbreak. Jansen said a quick prayer of gratitude. "Maybe you really are right about the light in Honfleur," Rich whispered to Laura as he basked in the beauty of the paintings.

> *Men's natures are alike, it is their habits that*
> *carry them far apart.*
> — *Confucious*

C H A P T E R
16

"So you're feeling better today?"

Gabe McAllister blinked several times as he studied the face of the blonde woman scrutinizing him. Frowning at the consequence of the slight motion of his head as he tried to dissipate the fog from his brain, he heard her continue speaking as if she could read the blurry, vague, and confused thoughts floating slowly through his mind.

"Gabe, I'm your doctor. My name is Lindsey McCall and you've been mostly out of it for the ten days you've been here in the prison emergency center."

Lindsey could see that her patient was having trouble tracking with her. She was not surprised, as she'd decided to do a CT scan of his skull last week and found that McAllister had suffered a severe concussion which concerned her greatly since she had been allowing liberal pain medication. For most of the week, Gabe had been in and out of consciousness; a result, she was sure, of the severity of the trauma to his brain.

But good news was revealed by the scan as well—the fracture of his lower mandible jaw was hairline and should heal quickly. She had removed the wires when she had first come in that morning, happy to see him staring at her now.

Lindsey was a cardiologist with a Ph.D. in Cardiovascular Research and would soon be licensed in Emergency Medicine. But she was not loathe to make use of her former colleagues about fifty miles south at the University of Houston Trauma Center. Once she had the films of the CT scan, she contacted Stan Nelson, one of the foremost trauma radiologists in the nation and Guy Corcoran, Chief of Neurosurgery at the medical center to seek their advice. Should McAllister be transferred to the University of Houston Medical Center in downtown Houston or should she keep him in Huntsville? Both men advised her to keep him at Huntsville and watch him closely; each had agreed to be on call, should signs of an intracranial hemorrhage appear. Guy had been willing to take call himself for the entire week just in case his friend Lindsey needed help.

The concussion was in the occipital lobe—that part of the brain where sight is controlled by the brain. Both specialists were reasonably confident that McAllister would recover but that his vision would be blurred and his thoughts sluggish while the contused brain tissue healed.

Lindsey had spent the early part of the week sleeping in the on-call room she had at the center because she wanted to take no chances with her patient. At the slightest signs of further damage, she'd have alerted Life Flight; and one of the fleet of emergency helicopters from her former employer, The University of Houston Medical Center, would have been in Huntsville within ten minutes to retrieve her patient. One of the changes McCall had insisted upon during the renovation of the Huntsville infirmary to a state of the art Trauma Emergency Center had been a helicopter pad on top of the new center. Thankfully, there had been no signs to warrant an emergency transfer.

Groggily, McAllister repeated, "Lindsey McCall … you're a doctor?"

Lindsey's smile widened. Although the words were muffled, clearly he was lucid and understood what was said to him.

Nodding, she replied, "Yep Gabe, I'm your doc and my husband Rich is your lawyer. One stop shopping here at Huntsville." Chuckling at her quip, McCall noted a new frown and guessed at its source.

"Gabe, Rich spoke with you a week ago today—you were pretty much out of it and in a great deal of pain so I am not surprised that you do—"

"Did he have a Doberman with him?"

Stunned, Lindsey nodded slowly. She'd read about the power of animals to heal ill and injured people, but had always been skeptical; watching Gabe's face now, she wondered. She remembered McAllister talking about a war dog that he had trained for a while in Afghanistan. His story had been garbled due both to confusion and the extent of his facial injuries, but he'd said something about the dog saving him and the nine men in his platoon when the dog discovered an IED.

"Yes, our Doberman was here when Rich came to see you."

"Max, his name is Max, right?"

There was only a shadow of the smile but nevertheless, it was there on the face that was now beginning to assume the typically recognizable contours of eyes, nose, lips, and jaw. Despite a rainbow of black, blues, and yellows adorning Gabe's face, Lindsey could see the face of a solid, maybe good- looking, man beginning to emerge. McAllister's gaze did not avoid her own. She held the stare as she replied calmly, "Right, his name is Max. Good memory."

"Any chance he could come by again?" McAllister covered well, but Lindsey could hear the crack in the ex-soldiers ragged voice, made coarse through disuse and dryness. Pretending not to notice the sheen in the man's hazel eyes, Lindsey nodded again.

"I'll be right back, you need some water."

Watching the tall, lithe figure clad in hospital scrubs walk away, McAllister clenched his teeth to avoid calling her back because he did not want to be alone with his thoughts. Gabe wanted to call her back but didn't; he didn't want to appear needy and she was most likely too busy to merely keep him company. He was rewarded with sharp shooting pains originating in his jaw and ending about a hundred feet over his head.

What the hell is the matter with you? Crying like a damn baby … this wasn't Baron. Hell, their Doberman wasn't even black like Baron. But the rationalizing was not working; he could feel the horror, the grief, and shock all over again.

Tears flowed freely as his mind brought him back to October 7, 2009 and his platoon's clean-up mission after the Kamdesh fiasco. Four days had passed since miscommunication and mistakes had led to one of the biggest losses of US troops. McAllister, Baron, and eight men were dropped into the mountainous valley to make certain that no munitions were left for the enemy to loot. It was dark, but McAllister's night vision goggles were dangling around his neck; he was worried and the glasses seemed to impede his senses.

The men were spread out behind Baron, a Doberman trained in detecting incendiary explosive devices. McAllister was spraying the night air with a light water mist so that he could determine the direction and intensity of the wind. He did this to help his dog interpret contradictory signs. Suddenly

McAllister saw Baron stop short, that silly stub of a tail wagging furiously, the sign that he'd found something. Then everything went to hell.

But McAllister knew the dog was merely one of the reasons he was feeling so uncharacteristically emotional. His memories were coming back; images of the attack in the shower by the gang of eight guys who assaulted him. He had heard nothing as he stood under the pounding water of the shower; had not sensed danger of any kind. One minute he'd been standing under the shower enjoying the feel of the hot water on his body; the next, he was on his back, dimly aware of the irony. He had survived four tours in Afghanistan only to die in this stupid prison. These guys were going to kill him.

They were screaming epithets at the top of their lungs about the varieties of depraved acts they were going to do to him once they had beaten him to a bloody pulp. He could recall only some of them because mercifully he was blacked out for most of it, but Gabe dimly remembered a huge black prison guard appearing out of nowhere.

Smiling at Lindsey and gratefully accepting the ice water she handed him, Gabe took two then three deep swallows.

"Easy there … you don't need to add vomiting to your list of woes."

Nodding in understanding, Gabe placed the mostly empty glass on the table next to his bed, and asked, "Who was the big black guy who stopped them? He must have been a guard?"

Confident now of the complete recovery of her patient, McCall grinned as she nodded in agreement. "Luke Preston is his name, and yes, he saved your life. He's been here to check on you every day since he brought you in."

Harvey and Tony should be arriving any time now ....

Max looked content as he dozed on his bed while Rich was preparing for Cunningham's two investigators, Harvey, and Tony. Cunningham had called Rich at home last night with "a few suggestions"; thirty-five minutes later, Jansen's legal pad was full with notes from their conversation.

Tapping his pencil while scanning his notes, he considered a few items which made him nervous. A slight understatement because this whole case, this whole crazy decision of his to change careers—again—had him tense and anxious. Rich almost wished for the calm and predictable days of being Chief Warden at Huntsville. Cunningham had spent over ten minutes explaining what he believed to be the key to the proof of McAllister's innocence and how they would find it. And it scared the hell out of Jansen.

Jansen did not doubt Cunningham's in-depth knowledge of criminal defense; he had read the court transcript of the appeal acquitting the Houston cardiologist Ted Ross. Cunningham's interrogation of Marcie Ross was brilliant. Despite the fact that Ross's ex-wife was a hostile witness and had brain-washed their child into believing that her father had sexually assaulted her, Cunningham's questions to Marcie had led skillfully to a most remarkable confession by Christy, the moment Marcie took the stand after being called as the next witness.

Through his measured and methodical cross-examination of Marcie Ross, Cunningham revealed the deception and fabrication of her story. During her progressively unfounded and inconsistent answers to Cunningham's cross, Marcie was reduced to calling the doctors, who had declared her daughter a virgin, liars and claimed they were part of a medical conspiracy against her and her little girl. Listening to the public hysterical rant of her mother just one too many times, little

Christy had exploded.

Reading the transcript was riveting; Rich could imagine the stunned, astonished silence in the Houston courtroom when the first few words of the child were uttered.

Mr. Cunningham: Good morning, Christy.

Christy: Good morning.

Mr. Cunningham: Thank you for being here today. I apologize in advance for the questions I need to ask you about the things you said your dad had done to you several years ago. Is it all right if I ask you about this?

The Court: Ms. Ross, please reply so that you can be heard.

Christy Ross: Yes, it's okay.

Mr. Cunningham: Several weeks ago, a doctor examined you. Do you remember the doctor, Christy?

Jansen knew Cunningham referred to a gynecology examination most likely performed by a Pediatrician. The exam had revealed an intact vaginal hymen and reported the absence of any suspicious scarring around the anus. The Pediatrician had stated she believed that Christy Ross was a virgin. Examination of her genitalia did not reveal the presence of any prior sexual activity.

Mr. Cunningham: I know this must be very hard on you, child.

Christy Ross: I LIED BEFORE. MY DADDY NEVER DID ANY OF THOSE THINGS TO ME. MY MOM MADE ME SAY ALL THESE LIES, THEY WERE ALL LIES. DADDY IS INNOCENT, HE NEVER TOUCHED ME IN THOSE PLACES, I'VE NEVER SEEN HIS PENIS; EVERYTHING I SAID WAS LIES. SHE TAUGHT ME THE WORDS ANNNN

....

Rich had read his share of transcripts. He'd never seen a court reporter capitalize the testimony of a witness; despite the fact that he'd read this section of the transcript at least ten times, it still stopped him cold. And if he'd been present in the courtroom?

Capitalizing the nine-year-old Christy's testimony was actually ingenious on the part of the court reporter, Jansen thought. Despite the fact that he'd not met Christy Ross as yet, he could see and hear the tortured body of a little girl, could hear the sobbing which would have accompanied the words that must have burst forth from the little girl's psyche, burning their way through to her heart where they had been festering for years.

"Are you Jansen?"

Simultaneously, Max scrambled to his feet and Rich started from his concentration on the file to see a pair who had to be Harvey and Tony, the two investigators Cunningham had promised would be in his office Monday morning. He and Max were staring at two of the most unusual looking women Rich had ever seen.

"Yeah, you two must be Harvey and Tony?"

Figures, with Cunningham 'and associates' nothing was what was expected. Harvey and Tony, right, of course they'd be women and bizarre ones at that. These two look like Mutt and Jeff, the ethnic version.

The tall skinny black woman replied, "Right, I'm Harvey." She nodded to the Hispanic fireplug-shaped woman to her left who was built like a linebacker for the Texans. "This is Tony."

Tony nodded as if in agreement that yes, she was indeed Tony as she jabbed a short fat forefinger at Max, "That's a Doberman, dude. I don't do Dobermans. Get him out of here now." Her voice was low and almost menacing as she stared at Max, who was suddenly rigid next to Jansen; the highly intuitive dog immediately sensed the threat, fear, and anger pouring off this woman.

Ignoring her order, Rich gestured a down command to Max with the flat of his palm; the Doberman dropped down to his bed, crouching on haunches and elbows as he anxiously surveyed the newcomers. Jansen's jaw worked and his teeth ground as he worked to get his reaction under control.

What hole did this bitch just climb out of?

A few minutes later

Jansen's Law Office, Downtown Houston

*It's life that matters, nothing but life—the process
of discovering, the everlasting and perpetual process,
not the discovery itself, at all.*
— *Dostoevsky*

CHAPTER
17

Rich, Harvey, and Tony were standing in the office that Cunningham's two investigators would use for the duration of their investigative work with McAllister's appeal. They were two doors down from Jansen's office with the offending Doberman inside.

Well aware of the fear generated by Dobermans among some people by mostly exaggerated stories of the aggression of the breed, Jansen calmly replied to Tony's continued protests against the presence of Max. And he nodded agreeably, "Tony, I understand. The dog won't be here after today. You'll not see him again."

The woman was breathing very rapidly, her brown eyes wide and dilated, fists clenched, her shoulders were hunched in a classic posture of fear covered up with anger. Before Tony could respond with another volley of epithets, Harvey took two steps to her left, gently clasping her partner's right forearm which was sleeved with an intricate pattern of pastel tattoos beginning at the wrist and disappearing beneath the a baggy sweatshirt with cut-off arms and squeezed the arm.

Surprised at the unexpected support from the tall lanky black second investigator of this bizarre dyad, Rich stepped back to watch Harvey subdue, almost "gentle" Tony. He realized that Harvey was really quite beautiful as he listened and watched the tenderness with which she spoke and touched her partner. Her long curly Afro hair hung in tendrils aside aquiline features and a wide, generous mouth which was curved into a soft smile.

"Toni, honey, it's okay, the dog is gone, he won't be back. We have a lot of work to do. Remember, Zach expects us to figure out how we can get Annie and Christy Ross together this week … that's gonna take some doin' on our part, girl!" Her long coffee-colored fingers were wrapped tightly around the light pinks, blues, and greens of Toni's forearm, her dark, almost black eyes with their long curly eyelashes focused intently on the now relaxing, coarse features of her friend.

Rich had assumed the two were gay, but now rethought that assumption when he noted Harvey's wedding rings, one a large diamond engagement ring, adorning the left hand now loosening its hold and gently patting Toni's arm.

Wait a minute, she just said that Cunningham's orders for his two investigators would get Christy Ross, the daughter of the Houston cardiologist whose lies about the sexual abuse of her father had landed him in jail and forced him to declare bankruptcy, and Annie, the little girl accuser of Greg McAllister, together. When did this decision take place? Why didn't he know anything about it? More than all of that, how on earth could such a meeting possibly take place? Why would Christy Ross ever agree to meet with a little girl whom she had never met? Why would she be willing to walk down a path that had to be fraught with guilt and sorrow?

His mind was a jumble of confused thoughts and emotions which ranged from humiliation and frustration to anger. Jansen had the ever increasing sense that he was a passenger on a train that had left a station that he knew, and was hurtling toward an unknown destination. Despite this increasing total loss of control, Jansen's studiedly neutral facial expression belied the riot of emotions churning within.

"We're here to help this guy Gabe McAllister, Rich." The statement was said flatly, like an announcement.

Expertly reading Jansen's perplexed and frustrated state of mind, Harvey took a deep breath, and dropped her left hand from Toni's right arm so that she could point to Toni as she continued, "Toni won that acquittal of Dr. Ted Ross for Zach." Harvey let the shards of that verbal bombshell pierce Jansen's anti-Toni Kevlar by dropping the remark casually, using the softest of tones and a mere whisper of a smile before continuing on with her deceptively ingenuous revelations about Toni Martinez, female sleuth extraordinaire.

Ignoring Toni's obvious non-verbal gestures of increasing dismay, "Toni here had the idea to go talk directly with Christy Ross. She had a 'feeling' about the claims of Ross's ex-wife, Marcie, and she wore Zach down but it took almost too long. Marcie Ross is kind of a quintessential Southern belle … beautiful really … at least physically anyway and she had everyone convinced of the sexual perversion of her husband. Everyone but Toni.

"At first, Zach put off Toni's insistence to 'attitude.'" Laughing now, Harvey's broad smile at Toni was infectious enough that Toni answered with a grin of her own that transformed her face from ugly to … well, not quite so ugly.

Rich felt like he was an unwilling participant in one of those magic shows where the magician appears directly in front of you while you're sitting passively in the audience. Then the showman persuades you up onto the stage to be sawed in half. As he watched these two women perform an act that was too smooth to just happen, he decided this had to be practiced.

"Zach had hired Toni just six months before the Ross case, so he'd had too little time to see beneath Toni's very effective cover."

Glancing at Toni, Rich was startled to see a blush climbing up her thick neck and heading up to her cheeks. Her formerly rage-filled brown eyes were now directed at Harvey and had lightened from an opaque dark brown, to amber with brown and hazel highlights; risking a quick glance at Jansen, Martinez failed to conceal her smile.

"Toni's Puerto Rican … she was raised by her grandmother, who was blessed with a highly developed psychic sixth sense, and who recognized that Toni also possessed the gift."

Harvey stopped speaking, regarding Jansen while she tapped a long and skeletal coffee-colored forefinger on her chin; her eyes were large, widely spaced, with long curly lashes. Quite obviously the woman was deliberating about how much more to tell him. Martinez looked about as relaxed as she probably could get; her formerly combative posture had been reigned in. Toni ceding control of new and potentially volatile situations to Harvey seemed like a path these two had trodden many times in their partnership.

The office was quiet while Jansen allowed himself to be studied by these two most unusual women; openly by Harvey and surreptitiously by Martinez. The silence was not uncomfortable.

Rich Jansen was no novice in the study of human behavior nor was he inexperienced in the art of leadership. His intuitive judgment was generally right on target and had served him well while under fire both literally and figuratively. But Jansen knew that his initial appraisal of Toni Martinez had been wrong, dead wrong; all emotion from his former reactions had bled away leaving him wondering, curious, even excited to learn more about these two unconventional characters who had entered his life. The change was tangible both on Rich's face and within the energy within the room.

Coming to a decision, Harvey asked, "Do you know anything about Santeria, Rich?" Without waiting for a reply, which was a really good thing from Jansen's perspective because he knew next to nothing about the word, Harvey declared, "Santeria is a syncretic religion." Smiling at Jansen's raised eyebrow, she explained, "Some consider all of Christianity syncretic, which means merely that the religion takes existing cultural beliefs, in this case, pagan ones, and builds the religion on top of them. Atheists love to point out that the pagan beliefs of virgin birth, death and resurrection existed long before Christ and, therefore, prove the spuriousness of Christianity and all of its claims.

"The thing is, most religions have done exactly that. The rapid spread of Buddhism in Asia occurred because of the merger of Shinto icons and practices with Buddhism. But," smiling once again and shaking her head, "the atheists don't complain about Buddhism, just us Christians."

By way of explanation, Harvey stated, "I have a Masters in Religion from Vanderbilt and was planning to go for a doctorate until I met and married Zach Cunningham and had our two children. The investigator isn't all that different from the religious scholar when you think about it. Both are detectives."

Of course these two would be married. This stunning black woman would naturally be attracted to one of the least attractive men on the planet; maybe there's someone less physically appeal-

ing but I've never met him. But the man was brilliant, that had to be the attraction between these two. Zach Cunningham looked as if he were a lot older, maybe by twenty years? Harvey has to be close to six feet tall, she's only a few inches shorter than I am. She could be a model; he could be a godfather in an African-American mafia. Zach is no more than five-four … at most, five-six. Paradox rules once again. Amazing.

By now, Rich was captivated by these two clever women, each of whom knew the recipe to assure that they were underestimated by the world. It was a rare art—he knew why Cunningham employed them: they were lethal.

Harvey paused, waiting.

Realizing that it was time to reveal a bit about himself, Jansen smiled, extended his hand first to Harvey and then to Toni as he declared with a grin, "Ladies, we quite clearly got off on the wrong foot."

Looking directly into Toni's eyes and holding onto her hand, he said, "I apologize for having Max in my office; I forget that everyone does not have the trust and affection for my dog as I do. He'll be staying with my wife, who is Medical Director for the Huntsville Prison System starting tomorrow; he'll not be back while you are here, you have my word."

Pretending that he did not notice Toni's widened stare at this disclosure, Jansen continued, "Until last week, I was Chief Warden at Huntsville. Although I practiced criminal law right after I finished law school, I left after a year and became a cop."

Still holding onto the unresisting Toni's hand, he continued, "It's been over fifteen years since I've defended anyone, so you two obviously are way ahead of me … feel free to treat me like any newly minted law intern in Zach's office."

Huntsville Prison

*Because I've known war dogs, I will never look at dogs the
same way again. Because I've known their keepers,
I will never look at the military, or the people
in its community, the same way, either.*
— Rebecca Frankel War Dogs

C H A P T E R

18

McAllister knew that Dr. McCall was keeping him in her infirmary long past his need for her medical attention; he was grateful, very grateful, but each time he tried to express his appreciation, something happened to shut him up. Good things, all good things. Like a few days ago, he had thought back for a few minutes, trying to orient himself to time and place.

Yeah, it had been Tuesday morning, early, it was just starting to get light in the infirmary. He'd not been sleeping, just hadn't wanted to open up his eyes to the day, when he'd felt the unmistakable pressure on his arm.

Gabe's eyes had snapped open because he knew that unique pressure … knew it well. And there stood their Doberman, Max, regarding him steadily with those incredible amber eyes. The dog had pushed his snout through the side rail of his bed and had fit his head through the space so that he could push his nose against McAllister's arm, gently but persistently.

Suddenly, he was back there again.

The handler at Lackland Air Force Base kennels in Texas who had taught him and Baron called it astronomical time; the night was waning, dawn was imminent but you still couldn't see colors, only shapes.

Both human and canine eyes see through retinas which are lined with rods-motion detectors and cones for color distinction. Scientists believe that evolution dictated the larger ratio of cones to rods in humans than in dogs because humans had learned to rely on color to find food during the daytime, while dogs were nocturnal hunters and relied on movement in order to detect prey. Therefore, dogs can see far better at night than can humans. Recent canine research has revealed that dogs are color-blind only to reds and greens, thereby painting their world in yellow and muted shades of blues and gray rather than the complete color spectrum that is seen by humans.

They were walking in on a narrow tortuous path next to what looked like an Afghan cemetery, erratically placed body-shaped mounds of earth with an occasional tombstone; an ideal place to bury pressure or remotely detonated IEDs. McAllister knew he should have his NVD (night vision goggles) on but he hated them, had never become accustomed to the damn weird and eerie green they shaded everything.

The high desert wind was blowing at about 20 miles per hour, not too bad for the 'dark side of the moon,' or Kamdesh, Afghanistan, the name that had been given to one of the bloodiest and stupidest battles of this endless war. It was too dark to see anything but the shapes of the large stones marking the graves.

McAllister and Baron were leading the small group of Marines who had been dropped into what had been one of the hottest war zones of the war to date. McAllister was watching Baron, straining to see ahead. Well aware that the cemetery was one of the more dangerous places for soldiers in Afghanistan because many of the bodies were identifiable simply by heaped mounds of dirt, a perfect place to bury a detonator plate for an IED, McAllister felt the acid of the hastily gulped black coffee trying to burn its way back up. He was more than jittery, he was scared.

Strangely, the United States Military seemingly has had to relearn just how powerful a weapon were dogs in war with each succeeding war. During the battle for Guam in World War ll, the Japanese placed far more value on an executed Doberman war dog than they did slain American soldiers. The fear of the soldiers for the dogs was so great that the Japanese soldiers called the Doberman War Dogs *Devil Dogs.* This name was appropriated by the American Marine handlers fighting for recapture of the island; they called themselves the Devil Dog Battalion.

Today, if one visits Naval Base Guam, the visitor can visit the National War Dog Cemetery where a monument to the twenty-five Dobermans who died saving Marines is topped by a sculpture of a Doberman named Kurt. Credited with saving the lives of two hundred fifty marines, Kurt was the first war dog to be killed in Guam. His sculpture is titled, "Always Faithful," or Semper Fidelis, the motto of the Marine Corps.

Then later, in Viet Nam, military training of dogs extended from Dobermans to German shepherds, along with many other assorted breeds.

But it was another forty years before the military dusted off their memory and decided to open MWD training facilities once again. By 2004, the military realized that the extensive and successful use of improvised explosive devices in Iraq and

Afghanistan warranted the reintroduction of dogs into the battle. The term IED was first coined by the British Army to describe the varied concoctions of fertilizer and semtex combined with a remote detonation created by the IRA. The widespread destruction of the hapless British soldiers either driving or stepping onto the homemade explosive devices back in the seventies was being repeated among the American and allied troops in the Gulf wars.

Anatomically, the nasal passages of canines seem expressly designed for purposes of detection and discrimination of odors. Dogs have four nasal passages concurrently inhaling the full new universe of scent around them while exhaling carbon dioxide and discarded odors. Unlike their human handlers, with only two nasal passages, dogs are compulsory nose breathers, they pant to sweat not breathe. Those cool, moist black noses serve to collect molecules from the swirling olfactory soup surrounding dogs and bring them into contact with specialized receptors in the canine nose. They have an ability to "smell in 3-D" was the way one dog handler creatively compared the superiority of the canine olfactory system to that of humans. On average, the canine nose has two billion olfactory receptors, while their human handlers have a mere fraction at forty million. Dogs can discriminate between and among countless ongoing odors to find and identify the scent they have been trained to seek. Dogs are, therefore, a natural partner in the dangerous business of identifying bombs before they explode.

In addition to their natural senses, recent canine research has revealed the extraordinary accuracy with which dogs read human facial expressions along with verbal and non-verbal cues. In studies comparing chimpanzees' and dogs' ability to interpret human gestures and expressions, dogs win, each and every time. Unerringly, it seems, dogs outperform their allegedly far more intelligent primate in simulated tests of interpreting and acting on human gestures and facial expressions.

Today all kinds of dogs are used as war dogs, with Labrador retrievers, German shepherds, and, the Belgian Malinois among the most commonly used breeds.

Baron had been classified as a 'misfit.' When McAllister got to Leavenworth and learned about the group of misfit dogs, he immediately asked if he could train with one of them. The name was given by an Air Force tech sergeant who had been one of the original war dog trainers. He and his Belgian Malinois had been the first dog/soldier team to be killed in Afghanistan. There was a plaque hanging on the wall of the Spartan entry way to the training center picturing lanky twenty-four-year-old Tech Sergeant Skip Anderson and fifty-pound five-year-old Romeo, both staring at the camera. The snapshot had been taken a week before they had deployed to Afghanistan, never to return.

Baron had been categorized as a misfit because the current head of the training program, Jerry Polowicz had flunked him out of the program for a number of reasons. Despite the dog's ability to consistently identify mortar shells, C-4, fertilizer, and semtex along with the numerous other ingredients used to create explosive devices at close to one hundred percent accuracy, Baron did so only with Polowicz, no one else. More worrisome was the Doberman's attitude toward each of the five soldiers Polowicz had assigned to work with the dog; Baron was not vicious to his handlers; in fact, he was almost exactly the opposite: he ignored them. If Polowicz didn't know better, he'd have sworn the dog was bored with everyone else.

For Jerry, the dilemma was painful: his deployment days were over, so the bond between this Doberman and him was of no use. Worse, Polowicz had no place to send the dog. Until McAllister showed up.

Baron and Gabe were a team almost from the first time they set eyes on one another.

Gabe had laughed when he walked into Baron's kennel, looking over the beautiful eighty-pound Doberman and said, 'Misfit, huh? Good, me too.'

Doberman pinschers were first bred in 1890 by the German tax collector, Karl Louis Dobermann. In looking for the perfect combination of fearlessness, speed, endurance, loyalty, intelligence, and obedience, Dobermann may have used as many as ten different breeds. Most believe the modern Doberman to have been produced from a combination of the German pinscher, Beauceron, old German shepherd, greyhound, and the Rottweiler.

Extremely quick learners with a deep need for people, Dobermans can become stubborn, willful and destructive if the people around them are incapable of achieving the healthy dominance required to train and exercise these unique dogs.

From the very beginning, McAllister and Baron were unbeatable in the contests with other dog teams at the Lackland training center. No matter how cleverly the pressure disc was hidden, or how well hidden behind a cupboard was the C-4, Baron's nose found it. During the twelve weeks of training, McAllister and Baron made over thirty jumps from the Chinook helicopters; they surpassed all the other teams in finding targets and returning to base once their mission was completed. Not infrequently, Jerry Polowicz found himself angrily swiping away tears as he watched Baron and Gabe McAllister playing tug of war with the dog's kong; or saw them stretched out together, both long lean bodies, the human and canine relaxing next to one another after a grueling mission in the Texas high desert.

Polowicz knew this team would save many soldiers when he pronounced the two ready to roll, relieved that he had not had to make a decision that he would regret for the rest of his life.

Baron had slowed down that day from his normal fast-paced trot. He was watching one of the tall gravestones on his left, nose up, moving ever so slightly more and more to the left. Watching his dog, McAllister raised his right hand to slow down the men following while he strained to look ahead, to the left where Baron was so intently focused. Suddenly, as if he had run into a cement wall, the big dog skidded to a halt and looked back at McAllister; eyes lit, stubby tail wagging furiously, alive with the knowledge that he'd found the target and was eagerly awaiting the play time which always followed the find. Those sensitive ears were quivering with anticipation: the tell-tale click of the pressure plate was barely audible to any but those sensitive canine ears; Baron knew he'd done it, he had sought and found: mission complete.

The explosion was deafening; McAllister only knew that he was screaming when Samuels, his second in command had wrapped his arms around him so tightly that he could not breathe.

•

Lindsey watched her patient from the radiology diagnostic area. Gabe could not see her, happily so because the ex-soldier had lowered the side rails of his bed so that he could get out of the bed to sit down in the chair next to the bed to get closer to her dog. She could not see his face because it was buried into the big chest of Max who stood still in front of the chair, staring at her through the window, calmly, as if sobbing soldiers were an everyday occurrence in his life.

She worried about this man; only twenty- eight but he had the eyes of a very old man and when she tried to get past the shield McAllister used to deflect everyone around him, his eyes took on a characteristic thousand-yard stare and he became unreachable.

Dr. Lindsey McCall was no stranger to trauma: she had suffered profound loss, betrayal, and like McAllister, had been imprisoned for a crime she did not commit. But Lindsey knew that the carnage McAllister had witnessed, the brutality and horrors he'd experienced, had changed his psyche and personality; they perhaps had permanently scarred him so profoundly that he may not be able to find his way back.

McCall knew how strange was her certainty that this guy had done nothing to the little girl. Unable to explain anything but the power of her conviction of McAllister's innocence to Rich, Lindsey knew she had swayed her husband, had caused him to look at this ex-soldier almost through her eyes. She also had complete confidence that her husband would get Gabe out of jail; it was only a matter of time. In the meantime, she was confident that Rich's successor, Warden Bob Cleary, would permit Dr. McCall to keep her patient in the infirmary until McAllister was released. Cleary was a good man and knew that if McAllister were released into the general Huntsville Prison population, chances were better than good that he'd be dead within a week. None of those "details" bothered her.

What she thought about when she awakened at three in the morning as she did frequently, was what would this ruined man do when he got out?

Could he pick up the pieces of his ruined life with the ease that she had?

During one of the few times McCall had sought and found a fissure in McAllister's protective psychic gear, she'd nonchalantly asked him a few questions while checking his neurological signs.

"Look up and to your right, now left, please, Gabe. Good … you're looking great actually."

Smiling, Lindsey gazed into the hazel eyes of her patient

expecting a response. There was none. For a moment, she got worried that he may have sustained more head trauma than she had thought.

Finally, she heard sound but could not make out his words.

"I'm sorry, can you repeat what you said just now? I couldn't understand you."

His mouth was smiling but, his eyes looked dead as he answered her, "I said, I'm the luckiest bastard in this prison, aren't I Doctor?"

A couple of days later when Lindsey had just completed a fairly extensive neuro exam, both physical and mental, all of which Gabe had passed with flying colors, Lindsey decided to ask a few probing questions.

"Gabe, are there any family members we can contact? I see that you've not had any visitors since you've been here."

"Nope."

Despite the obvious non-verbal invitation to shut up, Lindsey continued.

"Are you a believer Gabe, would you like—"

The vehemence of the "NO" which cut her off surprised McCall, not because of the lack of interest in God or religion but because the guy did not seem angry at her. If anything, the cause for her concern was the total absence of emotion, the one exception being the breakdown with Max. Wondering at the brief "conversation," if it could be called that, she thought that sudden flash of anger a good thing as she walked away.

Watching McCall walk away through lidded eyes still extremely swollen, McAllister's mind returned to the mental scab he'd been picking at with his recovering memory of all that had transpired since he quit the Corps. He deserved all this.

Eyes wide open, he'd made the decision to live with a

woman and a little girl who were each more damaged than he was. Mouth moving only slightly due both to the pain and to the bitterness of his thoughts, Gabe realized with a jolt that he'd been weirdly happy during those last few conscious thoughts. He had lain there completely confident that those prisoners would kill him. And he knew he deserved it.

I knew that Annie had been molested by other guys. Hell, it was written into those hundred-year-old-eyes that didn't want me to leave that first morning I woke up in Sam's apartment and couldn't even remember the name of the woman I'd screwed.

I was a coward … three combat awards—silver star, purple heart, and distinguished leadership—all lying somewhere in boxes I've never bothered to unpack. And the words that had been said to me: heroic courage under pressure; selfless disregard for self … their echoes are still audible. Captain Gabriel McAllister, solder extraordinaire. Right.

The disgust and self-hatred were rising to levels that threatened to consume him. He was surrounded by people with real guts. This lady doc who had somehow had the courage to climb out of a hole as deep as he was in, her husband who had been a Marine, homicide cop, and now a criminal defense lawyer—*his* defense lawyer, for some inexplicable reason. These were people who took the really extreme risks, like falling in love, getting married, deciding to help a loser like him. Were he the hero that all the combat rhetoric claimed, he would have confronted Sam with all the truths he saw in her child and in her, beginning with the addictions.

But he stayed silent. Never opened his mouth. Until that last night, when Sam, stoned and naked, brought her naked five-year-old into the shower with him. Stupidity and cowardice: a dangerous combination that gets you killed.

Kate's Condo in Montrose area of Houston

We are never prepared for what we expect.
— *James Michener*

C H A P T E R

19

"Zach's people have found Annie and her mother."

Kate Townsend startled out of her reverie to grab her phone just as it was about to go to voice mail. Grabbing her phone with a guilty start, she looked around her empty condo, half expecting to hear a deservedly derisive comment about the wasted time she'd just spent daydreaming in front of the half-finished second article in her *A Nation of Law: The Dark Side* series. Her deadline was, the reporter reminded herself ruefully, in a just a little over seventy-two hours.

Lifting the phone to her ear with her left hand, she found herself grinning ecstatically at the rainbow made by the sun on the diamond ring.

Townsend, you are incorrigible! Honestly, I feel like a freshman in high school who was asked to the Prom by the senior Quarterback of the football team! Who would have thought that the traditional diamond ring, the oh so traditional down on one knee proposal and the intimate conversation about the possibility of getting pregnant would cause so much joy in the heart of this oh so untraditional female?

Feeling the heat of the blush from Kate's memories of the weekend spent with Steve, she had to ask for a repeat of the statement so she could get reoriented from her daydreams back to her work.

"I'm so sorry. Can you tell me once again what you just said?"

The masculine laughter coming from the phone was warm and affectionate when Hank Reardon nailed her mood, "What's the problem, intrepid reporter? That diamond ring obliterating brain cells by the nanosecond?"

Nonplussed, Kate exclaimed, "Hank Reardon, how in the world did you hear about our engagement?" Shaking her head with a sheepish smile, "Okay, take pity on me, please. Was it Lindsey or Rich? We had dinner with them the Sunday before Steve returned to San Francisco."

Kate was surprised and delighted with the close friendship that Steve Cooper, her fiancé and Chief of Cardiology at the University of California at San Francisco had developed with Rich and Lindsey. She had wholeheartedly agreed when Steve had suggested that they join Lindsey and Rich for a celebratory dinner at their home in New Waverly.

"We billionaires have our ways, Kate."

Rolling her eyes at the statement that made Reardon sound like all the things he was not, Kate grimaced and said tightly, "Please tell me that I won't read about this on the gossip page of one of our competitors, Hank."

Hank Reardon was CEO of Andrews, Sacks, and Levine, the pharmaceutical company which manufactured and held the patent to Lindsey McCall's Digipro. The drug was a molecular modification of the drug Digitalis, which produced all of the beneficial effects on the heart of Digitalis but without the lethal side effects. Kate and Reardon had met during the intense months of Kate's investigation of McCall's conviction for murder and subsequent imprisonment at Huntsville Prison. Townsend's investigative series, *Murder in the Texas Medical Center,* had won the Pulitzer for her and for her newspaper. During the intense months of work which led eventually to McCall's acquittal and release from prison, Reardon and the reporter had developed a close friendship.

One of the wealthiest men in the world, Reardon had connections everywhere, Kate was well aware; she didn't think Reardon would say anything but now that she had a bit of a name herself ….

"Oh for God's sake Kate, you know better than that!" The exasperated and annoyed tone was classical Hank Reardon.

"Sorry, Hank, it's just that this is …."

"Brand new." Cutting her off without apology, Reardon added, "I know Katie girl—even though it's been a long time for me, I know how you feel." Kate heard a deep sigh, " Katie, my girl, if you could have seen me the night that my Peg agreed to marry me..." Reardon's voice caught and he had to clear his throat.

Reardon had lost his wife Peggy to ovarian cancer the year before. Despite the fact that Peggy had been in the last stages of the cancer, her warmth, hospitality, and genuine affection had been apparent to Hank, his daughter Liisa, and most of all, to Kate. During that week at the Reardon home, Kate had quite literally fallen in love with the Reardon family.

"But Kate, so sorry, I don't have a lot of time to let you know what is happening in your neck of the woods with your new guy, McAllister; we'll save this other discussion for later."

Kate listened as Reardon updated her on the progress made by Toni and Harvey, the investigators who worked for Zach Cunningham. Finally they had located the little girl, Annie, and her mother, Samantha Bridges, whose testimonies were crucial to the appeal.

During the dinner celebrating the engagement of Kate and Steve, it had taken no time at all for the foursome to make the switch from celebration to business; they had talked at length about McAllister. Steve Cooper had been intrigued by this case because of his acquaintance with Ted Ross, the cardiologist, who had been acquitted of similar crimes by his daughter Christy's admission that she had lied about the abuse. None of the four had any direct experiences with the sexual abuse of children and found the entire subject of the use of small children for sex appalling.

Equally atrocious, however, was the notion of using a child in the complex and perverse manipulation played by a mother against a father and husband or boyfriend. Both Cooper and Lindsey were dumbfounded at the estimates of women alleging that sexual abuse had been committed against their kids; an abuse which was later found to be false.

Since the first article in Kate's investigative series had been published on the front page of her paper that morning, the Pulitzer-winning reporter Townsend and the Houston Tribune were once again the talk of journalistic circles. The paper had hired a secretary for Kate to keep up with the correspondence coming in via the social media and snail mail following her *Murder in the Texas Medical Center* series. They were considering a second assistant even before her current series, *A Nation of Law: The Dark Side,* had hit the streets. Within hours after the first article, the volume of comments and mail was massive, leaving Kate's editor Jeff Simpson no choice but to hire a second person to handle Townsend's voluminous correspondence.

The irony of Monica Livingston, Lindsey's head nurse at the prison emergency center, and her incapacitating tsunami of memories of her childhood incestuous experiences with her father was not lost on the group. Monica remained on a medical leave of absence while she received treatment.

"Obviously, you all think this guy is innocent or you wouldn't be spending this kind of time and energy on him," Cooper's comment was said casually. The lanky doctor was seated on one of the brown leather couches in Rich and Lindsey's living room. One arm was wrapped around Kate, the other held a glass of wine which he was twirling in the dim light.

Steve felt Kate tense and pulled her closer.

"Honey, I'm playing devil's advocate and simply stating the obvious … in a way, I almost wish I'd urged you to walk away from this one, Kate." Steve had dropped the arm holding Kate close to him down so that his hand could grab her left hand, hold it and fiddle with her engagement ring while he talked. "On the one hand, we have Monica, abused by her own father for God's sake … for years as I understand it."

His statement was rhetorical and required no answer, but Lindsey, who was stretched on the floor beside Max, nodded and said, "Yes, you're right, Steve."

"And we have this soldier, this guy who's done four tours in Afghanistan. A man who most likely has the worst PTSD known to man and moves in with a gal he knew to be a drug abuser, a woman with a five-year-old-child. How utterly irresponsible can a guy be?" Cooper looked with deep affection at the agitated expression on Kate's face and continued gently. "But if we consider what had to be going on in his head resulting from his own trauma, we can get an approximate grasp of why a soldier, a Marine at that, might behave this way. We can get a take on McAllister's state of mind because we've been analyzing this case for several weeks and we have the benefit of this kind of conversation among ourselves.

"But if we four were on that jury, blind, deaf, and dumb

to anything but what we heard in the courtroom and we heard that little girl claim that he had raped her, that he had put his dick in her mouth and everywhere else, wouldn't we all find him guilty?"

Steve took a deep breath as he studied the uneasy faces of Rich and Lindsey, who were concentrating on every word he said.

"Unless, of course, this is another situation like Ted Ross's. Where someone manages to get a little girl to admit she's been lying … that her own mother had forced her to make all of these claims. In a crazy way, you can almost understand why Christy admitted the lies. This was, after all, her own *father*. But here we have a virtual stranger … someone with whom this kid has had no relationship at all. How likely is she to admit that she is lying? What possible incentive would she have other than screwing up her life even more than it already is?"

Cooper's tone was soft, but his words silenced the room completely; even Max seemed to feel the tension. The Doberman sat up, then went over to sit in front of Rich, whining as he placed his paw in Jansen's lap.

Still lying prone on the floor, Lindsey said softly, "After listening to Kate talk about Alexandra Allbrite and her experience as Juror Foreperson, Steve, I suspect you are right. We'd most likely vote that he was guilty, just like she did. And whether this little girl can admit her lies? Therein lies the rub."

A significant number of Americans, it seems, believe that no innocent person can be accused of a crime. Of the fifty states in the country, over half make use of grand juries in determining whether sufficient evidence exists for the district attorney to bring an indictment against an individual for cause. Grand juries were established as a "voice of the community" to protect a fundamental maxim of American jurisprudence: innocent until proven guilty. However, in less than five per cent of cases presented to them by the district attorney, does a grand jury vote against indictment: if you are accused, you must be guilty.

Lindsey sat up and scooted closer to the now agitated Doberman, who was being completely ignored by her husband.

"Come on baby, come back here with me." Voice soft, almost crooning, Lindsey looked up at the pensive face of her husband and knew that he was in deep thought, he probably hadn't even heard Max's pleas for attention. Continuing her high-pitched, lilting cadence, she whispered, "That's right, it's okay Max, come back over here with me, let's get some music for you, boy." McCall reached over to turn on the sound system; instantly, the room was filled with the muted strains of a Sibelius violin concerto.

Finally the dog stood, turned around and followed Lindsey to lie down once again, but not without a loud sigh of protest. Earlier in the evening, Jansen had entertained his wife and friends with the story of their Doberman Max's banishment by Cunningham's investigator Toni from his downtown law offices. And that Max was back at work with Lindsey at the Emergency Center in the prison. Cooper and Kate were smiling as they watched Lindsey and the dog.

"If only Toni could see this scary Doberman now," Kate muttered. "He's like a little kid, isn't he? What's with the music Linds? It's acting like a tranquilizer on Max."

Lindsey nodded in agreement as she sat, legs akimbo, stroking the now relaxed big dog. "Works like a charm; his breeders played classical music to his mother the entire time he was in utero, and then during the three months that he was with the rest of the litter and his mom."

Reardon's opening statement, "They have found Annie and Sam," was echoing in Kate's mind. She had about a hundred questions rolling around in her head; they had been building up since the night in the restaurant with Rich Jansen—the call from Hank in the middle of his night when he had given Jansen the name of Zach Cunningham. Cunningham had been the catalyst for this entire venture.

According to Ted Ross, Zach Cunningham was one of her admirers. An admirer whom she never had even spoken with. Undoubtedly Ross would never have agreed to meet with Kate, much less consent to his daughter Christy entrusting Kate with her story, if it hadn't been for Cunningham. Once again, Hank Reardon's impact on her career was colossal; there was only one possible source of Cunningham's admiration.

Hank Reardon, what is your interest in the sexual abuse conviction of some anonymous ex-soldier? How do you know this criminal defense attorney, Zach Cunningham? How did you persuade the guy to take this case ... are you paying him? Don't you have enough to do as CEO of one of the biggest pharmaceuticals in the world without getting involved in this lurid story? Why are you even tracking what is happening with McAllister and why would you know they have found the little girl who accused McAllister before Rich or I know? Why do you even care?

Swallowing these and all of her other questions, Kate declared instead, "Rich said something about this Toni person having some kind of psychic ability. Hank, apparently the other investigator told Rich that it was Toni who convinced Cunningham that Christy Ross had been indoctrinated by her mother into believing that she'd been abused by her father.

"Rich inferred from Harvey that Zach had been close to persuading Ted Ross that his only hope was to enter a plea of guilty and argue for lower sentencing. Has Cunningham spoken to you about her at all?"

"Toni was raised in Puerto Rico, Kate. An American state to be sure but one where the culture is anything but mainstream America."

He's going to say he knows this lady and probably that he introduced her to Cunningham.

Cutting off Kate's eminently prescient thoughts, Reardon continued speaking. "About six or maybe it was eight years ago, I decided to accompany a couple of our scientists on a research trip to the San Cristobal Canyon in Aibonito, Puerto Rico. Within an hour, I was tired of examining the underbellies of ferns and frogs so I wandered down into the village and met Toni. Have you met Toni yet, Kate?"

"No, I've only heard about her … shall we say … aggressive dislike of Rich's dog and that she sounds like quite a character. Rich said he thought she was right out of a poorly written novel. Until Harvey, who I take it is married to Zach Cunningham, who is also quite a character but in a very different way from Harvey, made it clear to Rich that Toni has," Kate paused, wondering how to phrase this discreetly, "unusual gifts. That Toni is more than she appears to be—a lot more."

Reardon chuckled at the phrase. "Toni must have been in her late teens, maybe early twenties, and spied me from across the plaza the minute I appeared in the town."

That would not have been hard. Kate easily imagined how conspicuous the blonde, wiry and dynamic Hank Reardon, most likely dressed in a plaid shirt and jeans, would have been among the natives of a remote rural mountain village of Puerto Rico. But she said nothing; she could not wait to hear the rest of this story.

"Toni made a beeline for the new touristico, yelling at the top of her lungs several yards before she got to me. Holding a strange-looking frog, she claimed she had one of the last remaining native crested toads in the whole country—worth thousands of dollars, and she would sell it to me for merely $500.00."

And so Reardon buys the frog-toad and hires her to be one of Ariana's lab assistants.

Townsend's sardonic thoughts weren't all that far off, but Toni's employment would have nothing whatsoever to do with the enormous animal research building complex at Andrews, Sacks and Levine in Lausanne, Switzerland, which were managed by the elfin French woman, Ariana.

"I'll edit this story, Kate, because we're getting short on time here. But I ended up staying for a couple of days with Toni and her grandmother—long enough for me to decide that Toni has rare intellectual gifts as well as … I guess Rich's description works—a powerful sixth sense in her world and the people in it. When I met her, Toni spoke four different native dialects in addition to Spanish and English. Toni's grandmother is full Arawak and is a direct descendent of one of the Taino chiefs Ameyro who became great friends with Diego Mendez, the Secretary of Christopher Columbus."

Answering Kate's question before she could put it into words, Reardon explained further, "The Taino were a peaceful indigenous Caribbean people with one of the most successful cultures of that time. That is, until they succumbed to the diseases brought by the Spanish when they came to 'civilize' them. As a people, they are extinct now, but most Puerto Ricans are at least partially Taino, or Arawak as they were later called."

This non-sequitur was fascinating; Hank Reardon's limitless curiosity about his fellow man never failed to captivate Kate, but generally the billionaire stayed focused on the vast array of responsibilities requiring attention. He was wandering a bit, she thought, which was unusual for him.

"I hired Toni to help run my portfolio. Within a year, she'd figured out a way to take the computer program designed by Stock Traders.com and add dynamic seasonality. Since then, all the major financial houses have been trying to get me to sell them my program, which was designed by a Puerto Rican teenager! Tom, my Wharton-trained financial planner, has been trying to get me to tell him how I made the new program." Chuckling to himself, Reardon said, "But I've never had the heart to tell him.

"About a year after that, Zach told me he was looking for help for Harvey; she'd threatened to quit if he didn't find another person. Harvey took five minutes to interview her; tells me that she owes me for the find." Reardon chuckled, "In fact, that's one of the reasons he was willing to take McAllister's case."

"Toni had been molested by her brothers and father as a little girl, apparently using girls in that way is not all that rare in the rural villages of Puerto Rico. But her grandmother found out and brought Toni to live with her when she was still very little, helping her deal with what had happened to her and helping Toni develop her abilities."

There it was, finally. The grandmother helped this lady use her early trauma, turn it around to help other girls. Coupled with the psychic abilities, this Toni had become quite a weapon apparently. Glad she's on our side.

In a characteristic lightning fast change of subject, Reardon asked, "Hey Kate, what are you doing for Christmas?"

Her mind still on her newfound awareness of Toni and wondering if Jansen knew all this, Kate took the phone from her ear to shake her head slowly in amusement and appreciation for him. Kate brought the phone back to her ear to hear Reardon continue, "Lindsey and Rich are on for a week; I thought it would be fun for you and Steve to join us, what do you think?"

Laughing, Kate quipped, "Anytime I am invited to Lausanne, I will say yes, especially during Christmas! I'll talk with Steve to make sure it will be okay with him.

There is just one life for each of us: our own.
— Euripides

C H A P T E R

20

Kate was nervous. Stupid, she knew, she'd proved herself. Hell, she'd more than proved herself many times even before she earned four Pulitzers: three for her reporting and one for her paper, The Houston Tribune. The second article in her series, *A Nation of Law: The Dark Side*, had appeared on the front page of the Trib on Sunday, just two days ago. She'd known her story would be controversial. All of her stories were controversial. But she'd never expected controversy of this magnitude; her office was reporting mail, texts, tweets, and phone calls on a scale that dwarfed those on the series that won the Pulitzer: *Murder in the Texas Medical Center.* Unimaginable.

Watching Kate try to hide the fact that she was incredibly nervous, Rich watched her try to fidget subtly. After the twentieth time she'd twisted her diamond ring around her finger, he decided the kindest thing would be to state the obvious.

"Kate, what is freaking you out here? You have established yourself as one of the top investigative journalists in the country … you've already won the top awards and you and Steve seem as if you have a relationship made in Hollywood—"Jansen cut himself off when he looked at her.

"There's nothing wrong between you and Steve." Intentionally, Rich had made his question a statement because he really liked these two; besides, he was really looking forward to Christmas.

"Kate? Say something, please."

He couldn't hear anything but mumbling. Looking closer, Rich realized she was crying. Like most men, he hated that. He had no idea what had prompted the tears and suspected that if she was anything like the two women he knew intimately, his wife Lindsey and his deceased wife Laura, that she had no idea either. Those two had taught him that frequently tears were what bouts of anger were to guys: bleed-off valves. But he had to ask.

"Sorry Kate, I couldn't hear you."

"I think I may be pregnant."

Jansen stared at the reporter, having not a clue what to say.

Just then, Harvey and Toni walked in.

"Sorry we're late guys, the traffic at the Starbucks was wicked." The two women were staying across the street at the apartment held by Kensington and Associates; the obligatory laughter following Harvey's comment was a little forced but no one seemed to care.

Following the introductions, the four took their seats around the large white block table in the center of Jansen's corner office. Kate took the lead, amazing Rich with the speed with which she regained self-control.

The morning August sun streamed through the vertical white window coverings, protecting the floor-to-ceiling glass northern-facing wall. The waves of bright sun highlighted

Kate's mahogany hair with red streaks. And they lit up that diamond on her left hand which rested on the table, firing delicate rays of violet, blues, and greens from her long fingers.

Smiling warmly at Toni, Kate said, "Hank Reardon and I are good friends, Toni. Hank told me just a little about you and your background; he sure thinks a great deal about you and your abilities. I am delighted to meet you!"

Jansen winced, thinking of the unpleasantness of his first interaction with Toni, but then decided to sit back and watch while Kate Townsend totally disarmed and completely charmed this prickly, enigmatic lady.

Kate grinned broadly as she added, "Hank told me you were the quant who showed his Wharton MBA financial manager how the real stock pros make it in today's volatile stock market."

Out of the corner of her eye, Kate could see the astonished expression on Rich Jansen's face as she continued to sound like what she was not: an expert in the stock market.

"Hank explained that you grasped the implications of volatility, application of Fibonacci numbers to the VIX along with the strategy of the Iron Condor and Butterfly in a way that permitted a brand new way to program in day-to-day seasonality, creating, in effect, a unique way to analyze the stock market. Apparently, he fights off seven-figure offers for the program on a monthly basis and says you and you alone have taught him—his team, actually—a relatively safe way to do options trading."

The grin on Toni's face transformed it.

Toni extended her tattooed arm to Kate and reached for that left hand to hold it.

"Mr. Reardon has been wonderful to me and Abu. He flies her to Mustang to visit me a few times a year. Because of him, we've accumulated enough money to build a beautiful new home in Puerto Rico for Abu and me."

Jansen sat there, transfixed by this woman and by how badly he had misjudged her. Just then, Harvey Cunningham happened to catch Jansen's gaze and winked as she took control of the meeting.

"They live in a condo off Richmond, not too far from the Galleria." Harvey's voice was soft; there was an accent, but Jansen could not identify the origin.

"What do you think we should do now that we've located them?" Kate was writing notes on a well-used legal pad, happily ceding control to the two investigators.

"Call Christy Ross and tell her we've found them. Make sure she and her dad are on board for Christy to talk with Annie, hopefully, to get her to tell her the real story. Find out where Annie goes to school. Check out her friends. See if we can get her friends and teachers to talk to us. Maybe same with their church if they go to church. Basically, we are aiming to catch the kid in lies."

Each statement was said flatly, dispassionately, by Toni who still covered Kate's engagement hand with her own. Apparently Kate was the bridge to Toni's savior, Hank Reardon, and Toni wanted to hold on as long as she could.

"Okay Toni, what do you want Rich and me to do?"

"Not a thing, give us two days. Let's meet back here in two days. We'll know more." Squeezing Kate's hand and smiling again to Kate as she rose, Toni nodded to Rich and walked out. Harvey smiled at him as she followed Toni, reading Jansen's mind with the comment she threw over her right shoulder as she walked out the office door. "Don't worry, your part of all this will start soon enough."

The door closed and Kate and Rich were alone again.

Rich said nothing. He had learned long ago that when you had no idea what to say that it was best to say exactly that: nothing.

The seconds, then the minutes ticked by. Idly, Rich considered what would be happening in his world in two days; September 5th had been ingrained in his memory for many months, the day Lindsey would take her Emergency Medicine Boards.

Like Kate, Lindsey was nervous. The last several evenings she'd been late into the night studying and was up earlier than Rich to head to her office. Jansen knew better than to console his wife with tepid comments of reassurance so conversation was sparse at home, too.

How could you have blurted out to Rich that you think you may be pregnant? How was that even possible? You are the most discreet woman on this planet and yet you blab that? To Rich Jansen, for God's sake? What if he says something to Steve before I do?

Jansen could feel the tension in the room. He was glad Max wasn't here: the dog would be pacing and whining, his barometer for tension well over the top.

"I am very sorry, Rich, I cannot believe I said what I did and worse began to blubber like a baby. Unconscionable, really." Lips compressed and dark head shaking slowly back and forth, Kate looked like an elementary school teacher admonishing her class of disobedient five-year-olds.

Jansen rose, walked the four steps to get around the corner of the white table and sat where Toni had been sitting and picked up the hand Toni had been holding. He squeezed it.

"Kate, believe me, you owe me no apology, none whatsoever. The comment you made won't be repeated to anyone, not even Lindsey; I'd guess you're worried about that in addition to a whole lot of other things you are apparently concerned about. This one you can cross off your list."

Jansen's gaze was deep and probing as he waited a beat to

see if she would say anything. When Kate stayed silent, Rich added, "You and Steve have become really good friends; Lindsey and I love spending time with you two … but if there are problems between you, serious problems, Lindsey and I will support whatever decision you feel is right for you, Kate."

He watched the tears reappear in the reporters big brown eyes. Her reply dumbfounded him.

"I'm crying because I'm so happy and I know it's completely idiotic! But I never thought I could have it all. I gave up marriage and family long ago when I decided to go after career, not just a job. I knew it meant sacrifice and I was willing to make it." Voice shaking, she said, "Now it looks as if having it all may be possible … how can that be?"

Enormously relieved, Jansen drew her to her feet and hugged her as he laughingly sang out, "Women—by God you are so different from men! Then there are women like you and Lindsey who act just like Steve and me … until suddenly, you don't!"

Rich and Lindsey's home in New Waverly

Don't try to put out fire by throwing on more fire!
Don't wash a wound with blood.
— Rumi

C H A P T E R
21

Lindsey and Rich sat in their living room staring at the fire. A norther had blown in and the early September air was deliciously cold. When Lindsey had returned from her day of testing for her Emergency Medicine Board Examinations, she'd dashed up the stairs, quickly changed into her running clothes and successfully persuaded her tired husband and not-so-tired Doberman to do a six-mile run in the woods outside their house. Each had agreed it would be the perfect appetizer before dinner. There was nothing like the restorative balm of copious sweat to alleviate anxiety and stress, but in weather like this, a long run in the woods was a tonic to man and dog.

Things had been so chaotic during the last few weeks, the couple had no time to talk alone, really talk.

Grinning at the soft contented snores of Max, Lindsey wiggled the toes of her feet, which were currently in Rich's lap, as a reminder not to slack off on the foot massage. Sighing, she stretched and arched her back as she murmured, "It just doesn't get any better than this, does it?"

"Nope.

"I accepted Hank Reardon's invitation to celebrate Christmas at his home in Lausanne, Linds. No way could I refuse again. Sorry that I haven't told you until now but it will be quite the Christmas celebration; Cooper and Kate will be going as well."

Rich didn't know why but he didn't explain the reason for the celebration—somehow it didn't feel like the right time; he'd tell her later in plenty of time for all the planning he knew she would want to do.

Over two years ago, Hank had set up a trust fund for Lindsey at his corporate bank in Lausanne; her income from the new drug Digipro was prodigious and growing steadily since McCall's new molecular configuration of Digitalis had revolutionized the treatment of acute cardiac failure. Reardon was not happy with the fact that seven figures and change was sitting in cash rather than investments. Hank had invited them countless times to fly over and tour the corporate offices of his pharmaceutical company, Andrews Sacks and Levine. He had also offered the counsel of his personal financial manager to present the options available for investments of this magnitude. Lindsey and Rich appreciated his concern and were well aware of the wisdom of Reardon's advice but their lives had been far too chaotic to consider making the trip, until now. This Christmas trip was going to provide an opportunity to address the concern.

Without diverting her gaze from the fire, Lindsey nodded slowly, in passive agreement.

Jansen watched her and wondered if she'd heard a word he had said. She looked exhausted. Just as he was about to suggest they go up to bed, the phone rang.

"Sorry to call so late, Rich. Harvey and I need to talk with you and Zach as soon as possible. Any chance that we could do a conference call now?"

Toni's voice was almost friendly and the apology sounded genuine; maybe by the end of this case, the two of them could be at ease with each other.

Looking at his watch, Jansen saw that it was close to eight thirty. Time for Lindsey to get some sleep. He doubted that she was worried about the oral exams she needed to take at the medical center tomorrow now that the written four-hour test was complete; but still, it was a test and tests were stressful, even for her brilliant mind.

"Sure, Toni, can you give me five minutes?"

Five minutes later, the distinct gravelly voice of Zach Cunningham intoned, "Okay, let's run through it. Toni, why don't you update Rich on what you and Harvey have uncovered in the last several days?"

Jansen was on his computer in his office, having successfully persuaded Lindsey to get to bed. He could see each of them individually; the four were logged in to Cunningham's office WebEx site. From the background behind Harvey and Toni, they were in the living room of the downtown apartment owned by Kensington and Associates located right across the courtyard from the offices. Cunningham must have been in an office either at his home office or his main office in downtown Mustang because all that could be seen behind Zach were floor to ceiling bookcases; it was a good guess that both of Cunningham's offices were stocked with reference books. Ruefully, Rich glanced around his home office and saw only novels on his bookshelves. Idly, he decided to unpack the stack of boxes of law books that stood in the corner of the large room. He needed to get that done tomorrow; Jansen was expecting a ton of work to come out of this meeting, so he'd need all these reference books and more, he wagered to himself.

"We've had a good deal of difficulty finding them, Rich. Our little plaintiff Annie and her mother Sam frequently move. In the ten months since McAllister's conviction, they have moved three times."

Instantly, Jansen began making notes on the legal pad sitting on his desk.

Moving three times in less than a year sounds like proof of McAllister's claim of the ex-girlfriend's source of pills. Each time one drive-in clinic starts to get suspicious, they move. There had to be records of those purchases.

Toni was seated on the floor in front of a coffee table on which was piled several folders. She grabbed one, opened it and took out two items, laid them flat on top of the coffee table and said, "Here are recent photographs of Annie and her mother, Samantha."

Pictured were two images of a woman who looked to be in her late twenties with long strawberry blonde hair and a miniature little girl version of her but with curly bright red hair. Jansen wondered how far away whoever had taken the shots had been, because the faces of the woman and child were crystal clear. The woman's gaze was clouded, almost obtunded, fitting what McAllister had said about her multiple drug addictions. The eyes of the little girl were huge, vividly blue and somber; too melancholy for a child of six or seven. Neither woman nor child was smiling.

"Did you take these, Toni?"

"I did, why?"

"Well, the clarity of their facial features makes me think you walked up to them and asked that they pose for a picture. These are really good photographs."

Jansen was staring at the child, thinking as he did so that Annie's eyes looked older than her mother's. Quickly catching himself in that thought, he looked again at both woman and child and confirmed the thought; the only phrase for the child's expression was world-weary.

"Harvey and I were only across the street from them and my camera is really good."

Quickly, Toni added, "Harvey finally found them at this new address out in Katy. We'd been waiting outside their new apartment for a few hours, but I am sure they didn't spot us. Especially the mother; she seemed focused on something and wasn't paying a lot of attention to anything around her. I'm pretty sure that the reason the lady moves her kid all the time is that she needs a new supplier."

"Hard drugs off the street, Toni?"

"No, it's pretty much all prescription stuff, Rich. Stuff like Ativan, Zoloft, Vicodin, Xanax and a whole laundry list of anti-depressants including those with some serious side effects."

This time it was Harvey talking. "It looks like these docs get alarmed after a while and cut her supply off—I'm amazed that she hasn't killed herself, Annie, or someone else while driving on these crazy Houston freeways."

Jansen nodded as he processed all the information. So far, all that McAllister had claimed about his one-time live-in girl-friend was being corroborated by the two investigators.

Good for our side but you have to wonder what kind of chance this little kid has for anything close to a normal life, never mind a childhood ... sure looks like that possibility has been wiped out, at the ripe old age of six or seven.

Looking again at the child's expression, he asked the others, "You guys see it in the kid's eyes, don't you?"

All three faces on his computer screen nodded slowly and deliberately.

"Yeah, this kid has been ... or more likely *is* being molested by someone."

Zach Cunningham's use of the present tense shook Jansen up. He was right, of course. More and more, Rich was sympathizing with his client. By just looking into the too-old eyes of this little girl, Jansen could completely understand wanting to rescue her, to try to do the impossible and retrieve her lost innocence, then package it up as childhood regained.

"What does the mother do for work, do we know?" Jansen's tone was matter of fact but not his emotions; they were reeling.

God, this case is every bit as bad as I expected. I'd like to get my hands around this woman and shake her until her teeth rattle.

"Unbelievably, she has a good job as an administrative assistant at Shell Oil. She has worked there for four years and makes a little over fifty-two thousand plus full medical and dental benefits for her and for Annie. They also have a daycare center which is free for Shell employees." Harvey's voice dropped a bit.

"I've talked with the woman who runs the Shell center quite a little bit over the last few days," Harvey continued. "She is a graduate of Houston's Depelchin Children's Center, a well-respected training program for child services in Houston. Claire tells me that she is very concerned about Annie on a number of levels and that she has tried to speak with Sam, Annie's mother, about her concerns several times but Sam simply laughs her off."

Watching and listening to Harvey Cunningham explain how she had managed to obtain confidential information about one of the woman's small charges did not shock Jansen. It should have, but it did not. Her bearing was close to stately, elegant and eminently professional; Rich had known Harvey for a little less than two weeks yet felt as if he could trust her with his life. With ease, he could imagine this consummate professional, Claire, dropping her defenses in the face of an act like Harvey's; of course, that was just it, the woman was not acting. Sincerity, legitimacy, and authenticity shimmered about Harvey Cunningham in waves.

"I have not broached the subject of trauma but Claire has come very close to suggesting that she believes that Annie may be at great risk. Claire told me yesterday that Sam's wide range of male dating partners is a subject of some concern among some of the Shell supervisors and managers."

Jansen was concentrating on finishing off some notes, questions and items to pursue over the next few days and did not hear Zach until he completed his statement which ended with something that sounded very like and "Rich, you'll do the interrogation of Annie to get her to admit that it's 'some other guy.'"

The SODDI defense is well known in criminal defense law. Jansen could not count the number of times that he'd heard a defense lawyer claim that "some other dude did it" while he was head of the Harris County Homicide Department. But here it was, alive and well and waiting for him to crack his non-existent criminal defense skills on.

No one on the call said a word, waiting for an acknowledgment from Jansen, who did not even try to hide his stunned reaction. Written all over his face were his shock, dismay, and fear at what had to feel like a red hot coal dropped right into his lap.

Nodding at Jansen, Cunningham finally broke the silence and the studied neutrality of his own facial expression. Grimacing, he acknowledged, "Man, these are the very worst kinds of cases. And for you? Just getting back after a hiatus of ten or fifteen years?" Zach shook his long Rastafarian locks slowly back and forth.

Cunningham's rasping voice was softer; in lowering the

volume, the gravelly voice became croaky—even more weirdly unique then when he spoke "normally." Jansen had heard no other voice like this guy's, ever. Despite the nausea he was currently fighting at the prospect of conducting the cross-examination of this child, Rich was fascinated by the multifaceted personality of Zach Cunningham. Jansen did not doubt Cunningham's instincts.

No one replied to Cunningham's question; both women knew it was rhetorical and it was painfully apparent that Rich Jansen was bowled over by what he had just been told.

"Foolishly, Rich," Zach continued, "I thought we might get a pass on this one. As you know, the plan had been to see if Christy Ross could get a relationship with Annie. Toni had come up with that one because she and Harvey feel, like you, that this guy is a victim just as Christy and her Dad were, and she knows the drill."

Cunningham was completely still. Sitting at his desk looking into the camera on his computer he suddenly brought a hand up to cup his chin while his gaze roamed from Jansen to his wife, Harvey, then to Toni, and back to Jansen. Suddenly, that left hand was up close to his mouth with his thumb under his chin and his forefinger curved over his lips at the far end of the scar running down to the chin, rocking his head back and forth; obviously, deep thinking signaled an unconscious gesture adopted long ago to hide the scar.

Hand returned to his desk, Cunningham squinted at Rich as he sighed deeply, and told them, "And the appeal to the state Appellate Court has been granted."

Startled, Jansen reacted, "Well, that's good news!" Then, looking at the three somber faces, asked, "Isn't it?"

Noting the glance passed between Toni and Harvey, Jansen got it about the same time that Cunningham replied, "Yes and no. Yes, of course it's good news because we now have a chance to free this guy."

The left hand moved back up to the exact place where it had been before, only this time, the first knuckle of his long, very black forefinger moved back and forth as Zach's very white teeth nibbled at the knuckle.

"But kinda bad news because my two other requests were granted as well."

Attempting a smile that came off more like a wince both because of his scarred mouth and his mounting sympathy for the plight of his co-defense counsel, Zach explained. "The Appeals Court judge approved my motion for a new trial based on our arguments of inadequate counsel and jury tampering; the new trial is set for September 28th. In Amarillo. The Judge also approved my motion for a change of venue based on the Houston media surrounding Townsend's series: *A Nation of Law: The Dark Side.* It is highly unlikely we can find a single person in Houston who has not heard about McAllister and the juror whose admission of jury tampering got him a new trial. All the publicity surrounding Townsend's articles has assured that. Ergo, she approved the change of venue. Connors from the Houston DA's office will prosecute the case again. And Jansen, in Amarillo, we'll likely be dealing with a white jury since fewer than five out of a hundred in Amarillo is black."

This time Cunningham's expression was sardonic as he asked, "Can you picture the reaction of our middle-America, conservative Amarillo white folks as they watch this black dude interrogate our precious little red-headed Annie? When they are still wiping tears away from Connors' heart-wrenching performance with her?"

Zach waited patiently while the graphically visual image he had painted appeared on Jansen's face before continuing.

"By now, much of the whole state of Texas and maybe the

country is aware of what's been happening with McAllister. After a lot of discussion, we know that Christy Ross cannot help us with Annie. She's heading into her junior year in high school; she doesn't need this trial to educe their local media's interest in what happened to her and her dad in Houston. Ted doesn't need it either—these end up being minuscule towns in which live a number of people with exceedingly small minds. They are the minority to be sure, but one's enough.

"Christy and Ted are both willing—eager even," Cunningham's gaze shot to his wife Harvey, then to Toni, who smiled and nodded back. This had been discussed, at some length. "But this trial will attract attention, the Houston media along with national. I'm hoping that we can keep Dr. Ted Ross and his daughter Christy as far removed from all this as we possibly can.

"I've told them thanks for the offer of their help but explained why I think it too dangerous. They understand."

Jansen had reached his tipping point.

Now, far past the point of being anxious and overwhelmed, he was into a well-known state of mind he knew well. In his mind, he thought about it in a sing-song cadence: *Got it, we don't know what we're doing! Been here before! I can sing that tune!*

The times he had lived there were too numerous to count: starting on his first day at Harvard University, a rural Texas kid with a heavy Texas accent, continuing on to his decision to join the Marines rather than continue on to graduate school like the rest of his classmates, and then his first day in the Houston Homicide department—former criminal defense lawyer turned cop.

Yes, this was familiar territory for Rich Jansen. And it was strangely comforting.

Laughingly he asked, "So that's all you have for me tonight,

Zach?"

For the first time since he had quit the job as Chief Warden at Huntsville and walked back into the offices of Kensington and Associates, Rich was comfortable. It wasn't that he was unimpressed with the experience and knowledge of Zach Cunningham and his two excellent investigators; far from it, the longer he worked with these people, the more he admired them. It was the familiarity of working with complex problems, people, and personalities; in the end, it was all the same, whether framed in the law, prison, combat, or marine corps: each situation was unique, unpredictable, and could go anywhere at any time. Finding the right words, the right tone and timing to open up Annie and her mother were skills that could not be learned in lawbooks. They had to appear spontaneous, natural, while being kind. Impossible.

We don't know what we're doing! And he loved it.

Huntsville Prison

Be firm and courageous for the sake of our people and our God;
make up your minds to be brave men.
Everything depends on you.
— *Maimonides*

C H A P T E R

22

"What time was it that she brought Annie into the shower with you?"

"I don't know, I had just come back from work, had learned I'd been accepted for the joint drug task force training so ..."

"Wrong answer, McAllister, you've had little else to do around here but think, so think. What time did you get into the shower?"

They had exactly twenty-one days before Gabe McAllister's trial began and to say they were under the gun was a massive understatement. McAllister, now healed from his wounds and living in the protected emergency center, was flustered by Toni's relentless hammering. They had been at it for only two hours, but it felt like a lot longer.

Seated at Lindsey's conference table were Jansen, McAllister, Harvey Cunningham, and Toni Martinez. Toni sat at the head of the table. This was her show and she was damn good at it, Jansen thought as he watched the ease with which she spun the alleged facts of McAllister's conviction. Their job was clear-cut. They had to take Allen Connors' eloquent arguments proving guilt, arguments which he knew well since this was his second time around, and sufficiently alter them to persuade twelve people to overturn the conviction. Everything, in this case, was biased in favor of Connors.

"During the year you lived with Sam and Annie, how many times did you take her into the shower with you and her mother?"

"I never did that. It was Sam who brought Annie into the shower. I instantly got her and her mother out of there. The three of us were in there for less than five seconds."

"How did it start, did you just start touching her?"

"I never touched her."

"You never picked her up or hugged her?"

"No, I mean I never touched her sexually."

"Where were you when you had her do oral intercourse with you McAllister. Were you in the bedroom, the living room?"

"I NEVER did this to this kid, NEVER—I NEVER TOUCHER HER."

McAllister had exploded out of his chair, towering over the three seated people around the conference table; his face was close to purple, not from the healing scars of the beating but from rage and frustration. Toni looked entirely at ease; there was no trace of fear, even of discomfort when the six-foot-five former soldier leaned down to get closer to her, glaring furiously at her.

Just as Jansen was about to stop this, Harvey laughed softly and stood. She walked over to McAllister and declared in that soft subtly-southern accent of hers, "Trust me, Gabe McAllister, none of us would be sitting here if any one of us thought for a shred of a second that you did any single one of these things to this little girl."

Once she had drawn herself up to almost meet McAllister's gaze, Harvey leaned close to him. And in a voice so soft that Rich had to strain to hear her, she told him, "But Gabe, if you think the grilling that Assistant District Attorney Allen Connors gave you in your first trial was terrible, the one you will face in Amarillo will make Houston look like a cakewalk. Allen Connors is one of the top Assistant DAs in Texas, and he has a ninety-five percent conviction rate."

Those beautiful ebony long-lashed eyes fixed on Gabe as she asked, "Can you guess just how outraged Connors is about Zach Cunningham's winning the appeal to grant a new trial for you? Connors is a very ambitious man. He believes a fairly major part of his future lies in persuading a group of ordinary people in Amarillo that you are an odious pervert, the dregs of humanity. He will treat you exactly like Toni is treating you. He will berate you. He will fire these questions at you, just as she is, in hopes that he can get you to do what you just did. He wants you to lose control, fill yourself up with rage and act like what he believes you are: a dangerous pervert who needs to be locked up. Any weakness you show him, Connors will exploit. So he can show the jury that you that you're dangerous.

"He wants only one thing: to make sure you spend your life behind bars. Our job is to make you impervious to all the slime he throws at you. To make you so comfortable with being accused of all the various labels for sodomy, rape, and fellatio with a six-year-old child that your Kevlar vest deflects all that filth. Because we know, and most importantly Gabe, Sam and Annie know, these are lies. None of this has happened … with you." Her voice lowered almost to a whisper, "But *someone* did do these things to this kid. And we believe *is* doing these things to Annie *now*, most likely ever since you left."

Gone were the rage, the dilated pupils, and the florid skin; McAllister quietly stood next to Harvey, mute, pale, and passive, looking as if his very skin hurt.

Smiling now, she extended her arm and flexed those long elegant coffee-colored fingers at the chair McAllister had just vacated. "Let's get back to work now please, Gabe; we have three months of work to get done in less than twenty-one days."

During the thirty-minute break for lunch, Rich called Kate to ask for a quid pro quo: for his updates of their changes in strategy, would she be willing to hold off on any more articles?

"No worries, Rich, I totally get what off-the-record means and will comply, but you're asking that we hold the piece Jeff is planning to run this next Sunday?"

Kate was talking about the third of what she planned as a four-article piece for her series. The first and second had been published sequentially on the last two Sundays and were already causing a stir in the Texas and national media. Her editor, Jeff Simpson was excited about the reaction and was anticipating heightening of national awareness with the next installment.

Jansen was well aware that her former series, *Murder in the Texas Medical Center*, had laid the foundation for his work in freeing the woman who was now his wife. Townsend had proved herself trustworthy during many parts of that intense and agonizing investigation during which Rich had risked several counts of ethical violations and even disbarment. While Chief Warden of the Huntsville Prison System, he joined Todd Kensington in preparing the legal brief that argued for an appeal of the murder conviction of Dr. Lindsey McCall. Although the petition was never filed, because of the suicide note of Lindsey's sister Paula, Jansen knew that Kate Townsend understood the phrase off the record with an integrity he had never encountered with another reporter.

"Yes, that is exactly what I am asking, Kate. If you need me to explain to Jeff personally what's at stake here, maybe the three of us can talk now?"

Kate was standing in the living room of her condo thinking wryly about how her carefully orchestrated plan for a run in Memorial Park was most likely squelched. Because she had worked late into the night and then had risen very early to polish off the third article in her series, she had free time during today: a rare commodity in her busy life.

She had promised Steve that she'd no longer run during the evenings. There had been recent assaults on female joggers despite the bright lights the city had installed in the park; there remained isolated patches of forest in the very popular Memorial Park where hunters could find unsuspecting prey.

Rich is right, Jeff likes him a lot; taking the time to explain what is happening himself is really the courteous thing to do. One of the few things I like about Texans is their intuitive sense of civility, something the rest of us seem to lack in our rush to expediency. And there is a bright side to this: I'll bet it's close to ninety out here with the humidity the same ... Lord how I hate their weather here. It's been close to four years now, but this crazy freeway system, horrendous weather, and the idiosyncratic behavior of Houstonian precludes my ever thinking of this place as home.

Kate placed a call to Jeff to conference him into the call with Rich. "Hey Jeff, I've got Rich Jansen on the line with me. Can you talk with us about holding Sunday's next article?"

"Hey Rich, how are you and Lindsey doing? We've not

seen you since … gosh, your wedding! That is way too long ago. Maybe you and Lindsey can break away from the country and meet Ellen and me for dinner downtown some Friday night soon? A delayed celebration for your latest change in careers?" Chuckling, Jeff asked, "So how is it on the other side, by the way?"

Kate smiled as Jansen replied to the questions and agreed to a tentative date for dinner, thinking as she listened to the two men, that Jeff Simpson, despite his Boston roots, had acclimatized very quickly to the Texas business culture: start with the personal and the casual. Were this Kate's conversation, she'd have started off with who, what, why, where, and how: the difference between a reporter and an Editor-in-Chief she guessed.

Rich laughed as he replied, "Well right, Jeff, that is the point here, isn't it? Life on the other side … gotta tell you, there have many times in the last few weeks when I have wondered just exactly why I made this decision. My first experience with criminal defense law was one I hope never to repeat and jumping back into a child sex abuse conviction …."

Both Jeff and Kate were silent as Jansen's voice trailed off.

After a beat or two, Rich continued, "But the truth is, Jeff, I was getting bored out at the prisons. Once Lindsey switched from inmate to Medical Director, things calmed down overnight out there. Funny how that happened." Both Jeff and Kate replied with an obligatory grunt of amused agreement.

"And in a way that seems close to providential, our intrepid reporter here, finds that piece about Dr. Alexandra Allbrite's admission of jury tampering, comes out for dinner, and asks if I'd be interested in helping with this guy's appeal."

Once again chuckling, Jansen said, "I sure can tell you that Governor Bell was not overjoyed to hear that we may have another wrongful conviction at Huntsville but he was more than happy to hear that his Chief Warden was planning to do this appeal the right way, as a criminal defense lawyer, rather than as his Chief Warden this time."

Very soberly, Jeff said, "Rich, I can honestly not think of anything more deeply perverse, lurid—the adjectives can continue for many more minutes—than the sexual abuse of little girls." Pausing with an audible gulp, Simmons continued, "Ellen and I have three girls and if anyone …." his voice trailed off, unable to complete the thought.

"But damn it Rich, I had no idea of the prevalence of guys being accused and convicted, wrongly. Kate and I were in Boston during that entire Ted and Christy Ross fiasco. As a dad, I cannot imagine the hell that man went through because of a greedy, crazy, wife."

A deep sigh later, "So, tell me Rich, what do you need from me?"

Quickly, Jansen summarized the facts and informed the editor of the date and place of the new trial, the fact that they had located the little girl and her mother and the strategy to prove that Annie had been molested but not by McAllister.

"Amarillo." Simpson's statement was bald.

"Isn't this Oklahoma guy … Cunningham, isn't he black?"

"Yep."

Simpson had been a newsman for his entire career. In his late fifties, he had been Chief Editor for newspapers on the east coast, west coast, and now Houston; there was little that missed his penetrating mind.

"I take it that our very own Allen Connors will prosecute in Amarillo?"

Simpson, like most reporters, was well aware of the Houston Assistant District Attorney with the highest conviction rate of any in the country.

"Yep."

"Kate had told me that Christy Ross had volunteered to speak with this little girl, from one brainwashed victim to another, in hopes that Annie will tell the truth."

"Right, Jeff, but Harvey and Toni, Cunningham's two investigators, have fairly solid information that Annie is being molested—now. The mother has quite a diverse dating schedule. We think this kid has had an extensive history of sexual abuse, and our job will be to prove to the jury that some other guy did and is doing it."

"So Annie will have to be cross-examined during the trial …"Simpson's mind was tracking quickly, "… but it can't be by Cunningham, which leaves …."

"Me, right."

"Good God, Rich, I cannot imagine getting an already traumatized kid to admit she'd lied, thereby traumatizing her even further."

"As you might imagine, Jeff, I'm using all the defense mechanisms that Freud ever constructed to deal with all of this."

"But you're really helping this kid, Rich. I have never been in favor of the state taking the role of a parent but this little girl needs someone to save her from her mother."

Kate's comment was the first she had made during the entire thirty-minute conversation. Perhaps it was the thought, still only a thought, that she may be pregnant but she felt protective toward this tragic little girl, Annie; a surge of what could only be called maternal protection for this child who was being so horrifically abused by her own mother.

"Look Rich, I just realized the time. You and Kate work out the time for the appearance of the next article. Kate, just let me know, gotta run, and looking forward to that dinner." He added breathlessly, "Kate, you and Steve, if he's in town or you alone, do join us, we're in the mood for an excellent steak.And we hear that Vic and Anthony's is the place to get one."

Home office of Zach Cunningham, Mustang, Oklahoma

The two most important days of your life are the day you were
born and the day you find out why.
— Mark Twain

C H A P T E R
23

Zach was pacing in his office. He'd not stopped since he had hung up the phone. Finally, he reached his decision and was about to pick up the phone when he heard his son.

"I thought we were going to finish this game of chess, Dad."

His office door was open just a crack because the kids were very respectful of their father's working space; most of the time when the door was closed, like now, it meant "don't venture in there." But his ten-year-old son was right; he had promised Thad they would complete the game they had started that afternoon. It was Sunday, after all, and Mom was away, working.

"Thad, come on in, son, it's okay, I won't get angry, promise."

Thaddeus Cunningham was named after his grandfather, a Texas oil rigger and Korean War veteran who had died too young. Through one of those mysterious quirks of genetic engineering, Thad looked nothing like his dad, a fact for which Zach was exceedingly grateful each time he looked at him. Thad was almost a facsimile of his mother: with Harvey's long, lean skeletal structure, big dark brown eyes, long curly eyelashes, and her coffee-colored skin, Thad was already fighting off the girls, both black and white.

Grinning as he walked in, Thad rubbed his hands in excited anticipation. "Okay, Dad, ready to be thrashed by my Queen?

Hugging his son, Zach realized it would not be long before he had to look up at the kid; it felt as if he'd grown two inches in the last few days.

"But let me make one phone call first and I'll come on out to finish our game. Why don't you make us some grilled cheese sandwiches while I make this call? I promise, Thad, it'll be ten minutes or sooner."

Cunningham's dilemma is one faced by every lawyer gutsy enough to take on a child sexual abuse defense, amplified about a thousand times because he was a black lawyer, defending his client against a white seven-year-old child. Not just coffee-colored black like his wife, but black like the deepest part of the night, like the Nigerian or the Congolese.

As a young law student at Columbia, there had been a few—very few—blacks and women among his mostly white male graduating class of 1968. While the women had tried to look and sound as masculine as possible and the blacks adopted the broad-toned speech and conservative dress of the Ivy League, Zach decided to flaunt the chaotic conglomerate of the physical and mental differences that composed who he was. Rather than shearing his coarse, curly black hair like the two other black guys in his class, Zach decided to grow long Rastafarian locks, corresponding perfectly to those heady and raucous years of the late sixties. As time passed, however, he realized that the look suited a most effective courtroom persona which he had been carefully cultivating over the years. He kept the wildly outmoded hairstyle.

The strange combination of his diminutive stature with a voice that sounded as if it emanated from a three-hundred-pound linebacker were gifts, Zach decided, which he used to great effect in law school, graduating as a James Kent Scholar during each of his three years at Columbia law school. Roughly equivalent to the magna cum laude honor awarded at Harvard and some of the other law schools, the Kent Scholar award was rarely earned for a single year, let alone for the entire three years.

Cunningham was one of the few Columbia law students who had ever earned the academic distinction, most likely a significant factor in his achieving a year-long internship with William Kuntzler.

Kuntzler was the speaker at the Columbia Law School 1968 graduation ceremonies, the year Zach Cunningham graduated. A class of 1948 Columbia law school graduate, Bill Kuntzler was well on his way to earning the New York Times sobriquet as "the most hated and also the most feared lawyer in America." Director of the American Civil Liberties Union and defender of radical groups like the Weathermen, Black Panthers, and the Chicago Seven, Kuntzler's legal philosophy diverged almost wholly from that of the faculty at Columbia.

"I only defend those I love," Kuntzler intoned to the stunned graduates and mostly silent law school faculty still reeling from the campus protests of those turbulent years. "I'm not a lawyer for hire; I defend only those with goals I share."

His statements were completely at odds with the fundamental objectivity assumed to be essential for the successful lawyer. The entire basis of law school training was the absolute detachment of the lawyer from her personal biases and prejudices. Lawyers were trained in the art of adversarial argument; they were equally prepared to discover and argue for the prosecution or the defense.

Following the completion of his talk and mostly ignoring the small group of graduates and faculty crowded about him, the famous lawyer strode over to where Cunningham remained seated, alone.

Extending his hand, Kuntzler jibed, "I'm guessing that what I've been talking about for an hour or so has not fit with the type of law you want to practice … which is—" Bill Kuntzler interrupted himself as he leaned down to ask, "may I sit?"

The embarrassed young Zach Cunningham nodded mutely and pointed to the empty chair next to him. Kuntzler sat, then continued in a low voice, "Prosecution. You want to put the criminals away just like your daddy taught you, am I right?"

Although the words seemed condescending, Zach did not feel belittled. Quite the contrary. There was a reason he'd been singled out, Zach understood. Apparently this guy wasn't all that fond of sycophants, and recognized that Zach was not among that group.

Cunningham also knew clearly why his choice of the law had been apparent to Kuntzler; his expressions gave it all away … to an expert in people. Zach was his father's son and believed in law and order; the radical rebelliousness of many of his classmates was of no interest to him; in fact, it seemed childish and boring. Cunningham's father had been one of the few blacks who had "made it" in the Texas oil industry until an explosion ended his life at the age of fifty. Therefore, much of Kuntzler's rhetoric had rolled off Zach's shoulders; he disagreed with more than ninety percent of what the guy stood for. But he also knew that no law professor at Columbia had so galvanized a roomful of people as had Kuntzler nor had any of his professors read him as clearly.

"You're right, Sir. But a year in your office as an intern could dissuade me."

It was Kuntzler who taught Zach that the courtroom was a stage and that every person was there to play a part, most especially the jurors, because they were there to be manipulated. The job of the criminal defense lawyer, Kuntzler believed, was quite simple; believing his client to be a pawn, a pawn of a system that increasingly favored the powerful and overrode the average citizen, the work of the lawyer was crystal clear. Cunningham smiled for he could hear his mentor speaking as if he were standing here in his office.

"And that's the terrible myth of organized society, that everything that is done through the established system is legal … it makes people believe that a person who is convicted has gotten all that is due him." He would then add his trademark punchline that he delivered to his juries, and his voice would soar with the threat, "If you do not decide this case on the evidence, someday, somewhere, you will wake up screaming."

Smiling now, Zach picked up last Sunday's Houston Tribune and scanned Kate Townsend's article once again.

A Nation of Law: The Dark Side. Hell of a title, Ms. Kate Townsend. Too bad Bill isn't alive to read this, he'd like what you've said here. Bill would feel some vindication, albeit far too belatedly. Has it really been over fifteen years since his death? Okay, my old friend, let's test out those acting skills you taught me all those years ago. If there has ever been a pawn of a system, it's this ex-soldier, who tried to help out this sad lady and her ravaged kid. And we will get you acquitted my soldier boy. I promise you that.

This is gonna be quite a case … hope we're ready for the ride of our lives my new friends.

"I'm timing you, Dad, and I'll burn them, okay?"

Despite the fact that they looked nothing alike, Zach and Thad were eerily similar. Thad already loved hanging around the courtroom when he was allowed. Of late, Zach had tried out some arguments on him to see what Thad could do as an imagined prosecutor. Thad had come up with some impressive logic. And the kid's chess game was improving by the day.

Harvey was a consummate healthy eater who cooked nothing but fresh and healthy for her family. While she was away, Zach and Thad liked nothing better than eating comfort food. Like mac and cheese, grilled cheese sandwiches, preferably burned hot dogs, preferably burned popcorn, and the other varieties of food and snacks that Harvey and their teenaged daughter, Mandy, despised. And the verboten potato chips.

"Great Thad, open up those salt and vinegar chips will you, and beer? Go ahead and time me! Five minutes and counting, starting …"his watch showed close to nine-thirty, "NOW."

As he sped-dialed Jansen's number, Cunningham grinned widely in sheer delight at the miracle of his family. Still a bachelor in his mid-fifties, Zach had decided that a wife and family were luxuries held by other men, not for him. But then he met Harvey, as beautiful as any model, who had for some reason he could not fathom decided she wanted to spend her life with him and had given him these two incredible little people. Not so little anymore. He shook his head at the sheer impossibility of what had become his life.

"Jansen, I'm sorry to bother you again this late, it's Zach."

At the other end of the line, Rich laughed, "You know what Zach? I knew it was you from the minute you opened your mouth … somehow you sound like no one I have ever met!"

"I've changed my mind, Jansen, listen up."

Rich's smile faded as he listened.

"I don't know you very well, Rich, but I'm impressed with what I have seen so far. Of course I'd read about your background as head of the homicide department and of the shooting that very nearly killed you.

"But more than that, you're different … unlike me, you don't advertise your differences; it takes a while to see just what kind of a man you are. When I just told you that you'd need to do the cross-examination of Annie, we all saw your expression; you didn't try to hide it.

"You looked scared shitless, as by God, you should be. But you didn't retreat—in the words of the Marines—" a dry laugh here, "my Dad was a Marine, a Drill Sergeant at Paris Island, once he gimped his way back from Korea, that is. Already, I like working with you, I don't remember the last time I said that to anyone, Jansen. Like my Dad would say, I know you have my back.

"But you're no more ready to cross-examine this little seven-year-old white kid than my ten-year-old son is.

"The strategy has changed once again. I'll fax you the prosecution's list of witnesses tonight but I'll take the star of this show, you'll take her mother."

Kensington and Associates Condominium, downtown Houston

*When…in the course of all these thousands of years has man
ever acted in accordance with his own interests?*
— *Dostoyevsky*

C H A P T E R
24

"For the last three days, she's home by six with Annie. Then changes into sexy bar clothes and by seven, is driving back mid- or downtown to frequent either Poison Girl, Pub Fiction, or The Dogwood. All advertised as the best place to hook up for an hour or a night. Then she shows back up with a guy around one or two in the morning.

"Figure she gets about two maybe three hours of sleep if that. From what I can tell, the kid is by herself at night. There is no sitter or friend I've seen go in."

Toni had her eyes on her IPAD notes as she spoke. Flipping to her phone, she pulled up photos of a four-room apartment and handed the phone over to Jansen. She explained, "Here are the pictures of their apartment. Ordinary place, two bedrooms, this small one is where Annie stays—the blue dog on her bed is the stuffed animal McAllister told us about. And the kitchen looks untouched; apparently she grabs takeout for Annie on the way home from work."

Harvey Cunningham, Toni Martinez, and Jansen were seated in the living room of the condo owned by the Kensington law practice where Toni and Harvey were living while working in Houston.

"How did you get into her apartment?"

Grimacing at another tangible jolt of the reality of working the other side, Jansen raised an eyebrow at the two investigators. He was unsurprised when Harvey leaned her long, lean torso down to reach into a side pocket of the purse at her feet, pulled out a leather packet of lock picks and brandished it proudly.

"Did anyone see you?"

Catching the look that passed quickly between the two women, Rich successfully suppressed his sigh.

"What time did you ..." *guess the phrase break and enter would be somewhat unpopular,* "get into Sam and Annie's condo?"

"Two thirty-three p.m."

The precision of the time most likely meant they'd used video. Toni had replied with the time so Jansen asked her, "So there's a video?"

"Yep."

Ignoring the video for the moment, Jansen asked, "Basically, what's your take on the kid and the current molestation the day care person at Shell seems to suspect? Seems hard to believe that anything could happen between one or two in the morning and six when they both presumably need to get up and make it to work."

This time the look between the two investigators was redolent with echoes of previous conversations.

Rolling his eyes slowly, deliberately and with exaggerated sound effects, Jansen let loose the sigh he'd been suppressing since he had walked into the condo early that morning.

"Toni, I know you don't like my dog, me, or this case." Holding up his hand to stop Harvey's immediate defense of her partner, Rich calmly and very quietly took his eyes from Toni's face, turned to look at Harvey and just said, "No."

The two women were seated on the wood floor and were using the square white-on-wood coffee table as a desk. The condo was furnished with an Asian theme, the eight pieces were modular and were placed in the areas with the best views of downtown Houston. As usual, the law firm spared no expense in the furnishings. The sparse utilitarian look was softened gracefully by several beautiful Oriental paintings of varying sizes hanging on the twelve-foot walls.

Rich had been sitting on one of the smaller couches but dropped down to a space opposite the women so he could see both of their faces.

"We're here to help this guy, Gabe McAlister, Harvey …" pausing for a beat, "and Toni."

He made the statement baldly, his expression now studiedly neutral. "Harvey, I believe those were your exact words a couple of weeks ago."

Harvey was staring back at him, eyes a bit wider than normal and Toni was staring down at her lap.

"I've had enough of the game playing: the looks between just us girls and picking the lock of the plaintiff's mother to film the inside of her condominium and probably planting video cameras in both bedrooms."

The blush slowly crawling up Toni's neck just starting to reach her cheeks told him he was right. They had installed a camera in Sam's apartment, thereby adding four, maybe five counts to the felony of burglary.

"I have been nothing but respectful to each of you since we met, do you agree?"

They stared at him, too shocked to open their mouths.

"Do I need to repeat the question?"

He waited a few beats.

And then stared at each one, eyebrow lifted.

Surprisingly, it was Toni who replied first with a very soft, "Yes."

Then Harvey followed with her assent.

"Do you think you have returned my courtesy?"

Both women shook their heads.

"Look ladies, this feels all too much like junior high school to me so I expect to have this conversation just one time, this time. And then I'd like it forgotten.

"And I'd like it to remain among the three of us; no need to let anyone else in on this foolishness but the games stop today, here, now."

Rich was speaking softly, very calmly. Conversations like this had been his bread and butter for years and his comfort with the words, with the confrontation, with the spelling out every last detail of what had been happening was painfully evident. He could do this for hours if need be.

"Part of this silliness has been my fault." Waiting for a moment to let those words sink in, Jansen once again scrutinized each of their faces and continued. "I've been walking on eggshells around you two," he admitted, as he tilted his head to the right as if to see each of them more clearly.

"That was for a whole bunch of reasons, beginning and ending with my own lack of confidence as a criminal defense attorney. Fairly understandably, you both figured you were on your own because this bozo Jansen doesn't have a clue."

This time, it was Harvey's lovely face suffused with color at the bluntness of his words. Gazing at her to rub it in, "And you know what Harvey? You're quite right. I don't."

The silence in the living room was a tangible thing. Even the noise of the morning weekday traffic seemed hushed.

Jansen suddenly smiled, but the smile did not quite reach his eyes.

"But here's the thing, Harvey. You are not the one who will need to make mincemeat out of this single mother doing her best to keep her kid, her job, and her men all in the air without colliding. She may be a total loser in our eyes but somehow she keeps a job and gives the kid a roof over her head. You're not the one who is going to do his level best to make certain this state takes her little girl away from her. A child who undoubtedly will do anything for her mother, even lie for her." His voice dropped almost to a whisper. "You're not the guy who will prove that her carelessness with strange men has led to the repeated abuse of her little girl."

His mouth was drawn down, the grimace accentuating the sordidness of this case.

Jansen turned to Toni, "And you're not the one, Toni, who will need to grill that kid with enough of her lies to make it apparent to twelve ordinary citizens of Amarillo that she was lying. It was not our guy Gabe McAllister who raped and sodomized her, it was some other guy. That'll be our job, Zach's and mine."

Shocking himself and them, Jansen added, "With a little luck, we'll get him on one of your cameras." Then he looked at them directly.

"Your actions may well provide the single advantage we have over Connors and could possibly allow us to get the real bastard. But guys, this is illegal as hell."

"Rich, I'm sorry."

"No need for any apologies, Harvey, none. I just need your assurance that you two will *never* go off on your own again without discussing what you are doing with me. The next time you decide to put my license on the line, talk to me first! And that goes for each of you, are we clear?"

"Yes, crystal clear."

"Toni? Please look at me and answer me."

That colorful sleeved arm reached out, hand extended; as Rich took it to shake her hand, he saw respect and a smile in her eyes as she said, "Yes boss, quite clear."

This time there were no exclusive glances between the two investigators.

"Good."

Pulling out his notebook, Rich handed out a copy of the list of witnesses that Zach had faxed him last night. Jansen had written his own name or Zach's name next to the witnesses that each would cross-examine following the state's presentation of the case. There were eight.

Jansen was assigned to the child psychologist, social worker, nurse practitioner, and Samantha Bridges, while Zach's name appeared next to the first witnesses for the state: the Houston detective, followed by their social worker, a pediatrician, and Annie.

Watching Harvey's eyes widen at the division of witnesses between the two lawyers, Rich waited a beat of two to see if she would say anything. When she looked up at him silently, waiting, he merely nodded and moved on.

"I'm thinking out loud now guys, so this is open discussion time." Getting up, Rich walked over to retrieve a small portable whiteboard that he'd worked on until early in the morning before grabbing four hours of sleep.

On it was a chronology of the entire case beginning with the meeting of Gabe with Sam at the bar. Then minor details of their life from the moment that McAlister had moved in with Sam and Annie, the date of the shower and of his departure. The timetable started with the call from the neighbor mother of Annie's friend, alerting the state to the possibility of child abuse. Some of Jansen's days of the police investigation were inferred based on what they knew took place during the three months. Guessing, Jansen had written a total of eight meetings between Annie and the five witnesses for the state by the time of his arrest, three months later.

"Here are the weaknesses of the state's case, as I see it." Jansen enumerated the curious timeline. A delay of six months between McAllister's departure and Annie's disclosure of the abuse to her six-year-old friend. Then the estimated eight sessions where Annie and her mother were being questioned by various medical and state personnel. The intact vaginal hymen and scant physical evidence and finally, the first notice McAllister received of any hint of a problem, his arrest.

"If we are allowed by Connors, we will demonstrate to the jury that the case against Gabe was wrapped up in a very tight package long before he was read his rights. Constitutionally, there is no explicit prohibition against working a case this comprehensively prior to the accused having any knowledge of it, but most everyday folks would be concerned if this were to happen to them. If we get the chance, we could spin the clandestine nature of the way this was done."

"But the mandatory reporting statutes specify that there is no obligation to inform the parent or guardian," Toni spoke carefully, warily.

"You're right, Toni, quite right; the neighbor was doing what she believed to be her duty." He knew that Toni and Harvey still smarted from his earlier outburst but expected them to get over it. And soon, they were too immersed in the work ahead to waste any more time on this.

Pointing to the whiteboard, Rich declared the most compelling witnesses for the state to be Annie herself and the child psychologist.

Five hours later, the three had a list of eight witnesses for the defense. Beginning with the original neighbor who had called the state and ending up with their own child psychologist, also an expert in child abuse cases.

*Everything in the universe is made by union and generation —
by the coming together of elements that seek out one another,
melt together two by two, and are born again in a third.*
— *Teilhard deChardin*

C H A P T E R
25

Kate had not called Steve to tell him she'd be there for the weekend until they were circling over San Francisco Airport. She'd made the decision after her editor had told Jansen that The Trib would hold the last two articles about the McAllister case until Jansen gave the green light. That decision had placed Kate ahead of her work schedule, a rare place to be for a busy crime reporter. Free time was not a luxury she had allowed herself of late.

She knew she *needed* to see Steve. Her most uncharacteristic outburst in Jansen's office still embarrassed and discomfited her, deeply, when she allowed herself to think about what was happening in her body. Understanding the effect of hormones on her body was one thing when the understanding was purely intellectual, but experiencing the emotional roller coaster that it felt like she was riding was another thing entirely. Immediately following that outburst, she had felt as if some alien being had taken over control of her body and then had realized that in fact, one had.

She'd been too freaked to buy one of those pregnancy kits but she knew her body, had lived in it comfortably for thirty-six years; something was very different. That her menstrual cycle was off by over three weeks confirmed her suspicions.

Steve had made reservations at one of their very favorite restaurants, Alfred's Steakhouse, at the corner of Kearny and Washington Streets. Alfred's was considered one of the best steak houses in the city and was known for huge martinis and custom cuts of beef. Securing the reservation was an accomplishment to be sure, especially on a Friday night in San Francisco with only two hours' notice.

They were standing at Alfred's iconic huge signature bar. Steve looked over at Kate in surprise as she declined a martini and asked for tonic water and lime.

"Are you feeling ill?" His forehead creased and he looked worried as he took Kate's hand.

"No, just not in the mood for a martini right now. It's kind of warm in here and I'd like a nice cool glass of tonic water."

They'd not seen one another since the dinner at Lindsey and Rich's place a few weeks ago so there was plenty to talk about. Steve was excited about a new cardiologist he had hired who reminded him of Lindsey because she was so good in the cath labs. Like Lindsey, she also had a doctorate in cardiovascular research.

Finishing their drinks, they followed the very friendly waiter over to a table in the far corner of the restaurant, away from other diners. As he approached the table, the waiter turned to Steve to ask if the table was private enough.

"Perfect, thanks very much," replied Steve as he pulled out Kate's chair and kissed her softly on the lips.

Once they were seated, he looked at her and said, "Okay, out with it, what's wrong? You seem …" he stopped while he scrutinized her eyes and facial expression, "tense, worried, and agitated and something else, too … but I'm not sure what it is. You're not drinking a martini to celebrate the astonishing praise for this new series you're writing. You're feeling warm in San Francisco where you are usually freezing. You look more beautiful than ever, your cheeks are actually rosy!"

Kate watched while Steve considered all the variables in front of him. His facial expressions hastily mapping and rejecting possible explanations. She felt like she was looking at her computer screen when it put up that circling icon, thinking.

Suddenly Cooper's face lit up with understanding, puzzle solved. "You're pregnant, aren't you? One weekend and you are—"Cooper's face underwent a thousand emotions in successive waves; worry won out.

"We need to get you to see my friend Sally asap. Sally is the head of OB at Stanford, I'll see if she can see you tomorrow." He broke off when he saw Kate's shoulders shaking and her head in her hands. Steve was sure she was crying and jumped up so quickly from his seat, the upholstered chair rocked and teetered before it landed back on its four legs.

Kneeling next to Kate, he gently pried her hands from her face expecting to see tears and was stunned to see the hilarity. She was trying to talk, but each time she'd get the first word or two out, the gales of laughter kept all the words incomprehensible. Several times she would begin to gain control of herself and try to talk but would only dissolve in laughter again.

Finally, she was able to say, "The nightmare of every sixteen-year-old, pregnant from the first time—it's just that it took me twenty years to get knocked up!" And then Kate began to laugh again, seized by so many emotions that laughter felt like the most genuine response.

Steve stayed by her side long enough to look closely at her glowing face, shining eyes, each of which he lightly kissed as he stood back up. Then he returned to his seat to enjoy the beautiful steaks and grilled asparagus that had just arrived. As he sat down, he declared, "Nine months having to drink martinis alone, Kate. What a bummer."

<hr>

"Sally, thanks for moving your schedule around to fit us in on a busy Saturday morning! Kate, this is Sally Cochrane, Chief of Obstetrics and Gynecology at Stanford; Sally, you've heard me talk about Kate ever since I got to Stanford,and here she is!"

Dr. Sally Cochrane was, in a word, delightful.

"I have never met a Pulitzer Prize-winning reporter before, never mind had one as a patient. The pleasure is mine. Here Kate, let's come back here to my private exam room. Steve, we'll leave you to your cardiology journals." Smiling at Steve, she explained, "Stanford treats its Department heads extremely well. Our offices are each outfitted with adjacent exam rooms, I don't know of any other med schools that do that for their Chiefs. Personally, I think it's a not too subtle reminder of the importance of patients in the sometimes rarefied air we breathe in the world of academic medicine."

Kate was nervous. She'd not slept well the previous night; although she tried to attribute the insomnia to the substantial late dinner and sleeping in Steve's bed rather than her own, she knew better. The changes in her life suddenly seemed overwhelming and when she stopped to think, she felt wildly out of control. The most peculiar thing about how she was feeling was that she was happier than she'd ever been in her life.

Once she'd figured that she was indeed pregnant, Kate had surfed the net to find out about pregnancy and had learned instantly that she was considered high risk because she was thirty-six.

Reading about the hormones which were being released by her body helped her understand the mood swings and the hot flashes. But the undeniable reality was that a new person was starting to take up residence in her body and Kate did not know how she felt about all of this. She had been to doctors only for the annual physicals required by the newspaper and those were normally less than five minutes.

Cochrane seemed to intuit Kate's extreme discomfort, and threw an arm around Kate's shoulder; not an easy task as she was maybe five-feet-two and Kate was five-nine.

Closing the door softly behind her, Sally Cochrane gestured to a couple of chairs across from one another next to the exam table. Taking one herself, the chubby doctor took off her shoes and wiggled her feet.

"I figure it's a little nicer to talk face to face before we get really up close and personal plus it gives me a chance to take off these heels. Saturday morning rounds are a killer—we round in all three buildings: the maternal-fetal ICU, the Post-Partum Unit and Labor and Delivery. I asked a med student to measure the distance a couple of years ago: three miles."

Grinning wryly, Cochrane wrinkled her pert nose. "Not that I can't use the exercise, it's just that my vanity will not permit me to wear running shoes like the med students and the residents. So it's heels—three miles in heels."

Kate knew what the woman was doing and was deeply grateful. She seemed to know exactly how to help an extremely skittish brand new patient regain her mental balance, or at least point in the direction.

But Kate doubted that Sally Cochrane was much less driven

than was she, so it was probably unlikely that future appointments would be this casual.

"Can I ask you some questions?"

"I was hoping you would."

Describing how she had been feeling over the last few weeks, Kate ended with her one overriding concern. "I've read all I can stand about high-risk pregnancies and honestly, I don't know which of the all terrible complications I'm most afraid of."

After listing the fifteen potential complications for a first time pregnancy at thirty-five or older more completely than any of Cochrane's med students could, Kate stopped and stared at Cochrane. But the physician said nothing, she sat waiting.

"Is this normal—crying one minute and uncontrollable laughing the next? I'm exaggerating, obviously but sometimes … no most of the time, I feel …." Kate's voice drifted off and she sat staring at her engagement ring.

Cochrane waited for a couple of minutes, then while Kate still sat mutely staring at the ring, Sally leaned forward so that Kate looked up and at her, "You feel ….?"

"Completely, totally out of control," came Kate's very soft answer.

Nodding approvingly, as if Kate had won the spelling bee for the fifth grade class, Cochrane repeated Kate's words, "Out of control, yep, that's it, completely, totally out of control."

"Do you have children?"

"Three," Followed by a deep sigh, and then, "I wish I could tell you that it goes away. That eventually you'll regain your sense of yourself, but it doesn't. Not really. I *can* promise that the emotional roller coaster will smooth out and relatively quickly. But the feeling you had before? That your life is your own? Nope, you'll never get it back."

Sally switched topics with, "But the list of high-risk problems for older first-time moms?" She stood in her bare feet and rooted around for some pamphlets, one of which she handed to Kate. You have already beaten the first five, Kate. For a host of reasons, I am confident you know as well as I, women over thirty-five have a much harder time getting pregnant. The next several I feel fairly sure won't be an issue with you: diabetes, high blood pressure, and pre-eclampsia tend to occur in overweight women more frequently. Women who exercise tend to have healthier pregnancies simply because they are physically more fit. But the chromosomal abnormalities and miscarriages can be an issue; we'll just have to see as your baby develops."

Smiling, the physician pulled Kate up to her feet. "Let's get to it, Kate, or Dr. Cooper will be knocking down the door to ask what kind of trouble I've found—speaking of someone else who has lost control over his well-ordered life."

***

Early Monday morning, Steve leaned over, kissed Kate, and said, "Man, I wish you weren't getting back on that plane to Houston today."

Stretching both hands over her head, Kate grinned and said, "I'm not." And laughing at the surprised expression on Cooper's face, she explained, "With the agreement Jeff and Rich made regarding the last two articles in my series, I'm way ahead of the game. The third one just needs some polishing and the last one can't be done until after the trial, so I decided to stay here until the trial in Amarillo on the twenty-eighth. I'll just fly to Amarillo from here, if that's okay? Yikes, Dr. Cooper, that's almost three weeks together! Do you think we might get on each other's nerves?" In response to Kate's question, Steve pulled her back under the covers where he kept her occupied for a while; then his phone buzzed.

Answering the phone with "Cooper," Steve listened for a couple of minutes and then said, "I'm thinking about taking the day off. Can you reschedule appointments for Friday at the earliest? Chuckling at whatever was said, "Yeah, maybe the whole week." Listening again, he replied, "Yeah, whatever, but can you find Alicia—is she around? I'd like her to check in on a couple of patients for me."

Five minutes later, Steve was rubbing his hands together and grinning, "Great!" I can clear most of the week and we can play we're tourists in San Francisco; there may be a couple of days I have to go in, though."

"No worries, Steve. I'd like to spend some time shopping if you can imagine me wanting to shop, that is! I've decided to enjoy the surprise of seeing who shows up in this new schizophrenic psyche of mine!"

Kate watched him watching her. "What?"

"Sometimes, Kate, I cannot believe all this," his eyes glistening. "You know how much I love you, right?"

Ducking to avoid the pillow she was throwing at him, Steve said, "You know what we should set up, don't you?" Answering his own question, "I'm going to call that realtor who has been bugging me to look at houses. She claims she has some 'steals.'" he informed Kate while laughing at the second pillow coming his way and Kate's return jibe. "Right, sure, a steal in San Francisco means an efficiency for only a million. Remember, I used to live here, Dr. Cooper."

September 18th
Houston

I understand the harmony of the world, when
will I grasp its melody?
— Paul Claudel

C H A P T E R
26

"Are you sure we have the right address?"

"I've checked it twice and confirmed it with McAllister through Dr. McCall yesterday."

Harvey was driving and Toni was navigating while they looked for the duplex where Gabe McAllister had lived with Samantha Bridges and her daughter Annie for just a little short of ten months.

"Let me take another pass down Westheimer and turn the other way on Montrose; I sure don't want to get back on that 59 freeway if I can help it." Harvey had driven in lots of cities but never one the size of Houston with a highway system that snaked around and over the city in ways that seemed labyrinthine.

Turning the rental Camry around for the fourth time in the last hour, Harvey glanced over at Toni.

"What are you doing?"

Paging through several apps on her phone, Toni muttered

something.

"I can't hear you Toni … wait, aren't we looking for the corner of Yoakum and Montrose?" Answering her own question, she nodded happily and squealed, "That's it, Toni!"

Turning right down Yoakum, she stopped the car in front of a fifties-era white, clapboard house, obviously a double family. "157 Yoakum, right?" Harvey asked.

Toni smiled and said, "Yes, good job! And I found it—their names, finally. Her name is April Clarke and her daughter's name is Emily. It wouldn't be terribly warm and friendly if we didn't have their names, now would it?"

Nodding in appreciation while walking up to the door, Harvey turned to Toni, asking, "You or me?"

"You."

A heavy-set mid-thirty-something ordinary looking woman stood in a baggy dress, having opened the front door, and looked at them warily from behind the protection of a closed screen door.

"Yes?"

Harvey smiled warmly, "Good morning, we're sorry to disturb you but we're hoping you can help us by answering just a few questions … that is, if you are, in fact, April Clarke?"

Disarmed by Harvey, the woman tried to suppress an answering smile as she replied, "Yes, I'm April Clarke. What can I help you with?"

Harvey was thinking rapidly. This lady could turn hostile in moments. Working hard to put herself in the woman's shoes, Harvey smiled again. "About a year ago, your daughter was a friend of a little girl who lived next door, here," Harvey pointed to the adjoining section of the duplex house. "Annie Bridges is the little girl's name. Annie told your daughter Emily that a former live-in boyfriend of her mother, a man named Gabe McAllister had sexually abused her." Noting April

Clarke's widened eyes as she stepped back from the closed screen door, Harvey quickly complimented the woman.

"And you did the absolute right thing after you heard what Annie Bridges told your daughter, Emily. That is exactly what the law requires, April. My partner and I would like to speak with you about Samantha Bridges, Annie's mom, for just a few minutes if we can? I promise you, we'll take no more than thirty minutes of your time."

April nodded and had opened the screen door but then stood in front of the door rather than stepping aside to let Harvey and Toni enter.

Turning to Toni, who was standing on Harvey's left-hand side, the opposite side of the open door, "April, this is my partner, Toni Martinez."

Toni was always fascinated as she watched Harvey Cunningham manipulate people. Pretending that April had stood aside and welcomed them into her apartment, Harvey subtly stepped forward. After edging around the right side of April, Harvey left the woman no choice but to step back to make room for Toni.

When Harvey's eyes lit on one of the few items of distinction in the cluttered living room, she declared, "Wow, a teen-aged Skipper collection—what a lovely display!"

Unable to resist, April walked over to the mantel and lovingly patted the five dolls displayed there. Smiling widely now at Harvey, she told her with pride, "It's taken me twenty years to find these. I want to order her friends Ginger and Living Fluff but I need to save the money to get them. They're really expensive you know, they run fifty to seventy-five dollars and that's not even including their little outfits."

As if she, too, were an aficionado of the Ken, Barbie, and Skipper collection of dolls, Harvey said, "Yes, that's true but you know I've seen them on EBay for half that price."

"Wow, thank you. I'll make sure to check that out this week!"

Noticing Toni for the first time, she asked, "Toni, right? Awesome tats. Wow, those colors are gorgeous!" April examined Toni's sleeve tattoos then pointing to the geometric design on her own arm, suggested, "I should get these colored in, a little like yours, maybe."

The two women smiled at one another as Toni thanked her.

Gesturing to the worn patterned couch, April said, "Make yourselves comfortable. Would you like some coffee?"

"Sure, that would be great, if it's not too much trouble, thanks."

As April walked out of the small living room into the kitchen, the two investigators signaled a "so far, so good" thumbs-up to one another.

Munching on a cookie, Toni took a sip of the coffee and swallowed. "Gosh April, this coffee is better than Starbucks and this cookie is great—you made them yourself, right?"

Pretending to listen as April explained in painstaking detail how easy it was to make the cookies, Toni then offered, "Well thanks, that sounds like a secret family recipe, I appreciate you giving it to us." And looked at Harvey.

Catching the signal, Harvey said, "April, I'm sure you have a bunch to do like all of us in these crazy days so let me explain why we're here. We work for the lawyer who will defend Gabe McAllister in a new trial in about a week and a half." Ignoring April's sputtered and escalating angry response, Harvey leaned over to April and said very firmly, confidently and quietly. "I am sure you agree with me when I say that Sam Bridges did not like to sleep alone. Before Gabe moved in with her, there were very few nights when Sam did not have a guy with her."

April's mouth opened, then closed. The surge of aggressive

reaction to the feeling of being manipulated by Harvey began to dissipate visibly. Her mouth opened a second time, then closed again.

Harvey sat as still as a stone, waiting. Still leaning toward April, Harvey's gaze fixed on the other woman, willing her to open up, to think back to all those nights or early mornings when she'd been awakened by laughing male and female voices on the shared porch of the house. Harvey calculated that April Clarke made that call because she thought it the right thing to do; not out of any malevolence toward McAllister, but rather, from the concern of a mother for the welfare of a child: exactly what she had said to April upon meeting her.

The other reason Harvey was gambling was simple. They had evidence proving Sam's promiscuity, but it was inadmissible because of the illegal cameras which had been hidden in Sam's and Annie's bedrooms. Therefore, the testimony of someone who had witnessed the wide variety of men with access to Annie's bedroom before McAllister moved in was vital.

Toni watched and counted the minutes of silence. She and Harvey had downloaded the bugged footage of Sam's current condo and had video proof, albeit illegal, of a man creeping into Annie's bedroom. He seemed to be a regular "date" of Sam's. He waited until she passed out from the alcohol and drugs and went to Annie's room at about three in the morning. They had seen this on three different nights.

Toni was no stranger to this scenario; Toni's uncle and brothers had messed with her starting when she was about five, back in Puerto Rico. But Toni was lucky, she had her Abu. And Toni had had a big mouth; when she'd talked, her Abu listened and brought her to live with her. But this kid Annie had no one at all, no one but this guy Gabe who tried to help her and ended up being accused of what everyone else was doing.

As if she were reading Toni's mind, April suddenly looked over at Toni, suspiciously, and asked Toni, in staccato fashion, "What do you know about all of this? Why are you so quiet? Am I going to be arrested? Am I in trouble?"

And suddenly April burst into tears, sobbing as if her heart were breaking.

After a few minutes, April took her hands away from her face, picked up a napkin from the small tray with the cookies and wiped her eyes then blew her nose.

Toni looked at April and said, "You asked what I know about all of this, April. And my answer to you is that I know quite a lot, a lot more than I wish I did. But let me assure you that you're not in trouble, you are not going to be arrested because you've done nothing wrong. But Harvey and I need your help so that we can help Annie, as well as our client Gabe McAllister.

"We have proof that Annie is being molested now." Toni waited while the shock registered on April's face and eyes. One of Sam's 'dates'" Toni said the word as if it were a slur, "sneaks into Annie's room around three in the morning. He does all he wants to Annie while her mother is passed out in her bedroom. We believe that Gabe McAllister stayed with Sam, moved in with her and Annie, because he could see how damaged Annie was." Waiting a long beat and holding April's gaze, she clarified, "Damaged by other men, other boyfriends. You could see it, too, couldn't you April? You suspected this was happening even before McAllister moved in with Sam, didn't you?"

This time the tears fell silently as they rolled down April's face.

"Yes, I could see it, too."

The emotional landscape of the room had changed. Suddenly the three women were on the same side, working together to get Annie help.

"Can you remember the details of that first conversation with your daughter about what Annie said?" Harvey's posture had relaxed and she had her hand lightly touching April's as if to remind her that she was not alone in this.

"Emily was crying when I walked into her bedroom after Annie had left. She was holding a drawing of two stick figures. A big stick figure and a little one, posed in different positions, crudely, but clearly demonstrating a picture of a man with his penis in the little stick figure's mouth and butt.

"I grabbed it from her and started asking her where she got it. She told me Annie had given it to her and she told Emily that was what the man did to her at night."

"Gabe had moved out more than six months before Annie told Emily about this. Did you remember that?

April nodded, "I did, and I thought it was strange because I—" She cut herself off suddenly.

Gently, carefully, Harvey probed, "Because you …."

"Because I'd seen one of the guys Sam brought home after Gabe moved out and he seemed … creepy, a little too interested in Emily."

"Did you tell the social worker this?"

"Yes, but she wasn't interested. She didn't write anything but Gabe McAllister's name down. Annie had told Emily that it was Gabe."

"Did you and Sam ever talk, April? Enough for her to say anything to you after Gabe moved out, like telling you that she was sad or—"

Interrupting Harvey, April burst out, "Sam was furious. She wasn't sad, she was mad. That he had just left like that, not saying anything just leaving to go to some training camp. Then never coming back, she said she'd make him pay for leaving her like she was some slut or something."

Harvey and Toni spent another hour with April Clarke, reassuring her, answering her questions, several of them repeatedly and making certain that April understood the critical nature of her testimony would be to McAllister. To allay her fears about the costs of getting to Amarillo to testify, they explained that the lodging and flight for April would be covered by the firm.

April agreed that she could take off three days from her job at the nearby Walgreen's and would arrive in Amarillo on the evening of the twenty-sixth so that Rich Jansen could review her testimony with her.

Huntsville Prison

The essential is invisible to the eyes.
One can see rightly only with the heart.
— *Antoine de St-Exupery*

C H A P T E R

27

"Hi Gabe, I'd like to talk with you for a few minutes before you leave tonight for your trial."

Lindsey was standing in the door of a seclusion room that had been modified as a temporary cell for McAllister. The prisoner was sitting in a chair, staring at the floor. Looking up and over to her, he shrugged and mumbled an apathetic, "Sure."

Walking into the small room, she looked around for a bit then walked out, calling over her shoulder, "I'll be back in a sec."

In less than a minute, she was back with Max and was carrying the dog's huge dog bed that looked as big as she was. Jumping up to help, McAllister was transformed. "Hey Max, don't you have it made, a bed wherever you go? I don't think you'd care for the way you'd have to sleep in the Marines— the other war dogs would call you a wuss."

But the grin on his face was as big as Texas when he carefully placed the dog's bed right next to his chair and watched the big Doberman circle twice, plop down and start sucking the Berber chewie that he loved.

For McAllister, this was a speech, more words said than Lindsey had heard out of the man's mouth the entire time he'd been here.

Lindsey was in scrubs, her typical attire while working, and was feeling great on a few counts. The Emergency Medicine boards were over and done, she had passed and was now an official emergency medicine doc. It felt good; she was sick of studying. But more importantly, she had a plan for Gabe McAllister. One that she'd been cooking up ever since Rich had told her they were spending Christmas in Lausanne, Switzerland, and the reason for Reardon inviting them along with Kate Townsend and Steve Cooper. She was excited and happy for Steve, whom she'd known since their cardiology residency at Houston Medical. And Kate Townsend had become one of her closest friends.

Last night, she had broken tradition and cooked dinner. Rich had been so immersed in this case that he had forgotten to eat. She'd figured that she couldn't do too much damage to steak and baked potatoes and she'd been right. The meal was delicious and it had provided the context for telling Rich her idea.

Given that she was right and she was certain she was, Jansen thought it a splendid idea that would work well for them all.

Now that McAllister was behaving like a human, a transformation that occurred only when he was with Max, Lindsey decided to give it a shot. After all, what did any of them have to lose at this point?

"Gabe, I have a proposition for you ... once you get acquitted, I mean."

McAllister jerked as if he'd been shocked; in a way, Lindsey supposed, he would be shocked. After all, how long had it been since someone had offered him something … hope, a place to stay when he had none, anything at all?

"Acquitted."

The word was said slowly as if being tasted for hidden explosives.

"Right, acquitted."

This time, the ex-trooper stared at her, his mostly healed mouth agape. "You sound confident that I will be acquitted."

"I am."

His stare said it all.

"You said a proposition, what do you mean?" Although he was trying to hide the curiosity, it was there. The thousand-yard stare was gone, for the moment, and she realized with surprise, that he had beautiful eyes … hazel with highlights of copper … unusual.

"Rich and I have a guest house at our home in New Waverly. We'd like you to stay with us once you're out of here, at least until after the first of the year. By then, you'll have an idea of what you want to do next."

One of the very few adjustments the couple had made to the "cabin" that had belonged to the Governor of Texas before it became their home was the guest house. The drive to Houston was about ninety minutes. Too long a drive to enjoy dinner and drinks with friends out in the country.

Although the Governor's "cabin" was plenty roomy with four bedrooms, the guest house provided a great deal more privacy than was offered by a bedroom in the main house. Once the small house was built, they figured friends would accept invitations out to the Piney Woods without feeling they were intruding on the newly married Rich and Lindsey. They'd had fun supervising its building shortly after they returned from their honeymoon. They had furnished it with the furniture, dishes, and the other paraphernalia from each of their respective homes, giving the guest house an eclectic, eccentric, and comfortable look.

Lindsey could see the sheen in his eyes before he turned his gaze downward to Max, where it was safe.

She had some idea, not a lot, but some of what he was feeling right now. There was no one in the center right now, no patients, and the design of the center had included the best of insulation, for soundproofing. In the silence, the only sound was the one Max was making as he contentedly suckled the Berber chew toy. Lindsey's mind wandered.

"Why would you do this? Offer your home, a place to stay to me, a complete stranger?"

McAllister's words were choked out of his larynx, as if there were an enormous obstacle that precluded speech—he was clearly overcome.

"Because about two years ago, Rich was the Chief Warden here. The day I was released from here, he made the same offer to me. And I asked him the same thing in almost the same words."

"*You* were in prison? Here? A men's prison?"

"Yep. They made exceptions to the male-only policy here. They figured I'd be safer here than in one of the women's prisons. I was convicted of murdering my mother."

Well aware that McAllister was on the verge of overload and could shut back down at any minute, Lindsey added, "It's a long and very complicated story, Gabe. Someday, in the not too distant future, we'll tell you the details, but I'd like to get back to my proposition to you."

"What do you mean—like I would say no? Lindsey—I guess I can call you that? I'm using everything I've got right now to get past two facts: first, that you seem sincere and genuinely convinced that I'll get out of here, that I'll get acquitted. Honestly, I figured the best I could hope for was that when I came back here after this second trial, this time those guys would kill me. And second, that you and your husband, who used to be a Marine and was Chief Warden and a homicide cop and who knows what else, along with those two weird women, and their even stranger boss, are all working to get me out of prison. And now you're offering me a place to live? Why would you all *do* such a thing?"

Max stopped chewing his toy and looked up at Lindsey, then at McAllister, and whined so softly they could barely hear the sound.

"Sorry Max, forgot how tuned in you guys are." Gabe looked at Lindsey when he said, "These dogs are more like people than people, I'd forgotten." He smiled at Max then at her. "How great to be reminded!"

Smiling happily because Gabe had just provided her with his answer to the remainder of her proposition, Lindsey left Max with his new friend and then walked out the door to call Candace, who ran a Dobie rescue center in Conroe, and to tell her they had a deal. Baron, a two-year-old black and tan Dobie, had a home starting sometime within the next couple of weeks.

Just as she was about to close the door to Gabe's cell, he asked tentatively, "Dr. McCall … Lindsey, do you have another minute?"

Turning back around to face him, Lindsey replied, "Sure Gabe, what is it?"

"You asked a couple of weeks ago if I was a believer. I was rude when I said no. Are *you*?"

His eyes were bright, searching.

"Yes, I am."

Staring at her, he said, "But you're a doc. I thought you

guys were all atheists. What happened to you?"

Smiling, she answered, "Most of my friends in medical school were, maybe still are, atheists and I was, for most of my life. If not an actual atheist then at least agnostic."

He was watching her carefully, waiting.

"What happened? I achieved everything I'd ever set out to from the time I was a little kid, then I landed here where I could wonder what life, my life had been all about."

Lindsey's mind rocketed back to the month she spent alone at the monastery, shortly after she was released from prison and the conversation she'd had with Father John Tobin about forgiveness.

It had taken Lindsey just two days to read Jung's *Modern Man in Search of a Soul.* She had enjoyed the book so much that she had read it twice, the second time slowly, enjoying the thoughts of the man who had begun his career as a protégé of Freud, but who had diverged from the Freudian school of psychiatry after only six years with his brilliant but tortured mentor.

Lindsey reflected on the many surprises she had found in the book: Jung's nomenclature, for example. He was emphatic about the essential aspect of the confessional stage of the psychoanalytic process for the therapist and patient to establish a therapeutic relationship. Confession: the word had seemed to proclaim itself to her as she had read and then reread sections of his book. The power of the word itself and of Jung's conviction that the physician psychiatrist could not be of assistance to anyone past the age of thirty-five—for Jung, the onset of middle age—without the aid of some religious belief on the part of the patient, reverberated in her heart. She wondered if Jung's theories were perceived as radical when he wrote what would be the last book of his life? Radical indeed seemed an appropriate description in the contemporary age of psychiatry, one that predominantly relies on medication—the chemical cure.

"Talk to me about confession, Father," she had requested at the time.

They had been seated at a small table in a charming wine bar on the outskirts of Beaumont. Father John Tobin had turned to look at Lindsey. "You liked Jung's book, I take it." His gaze had been penetrating and unsurprised.

"I'd not been exposed to anything like that in medical school. I found it—" she had searched for the right word and looked at the priest, "*radical* is the right word, I think, Father. From the Latin, *root*."

Tobin had decided that he and Lindsey should see some of the sights of downtown Beaumont just for a change of scenery after her first few days at the monastery. He had appeared right about three that afternoon to ask if she'd like a glass of wine and cheese and crackers. He'd laughed at her jubilant response.

Later, while seated at a small wooden table covered with a brocade tablecloth, Father John had taken a sip of his cabernet and smiled. "Now that's a nice cab." They had each asked for a glass of house cabernet sauvignon when they arrived at the quaint and comfortable bar. Peering across the table at McCall, he prompted, "Radical."

Enjoying her wine every bit as much as the priest, she had just nodded while she sipped her wine and nibbled on a chunk of sharp cheddar cheese. When Father John had said nothing further, Lindsey had explained, "Radical in the sense of getting to the origin, the heart of things."

She had paused while she considered how much to reveal. And had then declared, "I've never thought of a therapeutic relationship as one that must include a stage of confession." She had looked over and grinned, as she continued, "But therapeutic is not a characteristic of my admittedly prejudicial view of Psychiatry. But once I read Jung's explanation and thought about how we learn to trust and love one another, I realized that confession is an accurate name for the way we do it." She had been thinking first of conversations with Rich, so like confessions, as she spoke. She had felt the blush in her neck move up to her cheeks.

"But it seems to me that confession must lead somewhere … to forgiveness, or else the process is just intellectual, academic."

She had looked over at the priest, who was gazing intently at her, motionless. "That's why Jung insists that some type of religious belief must be present in the patient for healing to take place. A psychiatrist cannot possibly forgive—even the very best friend cannot forgive. And how does one go about forgiving the unforgivable?" Her voice had trailed off, as she sat staring at the wineglass she had gripped with both hands. Her expression had been tense, her body rigid while she had stared at the half-filled wine glass. Finally, she had looked over at the priest.

"So that's why I'd like to talk to you about confession, Father." Her eyes had been glistening, her expression pleading, and her mouth had trembled as she stared at the silent priest.

Very gently and simply, Father John had asked, "Are you asking to join the Catholic Church, Lindsey?"

"Yes, I am, Father John. Yes, I am." The words had been breathed, not said, and her relief at the statement was palpable. Lindsey's eyes blazed, and her face had been illuminated.

She was surprised that Gabe had remembered her attempts to introduce the idea of faith, of belief in God back when he was still in a fairly rocky medical condition. But very soon he would be on trial again, and would have to endure all those people testifying about him. Total strangers in whose hands rested his future or complete lack of one.

McCall remembered all too well what her trial had felt like: the disorientation, sense of almost total bewilderment; she was profoundly grateful that she had not needed to endure a second one.

Looking at McAllister's face now, Lindsey told him, "There's a book I was given, Gabe—a most intriguing book, written by a psychiatrist." Making a face, she explained, "Psychiatrists are not my among my most respected colleagues so I was prepared to think what he wrote was more doubletalk. But instead, this book changed my life." Studying him, Lindsey said, "He wrote it for people in mid-life, which he considered over the age of thirty-five. I know you're not yet thirty but since you've lived a couple of lifetimes already, perhaps you'd like to read it?"

McAllister was staring at her. She thought it was with his thousand-yard stare but was surprised again when he shook his head, as if to clear it, focused on her and said, "I would, thanks. And, Dr. McCall ... Lindsey?"

She cocked her head and lifted an eyebrow.

"You never answered my question. Why are you doing all this?"

"You're right, I didn't." She smiled and walked out the door.

After McCall had left, Gabe picked up the well-read book and paged to an inscription a few pages into the book.

It was dated a little over two years ago. In strong clear script it read, "Lindsey, peace and all good, John Tobin."

*Facts are stubborn things; and whatever may be our wishes,
our inclinations, or the dictates of our passions, they cannot
alter the state of facts and evidence.*
— *John Adams*

C H A P T E R

28

"My esteemed colleagues will try to present Gabriel McAllister as a hero. This man served in the Marine Corps, did four tours in Afghanistan and then became a Texas State Trooper. All laudatory and most likely jam-packed with heroic acts. But we are not here to discuss Mr. McAllister's war record, impressive though it is. We are *here*, ladies and gentlemen of the jury, to seek justice."

Allen Connors had been standing still in the crowded courtroom. He stood between the judge and the jurors as he began his opening statement, then he paused for a few beats and lowered his voice so that it sounded almost like a whisper. Connors took one step forward, closer to the people seated in the courtroom; slowly, like the consummate performer he was, he raised his voice so much so that two of the female jurors jumped.

"Justice for little seven-year-old Annie Bridges. Annie was

subjected to the vilest, heinous, and odious of human perversions: sexual molestation of a *child,* for heaven's sake, a child!"

"Mr. Cunningham and his associate, Mr. Jansen, will use the fact of an intact hymen to cast doubt on the justifiable conviction in a Houston courtroom nine months ago. But the State will show that an intact vaginal hymen does not preclude sexual molestation; that rather, in a majority of these terrible cases of sex abuse in small children, there is no anatomic evidence. A fact which makes it *imperative – that – you – good – people – do – the – right – thing – and – keep – this – pervert – locked – up* where he belongs!" Connors had been pacing up and down but slowed his pace to match the pauses in his last sentence, a metered dance.

A short, wiry man, Connors was plain; he was easy to overlook in a crowd until he got in front of a courtroom. Suddenly, the man was transformed into a force: primal, compelling, and dangerous.

Jansen, Cunningham, and the investigators had arrived in Amarillo four days before on the twenty-fourth of April. Voir dire would start on the twenty-seventh and they had a good deal of work to do before the trial would commence on the twenty-eighth.

Cunningham's firm had rented three suites and a conference room at the Courtyard Amarillo Downtown for the week, to predict Connors' opening statement and major arguments, and review their own strategies for opposing his arguments. The hotel was practically across the street from the courthouse, and therefore, very convenient for the group. Jansen was delighted with the suite because Lindsey had asked his former secretary to stay at the house to take care of Max so that she could provide moral support for Jansen during his first trial. The couple had tentatively asked Wanda to stay through the weekend in case they wanted to remain in Amarillo for a mini-vacation.

Critical to their defense strategy was the element of surprise. They had several major pieces of new evidence that had not been introduced or explored in the first case but the timing to do so was key: too early in the case where Connors could adeptly sweep the information under the rug or too late where overloaded jurors would be unable to process due to overload—both situations were entirely possible and would guarantee conviction for McAllister.

They knew Connors would go directly to the reason for this new trial and were therefore expecting him to bring up the lack of physical evidence in the testimonies of the medical witnesses for the State. That Connors had come at it during his opening statement was a testament to his experience and talent in the courtroom.

Chief Justice Richard Montgomery presided over the Seventh Court of Appeals at the Potter County Courthouse in Amarillo, Texas. Harvey and Toni had been doing twenty-hour-days to complete the investigations of Samantha Bridges and Annie. Somehow they found time to research the three justices assigned to the seventh court so that Cunningham and Jansen would have some insight into their education, prior legal specialty, and potential biases. Both believed Chief Justice Montgomery to be the toughest of the three justices because he came from the prosecution side of the law. Montgomery had been District Attorney for San Antonio for over five years; prior to that, he'd been an average ADA in Lubbock for a few years.

When the two lawyers climbed the steps of the historic Amarillo courthouse built sometime in the early twentieth century, they passed through the electronic paraphernalia necessary to gain admittance to any courtroom in the twenty-first century USA; they then found their way to the second floor where the Seventh Court of Appeals was located.

"Montgomery, it is." Cunningham was reading the name of the presiding judge as Rich struggled with their bulging briefcases.

"Of course, it'd be Montgomery, Zach. But maybe he's developed a love for the dark side after all those years of prosecution."

Jansen stared again at Cunningham, smiling as he did so.

"Will you stop staring, Jansen?" The gravelly voice sounded as if it were packed with pebbles and was joined by a glare that attempted to be threatening but failed.

"Tell me again what your son said when he saw you the night following the dirty deed?"

"You know all that crap I said about you the other day— that I liked and admired you, that I think you're different? That I think you have my back? I take it all back, you're a royal pain in the arse, Jansen, that's what you are,"

By now, Jansen was laughing and Zach was working very hard not to join him. After making the decision to cross-examine the little girl, he finally called his barber who had been after him for years. Gone were the Rastafarian locks he'd worn for close to fifty years.

When he had walked through the door the night before he took off for Amarillo, Zach's daughter Mandy had been sitting in the TV room watching television while her thumbs raced on the tiny keyboard as she texted some friend and listened to something on her IPhone via her earbuds. Typical Mandy multitasking.

He had walked over to her and kissed her on the top of her head. Looking up she had smiled then turned to look again, and only stared, speechless.

At that point, Thad had come racing into the room, exuberantly yelling, "Dad, you're ho—" then had switched immediately to, "Wow Dad, you look just like Obama! Except your ears don't stick out."

Strangely, he did. If you ignored the scarred cheek and mouth, there was a strong resemblance.

Cunningham looked up at Rich as they walked together into Judge Montgomery's courtroom and said dryly, "If nothing else, Mr. Co-Counsel Jansen, these next four days will not be boring."

Voir Dire, or the judicial process of selecting an impartial group of twelve was a tricky, tedious and extremely time-consuming process. Because the rules for conducting the process are few and mostly vaguely worded, unlike most other aspects of trial law, practically speaking each judge seemed to conduct voir dire according to his or her preferences.

The defense team had spent many hours while still in Houston discussing their options for the creation of the ideal juror and eleven others like him. Once they learned who would be hearing their case, their list of options narrowed considerably for a number of reasons. While Connors' ideal juror was a married man or woman with children, the person Jansen and Cunningham believed most likely to be open to the arguments for acquittal was a single man under forty and childless with a military background.

Once they learned who would hear the case, the option of the jury shuffle was taken off the table, the risk of annoying Montgomery early in their case was far too high.

Jury shuffling is one of the ways to manage the composition of the jury; it is a request that the numbers dictating juror seats one through twenty-four be shuffled. The end result is that people seated in the higher numbered slots, and, therefore, are less likely to be selected, would end up with lower numbers.

But the jury shuffle had to be requested prior to the completion of voir dire and there was some controversy on just when voir dire began in counties where written questionnaires were used to qualify jurors. Counties like the one they were in.

The decision to take it off the table once they learned it would be the Chief Justice hearing the case, was based on two factors: use of the jury shuffle had been known to antagonize this judge before the case even got off the ground; and the Chief Justice was known to be fairly exacting and methodical with the process of voir dire.

For a case like this one, he would likely be even more so. The Chief Justice would do everything he could to assure an objective group of twelve citizens of Amarillo to judge this case; a very tall order in a case of child sexual abuse. There were somewhere around one hundred people in the court-room.

Groups of people were called in increments of sixteen: twelve jurors plus four alternates.

Prior to the seating of the first group of sixteen, Chief Justice Montgomery addressed all one hundred or so people seated in the gallery.

"Now, for those of you still in the gallery, when we ask questions, please listen. If you cannot hear the questions asked by me or the attorneys, please tell us. And as we ask the people who are seated in the jury box, think about your own answer because it's likely that some of you will be brought in to replace prospective jurors currently in the box.

"So, in the interest of saving time, if you are called to replace someone, I'll ask you, 'Are there any questions you would have answered in the affirmative?' If you can keep this question in your mind, and the questions asked of those in the box, we can save both your time and ours by not repeating the same litany of questions over and over again."

"The purpose of what we will next do is to determine if you are qualified by law to serve as a juror in this particular case. That is, to assure that you are unrelated to the parties and their lawyers, and have no evident bias or prejudice in this case, and can act as a fair and wholly impartial juror.

"To make this determination, I will ask a number of questions, then the attorneys will ask you questions on matters not covered by this Court.

"You are obliged by the oath that you just took to answer each question thoughtfully and truthfully. If any one of your answers reveals a legal basis for you to be excused as a juror, one of the attorneys will challenge you or ask that you be excused. If the Court agrees with the reason stated for the challenge, you'll be excused and another name will be drawn.

"Once we have an adequate number to qualify for cause, the attorneys are allowed to issue another type of challenge called a peremptory challenge. Each side is permitted to challenge you for a reason or for no reason at all and this Court has no alternative but to excuse you."

The word peremptory derives from the Latin word "peremptoruis" meaning final, destructive, decisive, and "periempere" meaning to destroy or cut off. Peremptory challenges have come under intense scrutiny because in some cases, peremptory challenges that were based on race or gender, were later determined to qualify as a mistrial on appeal. The Batson challenge refers to an overturned conviction in the appellate court based upon the use of peremptory challenges to strike all but white jurors. Although Jansen and Cunningham would love an all-male jury, the risks were too high.

The Judge leaned down and peered at the sixteen people in the juror box. "If this happens, it does not mean you have done something wrong or you are a bad person or that you need to worry. During the questioning, please understand that we have one goal only: to provide a group of twelve people who are impartial, unbiased, and unprejudiced. The integrity of our justice system depends on this."

Turning to the attorneys, Montgomery asked, "Please introduce yourselves and read the list of witnesses you plan to call for this trial."

Ten minutes later Connors and Cunningham had completed reading the names of their co-counsels, investigators and the total of sixteen witnesses who would be called to present the arguments for guilt and presumption of innocence.

"We'll begin now. Some of the questions I may ask require only that you raise your hand if your answer is in the affirmative; at that time, we'll explore the matter further. Please do not hesitate to raise your hand if you think it appropriate."

"Are any of the potential jurors acquainted with the defendant is this case?"

There were no raised hands.

"Are any jurors acquainted with the attorneys?"

No one raised their hand.

"Are any jurors acquainted with any of the witnesses?"

Once more, no hands were raised.

"Now, is there anyone acquainted with people in law enforcement?"

Several hands were raised.

One by one, Chief Justice Montgomery asked each of the five if they believed that the relationship provided a better understanding of the inner workings of the law, and all said no.

But when asked if listening to the testimony of a law enforcement officer would lend greater credulity than that of other witnesses, there were three jurors who agreed. Yes, they believed statements by law enforcement personnel to be more credible; the Chief Justice said, "I'll let you discuss this further,

Mr. Cunningham."

"Has anyone read or seen information in the newspaper, heard anything on the radio or television about this case?"

No hands were raised.

"Does any of you have anything other than a passing interest in the case?"

"What do you mean?" a woman named Smith asked.

"Have you an opinion about how this case turns out?"

"Yes, I think he's guilty."

"What?"

"I said I think he's guilty."

"You're free to go, Ms. Smith."

That opened up three more female potential jurors following suit.

By lunchtime, there had been thirty people dismissed. The reasons varied either from family relationships with law enforcement, a belief that they could not be fair based on the nature of the alleged crime, or merely a stated belief in the guilt of the accused. Three women had broken down in sobs when they answered Justice Montgomery's question about prior experience with sexual abuse and had to be escorted out of the courtroom by the Bailiff.

But by mid-afternoon, the tide swung and both sides got through to the next stage of acceptance or rejection for cause by the Defense and the Prosecution. There were twenty-four jurors who had qualified by negative replies to Chief Justice Montgomery's screening questions.

Intent on loading the jury with as many people who would likely be open to their respective point of view, the two teams were careful to use their three peremptory rejections for cause judiciously.

"Hello, Mrs. Davis. I see that you're a registered nurse who works in the Emergency Room at Amarillo General. How long have you worked at the hospital?"

"Five years."

"Mrs. Davis, you said you have three daughters under the age of fifteen. Do you think that fact would preclude your ability to examine the facts presented during this trial and arrive at a conclusion of guilt or innocence?"

"As a trained nurse practitioner, I have been required to adopt a professional and scientific approach to the patients under my care. I am confident I can transfer that same objectivity to the evidence presented during this case."

Connors probably loved this woman; she would have seen multiple rape victims and might be happy to have the opportunity to put one away for good. But Jansen wondered if she were being truthful. Perhaps she would be able to adopt the clinical detachment he had seen so frequently in his wife. Hesitant, Jansen looked over at Cunningham but Zach was concentrating hard on something he was writing and did not look up.

"Does the Counsel for the Defense pass this juror?" Montgomery's voice boomed from his lofty perch. A Texas A&M undergraduate, Montgomery was a 1968 graduate of the University of Texas Law School, making him around the same age as Zach Cunningham.

The two men could not have been more different in appearance and demeanor. While Zach's new "Obama" haircut had jettisoned his outmoded radical sixties look, he was one of only three blacks in the courtroom of about one hundred people, one of whom was his wife. He was wiry and slim; his trim body fit his pin-striped gray Armani suit with style and distinction. Montgomery looked as if he'd feel much more at home back on the Aggie football team where he'd been a tight end.

Just as Rich was about to say yes, for Zach, the defense

accepted this juror, he looked up and caught Toni's gaze. She'd been focusing on him and he must have sensed the intensity of her gaze. She was signaling a clear but subtle no.

"Object for cause, Your Honor." Connors was on his feet in seconds and the nurse left the room.

"Good afternoon, Mr. Martin, I'd like to ask you just a few more questions in light of the information you provided Chief Justice Montgomery a moment or two ago."

Connors was speaking with an early thirties-something former Army veteran.

"Are you married Mr. Martin?"

"I am not."

"Have you any children from a former marriage or relationship?"

"I do not."

Connors looked at the Chief Justice, "I object for cause."

"Ms. James, I would like to revisit your reply to the Chief Justice about whether you believe children lie."

Jansen consulted his notes, "Your reply, Ms. James, was 'Kids lie about little things all of the time, but I wonder if they could lie about something like this. But I believe I can be open to the facts of this case.' Ms. James, do you think it is possible for a child to tell a lie about having been sexually abused? To accuse someone of sexual molestation when that person did no inappropriate sexual touching of that child?"

Ms. James stared at Jansen.

"Please reply to counsel, Ms. James." Montgomery sounded tired. They had been at this for days, it felt like.

"No, I cannot believe a child would make up something like that."

"Dismissed for cause, Judge."

And on it went until finally, twelve people were grudgingly accepted by both sides. The twelve who later sat listening to the fourth witness presented by the State.

"Good morning, Dr. Davis. Thank you for breaking away from your busy pediatric practice to fly up here and testify to the sexual abuse of little Annie Bridges suffered by Gabriel McAllister over the—"

"OBJECTION on at least three counts: inflammatory, leading the witness and—"

It was the first time Zach had opened his mouth and that gravelly voice echoed in the crowded courtroom, startling everyone there including the Judge who interrupted the list of objections.

"Overruled. Mr. Connors, I'll not warn you again. Keep your comments to the facts and the rules of my courtroom," interrupted Chief Justice Montgomery as he glared at Connors and gave a surprised glance at Cunningham.

"Mr. Connors?"

Connors had turned his back away from the Judge and toward the jury. At the sound of his own name, he swiveled his body back to the Judge.

"Yes, Your Honor. I apologize, it won't happen again."

Thinking what everyone seated in that courtroom was thinking, Montgomery's voice lowered, his brows raised, and he instructed, "Counsels, please approach the bench."

Connors and his associate, a newly minted ADA named Grant along with Cunningham and Jansen approached the bench while the bailiff escorted the jurors out of the court-room.

"This case has been granted an appeal. Consider this a forewarning gentlemen, because there will not be another mis-trial on my watch. Do *not* play fast and loose with the rules in my courtroom. I don't give a rat's ass about conviction records or egos or anything but doing our best to present the best account of the facts and the evidence as we know them."

Looking directly at Connors, "Is that clearly understood?"

Connors conducted the testimonies of his next four key witnesses within boundaries until the day ground down to an end at almost exactly five in the afternoon. Jansen's cross-examinations were routine. The defense accepted the factual evidence of the case. There would be no attempt to rebut the testimony of the experts for the State.

———————◆————————

"Man, this is really great steak, maybe it's true that Texas has the best steak in the country," Cunningham quipped as he cut off another piece of a huge rib-eye.

Deciding to break from the seemingly endless non-stop work of the last several weeks, Toni, Harvey, Zach, and Rich were seated companionably in a booth at The Big Texan Steak Ranch. The restaurant was located on the old Route 66 right outside Amarillo

Taking a sip from her margarita, Harvey lifted it up. "Well, Rich, however this turns out for Gabe and for all of us, I want you to know how much I have enjoyed getting to know you and working with you. I think we are as prepared as we can possibly be."

The others lifted their drinks to clink their beers to Harvey's glass. "Anyone have any predictions?" she asked.

Taking a bite of her salad, she winked at Toni, expecting her to reply.

"My wife, Lindsey, is positive he'll be acquitted. She has been almost from the beginning."

Toni looked at Jansen in surprise. "Your wife is a doctor, is that right?"

"Yes, she is, Toni."

"Did she say why she thinks that?"

"No, but she has said this from the moment I decided to go back into criminal defense law and to take this case."

"That's interesting." Toni cut a huge piece of steak and began to cut it into smaller pieces. Looking up, she realized the others were staring at her expectantly.

"Well, it is interesting. I agree with Lindsey. We'll win this case." Toni studied one of the small pieces of steak, speared it, and added, "This case won't make it to the jury." She lifted the small piece of meat into her mouth and chewed, very slowly.

Potter County Courts Building, Amarillo

Before you embark on a journey of revenge, dig two graves.
— Confucius

C H A P T E R
29

"State your full name, please." Allen Connors was winding up the case for the prosecution with his two star witnesses.

"My name is Samantha Bridges."

"Ms. Bridges, did you live with the Defendant at 157 Yoakum in Houston Texas for a period of nine months and twenty days?"

"I did."

"Is the Defendant here, in this courtroom? If so, please identify him for us."

"Yes. Gabe McAllister, the man who is sitting there." Sam pointed over to McAllister, "The man sitting in the gray suit with the blue shirt and red tie."

"Okay thank you, and your daughter Annie was then five years old, is that correct?"

"Yes, that's right."

"Annie lived there with you and the Defendant during this period of time? When did you first realize that the Defendant was abusing little—"

"OBJECTION!"

Jansen was on his feet, "Your Honor, Mr. Connors' statement is prejudicial, leading and—"

"Sustained, Mr. Jansen."

Chief Justice banged his gavel hard. He leaned his massive torso over his desk to glare at Allen Connors while he queried him, "Counsel, do we need to go back in my chambers to review the rules of what is acceptable cross-examination in courtrooms?"

"I withdraw the question, your Honor, I'm sorry." Connors did not appear sorry; in fact, the quick look he gave toward his young associate looked amused and faintly contemptuous.

"One more cute little trick like that Mr. Connors and I'll cite you for contempt of court, are we clear here, Sir?" Montgomery's large jowls at the side of his face were quivering with the tension from the muscles jutting his jaw so far forward that he resembled a bulldog. An angry one.

Jansen caught Cunningham's gaze and lifted a quizzical eyebrow. Rich was wondering why Connors was antagonizing this judge; it made no sense.

Cunningham wrote "Arrogance—Houston ADA and hick small town judge, showing off to the kid."

Wondering, Jansen listened with surprise to a Samantha Bridges who seemed very different from the woman in the transcript in the first trial.

"Ms. Bridges, what happened on March 25th of last year?"

"The police came to tell me they had Gabe in custody for hurting Annie."

"Hurting Annie, Ms. Bridges? Can you tell us how the Defendant had hurt your child?"

Voice raised and eyes wide, angry, and defiant, she stated clearly, "He raped her and made her su—sorry, do oral intercourse on him."

Without moving his head from watching Connors, Jansen could see Gabe out of the corner of his eye. Following the training they had given him, McAllister's mouth was shut. His hands were visible on top of the table where he sat next to Rich. And he was staring straight ahead but a twitch in his jaw revealed the effort he was expending to keep from exploding.

Whether or not to put Gabe on the stand had been controversial from the very beginning. Toni and Harvey had put in herculean effort in getting him ready for Connors. The two investigators believed the jurors needed to hear from him, to hear him declare his innocence, to watch his face and mannerisms as he did so.

Jansen was wholeheartedly opposed. McAllister had only two ways of responding during the simulated cross-examinations: robotic or angry. The hours of repeated grilling had extinguished the physical, emotional responses, but Connors was among the best prosecutors in the country. Jansen worried about Connors pushing a button that could not help evoking McAllister's rage. Rich could see the consequences of the six-foot-five ex-soldier and ex-cop towering over Connors all too clearly—they would be toast.

"Ms. Bridges, prior to the police informing you, were you aware of any danger to Annie from the Defendant?"

Samantha turned big blue eyes to Connors and said demurely, "I should have known there was something wrong after the shower incidents."

Jansen clamped his left hand, hard, on McAllister's thigh to cause enough pain to stop him from reacting to Sam's testimony; testimony which was, Rich thought, a work of art.

Dressed in a conservative blue suit, with her light hair pulled back, Sam Bridges looked like a model for a young career woman. Her makeup was subtle and she seemed the soul of sobriety. Unmistakably, Connors' people had been working hard with Ms. Bridges.

"What do you mean by the shower incidents?"

"Well, this is really pretty embarrassing." A white slender forefinger snaked up from her lap to fiddle with the lace collar of her demure white blouse.

McAllister suppressed a low, growled, "Jesus."

Watching Sam's performance, Rich thought of another testimony in another trial by a woman with many of the same abilities to infer much more than their words and to adopt whatever persona suited the occasion. Paula Livingston, his wife Lindsey's dead sister, was better than Sam, but then she'd had many more years to practice her art.

"Ms. Bridges, answer Mr. Connors' question now please, we don't have all day." Montgomery was getting testy.

"Well, Gabe and I used to like to shower together as a way to … you know," clearing her throat, "arouse one another. And Gabe thought it would be good for Annie to join us so a few times, all three of us were in there making sure we were all squeaky clean."

Sam made a major mistake: she giggled.

The horror on the faces of the mostly female jury was priceless.

"Yes, well thanks but did you have evidence, Ms. Bridges, of the Defendant being sexually inappropriate with your daughter? Perhaps an occasion where you came home unexpectedly and disturbed—"

"OBJECTION LEADING THE WITNESS, your honor."

"Sustained."

Montgomery slowly stood.

"Bailiff, please escort the jury out of the courtroom for a short break. Counsel, my chambers now, please."

The Chief Justice's office was small but orderly. A large

scarred mahogany desk sat in the corner with a black ergonomic chair behind it. There were a few framed photos: one of a much younger Montgomery in position as a linebacker with the "Fighting Texas Aggies," another of the Chief Justice with a woman and two teenagers. A third was of Governor Greg Bell shaking hands with Montgomery.

Rather than going back behind his desk, Montgomery leaned against it, crossed his arms over his massive chest and stared at the four attorneys for a very long and very silent minute.

"Mr. Connors, I was once a prosecutor. Then I was elected to the office of district attorney. No, not in your town of Houston but in San Antonio. But I expect you knew this already, Mr. Connors."

Connors and his associate were dwarfed by Montgomery, but Cunningham looked Lilliputian as he stood in front of him; Montgomery probably weighed close to three hundred and Zach did well to hit one forty. Both Cunningham and Jansen avoided looking at Connors, staring everywhere but at him.

No lawyer enjoyed this kind of dressing down, even when it was well deserved; it was too loud an echo of pugnacious law school faculty and the derisive outburst aimed at the weaker students. Connors was behaving in ways that could only harm his case but did not seem to be able to stop himself.

Rather than just standing there silently and taking it, Connors stared back at Montgomery as if baiting him. "Your point, Sir?"

Shaking his large head slowly back and forth, Chief Justice Montgomery nodded at Connors, as if in recognition. "Mr. Connors, if it's hardball you want to play then by God, that's what we'll play."

<hr>

Back in the courtroom, Connors continued to question Annie's mother. "Did you ever witness the Defendant being sexually inappropriate with your daughter, Ms. Bridges?"

"No, I did not but …." Sam stopped for a moment, looked over at the jurors as if she wanted to ask them something.

"Were you going to add something else, Ms. Bridges?" Happily, it was Connors prompting his own witness, not Montgomery.

"I'm not sure of this but it seemed like Annie might have acted afraid of Gabe."

"What do you mean, can you give examples?"

"She'd tell me sometimes that she didn't want me to leave her with him. When I'd need to run out to the store, she was only five, so she needed someone to stay with her, of course."

"What ended your relationship with the Defendant?"

"I began to suspect there was something going on between him and Annie but I couldn't prove anything so I asked him to leave." She looked at the jury, slowly and deliberately. Then at the Chief Justice. Connors said, "So the reason you and the Defendant stopped living together was a direct result of your concern for the safety of your little girl. Is that right, Ms. Bridges?"

"Objection—asked and answered."

Wisely, Connors stopped here, "Your witness, Counselor."

Jansen approached Sam and smiled, "Good Morning, Ms. Bridges."

Smiling back, Sam said nothing and waited, warily.

"May I voir dire the witness briefly, your honor?"

Getting Montgomery's approval, Rich handed Sam a three-page document.

"Does this look like a copy of your testimony on November 10th of last year?"

Looking at Connors for help, Sam only sat there with the

documents in her lap.

Connors was scribbling furiously on a legal pad and did not look up.

"Ms. Bridges," Montgomery said her name so loudly that she jumped. "Answer Mr. Jansen's question, now please."

Sam took the three-page document and scanned it. "Yes, I guess so."

"Can you read the highlighted portions to the jury, please?"

"I never saw anything strange with the way he acted toward her. I had no idea that Annie had been hurt in any way by Gabe, I thought he loved her, as if she was his own kid."

"So which is it Ms. Bridges, did Mr. McAllister love your daughter as if she were his own or did he persuade the two of you to take intimate showers together?"

Sam sat staring at Jansen.

"Must I repeat the question?"

"No," the tears started to come. "I just get confused sometimes, I've been sick and sometimes need to take pills."

"Judge, permission to enter these documents into evidence?" Rich handed four pages stapled together.

"OBJECTION, the state has not seen these documents!"

"Judge, we received them two days ago and faxed them to Mr. Connors' office."

"Judge, my staff has been here in Amarillo for the entire week."

Montgomery attempted unsuccessfully to hide his smirk. "Mr. Connors, I believe there are fax lines between our two great cities, are there not? Objection overruled."

Jansen handed Sam a new set of documents, "Please read the highlighted sections here, Ms. Bridges."

This time, she took the document and read the highlighted portion without prompting, "Yes, I did make an accusation of the sexual abuse of Annie when she was about six months old. No, the man I accused was not her father."

Jansen waited just a couple of seconds in order for the impact of her words to sink in for the jurors. He then asked, "So Ms. Bridges, wouldn't you say there have been several men available to take advantage of your little—"

"OBJECTION!" Connors was on his feet screaming.

"Mr. Jansen, do we need to return to my chambers?"

"No, Sir, I will rephrase my question, I apologize to the Court."

"Ms. Bridges, you have had a number of boyfriends, would you agree?" Jansen's tone was courteous, flattering, "An attractive young woman like yourself must have many male friends."

"OBJECTION—relevance, Your Honor."

"Whether or not other men had access to Annie Bridges' bedroom at night is entirely relevant to this case, Your Honor."

Montgomery leaned over his desk so that he could see Jansen more clearly and squinted at him, "Counselor, I am giving you some latitude here. Use it judiciously."

"Overruled, proceed Mr. Jansen."

"Thank you, Your Honor."

Sam Bridges was fidgeting, visibly vacillating between the inference of popularity and suspicion; flattery won out.

"Yes, I've always been popular with the boys; I was a cheerleader in high school and have never had to worry about getting dates."

"Does the name Blaise Thompson sound familiar to you, Ms. Bridges?"

"No, I don't recognize that name." Sam was desperately trying to get Connors' attention, but he was studying a document very carefully.

"You filed a sexual abuse charge against Blaise Thompson when Annie was six months old, Ms. Bridges. Then when the police came to your apartment the following day, you denied it, you said it had just been a misunderstanding. Do you remember that misunderstanding, Ms. Bridges?"

The tears were back and Samantha Bridges looked lost. She was looking to the jury and over the courtroom for help, for someone to get her out of this pit she had neatly dug for herself.

"There was a note on the police report that night, Ms. Bridges. The officer wrote that you were so inebriated that you could not conduct a conversation with the officers. Do you remember that conversation or was that a misunderstanding as well?"

Jansen forced himself to look at his witness and not see her … to use the clinical detachment that he had seen on his wife so many times and had witnessed in himself. That phrase amused him. The implication was that clinical detachment was conferred with the medical degree or with graduation from the police academy or with the first kill shot. But there was no such thing. What clinical detachment actually meant, Jansen knew from experience, was that you either learned how to detach yourself from the deaths, injuries, and the wounds by numbing yourself to the fact that the virtual Uzi you were using would cause irreparable damage, or you had to quit.

"What do you mean?" The artfully applied makeup was smudged and dark streaks of mascara ran down her face. Jurors were shifting in their chairs and Connors had his face buried in his papers, the young associate ADA looked like a deer in the headlights.

"I mean that the police thought you were either high or drunk and were incapable of carrying on a conversation. Have you had a drug and alcohol problem, Ms. Bridges?"

"Objection, your honor, relevance."

Connors' associate was on his feet making the objection. Connors continued to stare at the pile of documents in front of him.

"Your honor, the veracity of this witness is entirely relevant; an individual under the influence of drugs and alcohol demonstrates clear and compelling evidence mitigating their ability to give credible testimony."

"Objection overruled. Proceed, Mr. Jansen."

"Well, I may occasionally drink a little more than I should but I certainly have no 'drug and alcohol problem' as you say. I have complete control over myself and my actions." Sam had recovered her former defiance and had reacted exactly the way that the defense team had predicted she would.

"Permission to approach the bench for a sidebar, Judge."

"Permission granted, Mr. Jansen."

The request for the sidebar roused Connors from his meditative trance; together, the four attorneys walked to the side table where they could speak with the Judge without being overheard by the Jury.

"Judge, Defense wishes to enter these materials into evidence to demonstrate the drug and alcohol problems of this witness." Just as Rich was gathering the materials to place before the Chief Justice, Connors began to argue his objections.

"This is the fruit of the poisonous tree, Judge. We knew these two would stoop to spying on a principal witness for the State and that's why I am prepared to—"

"Mr. Connors," Montgomery almost hissed the name, "How can you decide his information was obtained via the exclusionary rule? You have not even seen it as yet."

Montgomery and Connors were referring to a rule of law stating that evidence secured as a result of an illegal search, illegal arrest, or coercive interrogation must be excluded from trial.

Connors reviewed the police report from the original complaint of sexual abuse of sixth-month-old Annie with a graphic description of the drugged and intoxicated condition of Bridges. There were three other police reports in the packet which detailed calls from neighbors calling about Annie's being alone in the apartment for hours at a time. Two of the calls had been placed by April Clarke, who would testify for the defense the next day.

As Jansen watched, Connors' face became even paler and he closed his eyes for a moment, looked at Jansen then at Montgomery and nodded grimly. For once, the Assistant District Attorney had nothing to say.

"Ms. Bridges, please read the yellowed sections of these three reports to the jury."

*If you aren't in over your head, how
do you knowhow tall you are?*
— *T.S. Eliot*

C H A P T E R

30

"Good morning, Annie, my name is Zach Cunningham and I would like to ask you some questions. Would that be all right with you?"

Connors had ended the State's case against Gabe with the anticipated coup de grace: the testimony from Annie. The ADA had done a masterful job with her testimony. Whether strategy or serendipity, the methodical devastation of the truthfulness, character, and even maternal competence of Annie's mother by Rich Jansen in the minds of the jury had faded over last night's dinner and sleep.

The twelve had been riveted by Connors' gentle, artful, and skilled examination of the little girl. Now six, almost seven, Annie was tiny, weighing maybe sixty pounds. Connors' artful questioning of Annie ended with:

"Annie, I can only imagine how terribly difficult it has been for you to talk about what has been done to you. I have only one last question."

Upon taking the stand and replying to the first several moments of testimony, Annie was smiling, happy and endearing as she replied to Connors' easy first few questions of name, age, and truth versus falsehood. She had positioned herself on the edge of the huge chair, legs swinging as she spoke engagingly and brightly with Connors. The moment his questions turned to the abuse, the total transformation was alarming. The child scuttled back into the depths of the huge wooden chair and curled into herself looking for all the world like a feral cat. Her response to Connors' last question of who had performed all of these evil acts on her had been to point at Gabe McAllister with silent tears coursing down her face.

"I solemnly swear it was Gabe. Gabe McAllister."

The silence in the cavernous courtroom was a tangible thing; it felt as if there was a collectively held breath, everyone waiting for someone else to start breathing again.

The sound of Zach's shoes had echoed in the silent courtroom as he approached Annie, all eyes on him wondering; several of the female jurors had tissues and were wiping their eyes.

The child stared at Cunningham, one of only two blacks in the courtroom. Her natural curiosity drew her out of the protective shell she had climbed into during her previous testimony about penises, and vaginas and cum, a language known, spoken, and understood.

Annie sat up, pushed her little bottom to the edge of the chair and cocked her head at Cunningham, intrigued by the blackness of his skin. She smiled shyly at him.

"Can I ask you a question first?"

Carefully, the jurors and the observers in the gallery dared to take a breath and then another at the resiliency of this little girl, at what could only be described as spunk.

"Sure Annie, what is your question? You can go first, ladies always before gentlemen, that's a rule … did you know that, Annie?"

Her huge blue eyes on Zach, Annie shook her head slowly back and forth signifying no she did not know the rule. And then smiled, a thousand-watt smile as she declared, "I like that rule."

Legs swinging happily, she beamed at Zach, "Am I a lady?"

The women who had been crying in the juror box began again, one loudly, but Annie seemed not to notice.

"Right now, Annie, you're a little girl but when you are grown up, you'll be a lady … I predict a great lady."

The sound of the juror crying grew louder causing Montgomery to look balefully over at the juror; she caught the look and quieted herself.

It was a strange sight. The slight, wiry black man, clad in a custom-tailored Armani suit, today a soft light gray with a light blue striped shirt and mahogany and light gray tie, standing in front of a tiny red-headed little girl in a pink dress and white patent leather shoes swinging at the end of long spindly, white legs. Strange but endearing, particularly so because those close to Zach could see the consummate gentleness, respect, and total lack of condescension on his face. Like Chief Justice Montgomery and the jurors.

"Annie, you said you had a question for me," Zach's words and his smile had the gentleness of a spring breeze; impossible with that gravelly, pebbly voice of his.

Reaching out, she commanded, "Come here, will you please?"

Cunningham walked closer, waited, and then she directed, "Lean down here to me, please."

With a tiny white forefinger, the child traced the long scar which started in Zach's left mid-cheek and extended almost a third of the length of his mouth. Then she stopped there, brought her finger back to her mouth, kissed it and then brought the kissed finger to retrace the contours of the long and ugly scar.

"Someone hurt you, didn't they Mr. Cunningham, someone hurt you really bad."

Even Chief Justice Montgomery was wiping his eyes at the tender tableau made by the black lawyer and the small girl caressing leaning forward, stretching her skinny arm to reach and console.

Despite the discomfort it had to have caused his back, Cunningham stayed twisted in the awkward position he was in until Annie leaned back and grinned at Zach, releasing him.

"Okay, Mr. Cunningham, you can ask me your questions now."

Zach only straightened up. But he did not move back, away from the child. He stood, maybe a foot away from her, kept his eyes focused on hers and said, "Yes, Annie, we've both been hurt really bad, haven't we?"

The silence in the courtroom had taken on the character of something else; something was happening between these two, something rare and precious, maybe even sacred. No one, not even Connors, wanted to disturb it.

Somberly, Annie nodded. Her blue eyes, huge, did not leave his; it looked as if she didn't even want to blink, didn't want to look away even for a fraction of a second.

Cunningham's voice still held that almost magical combination of gentleness and grace.

"But mine happened a long time ago, Annie, about when I was your age. That's why it's a scar now. No one is hurting me anymore." Zach took his finger and traced the outline of the scar.

"But you are being hurt now in the middle of the night in your bedroom by a friend of your mother's, just like what happened before Gabe moved in, aren't you, Annie?"

The child's eyes already huge eyes seemed to double in size, her gaze started to shift in the direction of her mother who was crying now, loudly. As Zach moved to his right, to keep the child fixed on him, Cunningham was dimly aware of a signal from Montgomery to the bailiff. In seconds, the court-room was once again completely quiet; there was an air of almost reverence, recognized and embraced by everyone there.

"The man hurting you now, hurt you before Gabe, didn't he Annie?"

Very deliberately, slowly, Zach brought his finger up to trace the outline of the scar on his face, making sure Annie followed.

"He hurt you last week, didn't he, Annie? In the middle of the night, he still comes into your room and does those things to you that you said Gabe did, doesn't he?"

The child nodded almost imperceptibly, fear written all over her face, her little face starting to contort.

"Honey, *we,*" and he gestured to include the general body of adults in the room, "are the adults here. It is our solemn obligation to protect our little ones from what is being done to you."

Cunningham's voice, although low, could be heard clearly, almost resonating from the impassioned fervor of his words and depth of emotion he was feeling.

"Gabe never hurt you did he, Annie?" There was that almost imperceptible shake of the red head, this time signifying no and the fear ramping up.

Having absolutely no clue as to what would come out of his mouth next, Zach crouched down a bit so that he was more on her eye level, keeping the child's gaze locked on his.

"Your mommy was upset at Gabe leaving you, and you love your Mommy. You thought if you said this stuff about

Gabe, she would be happy again and you want your Mommy to be happy, Annie."

A tiny voice said, "Yes, I want Mommy to be happy but I can't make her happy, no matter what I say or do, I can't make Mommy happy. I lied about Gabe and I should never have lied."

The child nodded yes, over and over, silent tears streaming down her face, made more heartbreaking by the soundlessness of the tears, the unmistakable confession that a man was sodomizing this child now. Her blue-eyed gaze remained on Zach, unmoving, replaced by the thousand-yard stare of a wounded warrior.

"Annie, we'll stop him. He'll no longer touch you. Starting right now, *no one* will ever touch you like that again ever, I solemnly swear to you, Annie Bridges."

Cunningham's voice was loud enough to be heard outside the closed doors of the courtroom with a Baptist preacher-like intonation and cadence to it.

"Do you believe me, Annie?" Cunningham was still leaning down at her eye level.

Her answer was to scramble her little body up in the chair. And then fling itself into Cunningham's arms with a force strong enough for him to stagger with the sudden weight, then she held on for dear life.

It was over.

Chief Justice Montgomery recovered first.

"The case of the State of Texas v. Gabriel McAllister is dismissed. The State finds Mr. McAllister not guilty of the charges against him. Ladies and Gentlemen of the jury, you are dismissed. I thank you for your service."

Amidst the slowly building chorus of conversation in the gallery, there was the sound of a person clapping. Jansen looked up to see a woman, standing next to Kate Townsend, on her feet and clapping. As he watched, she began to make her way down the crowded courtroom to the front. Others took up the applause. Montgomery started to pick up his gavel and then stopped and smiled.

That must be Dr. Alexandria Allbrite, the woman who started all of this with her admission of jury tampering. Bet she is coming down here to talk with McAllister.

Just as Jansen completed the thought, Montgomery looked at him and then signaled to the four attorneys, "Counselors, my office, now."

Certain they would be called on the carpet—or worse—because of the illegal cameras installed in Samantha Bridges' condominium, Jansen walked slowly, reluctantly back to the chambers. He was thinking sardonically that his second career in criminal defense law had lasted about as long as the first: one trial.

No way would he let the Judge pin the decision to bug the condo on Cunningham; tacitly, it had been his idea … and a damn good one at that.

———

"My name is Alexandria Allbrite, Mr. McAllister. May I speak with you for a moment?"

Gabe was dazed. Within a matter of seconds he had watched a uniformed guy take Sam away followed by Annie's admission that he hadn't done those awful things to her. Followed by the Judge dismissing the jury because his case was dropped. And then he watched the Judge and all the lawyers walk out the rear of the courtroom leaving him sitting here, wondering what had just happened.

Roused from his stupor at the sound of the voice, Gabe looked up and saw a chunky fifty-something-old woman talking to him. Standing next to her was an attractive, tall, dark woman. They both looked familiar, but his brain was fried.

Standing up, he took the extended hand of the chunky lady who was apologizing to him.

"Ma'am." When all else fails he had learned as a Texas teen, revert to manners. "I'm the one who should be sorry. I have no clue what you are talking about, I'm kind of at a loss here."

Kate stepped forward and murmured in a less than gentle manner, "Alex, you have nothing to apologize for … if you had not written that letter, we wouldn't be here, he would still be in prison."

"Gabe, I'm Kate Townsend and this woman who insists she owes you an apology is Dr. Alexandria Allbrite. Dr. Allbrite was the Foreperson of your first jury, the woman who admitted to jury tampering, the woman who singlehandedly gave you a second chance."

Kate ignored Alex's protests; she was sick to death of listening to Alex's litany of recrimination, guilt, and refusal to give herself credit for doing what she could. More than most would have done. When Alex had called Kate asking if she could attend the trial in Amarillo with her, Kate had agreed without hesitation. But after listening to three days of the same self-deprecatory conversation, she'd had it.

"I remember you!"

Suddenly, Gabe remembered Allbrite. He could see her frown at the testimony about Annie's intact vaginal hymen, the notes she had been taking and the questions she had written down and handed to the Bailiff.

"You were the only juror asking questions of the witnesses." McAllister glanced quickly at Kate, "You testified at the hearing about the internet research you had done. That you weren't supposed to do!"

For the first time in years, through all the combat experiences and then trial days of tension, Gabriel McAllister heard the sound of his own laughter.

And the tall, some would say menacing former Marine, former Texas State Trooper leaned down to embrace this woman, this ordinary-looking woman who had given him his life back.

"Dr. Allbrite, I have served with some of the toughest guys in the Marine Corps. I have never met anyone with the guts to take on the United States Justice system … until you, Ma'am, until you."

Gabe stood, placed his hands on Allbrite's shoulders and nodded in Kate's direction, "She's right, you have nothing to apologize for, nothing."

Then smiling a smile that transformed his entire face, still holding onto her shoulders, McAllister stared into Alexandra Allbrite's eyes to ask, "How, in the name of God, can I ever thank you for what you did for me?"

This time, Chief Justice Blaise Montgomery was standing in front of his desk. Although he was leaning on the corner, Jansen could see how big he was. The only one not dwarfed by the man was Jansen: the other three were several inches shorter but it was the beefy heft of the guy that screamed out linebacker.

When all four men were standing in front of him, the Judge turned to the court reporter seated to his right and a little behind him with her machine perched on her lap.

"Stephanie, don't take anything down until I tell you. The first few minutes are off the record." The small woman looked somewhere between thirty-five and seventy, her skin and face weathered, half-glasses perched on her nose, and she nodded wordlessly.

Montgomery turned first to Connors, extending his hand as he did so, "Counselor, I am confident that you agree that justice has been done here, albeit, quirkily. I commend you on your conduct during this most unconventional trial and am sure you'll agree that our next steps are to find the man who has been perpetrating these atrocities on this little girl."

Jansen began to breathe and relax as he grasped what was happening here. The extraordinary decency of this man who was choosing to overlook if not condone the unmistakable inference that the sole reason Jansen and Cunningham had known to cross-examine Sam Bridges and her little girl the way they had was with "fruit of the poisonous tree," exactly what Connors had objected to. And he was persuading the prosecution of the essential integrity of his decision.

Montgomery nodded approvingly at the pale and somber expression on Allen Connors as the Houston ADA declared, "Your Honor, I agree with you entirely. Justice has been done in this courtroom today." And then Connors stared at Zach Cunningham who was standing next to him when he declared, "I have never seen a cross-examination like that one. What happened between you and that little girl was nothing short of miraculous."

"Good, because I am going to ask a few things from you, Gentlemen. Both the Defense and the Prosecution. Continuing in the miraculous nature of what has transpired here today, I will," Montgomery glanced back at the court reporter, "Stephanie, we are on record now, please."

The soft tapping of the reporter's fingers filled the small room.

"I will request that the District Attorney of Amarillo in

collaboration with the District Attorney of Houston warrant ADA Connors to search for and arrest the man who has been molesting Annie Bridges. And to request the assistance of Attorneys Jansen and Cunningham in that search."

The Chief Justice regarded Jansen and Cunningham for a long moment wordlessly, visibly weighing his next words, mindful of the exceptional, perhaps historic nature of his words.

"When I first presided over the appeal of *The State of Texas versus Gabriel McAllister*, I did so with the conviction that there were few more heinous crimes than that of the sexual abuse of our nation's children.

"But you two gentlemen have shown, without a shadow of a doubt that an innocent has been wrongfully convicted through the vengefulness of an incompetent mother and her emotional manipulation of her own child.

"Mr. Cunningham, I was up until four in the morning reading your brilliant defense of Dr. Ted Ross in Houston a few years ago. I also read the first two articles by that Houston reporter, Kate Townsend's *A Nation of Law: The Dark Side*.

"Two cases where innocent men have been victims are two, too many. I include a request to both Houston and Amarillo District Attorneys that a task force be established in this state; a task force with the express purpose of examining the current evidentiary laws governing sexual abuse in Texas; one which will examine also the current mandatory reporting of sexual abuse against children with the intent to identify triggers for wrongful conviction.

I am asking to chair this new task force and hope that you four will join me. Our goal will be a simple one: to synergize and augment the already remarkable gains in decreasing the prison population in this great state of Texas through an exhaustive analysis of the existing requirements for conviction of sexual abuse of children with particular attention to two cases: The State of Texas v. Theodore Ross, MD, The State of Texas v. Gabriel McAllister. To use these two cases significantly decreases the chances of future wrongful conviction."

Within the last several years, Texas had made national news when a right-wing Republican state senator had been appointed to a new committee called The Prison Reform Committee. The state had become alarmed when the rapidly growing prison population forecasted the need for seven new prisons at a cost of over two billion dollars. In twenty years, the population of imprisoned Texans had tripled with recidivism of close to forty percent. Awareness that the judicial system was "totally broken" had created a bipartisan era of cooperation in creating new "liberal" methods of dealing with drug offenders. New courts for drug offenders were created where judges came to work dressed in jeans, not judicial robes and were prepared with a wide list of drug rehab and group programs with which to work.

The new program was working. Prison populations were dropping and people without the benefits of homes and families were finally getting the help they needed to learn work habits once they were clean. Remarkably, the rates of return to prison had dropped like a stone. Notably, other extremely conservative southern states were beginning to implement prison reform as well, the rubric, "if Texas can do it" working well to get the attention of state legislators.

Reason says, "I will beguile him with the tongue."
Love says, "Be silent. I will beguile him with the soul."
— *Rumi*

C H A P T E R

31

Kate stood looking at a self she had never thought would materialize. Alone for the first time since she left Steve's house in San Francisco, she was standing in front of a floor-length mirror in what had been Peg Reardon's dressing room. She looked, Kate realized with surprise, stunning, even beautiful.

Her host, Hank Reardon, her husband-to-be, Steve Cooper, the matron-of-honor, Lindsey McCall and her husband Rich Jansen, had all insisted she spend some time collecting herself before they all headed to the Chateau D' Ouchy in Lausanne's Ouchy district where her marriage would be celebrated.

Reflected by the mirror was a tall, dark-haired woman adorned in an ivory-champagne lace wedding dress that managed to look modest with its long sleeves, illusion neckline, long fitted bodice, then gently flaring skirt; but yet elegant, refined, and tremendously expensive. The dress was an Oleg Cassini and had cost Lindsey close to five thousand dollars; Kate knew because she had googled the dress and found the original price.

One of the September weekends she had stayed out in New Waverly in Rich and Lindsey's guest house, Lindsey had insisted Kate try on the dress. Lindsey laughingly dismissed Kate's objections to borrowing a two-thousand-dollar dress and her worries that the dress would be too tight.

"Listen Kate, something borrowed … we have that covered in spades!"

Lindsey had helped her into the dress, stood back, and whistled.

"Kate, it looks better on you than it did on me!"

Kate had to admit that the dress was a perfect contrast to her long dark hair and olive complexion; hair that was now coiffured in a complicated style. The hairdo was somewhere between a chignon and French knot constructed by Liisa Reardon, Hank's daughter and head of the Research and Development Department at Andrews, Sacks and Levine, the pharmaceutical company located in Lausanne which Reardon led. Never would she be able to re-create what Liisa had done but the look was sensational. She felt foolish, almost narcissistic as she slowly turned her body, watching the train follow her … but kept doing it all along with a guilty half-smile. To her relief, there was no evidence as yet of the being that she and Steve had decided to call "Himher," having decided their child would be one or the other. And they wanted to be surprised when the baby decided to enter the world.

The last three months had dissipated in a blur for Kate. The response to the final two articles in her series, *A Nation of Law: The Dark Side*, had been overwhelming. The Houston Assistant District Attorney Allen Connor had graciously allowed her the scoop on the discreet arrest of a Shell Oil Senior Vice President and Sam Bridges' boss, Richard Bentley. Bentley, fifty-two years old, married father of three teenaged boys and a committed Christian, had initially denied any involvement with Sam and her daughter. He had folded when Toni showed him the video and threatened to release the videos showing his molestation of Annie on YouTube. Bentley's lawyer convinced him to plead guilty and take a minimum sentence of twenty-five years.

The mail to Kate's newspaper, *The Houston Tribune* and to Kate herself was voluminous. The paper had hired two people to answer the phones, answer emails, and answer written letters; both women exceeded forty-hour weeks in attempts to reply to people and to assure them that their concerns were noted. For the most part, the mail was in support of the material Kate had included in her series and in the acquittal of Gabe McAllister. However, there was a small number of calls, messages, and letters which could only be described as threats. Despite changes to Kate's personal emails and phone numbers, there was one person who seemed to be able to discover the new addresses and numbers.

The police had been notified of course, but there was little they could do with anonymous threats, despite the ominous, dark and ugly content of the messages. Mostly, Kate had successfully dismissed the threats as the work of someone with too much time on his hands. But during a weekend spent out with Rich and Lindsey, she had mentioned the calls and messages and had been startled to hear how gravely Rich had responded.

In fact, it had been at Rich's suggestion that she spend most of her time with Steve in San Francisco.

"You don't think you're a bit over- protective?"

At Jansen's request, Kate had shown him the deleted hate-filled messages that had been sent to her email address at the Trib.

Kate's teasing smile had faded quickly when she saw the

frown and concern on Rich's face as he scanned the content of the messages.

"Have you received anything by mail either at home or at the office, Kate?"

"Our new staffers manning the phones and messages, Pete and Jan, said there were a few. The same weird fonts as in the emails—I asked them to save them until I got a chance to look at them but," Kate wrinkled her nose in a grimace, "I've been dragging my feet because I really don't want to see them."

"Would Jeff be okay with you working from San Francisco starting Monday?"

"You're really worried about this, aren't you, Rich?"

Since that late September conversation, Kate had spent hardly any time in her Houston condo; in fact, she'd finally decided to put it on the market. Before leaving for Lausanne, Kate and Steve had found a perfect house in Sausalito and had made an offer on it.

Little by little, Kate was digesting this precious time alone. Liisa and Lindsey had insisted on her forty-five minutes alone before the most momentous event of her life to date and she was only now beginning to understand their insistence.

Kate smiled as she fingered the cerulean sapphire earrings Liisa had lent her with a whispered, "Something blue." They were almost exactly the shade of Hank Reardon's eyes, Kate realized as she stared at delicate teardrops dangling from her ears.

Hank Reardon. When we met, I thought of him as another father and now that Dad is gone....

Stopping in mid-thought, Kate reflected on the sudden death of her father last year. It had been almost exactly a year ago and she was once again surprised when she felt grateful—the sorrow was there, of course—but she was ever so grateful that her dad had escaped the slow erosive death that her mother suffered as she had battled with ovarian cancer, exactly like Peg Reardon, the woman in whose bedroom she now stood. She smiled at what she had been told by her dad's three friends who had been hiking with him when he died. A cardiovascular surgeon long retired from Stanford Medical School, her dad had been speaking about the beauty of the mountains, the perfection of the trip and had said, "This would not be a bad place to die." And then he did just that, most likely from a sudden onset of a lethal cardiac arrhythmia; he had just turned eighty-four.

I knew Hank had something up his sleeve when he asked me out here for Christmas … but this ….

Kate suddenly felt overwhelmed by the generosity and love showered on her by one of the richest men in the world and felt two tears roll down the expertly applied makeup by Liisa, the consummate researcher, and cosmetologist.

Just then, she heard a double banging on the door, as Lindsey and Liisa burst in wearing matching bridesmaid dresses.

"Okay Lois Lane, it is time to end your life as a single woman!"

The Chateau D' Ouchy, Lausanne

Give your hearts, but not into each other's keeping.
For only the hand of Life can contain your hearts.
And stand together yet not too near together:
For the pillars of the temple stand apart,
And the oak tree and the cypress grow
not in each other's shadow.
— On Marriage, *Kahil Gibran*

C H A P T E R

32

The Chateau D' Ouchy was a spectacular medieval castle, built in the twelfth century and renovated frequently to a five-star luxury hotel, situated on the shore of Lake Geneva. Ouchy had been a fishing village until it was incorporated into Lausanne in the mid-nineteenth century to serve as a port of Lake Geneva.

On their trip from Houston to Switzerland, Kate had played tour guide to Steve, Lindsey, and Rich since they re-created the trip she had made three years before in their flight to Zurich in Swiss Air and then the train ride from Zurich to Lausanne.

Lausanne, known as the Olympic Capital since it is the headquarters of the International Olympic Committee is a city in Romandy, the French-speaking part of Switzerland, and is located on the shores of Lake Geneva with a panoramic view of the soaring peaks of the Swiss Alps.

Kate had felt like the consummate world traveler when they arrived the week before at the metro train station in Ouchy, pointing out Old Town and the direction they would go to get to Hank Reardon's home. The city is built on an ancient river called the Fion. The dry river bed forms a deep gorge which runs through the Ouchy then rises over fifteen hundred feet to the mountainous northern edge of the city requiring several bridges to connect the adjacent neighborhoods. Negotiating the streets of the city can be tricky for the uninitiated because there are extreme differences in elevation.

Liisa was driving her Dad's Bentley, with Kate seated carefully in the passenger seat and Lindsey in the back. Liisa and Lindsey had persuaded the men to go on ahead. Playing fast and loosely with an old axiom, Liisa had claimed that it was bad luck for a bride to be seen by a man in her wedding regalia until the actual ceremony. She had said it with such conviction the night before at dinner, that no one disputed her.

It was snowing. The weather people were predicting that it could be a major storm so Liisa was driving the Bentley. The big heavy car moved very slowly down the mountain roads, and she was quite happy that her father had insisted on putting chains on the tires. They could see the fat snowflakes filling the sky, illuminated by the headlights of the Bentley, and on either side stood the majestic snow-covered firs of the Jorat Woods. The silence was immense as if in honor of this holy night: Christmas Eve in Lausanne, Switzerland, the three women were quiet, each with her own thoughts or prayers.

The wedding was scheduled for seven, she had left about a quarter to six, giving them over an hour to get to the hotel. The drive from the Reardon home on the outskirts of La

Mont-Sur Lausanne down to Ouchy generally took only fifteen minutes, but Liisa was keeping her speed right around twenty-five to thirty miles an hour. The roads had been sanded earlier, but she was taking no chances.

At six-thirty on the dot, Liisa pulled the Bentley up to the front of the spectacular hotel. The three women took deep breaths in unison, each exhaling sighs of delight in wordless exclamations at the beauty of the Chateau D' Ouchy. Its snow-covered neo-Gothic turrets twinkled in the bright night lights of the castle.

Three people approached the car. The fastest was the doorman.

"Enchantez Mademoiselle." Taking the keys from Liisa to park the car, the young man walked swiftly over to the passenger side, bowed as he opened the door and regally said, "Ici, ce est la mariee."

As she was guided quickly around the front of the car and out of the increasingly heavy snowfall, Kate was stopped by two women, Eleanor Philbin and Harvey.

"Eleanor!"

Stunned and delighted to see Eleanor Philbin, one of the owners of the Houston Tribune, Kate felt the sting of tears once again as she leaned down to hug her. And heard her whisper, "And something old, my dear, dear girl," as she clasped a triple strand of pearls around Kate's neck. "They were our grandmother's and now they are yours."

"Eleanor, thank you for these, how generous of you and what a wonderful surprise to see you here! Is Marguerite here, too?" Kate was stammering, her thoughts almost concussive as tidal waves of emotion threatened to bowl her over.

Owners of the Houston Tribune, the two sisters had become dear friends to Kate, Lindsey, and Rich during those months of chaos and confusion of the work several years ago.

"Did you honestly think that we would miss your wedding, my dear?" Eleanor's face was wreathed in smiles as she reached up with her barely five-foot height to place both hands on Kate's face. "But I think," checking her watch, "that you have somewhere to be very soon and Harvey has something for you, too."

Eleanor stepped to her right to hug Lindsey, whispering a quick, "Don't you look lovely tonight my dear and I love her in your dress. What an outstanding idea!"

The tall, lovely black woman took a small pearl headpiece out of the wool shawl covering the floor-length glittering evening gown she wore and adroitly affixed it to the back of Kate's head.

"We didn't know each other, until yesterday, that is, and began to conspire." Harvey directed a grin at Eleanor Philbin, and then said, "Something new …."as she patted the headpiece in place.

Her smile was dazzling as she explained, "Hank and Zach have been friends ever since they met in graduate school at Columbia. Hank has been inviting us to Lausanne for close to forty years now!

⎯⎯ ⋯⋯◆⋯⋯ ⎯⎯

"May I have this dance?"

"I understand that you commandeered this entire hotel for my wedding, Mr. Reardon." Kate's face was flushed as she dipped and swayed and covered the ballroom floor to the strains of a small orchestra that was playing a Straussian waltz of either Johann's or Richard's.

The ballroom was exquisite. To accommodate the orchestra and all fifty guests, the hotel staff had emptied the restaurant and adjoining lounge bar of its white ultra-modern Danish art deco furniture. They had set up what looked to be thirty to forty small tables and chairs for four along the edges of the long length of the gleaming dark parquet wood floor.

Single white, long-stemmed roses adorned each table. Along the back of the room to the right of the orchestra was a long table with a wide assortment of canapés on either side of a wedding cake that had to be over four feet tall. There were three cakes on top of one another. The bottom and largest of the three was decorated with intricate designs of roses large and small with the subtlest of rose delicately tinting the edges of each exquisite design. The middle cake, the same in its one-and-a-half-foot height but smaller in diameter was white frosting with a decorated edge. The top of the cake was completely covered with perfectly constructed pink roses lying on their green leaves.

"I did, Katie girl, I did, and happy to do it!" Reardon looked good, Kate thought as she pirouetted in response to the gentle and expert lead of Hank. He was in his element and looked proud and happy to hold and dance with a woman he loved almost as much as he loved his own daughter.

Looking about the room at the fifty people who had flown to Switzerland for her wedding, Kate was finally able to begin to take it—and them—all in.

When Kate had arrived into the foyer of the hotel—had it been only ninety minutes ago?—- she had felt like a princess or queen with the royal treatment her friends and this staff had provided her. Liisa and Lindsey had swept her into a dressing room to approve makeup and hair and then had led her out into a hallway and down a hall where they took a right and entered another hallway.

Along the corridor covered with a trellis of white roses throughout the length of the fifteen or twenty yards stood six men and women smiling and rose petals covered the floor at her feet. Each man was dressed in a white tuxedo and the women in white long skirts with sequined tops. When they reached the end of the hallway, Hank Reardon stood waiting for her, clad in his white tuxedo jacket with black pants, blue eyes shooting electric arcs at her as he extended his arm. At that signal, the beauty of Beethoven's *Ode to Joy* filled the room.

That was when Kate started to cry. Taking her hand, Reardon gently took his finger and wiped the tears away. "No tears tonight, Katie girl; he is watching I'm sure and what a privilege it is for me to stand in his stead and give his daughter away in marriage this Christmas Eve. Thank you, my dear, for this honor."

Sniffing loudly, Kate began to walk into a large banquet style room where about fifty people stood on either side of her, many of the women crying unashamedly through their smiles.

Lindsey and Liisa strolled behind Kate and Reardon toward a simple altar at the front of the room. There stood Steve next to a tall, thin man clad in black, holding a book of prayer. From that moment on, she could see only Steve, could sense only him.

Only later as she danced with Hank was she aware of the people who had come to her wedding. Jeff and Ellen Simmons, her editor and his wife, she saw as she and Reardon twirled by and then she realized that Ted and Christy Ross were there as well.

"May I dance with my wife, Mr. Reardon?"

"My, that sounds neat, Dr. Cooper."

"What?"

"May I dance with 'my wife'—that's me!"

Steve tipped up her head with one hand, pulled her closer to him with the other, and kissed her, making her insides melt.

"Yes, that is you, my wife." His eyes were warm, dark, and oh so sensual.

"Hank said we have the Riviera Suite," Kate's eyes were dancing, "Shall we go try it out?"

Pulling her closer, Steve whispered, "There is nothing I would like better than to unzip this zipper here." He touched the zipper at the top of her wedding gown and continued, "Unzip it to have my way with you, wife, but there are a few obligations of the bride and groom that must be attended to."

"You haven't spoken to Father John, Rich and Lindsey's priest friend who just married us. And I think that convention has it that you will cut the first piece of wedding cake sitting over there on the table to the right of the orchestra. Oh and then, you need to take your bouquet and throw it over your shoulder, making sure that Liisa Reardon catches it. Also, you may want to spend some time with all of these people who flew here for you, darling. Plus I should say a few words to George and Sally since they are my boss and your obstetrician.

"By then it will be after midnight. And if I know my wife, Kate Townsend, she will be out like a light as soon as her head hits the mattress, all of her best romantic intentions disappearing into her dreams."

Sighing theatrically, Cooper faked a groan as he asked innocently. "Is this what it's going to be like when Himher arrives … .honey, did you feed the kid … honey, did you pull up the side of the crib, honey, did you …." and ducked to avoid a sharp elbow to his side.

Hank Reardon's home

Humility is the agreement of the mind with reality.
— St. Thomas Aquinas

C H A P T E R

33

"Man, I could use a run. I have done nothing but eat since we came here a week ago! Maybe we should have taken Steve and Kate up on their invitation to stay at the hotel over the weekend."

Groaning, Rich Jansen opened one eye to look at the clock, "Lindsey, it's not even five in the morning!"

She was sitting up in bed looking way too awake, eyes bright and a huge grin on her face, like a kid.

"Okay, what do you want to do? I think the six-foot-drifts outside preclude running even for Lindsey McCall so what's going on in that lovely head of yours?"

"Hank told us he'd built a gym, remember? And said it's the building next to the cottage where Zach and Harvey are staying so it's about a five-minute walk. Come on, I'll race you there!"

Complaining good-naturedly, Jansen talked himself into thinking this was a good idea, knowing that if he did not, he would never get back to sleep if she went by herself. The

Reardon guest cottage was not unlike the one he and Lindsey had built back in Texas, at least in its simple floor plan if not décor. There were three small bedrooms, a good sized living and kitchen area, and fireplaces in the master bedroom and living area. The décor reminded Jansen of the antique chairs he had found for his office. The overstuffed chairs in all the rooms were all done in splashes of rose, mauve, and violets, similar to those in the main house but lighter, airier.

He could hear Lindsey in the bathroom brushing her teeth. She was already dressed so he grabbed running shorts and a t-shirt from the small oak chest of drawers currently accommodating their clothes, and his running shoes and then went to the living area in the front of the house to dig out boots and jackets for the walk to the gym.

And then Jansen smiled when Lindsey appeared, in her stocking feet, looking much more like a med student than the accomplished physician she was.

Once outside in the shockingly cold mountain air, Jansen's flashlight played on the snow piled several feet high on both sides of the shoveled walkway.

"There must be over seven feet of snow here!"

She was whispering, but Lindsey's voice carried in the still silence of the early morning.

"Bet it's more like eight feet," Jansen replied, also trying to keep quiet as they made their way past where Harvey and Zach were sleeping.

Suddenly they both stopped short. They shut off the flashlight and gazed upward to see a sky that only poets write of; the spectacular winter sky was dazzling in its intensity, revealing details of the Milky Way seldom seen.

Silently, they reached for one another's hands and stood there in silent rapt wonder.

"Even in the middle of the night, at the top of a mountain

in the middle of nowhere, a man cannot get a minute of peace!"

The unmistakable growl of Zach Cunningham was close … like directly behind them.

Turning in unison, Lindsey and Rich began to laugh at the sight. Zach had ear muffs and a hat and was practically dwarfed by a commodious down jacket.

Recovering first, Lindsey covered her mouth and managed to apologize through her laughter as she said, "We don't want to wake Harvey, I'm so sorry we've made so much noise Zach!"

"Nothing will wake Harvey, Lindsey; Harvey can sleep through anything, including the crying of her own kid."

At that comment, they all exploded into gales of laughter.

<hr>

"You know, Stella, we heard about these Belgian waffles of yours. Kate told us on the plane about these! I sure am glad I worked out this morning so I could enjoy these. What a treat!"

Placing her hands on more than ample hips, Stella looked first at Lindsey, then Harvey, and frowned. "Are all American girls like Liisa, you two, and Kate?"

Delivered in her thick Irish burr, Stella's comment was decipherable only to the initiated. Lindsey and Harvey looked at one another as to confirm the mutual lack of understanding and then shrugged at Stella about to feign ignorance.

Just then, Liisa appeared to translate.

"Stella thinks we're all too skinny and need to stop with all the compulsive exercise."

Scanning the detritus of the table, the three empty plates and chairs, Liisa observed, "I take it that Rich, Zach, and Dad have gone off somewhere?"

"Yes, they've gone to get Kate and Steve, said they would

be back in a couple of hours. Why?"

Liisa looked at Lindsey thoughtfully.

"Liisa, will you have some breakfast now, Miss?"

Smiling at Stella, "Yes, thanks, I will, Stella. I'll dig into this stack of waffles right here."

Lindsey had noticed Liisa's evasion to her question and the contemplative look on Liisa's face but decided not to ask for an explanation. She wondered if there were resentments left over from the days when Lindsey had been conducting the clinical trials for her experimental drug, Digipro. Thinking back to those days, she was aware of how difficult she had been to Liisa, who was merely working to re-create Lindsey's results in her lab here in Lausanne.

Picking up her coffee to take a sip, Lindsey thought about how to broach the subject and declared, "Liisa, I owe you an apology. I was an exceedingly difficult partner and …."

When Lindsey began to speak, Liisa put down her fork with a generous piece of waffle and raspberries on it and looked incredulously at Lindsey.

"You think I'm upset about those trials, don't you? Lindsey, you have no idea …."

Suddenly, she rose from her chair to come around to Lindsey and hugged her. "You were right, the study was far stronger because we used a control group of patients already on Digitalis, you were right! It was all the rest of us who were wrong!"

Both women looked over at Harvey, who was watching their interaction with a faint smile.

"Harvey, I apologize for being so rude to a guest. It's just that Lindsey and I worked together on this drug she created, Digipro, a drug that is having an astonishing effect on the treatment of heart failure. We disagreed about the methodology of the study; in fact, we fought about it. Her former colleagues at the medical school where she used to work and I were unanimous in our opposition, but since she was the PI on the clinical trials, she won out … I'm sorry to run on so and I'll bet I'm boring you so—"

Harvey flashed those brilliant white teeth in a broad smile. She interrupted Liisa by placing her long elegant fingers on Liisa's waving hand and stilled it as she replied to her in that unruffled, serene manner of hers.

"Liisa, I know boring. Boring is sitting hour after hour waiting for one of Rich and Zach's witnesses to move, leave the house, *do* something: now that is boring. Listening to you and Lindsey discuss something that is altering people's lives, helping them, is anything but boring." She blinked those beautiful long curly lashed obsidian eyes in sudden awareness, "Unless, the two of you would rather be alone to discuss unfinished business between you? If you need some time, I'd be happy to wander around your beautiful home if that is the case."

Simultaneously, Lindsey and Liisa laughed, "Not at all, it's healthy for us to have a non-medical person around—keeps us able to communicate with regular people!"

"But if you are interested, Harvey, I'd love to take you and Lindsey down to the lab." Glancing at her watch, "It's just a little after ten. Lindsey, would you like to see some of what we have been doing with the Digipro patients? And you may be interested in taking a look at our new protocol, Longevive, while we are down there. If we leave soon, we could spend a few hours down in the labs. I need to check on some things so it would help me out. Dad said that he wanted to show Steve and Kate around Old Town before they fly out in the morning and maybe grab some lunch down there.

"If we're back by three this afternoon, we'll beat them back here, I am sure." Liisa looked at Harvey and Lindsey, "So does this sound like something you'd like to do? If not, no worries at all."

Lindsey's face was alight with excitement. "Are you kidding, Liisa? Wow! It feels like the old days! Harvey, are you up for this?"

"Absolutely, would not miss this for the world! Thanks for including me, Doctors!"

All three were scurrying for boots, heavy jackets, and hats. As they walked out the front door, Lindsey asked, "Your new protocol, Longevive, what is that Liisa?"

"I'll show you when we get to the labs, Lindsey."

———————◆————————

Five minutes later the three women were crowded into Liisa Reardon's bright green Jaguar convertible, Lindsey and Harvey enjoying the beauty of the car.

"What a splendid car, Liisa," Harvey exclaimed as she settled into the rich camel leather of the passenger jump seat.

Lindsey had insisted that Harvey take the front seat since she was over five feet ten inches tall. Lindsey was not short at five feet seven, but it would be a lot easier to fold her legs under themselves in the tiny back seat of the sports car than it would have been for Harvey.

"Cars are one of my vices," the attractive blond woman replied, "especially sports cars. I just got this Jaguar last month. We'll see how well it performs on our mountain roads."

Liisa was downshifting as she expertly guided the powerful car down the twisting road heading into Lausanne. The slender young scientist was dressed in an emerald green sweater, which almost matched the sports car and jeans. She looked more like a college grad student than a scientist, a scientist who ran the research and development departments of one of the world's largest pharmaceutical companies.

The snow was piled high on the sides of the mountain road they were taking, but the last few days had been clear and sunny, leaving the roads dry.

"Liisa, what are the average costs for a company like yours to bring a drug from its experimental stage to market?"

Liisa looked into the rear view window at Lindsey with a grin, "Dr. McCall, you want to reply to that question?"

"You caught me daydreaming, Liisa sorry, what did you just say?"

After listening to the repeat, Lindsey replied, "Harvey, that's a tricky question depending on what you mean by a new drug. If it's simply a variation on dosage or for a different condition from the one for which the original clinical trials were performed, probably only ten to twenty million but I've been out of this for a while. Liisa is that about right for a non NME drug?"

"Pretty much on the money."

Harvey was shaking her head and laughing as she repeated, "*Only* ten to twenty million dollars, gotta love it … no wonder these drugs are so expensive. But …" Harvey chewed on her forefinger thinking, "at breakfast, you and Liisa had been talking about your methodology being different, more complicated and, therefore, more expensive, so we would be talking a whole lot more invested in Digipro than *only* ten to twenty million to bring that drug to market, correct?"

Liisa caught Lindsey's gaze once again in the rearview window; both smiled in appreciation of Harvey's astute observation about a field she knew nothing about.

"Absolutely Harvey. Lindsey's drug was a new molecular entity. For the NME she just mentioned, ASL's costs were close to three-quarters of a billion by the time we got it to market almost two years ago."

Liisa had turned off the mountain road and onto a wide two-lane highway with rows of huge snow-flocked aspens and birch trees lining the road. At the end of the road lay the campus of Andrews, Sacks and Levine. The corporate head-quarters comprised ten, maybe fifteen sculpted steel buildings of various shapes and sizes. Since it was the week between Christmas and New Year's, there were only a few cars parked in each of the five parking lots arrayed through the area.

Lindsey was speechless; she had expected Reardon's cor-porate headquarters to be big, but this was mammoth.

Liisa cast a glance at Lindsey as she pulled up to the main animal research labs. Liisa had been in the tiny, ugly lab at Houston Medical School where Lindsey McCall had spent untold hours during her "off time" battling the hundreds, perhaps thousands of failed attempts to create Digipro. Liisa could only imagine the nature of the thoughts racing through Lindsey's head at the mere exterior of the company complex.

Private industry versus state or federal; there is really no comparison. Just wait until she sees the labs.

Liisa pulled the Jaguar into what looked like the main parking lot, and parked. And suddenly the three women were entering the building foyer where a uniformed security guard addressed Liisa by name and rapidly produced two guest passes at Liisa's direction.

Liisa took the stairs very quickly with Lindsey and Harvey following closely behind her. When they arrived on the second floor, Liisa turned into an enormous open space with at least twenty, maybe thirty, men and women sitting or standing in groups of twos and threes among a variety of cubicles.

Looking around at the almost-football-field-sized lab, Lindsey was struck by the brilliance of the stark-white walls on one side. The external wall, composed almost entirely of glass, permitted the brilliant winter sun to diffuse throughout the cavernous room. Looking out the window, Lindsey could see acres of snow-covered grounds covering a variety of mounds. She bet in the spring these grounds were ablaze with marigolds, geraniums, impatiens, and all kinds of other plants she'd not be able to name but would recognize them when she saw them.

Lindsey was smiling, shaking her head in wonder as she looked around the artfully designed areas and catching the expressions on the faces of the young scientists as they worked.

Unexpectedly, Liisa clapped her hands. Instantly everyone turned to her.

"Merry Christmas, everyone! Remember I told you before the holidays that I had a Christmas present for you?"

Liisa walked over to Lindsey, took her hand and led her through an opening that divided the hallway from the individual cubicles where the researchers were working. She closed the distance between the groups and them by about twenty feet.

Grinning for all she was worth, Liisa said, "I cannot tell you all what a privilege it is to introduce you to Dr. Lindsey McCall!" Looking at one young man whose mouth had formed an "o" of astonishment, Liisa clarified, "Yes, Eric, this woman is the real thing. The woman who created Digipro—and guys, if I could show you the lab she did it in back in Houston, none of you would believe it!"

As Liisa was speaking, one by one all the researchers had begun to stand. By the time she had stopped talking, all were standing, clapping, cheering, the quiet research library-like atmosphere they had walked into had devolved into chaos.

Fifteen minutes later, they were back outside.

Lindsey, still trying to recover from an onslaught of emotion that had staggered her, observed drily, "So, Dr. Liisa Reardon, this wasn't just a 'Hey Harvey, would you like to see the labs, was it?'"

Once again, Harvey's social dexterity emerged. Harvey and Zach had known Liisa since she was a teenager, had done their best to advise Hank about the best way to raise a genius little girl. Liisa had lived a mostly privileged life as the daughter of a billionaire who had done all he could to assure that his little girl would be as psychologically healthy as was possible. Mostly, he had succeeded, Harvey thought.

Liisa was not an easy person to "hang out with," she was too intense; but she was not malicious or devious. And Harvey did not think Lindsey was either. She decided these two were simply too much alike.

Smiling innocently, she placed a hand on each arm of the two women between whom she walked and said, "But Harvey really did want to see the labs!" and squeezed. "By the way, Lindsey, I'd hazard a guess that you've not ever experienced a standing ovation from a room full of scientists before, have you?"

Despite herself, Lindsey smiled, her wildly careening emotions finally subsiding. She looked sideways at the elegant Harvey Cunningham, looking like a model as she strode down the walkway between the ALS buildings on the way to the animal research labs. Harvey was clad in her white cashmere coat with a wool leopard scarf and huge sunglasses protecting her eyes against the intense white of the sunlit snow banks all around them.

This lady is different. She sure is bright; I can see why Rich appreciated her help so much with the McAllister case.

"We've reached the animal labs." They had reached the door of the first building where Liisa stepped up to the unmarked, black metal door. She took off her name tag, which hung on a lanyard around her neck; and slid it through a small, rectangular black object at the right side of the door. It looked similar to the lock on the door of most hotels. The lock flashed green, and there was an audible click. Liisa grasped the steel handle and opened the door, then stood aside to let Lindsey and Harvey precede her.

"We have almost twenty-five thousand animals at ASL." Nodding at Lindsey's gasp, Liisa continued, now comfortably re-ensconced in her role of ASL tour guide. "Over seventy-five hundred of those are white mice and rats because all animal research begins with mice or rats. This building is mostly mice and rats and—"

Suddenly a slight figure emerged from a doorway to Liisa's right. They were standing in a small vestibule with a plain wooden table and chair serving as the sole furnishings. The newcomer was dressed in blue scrubs that read TMC in large block letters on the top and bottom. Until she smiled, Kate realized that her gender was indeterminate given the surgical paper hat covering her hair and booties covering her shoes.

Extending her hand, she simultaneously handed the three of them similar piles of clothing while shaking Liisa's hand.

"Merry Christmas, boss!" Smiling broadly at Lindsey, she extended her hand, "Hi, my name is Ariana. I'm the senior tech for the animal labs here at ASL." Lindsey smiled back and shook the young woman's hand, calculating that Ariana must be about twelve years old and to weigh no more than eighty pounds. Lindsey did not think she had ever met such a diminutive person. Ariana was French but spoke English perfectly with just the right amount of accent to fit an Edith Piaf impersonator. Ariana turned to Harvey, smiled, and went through the same routine. She handed her the pile of scrubs, booties, and hat, but the two looked comical as Harvey bent nearly double to accept Ariana's offering.

"Ari, please meet Dr. Lindsey McCall and Harvey Cunningham."

The young woman suppressed her reaction to Lindsey's name and just replied, "Welcome, we're delighted to have you here."

"She may be tiny, Lindsey, but no one comes in here without Ariana's okay. She runs the best animal labs in all of Europe, maybe even including the States. Before Ariana was hired, we lost hundreds of thousands of dollars caused by frequent epidemics among the animals."

Lindsey nodded her understanding as she deftly donned the protective covering for her clothes, shoes, and hair. She'd helped Harvey suit up as well by the time that Liisa had her isolation gear on.

Harvey and Lindsey had followed Liisa and Ariana into a large open room with what looked to be over ten thousand white mice in steel cages scurrying around and through a variety of mazes and miniature toys. Ariana stood in the center of the room, gesturing to all the cages and explained, "This is the intake room. We breed our mice in another facility, then bring them in here at about three weeks of age to assure normal growth and development for another two to three weeks. There are fifteen thousand white mice here at any given time."

Harvey was staring in fascination at the busy little white bodies engaged in what looked like normal mouse behavior to her untrained eye. There were three or four to a cage; each cage was meticulously clean; surprisingly, the only odor Harvey could detect was a slight whiff of disinfectant.

"Once we've ascertained normal weights and development, the mice are available to the scientists for experimentation." Ariana raised an eyebrow at Lindsey as if to ask if she had any questions. She then nodded briskly in response to Lindsey's negative shake of her head, and opened the door while she stood back to permit Liisa, Harvey, and Lindsey to pass through and back into the hallway.

"Onward to Laputa," Liisa intoned.

"Laputa? You must be kidding, aren't you?"

Ariana had joined them and replied, "No, she's not kidding at all, Harvey. It's Mr. Reardon's not-too-subtle message to his scientists." But the tech was looking at Harvey in surprise and turned to Liisa to remark, "The first in two years."

"The first in two years to do what?"

Smiling at each other, Liisa and Ariana chorused, "Laputa. No one ever comments on the name, ever!"

"Kate Townsend was the last one to understand the allusion."

"We Americans are just more literate than the rest of the world," Harvey said teasingly. "But knowing Hank Reardon, I'm certain he had a reason for naming his research lab after Swift's metaphorical satire of a people who are so bounded by theory and intellect that they are fundamentally inept and incompetent." Harvey was looking at Liisa expectantly.

But it was Ariana who answered.

"Harvey, you are quite right, of course." Ariana's expression was suddenly very somber as she explained.

"See, Hank Reardon's 'whimsical' naming of our basic science research labs serves as a grim metaphor for our work here at ASL. Either Hank or Liisa personally interviews each and every scientist and postdoctoral fellow employed or studying here at ASL. In that interview is a review of the extensive battery of psychological tests required for employment. The Reardons do everything in their power to avoid hiring cowboys and to assure that each is committed to the high road of drug research.

"They meet with us all at the end of each quarter to report on the financial state of ASL and update us on all ongoing projects. And the ASL bonus program is the best in the industry; with the FDA approval of Digipro, we all received a 20 percent bonus check."

Lindsey had been quietly following, listening and absorbing everything that the chief tech was explaining. Her response was a long low whistle that coincided with a breathy wow. "I have never heard of anything like this … ever."

Ariana nodded vigorously at Lindsey's comment and stated proudly, "My tech turnover is less than 10 percent; most research labs lose 50 percent of their techs each year. Here, they leave because we fire them for cause or because they decide to move elsewhere. No other research lab pays bonus checks for their techs—that I know of anyway.

"Our low turnover has a significant effect on the health of the research animals and therefore on the cost and quality of the animal experiments here at ASL."

The trio had been walking down the corridor and had reached the Laputa labs; once more, Ariana stood aside to permit Liisa's, Lindsey's and Harvey's entrance. Another vast room lay in front of them but was radically different from the lab where the mice had been happily chasing about in their cages. The design was somewhat similar to Eric's suite of lab facilities, in that the S-shaped design was continued here but with twice the space to accommodate the equipment necessary for the tiny research subjects.

Lindsey and Harvey blinked several times because the busyness of the scene before them took their breath away. Lindsey guessed, of course, but there looked to be thirty to forty white-coated people attending to one or two rats in his or her open cubicles. Upon entering the door marked with a huge sign "Silence! Live Experiments Under Way," the women had not needed Ariana's nonverbal finger to her lips; but suppressing gasps of astonishment was not easy. The silence in the lab was a tangible thing, yet it was not the silence invoked by a cathedral or the majesty of a sunrise; rather, it felt alive.

Lindsey could feel the energy in that room pulsing through every nerve in her body. Crazily, Lindsey wondered if her energy had somehow tuned into the frequency of the miniature monitors and other machines that most of the mice were attached to. It had been such a long time since she had felt this excitement.

After leaving the live experimental lab, Lindsey asked, "Okay, Ariana, then why does ASL allow visitors to view their primary research labs so openly?"

Ariana looked at Liisa briefly and then replied, "Excellent question, Dr. McCall. You're right. Most companies do not permit access to anyone other than authorized personnel. In fact, the previous CEO of ASL kept the place in lockdown mode 100 percent of the time, we are told by some of the old-timers here." Once again, the tech looked at Liisa, who nodded her okay to continue.

"Apparently, the former managers of ASL believed that keeping visitors out would preserve the integrity of the animals and, therefore, the experiments. When I arrived, the lab we just visited was designed very differently. There were extremely expensive negative air pressure systems in all labs, including those we'll see shortly, and the entrance was locked, requiring a pass key to enter. Those open cubicles were closed and per-mitted room for only one tech; that tech was surrounded by four walls that were also negative pressure and required a pass key to enter. Can you imagine working in total isolation for ten to twelve hours each day?" This time the amplified French accent was genuine due to the young woman's surge of emotion; the compassion evident in those amber eyes flecked with dark brown was deep and powerfully felt.

"I came here just about six years ago." Ari darted her eyes at Liisa for confirmation, got it, and continued, smiling at the memory. "Liisa recruited me, and I really didn't want to leave

Paris. I loved my job at the Pasteur Institute and was not looking to leave, but Dr. Liisa Reardon is a very persuasive woman … and truthfully? I really liked the idea of working for a woman ….”

Liisa, listening, only smiled.

“I told Liisa that I would take the job on three conditions, knowing that she couldn't meet them even if she wanted to: first, that she redesign all the labs so that the technicians could work under decent and humane conditions; second, that she allow me to write the policies governing access to the labs; and last, an entirely exorbitant salary. She met all three.” Pausing in her narrative, Ariana picked at a loose string on the sleeve of the baggy paper covering she wore.

Carefully breaking off the offending thread, Ari looked at Liisa and shook her head in wonder. “I don't know how you did it, Liisa. From what I'd learned about ASL, the company was close to receivership. So there was no money to undertake a major renovation of all research labs, but construction was completed two months after I got here.”

Liisa shrugged and replied quietly, “Dad and I knew we had to do it, Ari. We'd interviewed loads of people but never encountered anyone whom we needed more than she needed us!”

Liisa looked back behind her at the busy scientists, “Lindsey,” she asked quietly, “Have you seen enough for this trip? And yes, I am hoping you'll be back! I'd like to show you just a couple of other new protocols before we get back to the house.” Liisa checked her watch. “It's after one, are you guys okay or do you need something to eat or drink? We have really good coffee and the cafeteria is really quite good.

“Sorry Harvey, before we leave, do you have any questions?”

Within fifteen minutes, they were back in the main building and were on the first floor in Liisa's office. If it weren't for the spectacular view out the huge plate glass window, Lindsey would have thought she was back in her old office in the medical school. There were several institutional-looking file cabinets, assorted open files open on the round table where the three women now sat, and files cluttering the enormous wooden desk in the corner surrounding a desktop computer.

"How did you actually come to that multi-million dollar renovation, Liisa? I know you must have done a good bit of research about Ariana's claims before investing in that level of restoration and imposition of discipline among your, what …" Lindsey stopped and calculated silently for a few seconds, "five thousand employees?"

Liisa nodded, "Close. Six thousand."

"ASL has oppugned the experts. No research lab has done away with their negative pressure labs nor their isolated cubicles for research; rather, they choose to live with occasional epidemics among their research animals and extremely high turnover among their techs.

"Ari had persuaded the powers that be at the Louis Pasteur Research Institute in Paris to convert their labs five years before she came to ASL. Although it was a risky decision, the head of the institute backed Ari. Two years after the conversion, the Institute was just a few hundred thousand euros short of breaking even with their multimillion-euro investment: exactly what Ari had predicted, the savings were incurred by the drop in tech turnover, infectious outbreaks in the animals, and fewer tech errors in their experimental research assignments. After I'd talked with the head of the Pasteur Institute I was sold, and we committed to the redesign of all the labs."

Closing her eyes, Liisa said, "The conversions were a nightmare. Endless weeks of round the clock meetings with six thousand employees, explaining, justifying, and when needed, coercing and, of course, firing."

Lindsey looked around at the Spartan office. No diplomas, no personal photographs: this was private industry Lindsey mused, with no need to display academic achievements as in the world of academic medicine she had inhabited for so many years. Liisa had two doctorates, one in physiology, the second in biology; but in this world of private industry, only one thing counted: the bottom line.

"What did the switch cost you, Liisa? Unimaginable time, anxiety and energy I am sure but what was the cost in dollars?"

Liisa smiled grimly, "Exactly what it cost us to get Digipro to market: Seven hundred fifty million."

Shocked at the figure, Lindsey whispered, "Holy shit. The only way you could have funded an investment that massive—" Interrupting herself, Lindsey asked rhetorically, "wasn't this company almost in receivership when your dad took it over?" Thinking out loud, McCall said, "Yeah, I remember Simon telling me that was the case before I met your dad, he had just assumed the position of CEO for ASL. And the company was desperate … so the only way you could have funded all this was through venture capitalists."

"Precisely!" Liisa's face was lit up with excitement at Lindsey's quick grasp of the enormity of the risk. She framed her mouth to continue speaking, but McCall either didn't notice or care and said, "And you … you were at Stanford doing postdoc work on epigenetics as I recall. So what was it about a failing drug company that lured you away from Stanford's Department of Biology's research department?" Stanford, McCall knew, had one of the top basic science research agencies in the world.

Liisa only stared at Lindsey with a strange expression on her face.

Watching the exchange between the two women, Harvey

was fully conscious of the fact that neither Lindsey nor Liisa was aware of her existence, they had completely forgotten her presence. She knew very little about Dr. Lindsey McCall but was learning quickly: like Liisa, the woman was a genius; unlike Liisa, however, she wagered that Lindsey did not have a father like Hank Reardon. Of course, who could?

Just as the thought hit her frontal lobe, she heard McCall whisper in a voice so soft it was barely heard, "*Of course*, you get to work with your dad …." There were tears standing in her eyes as the realization hit her.

Harvey, accustomed to following her gut, just as softly, asked, "What happened to *your* dad, Lindsey?"

"He died in an experimental plane he was testing for NASA; I was a freshman at Rice University when it happened." Silent for a few seconds, she smiled widely at Liisa and Harvey through a sheen of tears, "I'd have given anything to work with my dad …." The joy of the deep love Lindsey had for her long-dead father was almost painful to watch. "I'm happy for you that you get to do that." There was genuine affection and sincerity in her words and expression.

Harvey wondered if Liisa had known about McCall's father, if Hank had told her about a loss which had to have been devastating for the young Lindsey.

"I get it, Liisa, please continue. I'm intrigued about how you two managed to induce venture capitalists to invest in a company with such precarious finances." Then, courteously, she turned to Harvey to ask for permission.

The energy between the two scientists was changing. The coolness, mostly it seemed from Lindsey toward Liisa, was evolving into something else: not yet friendship, but respect and understanding; whatever had gone between them in the past was being resolved. No way would Harvey miss this, she found it more than fascinating.

"We tried to place ourselves in the shoes of a venture capitalist. And figured that these people are risk takers, sure, but that they needed all the reassurance we could give them to invest in us rather than in our competitors. Ariana had already sold all of us on the data supporting the removal of all the negative pressure controls within the labs.

"However, the complete gowning procedures that Ariana wanted to employ as a universal for all the labs and for all the animal labs took more than a bit of persuasion. ASL research techs had made the same erroneous assumptions that all of our competitors still make: the presence of the semi-vacuum in the labs is adequate protection against infections in the animals. No one was interested in taking the time to don all that protective gear.

"That is why we had to have the round the clock meetings while dressed in protective gear. The data from the Louis Pasteur Institute made a clear and compelling argument, and if that were not enough, Dad and I made crystal clear that noncompliance with the new protocols would be met with termination. Most of the employees believe to this day that the new system was my invention, not Ariana's."

"Was the decision to 'open up' the research labs made at that same time?" Harvey watched as Liisa and Lindsey exchanged a glance.

"No, that decision came about a year after the conversion was complete. Ariana was opposed to it in the beginning."

Lindsey cocked her head at Liisa. "Why?"

"Ariana had worked only at the Pasteur Institute, where they have no need for venture capital. It is financed entirely by the French government."

Lindsey nodded in understanding.

"Do you think ASL's 'open labs' have made that much difference, Liisa?"

"The very first group we allowed into the labs decided to invest with ASL, with great enthusiasm. That is what jump-started the Digipro project."

Liisa looked thoughtfully at Lindsey and at Harvey. "If you were allowed back behind the scenes, if you will, wouldn't you be a whole lot more interested in investing in something that you've had at least a virtual hands-on experience with?"

"And the new Longevive project, Liisa?"

"Yes!" Checking her watch, Liisa grabbed three files and handed them to Lindsey.

"Here are the protocols. Please treat them as if they contained the passwords for the nuclear codes; this is cutting edge, exciting stuff that our competition would love to sink its pointed little teeth into." Grabbing coats, she flung them at them.

"We've got to move, guys, it's almost two-thirty."

*Research is what I am doing when I don't know
what I am doing.*
— *Wernher von Braun*

C H A P T E R
34

"Before we get into the details of Lindsey's trust fund, Hank, I want to remind you of a promise you made a few months ago, right after I decided to go back to criminal defense law." Rich sat back, took a sip of his coffee and then carefully placed it back on the table.

"Zach Cunningham is one of the most exceptional men I have ever met Hank—I'm not sure if I'll take him up on his offer to partner with him, but I am sure thinking about it. That cross-examination of Annie Bridges was nothing short of astonishing."

Rich stared at his coffee cup as if transfixed by its contents.

There had been neither the time nor the opportunity for Jansen and Cunningham to talk at any length about the task force that Chief Justice Blaise Montgomery had instituted at the conclusion of the trial in Amarillo. That early morning workout in Reardon's gym had been the sole exception.

Cunningham had made his offer to Rich to join his firm as a partner in his customary phlegmatic manner. Both men had just completed four hard miles on parallel treadmills. Cunningham had told Rich that he and Harvey were hoping to adopt Annie if, as Cunningham had wryly phrased it, "two minor problems of race and age can be answered to the satisfaction of the state." Almost in the same breath, he had invited Jansen to join his firm.

"I know you and he have been friends for a long time and I'd appreciate it if you could give me a little background on him."

Rich, Lindsey, and Hank Reardon were each seated on two of the six overstuffed chairs and couches artfully arranged in the book-filled room. So it was fairly easy to survey the display subjects which composed the extensive Reardon library collection. The two predominant areas of interest were, quite naturally, business and finance. But there were also extensive collections of biology-, chemistry-, and physics-related texts; there were even large fiction, decorating, and gardening collections as well. Lindsey calculated that there must be over five thousand books surrounding them.

Hank noted the direction of Lindsey's gaze and declared, "You probably didn't know that I turned down a cardiac surgical residency with Bernie Levin back in the late sixties, did you, Lindsey?"

Reardon smiled at the dumbfounded expression on Lindsey's face.

Reardon's gaze then roamed over his library and the stacks of books contained in the floor-to-ceiling shelves. Lindsey's gaze automatically followed his and she was startled to see some of the same cardiovascular textbooks that she'd had in her office at the medical center. For some people, Lindsey mused as she watched the man surveying the beautiful wood shelves made brilliantly light by a huge window in the ceiling, their collection of books mapped their life and passion. This was certainly true for Hank Reardon.

"Rich, yes, I remember that promise I made you while we were planning our Katie girl's wedding here back in October and am happy to tell you the story. But it's complicated."

Rich grinned at that last comment, "Hank, I'd be disappointed if it weren't!"

"I was in the MD/Ph.D. program at Columbia, and I rotated through Simon Bayer's research lab while I was doing the Ph.D. In fact, we actually became friends when I decided not to accept a cardiovascular surgical residency at Columbia. Bayer was curious about why a plum residency under the famed Bernie Levin at Columbia would be turned down by one of its best medical school graduates. And when I told him that I couldn't stand being around sick people he laughed and told me to meet him at TJ's that night. TJ's is a bar right around the corner from Columbia and is a favorite of the med students and residents."

Hank stopped, thinking for a moment, then continued, "At least that's the story I tell the reporters. It's a little more complicated than that but now is not the time to get into it."

He looked at Lindsey in an expectant way, almost as if he were challenging her to ask what the real story was, but Lindsey said nothing. The name Simon Bayer had suffused Lindsey with so many memories that she was overcome with memories of the man: a mentor who had been a father to her throughout some of the most difficult times of her life.

Rich watched both Reardon and Lindsey and was reminded of the life she had lived as a world-renowned cardiologist and cardiovascular researcher, and of work these two had done together that had revolutionized the treatment of heart disease. There were many times he felt awe and privilege for having been given the gift of this special woman: this was one more of them.

As if reading her husband's mind, Lindsey looked across at him with tears in those incredible green eyes to say, "I wish you could have known Simon, Rich. Simon Bayer was the rarest of men, the rarest of physicians, how I loved that man …."

"And how he loved you, my dear! If it hadn't been for Simon Bayer, I'd never have listened to the quixotic dream of some kid researcher about altering the digitalis molecule to remove its inimical effects on the body."

Reardon and Lindsey smiled at one another in rapt mutual memory.

Reardon snapped back first, chuckled, then sat back in his chair and declared, "Bayer tried really hard to convince me that an intolerance of chronically ill people could be an advantage in medicine. Simon believed that the hatred of disease could act as a catalyst for the relentless drive to discover the 'cure.'"

"That night at TJ's I met Zach Cunningham. Bayer had left me to attend a meeting he had on the other side of town. And I was calling myself every name in the book for walking out of medicine, wasting all those years of study and was basically disgusted with myself. All I wanted to do was get really drunk, escape myself."

Reardon's face was grim, his intense blue eyes staring past the massive bookcases and out into the blinding white of the sunlit snow, caught up in the memories of long ago anguish and loneliness. The only sound in the light-filled library was the crackling of the logs in the fireplace.

"But I have never liked to drink alone and had decided to just leave when I saw Zach walk in." Reardon's face lit up and a smile teased at the edges of his mouth with the long ago memory of Cunningham.

"There weren't too many med students with a Rastafarian 'do' so Zach made quite an entrance."

Lindsey had never seen Cunningham without his 'Obama' haircut, but Rich was enjoying Reardon's story immensely and was remembering their first meeting at the Oklahoma City Airport.

"Zach took a seat alone so I asked if I could buy him drink to celebrate one of the stupidest decisions I had ever made, turning down one of the best residencies in the country. Zach told me 'no,'" somehow Reardon simulated the pebbly, gravelly sound of Cunningham's speech, "'he would buy the drinks because he had just made a much dumber decision than mine, he was sure.' He had just signed on as an intern with William Kuntzler, the crazy criminal defense lawyer when all he wanted to do was prosecution. We stayed at TJ's until they closed at two in the morning. Zach was my best man when Peg and I got married and is probably my best friend in this world."

Hank looked thoughtfully at Rich for a long moment.

"Cunningham always told me there was no lawyer he could trust well enough to have as an associate in his firm and that he'd stay a solo, he didn't want a partner. You must have impressed him immensely, Rich."

Reardon looked up as a tall chubby forty-something-year-old man walked into the library.

"Perfect timing, Carl!"

After introductions were made, Carl Reynolds, Hank Reardon's financial analyst, joined the group, opened his briefcase, and handed out three copies of a ten-page financial analysis for the Dr. Lindsey McCall trust. Both Rich and Lindsey were speechless when they reviewed the document, the eight-figure size of the principle and the speed with which the money was growing as residual income from Digipro compiled.

Lindsey was the first to break the silence. "This is great news because I'd like to donate two-and-a-half million to Liisa's new Longevive project."

Startled, Reardon asked, "You mean invest that capital in a joint venture with us, don't you Lindsey?"

"No, I mean donate this money, Hank. It's a gift. But another five million I want to use in a joint venture with you."

Reardon looked at Rich who sat looking as if his wife gave away two-and-a-half million on a daily basis. Shrugging, Rich smiled, "It's her money, she gets to do whatever she wants with it."

"I take it you went to the labs today."

"Looks as if you guys have other business to discuss; I don't think you need me here any longer. It has been a pleasure meeting you and please don't hesitate to call me if you have any questions." Reynolds shook hands again and handed out his business cards to Rich and Lindsey, rose from the couch, and quietly closed the door to the library as he left the room.

Grinning back at Reardon, Lindsey patted the files she had brought into the meeting unnoticed, and said, "Yes, Hank, I sure did."

Picking up the heavy folders, she handed them over to Reardon. "Liisa was right when she told me to treat these as if they held the nuclear passwords; this is revolutionary work, Hank. Potentially, this information could change medicine."

Her eyes shining, she looked at both men, "I don't mean a modification of medicine, a slight alteration: this could be total transformation."

Even during her worst moments, Lindsey McCall was a beautiful woman. But during those times when she was passionately engrossed in something new, something she needed to explore, like now, she became breathtaking.

"Imagine, gentlemen, a method of modifying human genes through epigenetics, thereby accomplishing a doubling of the average life span from seventy to the Old Testament prediction of one hundred forty years rather than seventy.

"Consequentially, *medicine,* as we know it now would undergo the kind of change it did in the last century, not just in the US but in the world. Rather than the paradigm of disease, doctors would necessarily be trained and would practice from a standard of health."

Touching the files, Lindsey looked at Reardon and at her husband to ask rhetorically and almost ominously. "How much would Liisa's data revealing her doubling of the longevity of her rats with some relatively simple changes in diet be worth?

"As a corollary, what might happen if we can replicate the startling changes in morbidity and mortality in a minuscule sample of patients in the Digipro group by introducing simple and cheap dietary changes?"

Jansen realized that in the three years he had known his wife, he had never seen her on fire like this, never. Neither Reardon nor Jansen missed the repeated "us" or "we" in McCall's language.

*The man who follows the crowd usually will get no further
than the crowd. The one who walks alone is likely to find
himself in a place no has ever been.*
— *Albert Einstein*

E P I L O G U E

Gabe McAllister awakened from a sound sleep at the not so gentle pressure of Baron and grinned. Then he stretched his long body as hard as he could and swung his legs over the bed onto a Navajo rug.

Looking at Max, still curled on his bed, Gabe said, "Well, Baron, at least one of us has some energy in this house!"

Grabbing running shorts and a light T-shirt, Gabe bent down to put on his running shoes and socks, yelling at the top of his lungs. "Anyone want to go for a run in the woods before breakfast?"

Magic words: within seconds the two dogs had bounded down the stairs and were standing at the front door, eyes alight with eager anticipation.

Just minutes later, the three were running in the slow drizzle of a January rainy day in the Piney Woods. The two dogs in the lead and Gabe followed, all at a slow trot.

Even after three months of "freedom" he was still stunned by what had happened in the last year. Stunned at the profligate goodness he had been showered with by Lindsey McCall, her husband Rich Jansen and the crazy but lovable team from Oklahoma; stunned with the wonder of why people like them would help him. McCall had been so confident that he would be acquitted; she seemed so sure of so many things, he thought.

After he'd been here for a month or so, Gabe and Baron had literally run into Lindsey and Max on the running trail, each pair going in opposite directions.

"I finished that book you gave me the night before the trial, Lindsey. I see why you liked it. I've gone back to read a few sections again. Would you like it back? I see that someone named John wrote a personal message on the inside cover."

"No Gabe, you can keep the book." Laughing, she leaned down to re-tie the laces of her running shoes.Straightening up, she added, "I think I read that book at least four maybe five times. I'm surprised the print is still visible after the deep inhalations I took."

Laughing now, too, Gabe looked at this uncommon woman, thinking maybe for the twentieth time how lucky Jansen was to have her: brainy, beautiful, and somehow untouched by all of it.

But it wasn't luck at all, McAllister was beginning to see. Rich Jansen hadn't won that trial by being lucky; the guy had worked, studied and taken risks, big ones. The information he had about Sam, her boyfriends … even McAllister could see that some of that info was pure intuition, some of it probably through bugging Sam's place. The man did nothing in a half-ass way; it was all or nothing, just like his wife's approach.

Incrementally, maybe through the mere fact of living around these people, McAllister was taking inventory of his life. Analyzing the decisions he'd made, he had come to accept the fact that few had been decisions, they had simply been a way to avoid something else. The Marine Corps had been a perfect antidote for the total boredom he'd felt in college; it had not been patriotic fervor at all. He'd joined the Corps because he'd had nothing better to do.

Like sleeping with Sam. He'd nothing better to do the night he quit the Corps than sleep with another nameless female; but had then had come against Annie. And although it was true, he'd saved her from eight months of sexual abuse, the fact that he had lived there had changed nothing: he had helped neither Sam nor her poor lost little kid. McAllister no longer suffered from the self-hatred at his inept, tepid, and gutless refusal to deal with Sam and what she had done to Annie. He'd come to realize that mistakes were part of this weird journey called composing a life for yourself. They come with the package.

But he'd made a couple of promises to himself, starting with the generous and loving offer from his former boss Ted Stanley: he could have his job back with the Texas State Troopers. Gabe knew that he had more work to do to become the man he wanted to be. And for a while, at least, that work had to be done alone. So he had gently and kindly said no to Stanley.

Later that day, he and Baron would take off for points unknown in a fifth wheel he'd purchased with some of the money he'd been paid for his wrongful conviction. Rich and Lindsey were due home any time now, their red-eye flight from Switzerland had landed about an hour ago.

Turning back to look at the "guest cottage" he'd been living in since late September, Gabe thought back to the flight back from Amarillo to Houston, then the drive from the airport to here.

He had been sitting in the back seat of their car, knowing he should talk, say "thank you," say something, anything at all. Then Jansen looked in his rearview mirror, caught Gabe's gaze and smiled as if prescient, said, "No need to say anything bud … or do anything. Take it easy."

Looking back at Jansen's face in the rear view mirror, illuminated by the passing headlights, Gabe was shocked. The guy looked as if he'd aged ten years over the five, or was it more like only two, months of this trial.

No one had expected the searing and poignant recognition by Annie of Zach Cunningham, her instant connection with the strange-looking man; a relationship which resulted in Annie's admission that the man who had hurt her was not Gabe, that it was "some other guy." Some other guy who had taken Gabe's place in prison and was there, now. A fact which gave Gabe no joy, none whatsoever. This whole year had been about learning the depths of depravity possible for man. McAllister had thought he'd seen the entire gamut of the evil that one man can do to another while in the Corps; but that was nothing compared to this. Nothing.

Once the Judge had declared his case dismissed, he'd called all four lawyers back into his chambers and left McAllister sitting there alone in the rapidly emptying courtroom. Alone, that is until the reporter Kate Townsend appeared with the woman from the first jury. He could not remember her name, but she'd been crying and asking him to forgive her.

Townsend and Gabe had seen eye to eye on that one … Townsend had been sharp and annoyed with her—Allbrite, that was her name. She had been the Foreperson of the jury that indicted him.

McAllister dimly recalled standing up to take the sobbing woman into his arms and telling her that he'd served with few men who would have had the guts to do what she had done: write a letter to a judge in admission that she had done something illegal. And then go testify in court, admitting to something that she feared could cause significant legal problems for her: jury tampering.

They had stayed there awkwardly talking for maybe ten or fifteen minutes. He recalled the reporter warning him that reporters would be trying to track him down, interview him, get photos, and all else that came with five minutes of fame in this media-saturated world.

Finally, the lawyers came out and all four walked over to him where he sat waiting, without a single clue of what he was to do next. The two prosecutors stood awkwardly in front of him, seeming more at a loss than had the reporter and the Allbrite lady.

Gabe had stood up, towering over Connors.

"I apologize, Mr. McAllister, for the injustice done to you by the State of Texas." They could not have been easy words to say and Connors seemed sincere, so Gabe shook his hand.

Jansen shook hands with Cunningham and they looked at one another for a long moment, then another, and seemed unable to find the words for what had happened between and among the others over the last two months.

Toni was the first to break the silence when she extended her hand to Jansen to say, "I'd work for you again, any time, Rich. You're a good man and a good lawyer, I hope we get the chance to work together again."

Zach Cunningham and his wife, Harvey, silently stood next to Toni while she stayed put, leaving her hand in Jansen's. Looking down at the short chunky woman whom he'd come to respect, Rich nodded at the sheen of tears he saw in her eyes. Then he pulled the hand that had held his toward him until he had Toni Martinez, hater of Dobermans, in a bear hug, feeling the sting of tears in his own eyes.

Watching, Cunningham regarded the four dazed, exhausted people, his team of three plus Gabe, settling his gaze on McAllister who was still seated, and declared, "There are no winners here."

Then he walked over to McAllister and placed his hand on Gabe's head as if in a blessing. "But son, you didn't deserve what happened to you, not for one moment did you deserve what you got. Go find yourself a life." Cunningham grabbed his wife and Toni and walked out of the courtroom, promising over his shoulder, "Jansen, we'll be talking soon."

McAllister's thoughts about the trial had been interrupted when the car turned onto an unmarked road that didn't even resemble a road. Jansen had stopped and parked the car in front of a stunning huge log cabin, complete with wrap-around porch, and two chimneys for what had to be an enormous fireplace. Motion detectors had lit up the property as if it were daylight. Behind and to the left of the big house was a perfect miniature: one chimney and wrap-around porch, plus a most inviting rope hammock at the corner of the porch.

By the time they drove in and showed him around, pointing out toothbrushes, supplies, clothes, (vaguely he remembered someone having asked his size in the blur of the last two months), it was close to ten in the evening and they were all exhausted. With the exception of the two dogs.

When the front door of the main house had been opened by Wanda, Max had been standing there beside a second smaller black and tan Doberman. Both dogs raced out and down the four wide stairs leading from the porch to the forest floor and proceeded to do exactly what Dobermans do: race around in circles, race up then away from the three of them and Wanda, Jansen's former assistant at the prison, the woman who had been caring for them.

Finally, when both dogs had calmed down a bit and stood panting, tongues lolling out of their grinned snouts, Lindsey said, "Gabe, this new addition to our pack is named Baron."

Her eyes on Gabe to check his reaction to the name of the

dog, the same as his war dog whom McAllister had watched die a horrific death, Lindsey continued chattering as if there was no significance to the name.

Glancing at Rich, she explained. "Rich and I have talked about another dog for Max; Candace has several over at the shelter that we could check out if you'd like. But Candace said this guy had been in a panic. He really needed to get out of the shelter and into a home with someone who knows how to handle Dobermans. His previous owner had to give him up because he's too dominant for her. If it's all too much right now, we can bring Baron into the house."

Lindsey stopped her chatter when McAllister slowly dropped to one knee and very softly whispered, "Baron, hey boy, come."

The dog stood, trembling, staring at Gabe.

McAllister said nothing more but stayed completely still.

Suddenly, the dog raced over to Gabe and sat, right in front of his face and slowly, eased his nose to touch McAllister's face. McAllister's was not the only face with tears streaming down it.

The next title from Lin Wilder …

A Price for Genius

P R O L O G U E
Lausanne, Switzerland

Suddenly regaining consciousness, Rich Jansen attempted to stand then instantly regretted the movement. The pain began at the base of his head and exploded in successive and increasingly intense waves of agony, forcing him to close his eyes, hang his head and wait motionless. Remaining on his hands and knees for a minute then two for the pain to subside, for the nausea to fade, Jansen risked opening his eyes. Squinting at the bright light, he very slowly and carefully moved his head from right to left.

So far so good. Linoleum floor, shiny black and white. That noise what is that noise? Aw no, don't tell me, please God.

The memories flooded back as Rich raised himself up enough to crouch. Gingerly reaching behind his head with his right hand, Jansen winced when his fingers probed a large, wet and sore swelling at the back of his head. Slowly he stood, swaying a bit while the vast room spun about him.

Got myself a nice concussion, whatever they hit me with carried a hell of a wallop.

The phone call from Reardon had happened last night? Or was it yesterday? The minute he hung up the phone, Rich had called the airport to secure a seat on the next flight to Zurich. Nine hours later, he had arrived at the animal research labs in the corporate offices of Andrews Sacks and Levine, one of the largest pharmaceutical companies in the world, located in Lausanne Switzerland. The elfin Ariana had been showing him where the test mice were kept when everything went black. Looking around for her Jansen saw only a few spots of blood and some scuff marks. He saw mice scrabbling all over the lab; for whatever reasons, whoever broke in decided to free hundreds of mice and Ariana was nowhere to be seen.

The letter...where is the letter?

Jansen reached into the pockets of his sports jacket, the copy of the one he'd had on since leaving Texas, thirty-six hours before and breathed a sigh of relief as his right hand pulled out the single page. A page now bloodied from his head wound.

Hello Mr. Reardon,

By the time you get this letter, it will be too late. We'll already have her.

Here are the steps you must not take:
   • *Do not call the cops.*
   • *Do not contact the FBI*
   • *Tell no one.*

We'll know if you contact the police or the FBI. We'll know and we'll kill her instantly. But we are civilized businesspeople; this is all about business after all. Do nothing at all until you hear from us. And you _will_ hear from us Mr. Reardon.

You must know Sir, there is a price for genius. We trust you will pay it if you want to see your daughter alive.

In the other pocket of his jacket, Jansen found his cell. He dialed the number from memory.

Please pick up, please pick up.

Heart hammering as he counted the rings, Jansen's knees nearly buckled with relief when his wife picked up.

"Lindsey, where are you?"

"Rich? Are you alright?

"Fine. Are you at your lab or at home?"

"Neither. I'm at the track, I was just starting a run with Max."

"Honey, you're in danger. Get off the track, take Max, get in your car and go somewhere safe."

"What's happened Rich, what is going on?"

"Please Linds, listen to me, you need to leave town *now*. Make sure no one is following you and then get on the freeway to head for San Francisco. You should be there in a couple of hours, I'll make sure that either Kate or Steve is home. You have their new address, right?"

"I'm looking now."

Rich waited anxiously while he looked at the disarray in the lab. Cages were overturned and he could hear the squeals of mice. That had been the noise he had heard when he was coming to. He was way too old for this crap and knew just who he'd call once Lindsey was safely out of San Luis Obispo.

"Yes, I have their address. Max and I will head there now, I'll get in touch with them once I'm in the car. Worst case, I'll go to Steve's office at Stanford but I'll bet Kate is home with the baby. It sounds like you have enough to contend with up there. I'll call you when I get to Kate and Steve's house. Don't worry about us Rich, please."

"Hey, McAllister, Rich Jansen here. Are you and Baron still roaming free around the country?

"Yo, Rich!" Rich could hear the smile in Gabe's voice.

"Are you still looking to work for Zach and me?"

"You mean like an investigator?"

"Right."

"Sure, how soon?"

"Can you get to Zurich, Switzerland on the next flight out?"

"Sure but I'm bringing Baron with me Rich."

"Good, we can use him."

"Call me when you have your flight arrangements and I'll meet you at Zurich Airport."

Then he dialed another number, this one he needed to look up.

"Hi Zach, I think we need Toni and maybe Harvey out here. But you need to know this looks bad, really bad. If you don't want them to take the risk, I'll understand."

Jansen smiled when he heard the reply.

And then he made one more call. Once again, the reply was yes.

"They have taken Ariana too haven't they?"

Hank Reardon stood behind Jansen. For the first time looking every one of his sixty-eight years, the slight billionaire CEO needed no reply to his rhetorical question as he looked around the research lab, the scattered cages, scurrying mice and the small pools of blood on the otherwise immaculate floor.